# *Resurrection*

# Resurrection

## KEN McCLURE

SIMON & SCHUSTER
A VIACOM COMPANY

First published in Great Britain by Simon & Schuster UK Ltd, 1999
A Viacom company

1 3 5 7 9 10 8 6 4 2

Simon & Schuster UK Ltd
Africa House
64-78 Kingsway
London WC2B 6AH

Simon & Schuster Australia
Sydney

A CIP catalogue record for this book is available from the British Library

ISBN 0-684-85128-8

Typeset by SX Composing DTP, Rayleigh, Essex
Printed and bound in Great Britain by
Butler & Tanner Ltd, Frome and London

*The only thing necessary for the triumph of evil*
*is for good men to do nothing.*

Edmund Burke (1729-1797)

# — *Prologue* —

*Edinburgh, Scotland*
*August 1997*

The children went very quiet. Their mother, who had been sitting on the grass happily reading her new Virginia Andrews in the sunshine, looked over her glasses at the ground in front of her and listened intently for a moment. No longer reassured by the background noise of laughter and argument, she called out.

'Jemma? Graham? Where are you? What are you up to?'

There was no reply so she turned round to face the trees and called out again. This time there was a response.

'Mummy,' said Jemma's voice, sounding very small. 'There's . . . a man.'

The woman dropped her book and scrambled to her feet in ungainly fashion to dash into the trees, still in stockinged feet, fearing some hideous assault on her children. She stopped as she came to the clearing where Jemma's voice had come from and saw the pair of them standing side by side, looking up into a tree.

Relief was quickly replaced by horror as she raised her line of sight and saw a pair of light tan-coloured shoes revolving slowly at eye level. She had the ridiculous thought that a man had levitated up into the branches before reality insisted she face facts.

'Oh my God,' she exclaimed. 'Come here, you two!'

The children rushed towards her and she gathered them in her arms, letting them bury their faces in her skirt as they sought reassurance and safety. She was left looking up into the tree.

At first she thought she couldn't see much from where she was because of the leaves, but a movement of the corpse in response to the wind alerted her to the fact that she could see more than she'd imagined. Brown cord trousers and a greenish-brown jacket were providing unwitting camouflage. She looked up to where the face must be and waited until the corpse had revolved to face her. She drew in breath sharply as she saw the lopsided purple face with bulging eyes and lolling tongue peer at her through the leaves.

'Is he dead, Mummy?' asked Jemma.

'I'm afraid so, Jemma. We'd better tell the police.'

The police arrived within five minutes of the call, a panda car followed some ten minutes later by three other vehicles, all using sirens and flashing lights to speed their passage. Chequered tape boundaries were set up and, almost before she knew it, the woman had told the police everything that she could, not that it amounted to much. She was obliged to give her name and address just in case they needed to get in touch again, but they doubted that would be necessary.

She walked away from the scene with her children on either side of her, feeling a distinct sense of anticlimax and maybe even resentment. She was responsible for raising the alarm; she had started the whole thing off and now, quite suddenly, she was being treated as irrelevant. She wanted to know more, who the man was, why he'd done it, but they weren't going to tell her. She was an outsider again after a brief starring role in a nightmare. The door had been closed. She and the children were surplus to requirements.

The children sneaked fearful backward glances at the trees as they walked away, holding their mother's hand. They would remember this picnic for the rest of their lives. The man in the tree would return periodically to decorate the trees of their dreams for all time.

'Well?' asked the inspector in charge of his subordinate after the corpse had been lowered to the ground and a preliminary examination carried out. 'What d'you make of it?'

'Straightforward suicide, I should think, sir. He's foreign. A postgraduate student at the university. He's carrying a matriculation card, name of Hammadi, Ali Hammadi.'

'Photograph on the card?'

'Yes, it's him all right.'

The sergeant handed over the card and sifted through the contents of the dead man's wallet. 'Thirty-five quid in cash, two credit cards, a few names and telephone numbers, a phonecard, an invitation to a party and an electronic key to a university building, the Institute of Molecular Science.'

The forensic pathologist arrived, a short bald man, overweight and out of puff by the time he'd reached the clearing with his bag.

'Well, this is a nice change,' he said.

'Nice change?'

'It's usually pissing down and the middle of the bloody night when Lothian's finest call me out.'

'Oh, very droll.'

The pathologist knelt down beside the body and started to carry out his scene-of-crime examination. As he worked, he asked, 'Do we know anything about him?'

'A student. Molecular science we think.'

'Obviously not physics,' said the pathologist, examining the dead man's neck. 'He got the jump wrong. Neck's not broken. He strangled himself.'

The inspector adopted an expression of distaste. 'Students,' he snorted. 'Why do they have to make failing their bloody exams everybody else's problem?'

'We don't know that he failed any exams, sir,' said the sergeant through gritted but still respectful teeth. He was a lot closer to the dead man in terms of age than his superior.

The inspector gave him a black look. 'It's the usual bloody reason, isn't it? Papers will probably describe him as brilliant. Always do.'

# ~ One ~

*Saudi Arabia*
*September 1997*

The wheels of the long-base Land Rover ceased their constant struggle for grip on the sand as the engine died and the vehicle came to a halt in a deep hollow between two flanking dunes. The four men aboard unwound the *keffiyeh* from their faces and stepped out to shake the sand free from their clothes and savour the velvet silence of the night. Above them the stars shone down from a cloudless sky, dwarfing them in an almost lunar landscape, making them feel like the sole inhabitants of a strange and distant planet.

'Time to take a look,' said their leader. Despite his Arab dress, he spoke English; they all did. One man stayed with the vehicle while the other three climbed to a point just below the crest of the dune on the north side to throw themselves flat and wriggle up the last few metres to start scanning the desert. They used top-quality night-vision equipment as befitted members of an elite British military unit. Officially they were attached to the Saudi forces as 'advisers'. Unofficially they wore Arab clothing, carried no formal identification and did their own thing. At present they were one of a number of units patrolling the border area where Kuwait, Saudi Arabia and Iraq met. If Saddam was up to anything in the area, they wanted to be the first to know about it.

'Quiet as the grave,' murmured one of the men.

'Sand, sand and more bloody sand,' whispered another.

Their leader checked his hand-held GPS navigational system and mentally thanked the American satellites above that had just given him his map position on the surface of the Earth to within three square metres. He noted it down in his logbook and checked his watch before adding the time.

'Skip, there's something happening over there,' said one of the soldiers. He said it quietly and without excitement. Understatement was a matter of professional pride among these soldiers. The others took their cue from his line of sight and picked up on two vehicles travelling on the Iraqi side of the border.

'Convoy of two, they're heading straight for the border.'

'Don't think it's a convoy . . . more like a chase.'

'You're right. We'll take an interest in this.'

Two of the soldiers kept their glasses on the approaching vehicles while the leader of the unit took a studied look around at their surroundings, mentally planning the best way for them to stage an interception, should the approaching vehicles actually cross the border into Saudi territory.

'Military vehicles,' updated one of the soldiers monitoring the action.

'One man in the first, three in the second,' added his colleague.

'So they're chasing a man who wants to cross the border. Guess that automatically qualifies him as a friend of ours. Let's go.'

The three men packed up their gear quickly and half rolled, half slid back down the dune to the Land Rover. The soldier who had stayed with it saw their hurry and started the engine.

'Move over!' The leader took the wheel and coaxed the vehicle into a sliding, wheel-spinning acceleration down the steep gully leading out from the dunes. The other three checked their weapons and rewound their *keffiyeh* across their faces.

'On their present course, they'll cross the border just north of a flat stretch that runs between two rocky outcrops about eight hundred metres west of here. The natural line will bring them between the two. We'll take up station on either side.'

The instructions had been yelled above the engine noise but all three men nodded to signify they'd understood.

The Land Rover came to a halt and the four men split up, two on either side of a narrow strip leading inland but with rock formations on either side. There was a steep entry to the pass ensuring that any vehicle entering would have to slow right down. As the four cradled their weapons and burrowed into a comfortable position in the sand they could already hear the engines of the approaching vehicles.

The first came into view and alarmed the watching soldiers with its seemingly erratic progress. It was weaving from side to side for no apparent reason connected with terrain. This was allowing the pursuing truck to gain ground on it.

'The bugger's pissed,' offered one of the soldiers.

'Thought they didn't drink.'

'Come on, come on,' urged their leader, ignoring the background comments; he was very much aware of just how much ground the pursuing vehicle was making up 'C'mon! You can make it, whoever you are.'

'Jesus!' they all exclaimed as the leading truck hit a large boulder and one side was forced high off the ground. For one long moment it looked as if it would capsize, but it righted itself with a huge bounce that made the watching soldiers wince, and continued to lurch towards them. The pursuing truck was now only a hundred metres behind.

As the lead truck hit the rise, it slowed dramatically and its wheels sank into the build-up of soft sand at the foot of the climb. Its engine screamed as the wheels lost purchase. It was still moving forward but in painfully slow motion. The other truck had almost caught up with it when it finally cleared the top of the rise and started to pull away again, but the slewing motion induced by the acceleration was not being corrected properly by the driver. Suddenly the truck lurched violently to one side, as if the driver had completely lost control. It crashed into the rocks immediately below the waiting soldiers.

The soldiers looked to their leader. He held up his hand to signify that they do nothing. For the moment, they would remain as spectators. He was waiting for the pursuers to clear the rise. This they did a few moments later and their truck came to a halt in the middle of the narrow pass. Three Iraqi soldiers got out and levelled their weapons as they moved cautiously towards the crashed vehicle. They seemed reluctant; it was almost as if they didn't want to get too close for fear of the unknown. This puzzled the soldiers above. They could clearly see that the driver of the first truck was unconscious and slumped over the wheel. What were his pursuers afraid of? Did they imagine he was playing possum?

The Iraqi soldiers approached cautiously, holding their weapons in readiness. Then, when they were about five metres away from the vehicle, they stopped and raised them. It suddenly became apparent to the men above that they intended to execute their quarry without further ado. The soldiers' leader sprang to his feet and shouted out in Arabic, 'Stop! Lay down your weapons!'

The Iraqis were taken by surprise. They looked up but only to see that they were in a hopeless position. Two soldiers on either side of the pass were pointing their weapons down at them. Common sense dictated that they should comply with the instruction but panic won the right to decide. One of the Iraqis dropped to his knees and began firing. The other two obeyed the herd instinct. All three perished in the hail of crossfire that was returned. The world returned to an eerie black silence

'Fuck. I hope to Christ they really were on our side of the

border,' said one of the soldiers.

'They were,' said the leader. 'But the brass still ain't gonna like it.'

'You can say that again.'

'Border incident threatens Middle East peace,' intoned one of the others.

'Shit, what d'we do now?'

'Let's check the guy they were chasing. If we find out why he was running, we might still come out of this smelling of roses.'

'They tried to open the driver's door of the crashed truck but it had jammed; the impact had deformed it.

'Bring him out through the window.'

One of the soldiers reached in through the window and managed to get his arms round the slumped figure. He pulled the man back from the wheel and manoeuvred him across to the window. The others helped pull him through while the first soldier guided them. The injured man was laid down on his back in the sand and his *keffiyeh* removed.

'Sweet Jesus Christ!' exclaimed the first soldier who saw the man. He recoiled and fell back on to the ground, looking shocked. The others looked to see what was wrong.

'Christ almighty,' said another. 'Look at him.'

'This is all we need,' said the leader as he looked down at the man lying in the sand, his features lit by moonlight. Every centimetre of his face was covered in small weeping pustules, his eyes just tiny slits in the suppurating mess of his face. This accounted for his erratic driving. He was practically blind.

'What the hell's wrong with him?'

The leader shook his head slowly. 'God knows, but he obviously thought he'd get more help this side of the border.'

'Saddam's been playing with his chemistry set?'

'Could be biological.'

'Poor bugger.'

'Christ, where does this leave us?'

'Now there's tonight's prizewinning question,' said the leader. If it's something biological like a virus, we've already been exposed to it. All of us.'

'Christ, is this why Saddam stopped the UN inspections?' exclaimed one of the soldiers. 'They were getting too close?'

'Something tells me you're not going to be alone in thinking that before the night's over,' said the leader.

'So what do we do?'

'I vote we put this poor bugger out his misery and get the fuck out of here,' said the third soldier, who was now squatting beside the unconscious man as if mesmerised by the sight of his disfigurement.

'We're not going anywhere,' retorted the leader sharply. 'We've all been exposed to this . . . whatever it is. There's a chance we'll spread it. We'll have to call in the brains.'

'If you do that . . .'

'What?'

The soldier paused for a moment before saying, 'You don't think some bugger might figure the safest course of action would be to wipe us all out in one tidy hit?'

'It might cross somebody's mind, but they won't,' said the leader.

'Why not?'

''Cos we're the good guys, remember?'

The silence of the unconvinced was eloquent enough. It forced the group leader to add, 'Apart from that, they'll want to know what this is all about.'

'I like that reason better.'

'Stow it. Get these three back in their truck and dowse it with fuel.'

'What about him?' asked the soldier who still squatted beside the sick man.

'Make him as comfortable as you can.'

The leader returned to the Land Rover to radio back to base.

It was something he hadn't planned on doing: radio contact was discouraged but circumstances dictated differently tonight. As expected, he was told to stand by. He'd thrown the shit at the fan and now it was spreading.

'Do we light the fire?' asked one of the soldiers who'd been dowsing the Iraqi truck in petrol.

'Not yet. Get up top and keep your eyes peeled. They may send more when this lot fails to report back. Any sign of trouble and we'll light the fire immediately. We want to dissuade any more of them from crossing the border while the brass contemplate their navels.'

Ten minutes passed without anything at all happening. The four soldiers sat huddled against the cold of the desert night while they awaited instructions. The sick Iraqi lay by his truck. He had been wrapped in blankets and a makeshift pillow fashioned for him.

'What if the brass know all about this already?' asked one of the soldiers. 'What if they don't need to get hold of this guy to find out what it is? The more I think about it, the more I think they're going to waste us. It makes sense.'

'Shut it!'

There was a crackle from the radio and the group's call sign of Sierra Mike Zulu carried to them on the night air. The leader went over to the Land Rover and sat down in the front passenger seat to take instructions.

'I think he's moving,' said one of the others, looking towards the Arab. 'Maybe we should give him a shot of something.'

'I doubt you'd find a place to give him a shot of anything. I think his entire body's like his face.'

'Poor bastard.'

'If that's a virus, it's gonna be poor us very shortly.'

'We've had our shots.'

'Let's just hope they were the right ones.'

'I'm going to give him some water.'

'You're a good man, Charlie Brown. I'm not going near him.'

The leader returned from the Land Rover. 'They're sending a chopper.'

'For him?'

'For all of us. Rendezvous is four miles south of here at oh three hundred hours. That gives us an hour and a quarter. Rig up something in the back of the Land Rover for our friend here and let's get started.'

The leader crossed to where the soldier was dripping water from his own flask into the mouth of the Iraqi. The man seemed only semiconscious but his lips and tongue sought out the moisture. 'How is he?'

'Alive but I wouldn't give odds on that being the case in fifteen minutes.'

'We're moving out. A chopper's on its way. Do what you can for him in the meantime.'

The leader unstrapped a petrol can from the crashed truck and sprinkled the contents over the second Iraqi vehicle before throwing the can itself back in through one of the windows.

When the Iraqi had been loaded into the back of the Land Rover on a makeshift pallet and they were ready to leave the leader lit two rags and threw one into each of the Iraqi vehicles. Orange flames leapt up into the night sky as the petrol ignited. He shielded his face from the heat for a moment before turning to run over to the Land Rover and climb into the front passenger seat.

'Move out.'

They heard the helicopter long before they saw it.

'It's a bloody Chinook,' said one of the men, responding to the engine note as they scanned the heavens. There was no mistaking the surprise in his voice.

'What the hell are they sending a Chinook for?' asked another.

'You did tell them it's only one bloke and not a bloody Iraqi regiment, didn't you, Skip?'

'They know. Keep clear, I'm sending the flare up.'

The signal rocket fizzed angrily up into the night sky and burst like a miniature dawn on the scene below. A few minutes later the powerful searchlights on the underside of the huge Chinook helicopter took over a more permanent role in illuminating the scene as its twin rotor blades brought it to a hover over the Land Rover and deafened the watching party below.

After what seemed an eternity the chopper moved about a hundred metres to the south of them and touched down. Its blades were kept turning. The driver of the Land Rover started the engine but the group leader put a restraining hand on his shoulder.

'Let's wait for instructions.'

He had hardly said the words when a loudspeaker crackled into life on the helicopter.

'Sierra Mike Zulu, this is Chopper Tango Charlie. Remain exactly where you are. Do nothing until our men are with you. Flash your lights if that is understood.'

The leader nodded and the driver flashed the Land Rover headlights.

'I don't like this,' whispered the soldier who was looking after the Iraqi.

The doors of the Chinook opened slowly and several men dressed in what appeared to be spacesuits emerged. They unloaded several boxes, then started out towards the Land Rover, bringing the cases with them.

'Sorry for the high drama,' continued the voice on the Tannoy. 'But you men will be going into quarantine until further notice. Is anyone ill apart from your prisoner? Flash once for yes, twice for no.'

'Why don't they just use the radio, for Christ's sake?' complained one of the soldiers.

'The Iraqis have had time to figure out they've got a missing patrol. They'll be monitoring everything right now,' replied the leader as the driver gave two flashes of the headlights.

'Good. Just stay calm.'

The men in spacesuits reached the Land Rover and circled the vehicle.

'Bloody hell,' whispered one of the soldiers. 'I know our personal hygiene isn't all that it might be after a week in the desert but this is ridiculous.'

'Bio-safety suits,' said the leader. 'Completely self-contained. Nobody's taking any chances.'

The man in charge of the spacemen signalled that they get out of the vehicle. They complied and stood there feeling very vulnerable while the boxes that the men in suits had been carrying were opened up.

'Looks like we're getting suits too,' said one of the soldiers as the contents of the box nearest them became apparent.

'Difference is, they're wearing them to keep things out, we'll be wearing them to keep things in.'

'Doesn't do much for your self-esteem, does it?'

The soldiers donned the orange suits they were given while the Iraqi was removed from the back of the Land Rover and given a short medical check before being fed into another of the suits — with some difficulty, as he was unable to help himself. When everyone was suited up and all the seals had been checked by the men from the Chinook all those in orange suits were sprayed thoroughly with a disinfectant solution before being led over to the waiting helicopter. The soldiers turned as they reached it to see an incendiary device turn their Land Rover into a blazing inferno.

'I think it just failed its MOT,' whispered one.

The inside of the Chinook had been partitioned to provide a plastic cocoon for the boarding men. It had its own air supply and filtration system and was hermetically separate from the rest of the aircraft. Food and bottled water had been left inside for them. Their quarantine had already begun.

No one could think of anything much to say on the flight. They fell to silence as each man faced his own thoughts.

An isolation suite had been readied for them at the base hospital in Dhahran, not that much preparation had been needed. It already existed for the purpose – it had been commissioned as a precaution in the war over Kuwait but as yet had not been used in earnest. This was its first real test.

For the soldiers it was a relief to get out of the cumbersome suits and have a long shower before dressing in fresh fatigues. When they were ready, their debriefing was carried out by closed-circuit television. 'You'd think we'd just returned from Mars,' said one of the men. 'I'm expecting the US president at any minute.'

Their side of the story was straightforward. Two Iraqi vehicles had crossed the border into Saudi territory and they had intercepted. The Iraqis had failed to comply with a request to drop their weapons and had opened fire first. Three Iraqi soldiers had been killed, one sick man had been brought in with them for treatment. Both Iraqi vehicles had been destroyed by fire.

'And the dead Iraqis?'

'Cremated with the vehicles.'

The debriefing officer drew in breath through his teeth.

The group leader felt compelled to defend his action. 'I thought in the circumstances and not knowing what the agent was, it would be best to burn everything,' he said.

'Well, so far the Iraqis haven't made any noises at all,' said the officer. 'We haven't heard a peep out of them.'

'Is that good or bad, sir?'

'In my view, bad. Silence usually implies guilt. If this had been a case of a patrol innocently straying across the line they would have been screaming the place down and calling the UN into special session.'

'How is the Iraqi we brought in, sir?'

'Still alive, I hear. We're waiting for the experts to arrive.'

'So no one knows what's wrong with him yet?'

''Fraid not. We'll keep you posted. In the meantime I'll have to ask you all to be patient.'

'Yes, sir.'

'Still feeling all right?'

'Yes, sir, we're fine.'

The four soldiers were encouraged to get some sleep but it proved difficult for all of them. Although well used to having to sleep where and when they could under operational conditions, lying on a clean comfortable bunk, alone with their thoughts in their present predicament, was not something they had been trained for. The enemy this time was completely intangible; it was something they could not get to grips with. It was invisible and deadly and, for all they knew, it was already inside them; chances were, it had already won the battle. They became hyper-aware of their own bodies. When one of the soldiers sneezed the others froze in apprehension. Was it the first sign? The slightest twinge of pain in their limbs or any suggestion of stiffness took on a whole new significance.

'This waiting is driving me mad,' said one of the men as they started their third day drinking coffee and playing cards.

'Surely they'll figure out something today,' said another. They had experts flying in all day yesterday. Porton Down, CDC Atlanta, a team from Sweden.'

'Sweden?' chorused the others.

'Apparently they have a great deal of expertise in mobile isolation facilities for disease outbreaks. They set up a team after one of their cities was threatened with an outbreak of *filo virus* a few years ago. They're top-notch.'

'So they think it's a virus then?'

'Seems to be, the way they're moving,' agreed the leader.

'Christ, we must have it,' said one of the soldiers, getting to his feet and starting to pace.

'It's been three days and we're still all OK,' countered one of the others.

'I know but . . . Christ, we must have it. It wouldn't be much of a biological warfare agent if we didn't, would it?'

'So it's a crap agent, I'll settle for that,' said the leader. 'It'll be on a par with Saddam's crap missiles. They would have been as well throwing rice pudding at the Israelis as these SCUDS as I remember.'

'Or maybe our shots are working against it. We could be immune.'

'Yeah, let's look on the bright side.'

This spawned a short chorus of 'Always Look on the Bright Side of Life', which had more bravado than humour about it. It prompted their Saudi monitors to ask if they were still feeling all right.

'Never better,' replied their leader, not bothering to explain any further.

At seven on the evening of their third day in quarantine the doors to the isolation unit were suddenly opened up and the four soldiers were joined by British and Saudi officers.

'Your incarceration is over gentlemen,' announced one. 'You're free to go.'

The men were taken aback. The Iraqi's OK then?

'No, unfortunately he's dead but not from any dreadful new plague virus I'm delighted to say.'

'Then what?'

'Our international team of experts tell us he died from something called disseminated vaccinia; he was just unlucky.'

'I'm sorry, sir, I don't think I understand,' said the group leader.

'Apparently the chap suffered an adverse reaction to a vacci-nation against smallpox.'

'A vaccination?'

'I'm told that there are a certain percentage of people in any population who are hypersensitive to vaccinia virus, which they use for giving protection against the disease. This poor chap was one of them.

'So we are OK then?'

'Indeed you are.'

'Thank f— goodness, sir.'

'Amen to that, Sergeant.'

# ~ *Two* ~

*World Health Organisation*
*International Disease Monitor*
*Geneva*
*September 1997*

It was a hot afternoon. The sun was shining brightly on the summer crowds that thronged the pavements but, inside, the room was pleasantly cool because of air conditioning and was comfortably shaded, thanks to half closed blinds. There were twenty-four people assembled in the room when the doors were finally closed and the chairman brought the meeting to order.

'Thank you for coming, ladies and gentlemen. I've convened this special meeting of the Viral Pathogen Group to scotch a rumour I've been made aware of and to relay a report that has arrived on my desk from our colleagues at the United Nations Disease Monitor.

'The facts of the matter are as follows. Two weeks ago a sick Iraqi soldier was picked up just inside Saudi Arabian territory by a routine desert patrol. His intentions were not clear in crossing the border but it seems he was being pursued from the Iraqi side so we can assume that he was seeking help or even asylum. He was too ill to give any information to the men who picked him up, but one of these men, who had special training in biological warfare, recognised the possible dangers of the situation and sought expert advice by radio. The sick man was subsequently airlifted, along with the patrol, to a hospital in Dhahran which had isolation facilities and where they were all put in quarantine. The immediate fear for the authorities was that the Iraqi had been subject to some biological- or chemical-warfare accident. One of the staff physicians, however, a man in his sixties, thought he recognised the disease as being smallpox.'

A slight hubbub broke out in the room.

'Quite so,' conceded the chairman. 'A full-scale alert was declared.'

'When specialist people arrived from CDC Atlanta along with a Niklasson team from Sweden it was determined that the disease was not in fact smallpox but an adverse reaction to vaccination *against* the disease. The man was in fact, suffering from disseminated vaccinia. He was one of these few extremely unfortunate people who cannot tolerate vaccinia virus – I can't remember the exact incidence figure'

'One in a hundred thousand,' said a man halfway down the right side of the table, who spoke with a strong Swedish accent.

'Thank you, Sven,' said the chairman. 'Of course, once it was established that it was not smallpox they were dealing with there was relief all round. The three- or four-day nightmare was suddenly over. Unfortunately the Iraqi himself died without being able to furnish us with any details of what exactly had happened. The patrol members, who naturally had been worried about their own safety, were released from quarantine and allowed to return to duty. But it was a very worrying time for all concerned.'

A murmur of agreement surfaced in the room. The chairman continued.

'In view of the rumour about an outbreak of smallpox, circulating in certain professional circles, both here and at the UN building, I thought I would put the record straight. I have also asked Dr Jacques Lang from the joint WHO/UN smallpox advisory group to join us today and give us an update on the world situation with regard to that disease.'

A tall man with a distinct stoop and dark unruly hair that he kept having to brush back from his forehead stood up and sorted his notes in front of him on the table. He took a sip of water before beginning.

'Colleagues, as you know, there has been no case of smallpox occurring naturally on the planet since 1977 when the last case, a man in Somalia, died from the disease. The WHO declared the world free from the disease some two years later. True, there was one more death after the Somali patient but that was a case of the genie getting out of the bottle – or should I say the test tube? – in a laboratory accident in Birmingham, England.

'I think we all learned something from that tragedy. It stood out as a tragic demonstration of the ability of the virus to get out of containment. Ever since that time, the storage of live small-pox virus has been strictly controlled. Currently it is only stored at two places on Earth, the Center for Disease Control in Atlanta, Georgia, USA, and the Russian State Research Centre of Virology and Biotechnology at Koltsovo in the Novosibirsk Region of the Russian Federation. Security at both establish-ments is of the highest order and containment facilities for the virus are as secure as man can make them.'

'Even in Russia?' asked a somewhat jaundiced American voice.

'I appreciate your scepticism,' said Lang. 'Russian infra-structure leaves a lot to be desired these days but the Koltsovo institute is beyond reproach.'

'So, if the virus is locked up safely at only two places on Earth and no one can get at it, why was the Iraqi soldier being vaccinated against the disease in the first place?' asked one of the women present, a German in her late forties. The murmur in the room said that she had just asked the question many other people had been thinking.

Lang grimaced and said, 'Frau Doctor Lehman has of course asked an intriguing question. Frankly, we don't know. It may have been some routine procedure that no one ever got round to changing. That sort of thing often happens in a military environment where people are not encouraged to question things. Routine becomes tradition. Another puzzling thing is that the Iraqis have not yet acknowledged the defection of their man nor, I understand, the deaths of three more of their soldiers in the border incident that led to his escape.'

'What exactly happened?' asked Lehman.

'I understand the sick man's countrymen were intent on killing him when the border patrol intervened. I don't have any more details,' interjected the chairman.

'Why would they want to kill a sick man if he was just suffering an adverse reaction to a routine vaccination?' Lehman persisted.

'Maybe they didn't know that's what it was,' said the chairman. 'Maybe they saw him go down with some awful disease and were frightened they might get it too so they took matters into their own hands.'

'That's possible if it was a local decision among border guards,' said Lang, 'but if the order came from higher up maybe the Iraqis didn't want anyone to know he'd been vaccinated.'

'In that case we'd have to consider the possibility they've got their hands on the virus and intend using it as a weapon,' said an American voice.

The German woman, Lehman, nodded vigorously at this.

'That's a bit of a leap, Hank,' said the chairman.

'I just don't see how they could have got hold of it,' said Lang. 'There has been no breach of security at either of the holding establishments and there is no animal reservoir for the virus in the wild. It's purely a disease of humans – that's partly why we were so successful in wiping it out. That and the availability of such an efficient vaccine. I think we are worrying unnecessarily.'

'Just for interest's sake, how would smallpox rate as a biological weapon?' asked an Asian man.

'That's really not my field,' replied Lang. 'But personally, I would find it almost too frightening to contemplate. Smallpox virus is one of the greatest killers the world has ever known. It's been around for over two thousand years. It killed an Egyptian pharaoh, several European crowned heads and countless millions of ordinary people before vaccination brought about its demise.'

'Worse than anthrax?'

'Just as deadly and more practical to use. Anthrax is an extremely effective killing agent but it's difficult to protect your own forces against it and once you've used it it's damned nearly impossible to get rid of. It lies around in the soil for decades. With smallpox you can protect your own people with a very efficient vaccine that is virtually free from side effects, kill the enemy, and the virus will quickly die out again in the absence of a human host. It was generalised vaccination of the public that prevented them using smallpox as a weapon.'

'But that was all stopped,' said the German woman, provoking a long silence in the room.

'Indeed it was,' said the American man. 'Vaccination against smallpox was stopped in the USA as long ago as 1971.'

'Around the same time in the UK,' added an English voice.

'So two generations have grown up without protection against the virus,' said the chairman.

'But there is no virus to protect against,' insisted Lang. 'To all intents and purposes smallpox is extinct.'

The room fell to silence again. No one argued with Lang but there was no discernible agreement either. People were worried.

'I wish we'd wiped the damned thing out completely when we had the chance back in '95,' said the English voice.

'Well we lost the vote on that one,' said the chairman. 'You'll have to wait until the next scheduled date for destruction. If there's no further delay, the only remaining stocks of smallpox virus will be destroyed completely in June 1999.'

'So what have all these scientists who objected to the 1995 destruction proposal been doing in the meantime if as you say live virus is only held at two places on Earth?'

'I assure you,' said Lang, 'very strict controls have been applied to any research involving smallpox. The virus had its DNA sequence determined so we actually know details of the entire blueprint for its existence. Once that was known it was possible to cut the DNA into defined linear fragments. Research labs are allowed to have access to individual fragments of the virus DNA, never the complete organism and never more than twenty per cent of the fragmented DNA at any one time.'

'What good is a bit of a virus?' came another English voice.

Lang smiled wryly and answered, 'When we set out to sequence the virus we expected it to be fairly routine. As with all viruses we thought its genes would be concerned with the structure and propagation of itself. Only half of them were. The other half turned out to be human genes.'

There were several instances of raised eyebrows round the table, despite the scientific credentials of many present.

'They were genes concerned with the human immune system,' Lang continued. 'In short, the smallpox virus knows more about the human immune system than medical science does. That's really what prompted the delay in destroying it completely. It can teach us a lot.'

'I'm uncomfortable about having all these bits and pieces of virus floating around.'

Lang shrugged and said, 'It's not as if just anyone could just join up the fragments to recreate a live virus. It would take a first-rate molecular biologist, someone who had studied the entire genome, and even then he or she would need a lot of luck. Having said that, if there was any evidence that someone was even contemplating trying such a thing we would step in immediately and put an end to it. Criminal charges would almost certainly be brought.'

'And rightly so,' said the chairman. 'In the meantime, doing nothing is not an option for us.'

He paused and the others waited in silence for him to continue.

'We are clearly not happy about the vaccinated man but I don't think we could recommend a return to wholesale vaccination. There are risks associated with all vaccination programmes and we would have to justify them to the people who might suffer side effects.'

'Perhaps a limited reintroduction might be in order,' suggested one man. 'Just to be on the safe side.'

'That would be a possibility but it's a decision I think we would have to leave up to individual governments.'

Israel was uppermost in everyone's mind.

'But before we do that or recommend anything else, I suggest that we ask the Iraqis outright why their man had been vaccinated against smallpox and judge them on their reaction.'

The suggestion gained universal approval.

'Then that's settled,' said the chairman. 'I will arrange for a joint WHO/UN delegation to draft the question. We will reconvene when I have an answer. In the meantime perhaps Dr Lang and his colleagues could check again with the institutes holding live virus and also on the state of monitoring of these fragments.'

Lang nodded. 'Of course, sir.'

*Eight days later*
*Same location*

'We have received a reply from Baghdad, ladies and gentlemen,' announced the chairman. 'They say that during a routine vaccination programme for some of their troops an old batch of smallpox vaccine was used in mistake for hepatitis vaccine. Apparently one batch of freeze-dried vaccine looked pretty much like any other to the junior medical staff who were involved in giving the shots. They apologise for the border incident and any alarm caused.'

'They apologised?'

'Makes me suspicious.'

The chairman took off his glasses and waited until the comments subsided before saying, 'It is just conceivable they are telling the truth. Unlike many vaccines, freeze-dried smallpox vaccine can be stored for a long time. Such a mix-up could have happened.'

'The question is, did it?'

'I think we must be very cautious,' said the German woman.

'Dr Lang, have you anything to tell us?' asked the chairman.

'We approached both the CDC and the Russian institute. Both report no attempted breach of security and stocks of the virus are all accounted for.'

'Good, how about fragment movement?'

Lang moved a little uneasily in his seat. 'That was a bit more difficult,' he confessed. 'Many labs across the world have requested viral fragments for their research programmes. AIDS research is very intense. There is a lot of competition.'

'There's a lot of money at stake!' came the cynical comment from one of the group members.

'Is the monitoring system to ensure that no one lab gets more than twenty per cent of the complete virus working or not?' insisted the chairman.

'Yes . . .' replied Lang but he sounded uncertain.

'Let me put it another way,' said the chairman. 'Is it at all conceivable that an attempt has been made to recreate live smallpox virus from these fragments?'

'I would really think . . . not.'

'But you're not absolutely certain?'

'One can never be absolutely certain. If someone is deter-mined enough to do something, then who knows?'

The chairman was reluctant to let Lang off the hook. He said, 'Supposing a scientist were to request a few fragments of virus at one institution and then move to another. Would it be possible for him – or her – to order some more fragments without you realising what was going on?'

'Our records are institute records,' conceded Lang. 'Frag-ments are not referenced against individuals.'

'So a university department or research institute might be credited with having three fragments when, in practice, an individual scientist working there might have brought three more with him from his last job and have access to six?'

'I suppose so.'

A great deal of unease had been created by Lang's answers. The chairman had to hold up his hand for quiet.

'Ladies . . . gentlemen . . . please. I suggest we keep a sense of proportion about what we've learned. I was deliberately trying to paint a worst-possible-case scenario. Let us pause and consider the facts as they really are.' The room returned to calm and order. 'I think we can be reasonably sure that stocks of live virus remain untouched and there has been no criminal attempt to obtain them.' People nodded their agreement. 'The situation pertaining to the fragments, however, may or may not be a cause for concern. We need more in the way of reassurance.'

'I vote we recommend a complete ban on the circulation of these fragments for the moment,' said the German woman, Lehman. It was a view that attracted considerable support from the others but one that made the chairman discernibly uncomfortable.

'I see two things against that course of action,' he said. 'One is the fact that we would undoubtedly interrupt aspects of AIDS research programmes all over the world. To what extent, we can't be sure – perhaps very little in view of the slowness of progress in that particular field – but it would certainly cause inconvenience and even some degree of resentment among the scientific community. Universal goodwill is important to both the World Health Organisation and the United Nations. I am loath to do anything that might damage it.'

'Chairman, there is also a view that being overly concerned with our image makes us impotent. I would like to draw the meeting's attention to the last report issued by the UN inspectors in Iraq before their work was interrupted. They uncovered the presence of a factory at Wadi Ras which they suspected was being used for the manufacture of biological weapons. The Iraqis successfully argued that it was actually being used for vaccine production. In the light of what we've heard, I don't think we can take comfort from that . . .'

Argument and discussion continued until the chairman said, 'Colleagues, we'll put it to a vote.'

Voting slips were passed round the table, marked in silence and returned to the chairman, who separated them into two piles in front of him. It was obviously going to be a close-run thing. With the last slip assigned, he stood up and announced, 'We have voted by a majority of two to recommend an immediate halt to the movement of smallpox viral fragments.'

Some people shrugged, others smiled.

'Dr Lang? You have something to add?'

'Perhaps I should just say that individual countries have already been asked to carry out an audit on the fragments their research institutions are holding.'

'Good, that would be helpful,' said the chairman. 'But let's hope than none of this is really necessary at all. Let's look forward to finding out that our fears are groundless and our suspicions nothing more than paranoia.' It was an appropriate note on which to end the meeting.

*The Home Office*
*London*
*October 1997*

Adam Dewar arrived at the Home Office with only two minutes to spare before his scheduled meeting. He thought he'd given himself plenty of time for the journey up from his flat by the river, but he had underestimated the sheer numbers of late-season tourists in the capital. He was feeling distinctly ruffled by the time he had circumnavigated the final group.

'Video cameras! There can't be one dog turd left unrecorded in London,' he complained to his boss's secretary, Jean Roberts, as he entered her office a little breathless.

'Tourism is good for the economy, Dr Dewar,' she replied with a smile. 'Nice to see you in good form. You can go straight in.'

Dewar worked for the Sci Med Inspectorate, a government body set up to provide preliminary investigation into potential wrongdoings in the hi-tech areas of science and medicine, areas where the police had little or no expertise. The staff comprised a number of medically or scientifically qualified people whose task it was to carry out discreet, occasionally undercover enquiries in the often blurred margins that separated incompetence from outright criminality. Highly qualified professional people invariably resented outside interest in what they were doing, regarding it as unwarranted interference, so discretion was of the utmost importance until, at least, the facts were established.

Adam Dewar was a doctor specialising in medical investigations. He was well aware that there was a no more sensitive or conservative body than the medical profession. Closing ranks was almost a knee-jerk response to outside questioning. The well-guarded mystique of the witch doctor was still extant in late-twentieth-century medicine. The less the patient knows the better.

Dewar had been on leave for the past four weeks. This was part of the pattern of the job. Investigations were often intensive, requiring long hours of work and high stress levels. Occasionally they could be downright dangerous or even life-threatening. When they were completed, leave was generous. Dewar had spent his free time staying in a small village in the south of France which he had known since childhood, enjoying the wine, the food and sunshine of Provence. He had, however, spent the final week preparing for his return in fairly hard physical exercise. He had swum three miles daily in the sea off San Raphael and used the cool of the evening to run respectable distances along the vineyard paths between neighbouring villages. He felt reasonably fit again, not that his last assignment had taken much out of him in a physical sense.

He had been sent to look into the apparently high death rate among patients of a Lincolnshire surgeon when compared with statistics for similar operations in other parts of the country. There had in fact been no criminal aspect to this case. The surgeon in question had merely grown old in his job and had been unaware of his failing powers. His strong personality — common in surgeons — had prevented colleagues from doing much about the situation. It was one thing knowing what was wrong, quite another saying it. The man was also very influential in senior medical circles, circles which could make or break careers. The situation had been allowed to develop until the Sci Med computer had drawn attention to the statistical blip.

Dewar had not been subject to the man's power and influence, and he had a strong personality too. Under the terms of the Sci Med Inspectorate he had the power to resolve the situation — and he had. The surgeon had been retired. Happily, the end result had been achieved without scandal or rancour, thanks to the application of common sense.

Dewar knocked on the door and responded to the immediate

invitation to enter.

A tall silver-haired man stood up behind his desk and held out his hand. He was John Macmillan, Dewar's boss and the director of the Sci Med Inspectorate.

'Good to see you, Dewar. How are you feeling after your break?'

'Very well, thank you, sir.'

'Good, What d'you know about smallpox?'

Dewar shrugged his shoulders. 'Not a lot, I'm afraid. It was a terrible disease in its time but it's been extinct for many years. A triumph for the World Health Organisation, as I recall. It was cited as an example of the power of vaccination programmes when I was at medical school. Quite poetic really when you think that the very first instance of vaccination was Edward Jenner's work on that very disease back in the eighteenth century. It took just under two hundred years to wipe out something that had been around as long as mankind.'

'Wipe out may be a little strong,' said Macmillan.

'You mean it's broken out again?' asked an incredulous Dewar.

'Not exactly but this has newly come in from a joint WHO/United Nations body. They'd like our help.'

Macmillan handed the documentation over to Dewar, who flicked through it and quickly realised he'd need more time to assimilate it.

'When you're ready, I'd like you to handle it,' said Macmillan.

# ~ *Three* ~

The door of lab 512 opened and a tall, distinguished figure walked in. He ignored the people working there and crossed the floor to open an office door on the far side. Finding no one inside, he turned and said to no one in particular, 'No Dr Malloy.'

'Give the man a coconut,' whispered one of the men present to a younger colleague working beside him.

'Did you say something, Mr Ferguson?' asked the tall man.

'I simply agreed with your observation, Professor Hutton,' replied the man who'd made the comment. Both men held eye contact for a moment, the tall man barely disguising his dislike, the older man seemingly inscrutable in the time-honoured tradition of dumb insolence.

'Are you expecting him in today?'

'He didn't say he wasn't going to be in,' replied a young, studious-looking man, wearing a black T-shirt with the name of a pop group emblazoned across it. His white lab coat hung open.

'I think he was pretty upset after yesterday's vaccine trial results,' added a young red-haired woman in her early twenties.

'Coming on top of Ali's death, I think it was the final straw.'

'We all have to accept setbacks in our research. It's part of the job,' said the tall man. He looked around at the work-benches in the lab and muttered, 'Ye gods, look at the state of this place. You people should take a leaf out of Dr Pearson's book next door. His staff keep the lab spotless; you won't find any clutter lying around there.'

'Not so much as an idea,' muttered Ferguson.

The tall man's nostrils flared in patrician anger and he took a deep breath but he said nothing to the offender. 'Tell Dr Malloy I'd like a word when he comes in.'

As the door closed, the young man in the T-shirt said to Ferguson, 'You're pushing your luck with him.'

'He's all front and no substance,' replied the older man.

'Peter's right, George,' said the young woman, Sandra Macandrew. 'You are pushing your luck. He really doesn't like this lab.'

'He can't do much more to me,' said the older man. 'If Steve doesn't get a new grant I'm out on my arse anyway come Christmas. *Herr Direktor* has fingered me for early retirement.'

'There must be a good chance Steve'll get the grant,' she said.

'Really? Let's face it. Yesterday's trial result isn't exactly going to help it along.'

No one argued.

'It's still a bad idea to get up Hutton's nose,' she persisted. 'He could still screw up your pension deal.'

'I guess. But it's my only pleasure,' said the older man with a grin.

'He *is* a bit of a pompous prick,' said Peter Moore, the graduate student wearing the black T-shirt.

'University's full of them,' added Macandrew, also a PhD student. 'Something we have to live with.'

'And something the British do so well,' added Pierre Le Grice, a visiting postdoctoral research fellow from the Institut

Pasteur in Paris. 'If you look the part and wear the right tie you can go far in this country.'

'Maybe it's because the university's an "equal-opportunity employer",' suggested Ferguson, the senior technician with the group. 'Being a brainless balloon is no impediment.'

The door opened and a man wearing dark glasses and black clothes came in. 'Christ, my head's got a brass band playing in it,' he complained by way of greeting.

'*Herr Direktor* was looking for you,' said Ferguson. 'Didn't look too happy but we still managed to make him less happy by the time he left.'

'You haven't been baiting him again, have you?' asked the newcomer with a look of resigned exasperation.

'He gave us a lecture on lab tidiness, said we should learn from the Pearson lab next door.'

'That'll be the day,' snorted Steven Malloy, the group leader. 'But he does have a point. Maybe just a wee tidy-up, guys?'

'OK, we'll do that while you see the man.'

'I need some coffee first.'

'And an aspirin?' asked Sandra Macandrew.

'You're an angel,' said Malloy waiting until the woman fetched a couple of aspirins from her handbag and handed them to him.'

'Right, I'll nip down to the machine and grab me a mouthful of caffeine before seeing Hutton.'

'Come back with your shield or on it,' smiled Peter Moore.

'And whatever he says, don't deck him. Peter and I would like to get our PhDs,' added Sandra.

'And *then* you can deck him,' added Peter.

Steven Malloy walked down one flight of stairs and along the corridor to the staff common room. In the lull between morning coffee and lunchtime it was empty. There was some coffee left in the Cona flask so he felt the outside; it was cold. He put some coins in the vending machine and selected black, extra strength.

Taking the plastic cup in both hands, he walked over to the window and put it down on the ledge while he unwrapped the aspirins from their foil and palmed them into his mouth. He washed them down with the coffee, wincing a little as he almost burned his throat. Two more gulps and he threw the cup in the bin and started out for the director's office.

The director's secretary, Hyacinth Chisolm, immaculate as ever in a mauve two-piece suit and smelling of expensive perfume, looked him up and down as he entered. She saw a man of medium height, in his mid-thirties, dressed in a black polo-neck sweater and black corduroy trousers. His glasses sat at an angle thanks to one ear being slightly higher than the other and his nose was crooked. He had a mass of black curly hair that belied his years. She thought he looked like a mop standing the wrong way up.

'Good morning, Dr Malloy,' she said, affecting a look at her wristwatch to check that it still was morning.

'Morning, Hyacinth. He wanted to see me.'

'I'll see if the professor's free.'

Hyacinth pressed a button on her intercom and said with affected formality, 'Dr Malloy is here, Professor.'

There was a pause during which Hyacinth remained glued to her intercom as if frozen in a moment in time. It was as if she were about to have some momentous truth revealed to her. When it came, it was, 'Ask him to come in, would you?'

'Ah, Steven, I thought it was about time we had a chat. I was looking for you earlier. You weren't in.'

'I had rather a lot to drink last night after hearing the trial results. I had a bit of a lie-in this morning.'

Professor Paul Hutton, director of the Institute of Molecular Sciences, winced at Malloy's explanation. He said, 'It must have been a bitter disappointment to you and your team.'

'We've been working a hundred hours a week on that project for the last eighteen months and we really thought we had it this time. It was going to be the first effective vaccine against AIDS and suddenly it all turns to dust when the animal trial results come out. No protection at all. Absolutely zilch. It was all for nothing and I've no idea why.'

'Perhaps if you had consulted more with your colleagues during the development period, aired your difficulties more, interacted with your colleagues, things might have turned out differently. Group meetings, seminars, that sort of thing are so useful in dealing with problems.'

'Sure. It would have taken us thirty-six months instead of eighteen to get nowhere,' replied Malloy.

'Interaction is an essential part of scientific life,' snapped Hutton.

'Some people interact so much they do fuck all else,' said Malloy. 'They just spend their days "interacting".'

Hutton lost his cool. He leaned forward in his seat. 'Let me tell you, Doctor, I am getting very tired of the attitude of you and your research group in this establishment. Your lack of respect for rules and regulations. You continually fail to deal with paperwork; you don't make reports when requested. We practically never see any of you at seminars and I don't think I've ever seen you attend a staff meeting at all.'

'If I did all that there wouldn't be any time left for research.'

'Other groups seem to manage and still carry out research programmes. Dr Pearson—'

'Dots other people's T's and crosses other people's I's. I don't call that research.'

'His work is well respected—'

'Among other scientists who do exactly the same thing. Find a rut and sit in it, make like-minded friends and scratch each other's backs. You review my grant application favourably and I'll do the same for you. Yuuugh!'

'This is outrageous! I don't know why I don't just-'

'Three papers in *Nature* last year and grants totalling three hundred thousand pounds, of which the institute skims forty per cent off the top as "overheads" before we even start. That's why you don't just . . .' exclaimed Malloy equally angrily.

Hutton looked away to the side, deliberately taking time to compose himself. He seemed to be biting his tongue. When he finally looked back at Malloy he said in controlled fashion, 'I appreciate you have been under a lot of strain recently, Steven. Ali's suicide must have been a great shock and now the trial results on your vaccine suggesting it might be less effective than we'd hoped . . .'

'The word you're searching for is "useless".'

'Be that as it may, we sometimes have to accept setbacks. Learn from our mistakes. Pick ourselves up.'

Malloy had to consciously stop himself turning the interview into a musical – 'And start all over again'. He kept quiet.

'I suggest we forget our little altercation, put our differences behind us and start afresh. I would be the last one to insist on robotic behaviour among the staff but we must have some standards or we'd have anarchy.'

'I appreciate that,' said Malloy quietly.

'Good. Perhaps you could take a look at some of your paper-work backload, especially the staff appraisals. They're long overdue.'

'They used to say that life was what happened to you while you were planning for the future. Now it's what happens to you while you're filling in forms.'

'I can sympathise to a certain extent but the institute insists that every member of staff be interviewed by his immediate superior at least once a year and an accurate record kept of performance to date, achievements, plans for the future et cetera. It's modern practice.'

'Modern doesn't necessarily mean it's good,' grumbled Malloy. 'What happens to these appraisals, anyway? Where do you send them?'

Hutton moved in his chair. 'Actually, we don't.'

'You don't send them anywhere?'

'They remain here on file.'

'You file them?'

'It's useful to have accurate progress records of everyone on the staff.'

Malloy wanted to scream out, 'But is it necessary?' But he didn't. In the interests of harmony, even pretend harmony, he kept his mouth shut.

'I'd also like you to have a word with that technician of yours, Ferguson. He's not been attending mandatory safety courses on the handling of infectious material.'

'George Ferguson has been handling infectious material for thirty years,' pointed out Malloy. 'He was handling typhoid and tuberculosis in an open lab while I was still playing with my train set.'

'That's beside the point.'

Malloy bit his tongue again but Hutton caught the look on his face. 'The rules don't differentiate. All technical staff are required to attend refresher courses. Frankly I don't understand why you took him on in the first place. He's a constant thorn in the side of the admin staff.'

'I took him on because he's been moved around from pillar to post ever since his hospital closed; I needed a good technician. The trust turned down the technical post on the grant application I put in but funded the rest of it. It was like giving me a car but saying I could only have three wheels on it.'

'I'm sure they had their reasons.'

'It's just that they're not obvious to anyone but themselves. Anyway, George has had a lot of experience. He may not be the most diplomatic of people but I don't need a diplomat. I need someone who can handle viruses.'

'Let's agree to disagree on the merits of Mr Ferguson,' said Hutton. 'What I really wanted to talk to you about this morning was the use of fragments of the smallpox virus. You use them I understand.'

'Sure, we've been trying to understand some of the tricks that the virus performs to get round the human immune system. It's a pretty fascinating bug.'

'Well, I've been officially informed that there is now a complete ban on the supply and movement of these fragments until further notice.'

'What?' exclaimed Malloy. 'But I was just about to request the fragments carrying the DNA upstream from the region we've been working on. We suspect the control region we were looking for had been cut through during the fragmentation.'

Hutton shrugged and said, 'I'm sorry, it's a joint WHO/UN recommendation that the government has endorsed with immediate effect.'

'Shit, but why?'

'No explanation but they also want us to audit and declare all the fragments we're holding. Sounds like someone has been doing something they shouldn't.'

'Joining up the fragments, you mean? God, you'd have to be a pork pie short of a picnic to do that to any great extent. Mind you . . .'

'Yes?'

'In some ways I can sympathise with the people who'd like the complete virus to work on. The trouble we've been experiencing is largely down to working with fragments rather than the complete genome. They thought in the beginning it would be just as good but it's not. Lots of important genes have been cut through when they cut the DNA into fragments. So anyone interested in finding out how the whole thing operates might be tempted to try a bit of reassembly. It may be stupid and against the rules but it's understandable.'

'It may not be being done for reasons of scientific curiosity,' said Hutton.

Malloy looked at him questioningly, and then it dawned on him what Hutton meant. 'God, you can't be serious. Someone trying to reconstruct live smallpox virus? They'd have to be out of their tree.'

Hutton shrugged his agreement. 'Be that as it may, can you let me have a list of the fragments you're currently holding?'

'Of course.'

'I've also had a letter from Ali Hammadi's parents.'

Malloy's face clouded over. 'Oh yes,' he said quietly.

'They'd like to endow a PhD studentship in his honour. Some kind of lasting memorial. Your thoughts?'

'I still find it hard to believe Ali's dead. He was a good student, easy-going, easy to get on with. Everyone liked him. His work was going exceptionally well and then suddenly in the space of a few short weeks his whole demeanour changed. He turned into a morose recluse who wouldn't speak to anyone and then he took his own life. I just don't understand it.'

'We'll have to assume it was some kind of mental aberration. Clinical depression can strike at anyone at any time and for no discernible reason to the outsider.'

'And bright people are more susceptible, yes I know all the get-outs. I've been using them for the past few weeks but I still feel guilty. I should have realised how serious his condition was. I just kept thinking it was something he would snap out of if we gave him time. Girl trouble or something like that.'

'Not your fault. Graduate students are adults. We can't babysit them. Now, about the studentship?'

'OK by me. I think it's a nice idea.'

'Good. I'll tell them we're delighted and have admin start the paperwork. The Ali Hammadi Research Fellowship in Molecular Science. Has a nice ring to it.'

Malloy returned to his lab and told the others what had been said, starting with the government ban on smallpox fragments.

'But that's crazy,' protested Le Grice. 'If we can't try out the upstream region we can't find out what's wrong with our system. It's going to put a complete stop to our research.'

'Well, shit happens and it's been that kind of a month really,' sighed Malloy, sounding both tired and world-weary.

'But why?' persisted Le Grice. 'Why are they doing this?'

Malloy shrugged his shoulders. 'Hutton hasn't been told but you know how careful the powers that be are about smallpox. There must have been some kind of scare somewhere.'

'Probably some kid got a bad dose of chickenpox in Outer Mongolia and the WHO got diarrhoea. Don't these people realise what they're doing when they suddenly come out with crazy bans like this?' retorted Le Grice angrily.

'Let's give them the benefit of the doubt and suppose that they do in this case and that they might have good reasons for introducing the ban,' said Malloy.

'Look, if we can't get the fragments we need from the official sources any more, why don't I phone around? Maybe the Beatson in Glasgow has them or the guys in Manchester.'

Malloy shook his head. 'The ban is on all fragment movement, not just from official sources.'

'Sure but if they don't know . . .'

Malloy's look was enough to make Le Grice change his mind about what he was going to say.

'I know it's tough on all of us but we're going to play by the rules on this one. Apart from anything else there are certain factions within this institute that would not be averse to seeing us get into really deep shit and deliberately flouting a WHO/UN ruling is as deep as it comes.'

'Any idea how long the ban is going to last?' asked Sandra Macandrew.

'None.'

'This could screw up our PhD work,' said Sandra looking at Peter.

'You don't have to achieve success to get your degrees. You just have to show that you've carried out your research programme in a controlled and methodical scientific manner. Demonstrate that you thought things through and acted accordingly. The work you did on the first vaccine will probably be enough.'

'But it's not the same, is it?'

'No. A successful vaccine would have been nicer,' conceded Malloy.

Le Grice gave a snort at the understatement. 'So what do we do in the meantime?'

'We get the smallpox DNA sequence out from the database again and study it. See if we can figure out what's going on in the region we're interested in without actually working with it.'

'Not for the first time,' said Le Grice.

'I know we've done it before,' said Malloy, coldness creeping into his voice as his patience wore thin. 'But we're going to do it again. All right?'

'Sure.'

'In the meantime, George, we have to submit an audit of what smallpox fragments we hold at the moment. Maybe you could run a check on that?'

'Will do.'

'There's one other thing. Ali's parents want to set up some kind of memorial thing for him. They're thinking of endowing a studentship.'

'That's nice,' said Sandra. The others smiled and nodded, unsure of what to say.

'It's nice to know they don't blame us,' said Malloy quietly.

'It's about time you stopped blaming yourself,' said Sandra. 'All of us are to blame and none of us are to blame. We'll probably never know why he did it because he didn't tell us what was wrong and it wasn't for the want of asking. We all liked him. We all cared about him. He just wouldn't open up to us.'

'Not even after a couple of pints,' said Peter.

'Ali drank beer?' asked Malloy.

'George introduced him to McEwans eighty-shilling ale.'

'He was a willing student,' said Ferguson. 'He enjoyed it. Ali was a bright bloke. He figured out that Allah probably wouldn't hold it against him.'

'How often did you two go drinking?' asked Malloy.

'Don't read too much into it,' laughed Ferguson. 'Ali wasn't an alcoholic and he didn't get depressed. That isn't why he topped himself. We had an occasional couple of pints at the union on a Friday night, that's all.'

'But he never loosened up enough to tell you what was wrong?'

''Fraid not.'

# ~ *Four* ~

*The Sci Med Inspectorate*
*The Home Office*
*London*

'Jean has prepared a file for you,' said the director, John Macmillan, to Adam Dewar as he showed him to the door. I think the WHO are erring on the side of caution in banning the movement of these fragments but it certainly seems the side to err on as far as this bug's concerned. I've taken the liberty of arranging a meeting for you with a leading virus consultant at the London School of Hygiene and Tropical Medicine this afternoon, a man called Hector Wright. He'll give you a crash course on the disease; he's expecting you at three.'

'Right you are, sir,' said Dewar.

'I think this one is probably just a paperwork exercise, but good luck anyway.'

Dewar had lunch at a pub by the river on the way back to the flat. It was sunny so he sat outside in the autumn sunshine with a pint of Guinness, watching the river traffic go by and thinking it might be the last time he'd do that this year. He was pleasantly surprised at how quiet the pub was. It encouraged him to open his briefcase and take out the folder he'd been given. He flicked through the contents while he waited for his prawn salad.

Basically it was a list of the universities and research institutes currently holding DNA fragments of the smallpox virus. There were twelve, two in Scotland, the rest in England. Eight had already complied with the audit request, four were still to file. The two in Scotland were among the four. Of the eight that had made returns, seven had submitted lists that agreed with the central source file. One, the Institute of Biosciences in Manchester, appeared to have two more frag, ments than they were officially credited with. That seemed like a good starting point, thought Dewar as he put away the file and took a sip of his beer.

Hector Wright turned out to be a short fat man in his late fifties. He had a shock of white hair, a pugnacious expression and eyes that looked and learned all the time. He would never manage to look elegant or distinguished, whatever he wore, but no one would ever sell him a vacuum cleaner he didn't want.

'So you want me to tell you all about smallpox,' said Wright as he slumped back down in his chair behind his desk after shaking hands. Dewar caught the body language of a man about to launch an interrogation. 'Why?'

'I understand you're a leading expert on the subject,' said Dewar, deliberately misunderstanding the question.

Wright nodded thoughtfully. He knew that Dewar had sidestepped the question. He also reckoned that he wasn't going to get anywhere by pursuing it. 'I don't know if anyone can ever claim to be an expert on that little bastard,' he said with feeling. 'When I worked with it all these years ago it always seemed to have some new trick up its sleeve. You'd think you understood it then — I know it's stupid to say this about a virus, for God's sake: it's about the most basic life form you can get and some people would argue that it isn't even that — but it was almost as if it had a mind of its own, that it was malevolent, if you get my meaning, that it wanted to kill you.'

Dewar saw that the man meant what he was saying; he wasn't just coming out with it for effect.

'I don't mind telling you I got pretty mad when these people put a stop to the WHO proposal to wipe it out altogether back in '95,' Wright continued. 'All that rubbish about destroying something that God had created and what an interesting little beast it really was. Jesus! The only function a smallpox virus ever had on this Earth was to kill human beings. There's no intermediate vector, no animal hosts, no life cycle of its own; it only affects us and we're talking about a fifty per cent kill rate with variola major.

'As much as that?'

And that doesn't mean to say the other fifty per cent get better like nothing ever happened. More often than not it leaves the survivors brain-damaged, sometimes mad, often blind, always disfigured. If you come out of it with only a face that looks like you stood in front of a grenade when it went off you can count yourself a very lucky person indeed.'

'It's that bad?'

'The worst.'

'You've actually experienced it in the field, then?'

'Nineteen seventy-five, Somalia. I was with the WHO team who encircled the last outbreak. Like Apaches round a wagon train we were, closing in for the kill, vaccinating everything that moved so the disease couldn't spread out from its epicentre.'

'It must have given you a tremendous sense of achievement when you finally realised that you'd actually done it, wiped out a disease that's plagued man throughout recorded history and probably before that.'

'Damn right. Me and a few others, mainly Americans, got pie-eyed for a week but you know, it hardly made the papers back here.'

'Really?'

'People in this country had already forgotten what smallpox

could do. By that time it was something that happened in far-off lands. If we'd wiped out something that affected Cheltenham it might have been a different story — but Africa? Bottom of page five if we were lucky. Until, of course, the accident happened.'

'Accident?'

'Birmingham. Everyone thought it was OK to work on the virus under lab conditions. After all, you know exactly where the virus is at all times in the lab. Glass containers are much more predictable than human beings: they don't cough, spit, throw up over you or bugger off to Majorca when they feel like it. We didn't have the fancy containment facilities they have today and all the rules and regulations to go with it but we were still pretty careful in our own way. Each lab did its best; some were better than others of course. It was up to individual consultants to impose their own rules but Birmingham was a lesson to us all.

'The damn thing got out of what everyone thought was a secure lab. It killed a woman medical photographer almost before we knew it, and you know what the worst thing was? To this day we don't know what really went wrong. We don't know how it got out.'

Dewar was picking up a lot from Wright. The man was just talking conversationally but he found himself already developing a more than healthy respect for the virus.

'After that there was no more working in hospital labs and the like with live smallpox. Thank God. There could have been many more accidents.'

'My information is that there are only two places on Earth that are allowed to store live smallpox,' said Dewar.

'That's right, Atlanta and Koltsovo, although some pessimists think it still might be viable in corpses of people who died of the disease.'

'You're kidding,' said Dewar.

'I'm not talking about bodies that have undergone normal decomposition,' said Wright. 'I'm talking about bodies subject to special environmental conditions. It's been suggested that the permafrost regions of Russia might still harbour live smallpox in bodies buried there nearly a hundred years ago. The ground conditions would be just right.'

'*Requiescat in pace,*' said Dewar.

'Amen to that,' agreed Wright.

'I'm told the entire smallpox genome has been DNA-sequenced,' said Dewar.

'That's right. We know every last base pair of its evil little self. A string of letters you can't even make a word out of and it's killed millions.'

'Does that mean you could actually build it in the lab if you wanted?'

Wright smiled as if recognising the real reason for Dewar's interest. 'Who in their right mind would want to do that?' he asked innocently.

'I didn't say anything about right mind.'

'Point taken. No, there are easier ways of playing God. The genome has been cut into fragments so that researchers can work on bits of the virus.'

'So I understand.'

'And I've just heard about a ban being placed on the movement of these fragments,' said Wright, putting two and two together. 'Does that mean that you suspect someone of trying to reassemble them?'

'There's no real evidence of that. It's just a precaution,' said Dewar. He didn't want to insult a man of Wright's intelligence by pretending that nothing at all was amiss.

'But it's something you're looking into?' Dewar nodded. 'I wish you luck and hope to God it really is just a precaution.'

'For the sake of interest, Doctor, how would *you* go about doing it.'

'Reconstruct the virus? I wouldn't even consider it.'

'But if you had to?'

'I suppose I'd ligate the fragments or maybe start with another pox virus, something like cowpox, and try converting it into variola major with appropriate DNA changes.'

'Would that be easier?'

'Not necessarily, but not having tried it I couldn't say for sure.'

Dewar admired the scientific answer. 'I take it the authorities would know all about the possibility of altering another pox virus to become smallpox?'

'Of course,' replied Wright. 'There's not only a ban on any institution having more than twenty per cent of the smallpox genome in terms of DNA fragments, there's also a ban on having any other pox virus in the same institution at the same time.'

'If I were to tell you that an English lab has admitted to having two more fragments of the virus than it's registered to have, would you find that suspicious?'

Wright threw back his head and laughed. 'God, no,' he exclaimed. 'You know what university labs are like. The only paperwork they're interested in is the kind you publish to advance your career and get more grant money. Anything else is a pain that someone else will do but no one ever does. When the complaints come in they just scream "infringement of academic freedom" and it works like a magic mantra. Politicians back off like vampires from a crucifix. They don't like to be thought philistine.'

'I know how it goes,' agreed Dewar.

Wright opened his desk drawer and took out a sheaf of papers. 'I got these together for you,' he said. 'Everything you wanted or didn't want to know about the smallpox virus.'

'Thanks. I'm grateful.'

'Don't be. They paid me a consultancy fee. There's one more thing they asked me to do.'

'What's that?'

'Vaccinate you.'

*Institute of Molecular Sciences*
*Edinburgh*

'I've got that list you wanted,' said George Ferguson.

'Good,' said Malloy. 'Everything check out?'

'Sure, I've been through all fridges and freezers, checked all the fragment stocks. Mind you, there were quite a few tubes and bottles among Ali's stuff that I didn't recognise. I don't know what you want done about these.'

'I'll ask Pierre to take a look, see if he recognises anything, maybe clear out what we don't need,' said Malloy. 'Admin sent me down the official fragment record for the lab. Maybe you could do a final check, your list against theirs before we submit it. I don't need any more shit in my life.' Malloy rummaged through his desk drawer and came up with a brown internal-mail envelope which he flicked open to check it contained the right thing before handing it to Ferguson. 'There you go. Have you seen Pierre this morning?'

'He's in the computer room, working on the sequence data.'

Malloy nodded. He was just about to say something else when the air was filled with the deafening sound of a siren. Ferguson and Malloy looked at each other but speech was pointless until the sound subsided. When it finally did, the noise was replaced by deathly silence. All extractor fans and air conditioning had shut down. The continual hum that no one noticed was suddenly seriously missed.

'Bio-safety alert,' said Malloy. 'First we've had. Let's hope it's a false alarm.'

Under the terms of a bio-accident alert, staff had to remain exactly where they were until further notice. Doors were sealed so that no one could enter or leave; the windows in the building were designed not to open anyway. The main objective was to contain any infectious agent at large inside the building.

Five minutes passed before the telephone rang. It had never sounded so jarring before.

'Malloy.'

'Paul Hutton here. We've had an HIV incident on Level Three. There's been a spillage in the containment lab.'

'So what's the problem if it's in the containment lab?'

'The airlock was open when it happened.'

'What?' exclaimed Malloy.

'Two of Cairns's people had been working in there. When they were preparing to leave one turned back for some reason — maybe he forgot to do something or maybe just to check something — but he knocked over two vials of live virus almost at the same moment as the other one opened the airlock.'

'Sod's law,' said Malloy. 'But it's been contained within the outer lab?'

'As far as we know. Cairns's people seemed to know what they were doing. They stayed where they were inside and sounded the alarm.'

'You've arranged a decontamination team?'

'There's a bit of a problem.' Malloy closed his eyes. 'Malcolm Cairns and his two postdocs are away at the AIDS meeting in Chicago. There are only a couple of first-year PhD students left in Cairns's group.'

Malloy let out his breath in a slow sigh. 'You mean it's going to be down to somebody else to clear up the shit?'

'In a manner of speaking,' said Hutton, suggesting that it wasn't his manner of speaking.

'I suppose volunteers have been tumbling over themselves?' said Malloy.

'Well actually, I thought as yours is the only other AIDS lab you might agree to help out.'

Malloy paused before replying, 'OK, I'll do it and I'll ask for one other volunteer from my people, but I'm not putting any pressure on them . . .'

'Count me in,' said George Ferguson, who'd picked up the general gist of the conversation, standing beside Malloy.

Malloy looked at him, as if needing a second affirmation.

'It's OK. Count me in.'

Malloy, still holding the phone, said, 'I've got my volunteer. George Ferguson has just signed on.'

'Ferguson?' exclaimed Hutton. 'I'm not sure if that's entirely—'

'In the present circumstances it's what *I* think that's important,' said Malloy edgily. 'Unless, of course, you're telling me that you are prepared to take George Ferguson's place, Professor?'

'You know very well that I've not worked with live viruses for many years and never with that particular one.'

Ferguson, who had now been listening in to the conversation in the unusual silence of the room, smiled wryly and whispered, 'Another bugger who learned to swim from a book. Bugger'd drown if he ever hit the water.'

'It's George and me then. Perhaps you'll arrange for the suits and decontamination fluid to be ready for us on Level Three when we get there. Oh, and is the phone line still open to the two inside?'

'Yes, I have contact.'

'Maybe you could close your end so that I can speak to the people inside?'

'Of course.'

'Who are they, by the way?'

'Simone Clary and Gregor White.'

'Postdoc and third-year student. OK, ready when you are.'

The phone went dead and Malloy allowed ten seconds for Hutton to close the other phone link before dialling the Level Three lab. It was answered first ring by a woman's voice.'

'Hello, Simone, this is Steve Malloy. What's your situation?'

'I don't think it's too bad but Gregor . . .'

'What about him?'

'He's upset.'

Simone had lowered her voice to say it. Malloy guessed it was so that White wouldn't hear. He became aware of a whimpering noise in the background and sussed the situation.

'OK, Simone. I have to ask some questions before George and I put on the noddy suits and come and clean you up. Was the spillage contained within a given area?'

'Yes, one vial broke open on the floor, the other one survived.'

'So there is a puddle of liquid on the floor in the containment lab?'

'Yes.'

'Did either of you come into contact with the liquid?'

'No, I don't think so.'

'Did you see the vial hit the floor?'

'Not exactly. When I turned round Gregor had knocked over the vials but he made a brave effort to catch them before they hit the floor. He didn't quite manage it but he did catch one and interrupted the fall of the other so that the impact was lessened.'

'Good, that probably means there was minimal splashing and aerosol formation. I'm going to ring off now, Simone. George and I will be with you soon.'

Malloy put down the phone and turned to Ferguson. 'You heard?' Ferguson nodded. 'What d'you think.'

'Piece o' piss. Puddle on the floor, no aerosols. You could deal with that with a mop and some Dettol.'

Malloy smiled. 'Probably, but we'd better put on a show for the lieges. There is one worrying thing, though. Sounds like young White is throwing a wobbly. We don't want him making a charge for the door as soon as we get in there.'

'Maybe you could get Simone to keep him out the road till we do the needful.'

Level Three was almost deserted when Malloy and Ferguson entered from the stairwell. Their footsteps didn't quite echo but were certainly audible as they walked along the corridor to the anteroom and to the outer door leading to the high-level containment facility. Two bio-safety suits had been left outside along with a pressurised container of decontaminant fluid with a hose and steel spray head attached. The corridor phone rang; Ferguson, who was nearer picked it up.

'Put me on to Dr Malloy,' said Hutton's voice.

'*Herr Direktor*,' said Ferguson, passing the phone.

'Steven, the engineers have decreased the air pressure on Level Three so there can be no outflow.'

'Right,' said Malloy.

'A comfort,' whispered Ferguson.

'Good luck, you two.'

'Thanks,' said Malloy.

Ferguson made a face.

Malloy dialled Simone and got an engaged tone. 'Fuck!' he said.

'It'll be *Herr Direktor* trotting out sterling British claptrap,' said Ferguson. 'We're all with you Simone, although I'm three floors below heading for a taxi.'

Malloy thought about phoning someone else to tell Hutton to clear the line, then decided against it. Instead, he banged on the outside door of the suite, figuring Simone would understand. The phone line cleared.

'Simone, we're about ready to come in. Can you make sure you're both well back from the door?' He stressed the word 'both'.

'Of course.'

The two men suited up in silence and checked each other before closing their hoods and again checking the seals. Malloy sprayed the exterior surface around the door they were entering through and turned the handle.

The slight rush of air into the lab, which caused several pieces of paper on a notice board to flutter, was taken as a comforting sign. If air was flowing into the lab, nothing was flowing out.

Simone Clary and the student, White, were sitting together at the far end of the lab. Simone had her arm round the shoulders of the young man as he sat, round-shouldered, staring at the floor. Simone obviously mentioned the entrance of the newcomers because he looked up and regarded the presence of Malloy and Ferguson like a rabbit seeing an advancing car.

'Everything's going to be OK,' yelled Malloy, trying to overcome the sound-deadening of the hood he was wearing. He realised just how difficult it was to persuade someone who wasn't wearing a spacesuit like his that this was the case. 'Just stay still and wait till we clear up the mess.'

Simone's hands tightened on White's shoulders to stop him getting up. Ferguson remained in front of the door to block any panic-fuelled rush. White seemed to settle so Ferguson joined Malloy in walking into the BL3 lab, where they both saw the wet patch on the floor interspersed with broken glass.

'No problemo,' announced Ferguson. He poured concentrated disinfectant into the puddle and then sprayed the surrounding area with the pressurised disinfectant spray. 'Are we having an encore?' he asked.

'Suppose we better,' replied Malloy.

'One grenade or two?'

'Better make it two. Give everyone their money's worth.'

'That old yen for show business, eh?'

Ferguson prepared two disinfectant gas shells and then waited while Malloy finished checking inside the BL3 lab before retreating to the exit and giving Ferguson a nod. Ferguson pulled the toggles on both shells and stepped back smartly to join Malloy as the first spiral of gas escaped. They closed the airlock behind them allowing the gas to fill the interior and destroy any rogue virus particles that might have escaped the decontamination fluid.

'Shower time, folks,' announced Malloy as they rejoined Clary and Wright. All our clothes stay here for decontamination. We'll use the surgical smocks in the cabinet to the right of the shower room. You first, Simone.'

Simone appeared reluctant to leave White but Malloy nodded reassurance and she relinquished contact slowly with White and made for the shower.

'You'll be next, Gregor,' said Malloy.

'What's the point?' mumbled White. 'We were exposed to concentrated HIV virus, for Christ's sake!'

'It didn't splash on your skin and you've no obvious cuts or grazes it could have got into, so what's the problem? HIV's a bastard but it's not that easy to catch in a lab situation. Just thank your lucky stars it wasn't something like typhoid or plague you were working with.'

'You've got suits on, haven't you?'

'We like making a drama out of a crisis,' announced Ferguson, taking his hood and visor off. 'If you catch AIDS, son, it's because of what you've been doing with your dick, not because of that wee puddle in there.'

The comment forced a wan smile from White.

'Go have your shower,' said Ferguson, seeing that Simone had emerged from the shower room, wearing a white surgical smock and nothing else. Her wet, black hair hung round her face making her appear younger and more vulnerable than before.

'What happens now? she asked.

'When we've all showered, we'll bomb this place too and leave it for a while. You and Gregor will be seen by the university health people and probably put on AZT treatment for a few months as a precaution. You'll probably be offered counselling as well.'

'You get that if someone as much as farts in the same room as you these days,' interjected Ferguson.

You'll be blood-tested for HIV right now and then again in a few months' time, but chances are you're perfectly OK. I'd put money on it.'

'Thanks, Steve, and you, too, George,' said Simone.

# ~ *Five* ~

It was raining in Manchester when Dewar got off the train but he'd expected it would be. That was the thing about reputations: once acquired, justified or not, they tended to stick. The thought led him to think of one head of a university department he'd known, now retired, who was not remembered for any of the work he'd done in his professional life but solely for the fact that he'd made his tea with other people's used tea bags in the common room rather than contribute a few pence a week to the fund himself. Dewar was convinced that Manchester would not get the Olympic Games it craved, not for any locational or logistical reason, nor for any lack of facilities, but because people had an image of runners splashing through rainwater.

The taxi driver asked if he'd seen 'the game' last night on television. Replying that he hadn't, ensured that he got a ball-by-ball account until they reached the university some ten minutes later. Standing out in the rain was suddenly a welcome experience.

'I've an appointment to see Professor Kelman,' he said to the man behind the reception desk after shaking the rain from his hair.

'Third floor.'

With apparently no more information on offer, Dewar took

the lift to the third floor and found what he needed to know on a board facing him when he got out. It even had personnel photographs on it. He was now looking for a bald man in room 317/18.

'Can I help?' asked the woman who occupied the outer office (317) and whose severe features suggested that helping anyone was the last thing on her mind.

'I've an appointment with Professor Kelman.'

'And your name?'

'Dr Dewar.'

'Ah yes. From . . .' She slipped her spectacles down to the end of her nose and tilted her head back slightly to ease reading from the diary in front of her. 'The Sci Med Inspectorate.'

Dewar was shown into a well-appointed room by university standards and greeted by Kelman, a tall, angular man with sloping shoulders and a university tie drawing his shirt collar a little too tight. He had very large hands and feet and wore fawn-coloured twill trousers that ended a couple of inches short of where they should have. This, in turn, exposed chequered socks that Dewar assumed could only have been a Christmas present from a close but colour-blind relative.

'I understand we have been naughty boys,' said Kelman.

Kelman's seeking to diminish the crime at the outset did not endear him to Dewar. Apart from anything else it cast him in the role of petty official come to annoy an important man with better things to do.

'You do appear to be in contravention of a WHO/UN ruling endorsed by HM Government, Professor,' he replied, pushing the stakes right back up again.'

'Oh dear,' replied Kelman, now unsure which facial expression to adopt. It was too late to play the contrite card, and trivialising the infringement clearly hadn't worked. 'What exactly is it that we're supposed to have done?'

Best you could do in the circumstances, thought Dewar.

Ignorance of the crime. Not acceptable in law but always a good first step in moving yourself sideways away from blame.

'You are licensed to hold two fewer fragments of the smallpox virus than you admitted to in your recent audit submission. This actually brings you above the twenty per cent of the genome limit that the WHO has recommended.'

'Recommended?' said Kelman, thinking he'd found a linguistic loophole.

'Enforceable by law in this country,' added Dewar, closing it off.

'I see,' sighed Kelman. 'Well, this appears to be more serious than I thought and it's Dr Davidson's territory, I fear.'

It was bound to be someone else's, thought Dewar. No matter, the buck stopped with the head of department, as far as he or anyone else in authority was concerned. It was now just a question of how many others Kelman was going to take down with him.

'Perhaps I could have a word with Dr Davidson?'

'Of course. Would you like me to be present?'

'As the responsibility is finally yours, Professor, I'll leave that up to you,' replied Dewar.

Kelman's grin lacked conviction.

A small, thin man wearing Levi jeans and a crushed, grey T-shirt came in through the door. Dewar thought he knew the type. They were common enough in academia: undersized, spectacles-wearing, Mummy's boys, bad at games, lousy at PT, unattractive to the opposite sex, guys with more hang-ups than a washing line, guys who'd finally found a safe, secure environment in the institutionalised world of academia where they could relax and call themselves Mike or Steve, where on the outside they'd always been Michael or Steven. They could now wear jeans and be 'team leaders' whereas before they'd always been the type nobody wanted on their team in any capacity, let alone as leader. For them an academic appointment was get-your-own-back time.

'Alison tells me there's some bureaucratic problem,' snapped Davidson, pointedly looking at his watch. Dewar noted it was a double-Y-chromosome man's watch, one that could probably tell you the time, in Tokyo, at two hundred feet under the Baltic Sea. It looked like a soup plate on Davidson's scrawny wrist.

'There's a problem with your audit return for the smallpox virus fragments you've been using, Mike,' said Kelman.

'Jesus,' exclaimed Davidson. 'Why don't we all stop doing research and just fill in forms. That's what it's coming to.'

If he expected an apologetic response from Dewar, he was badly disappointed. 'If you don't come up with good explanation for the discrepancy in your return that's exactly what you're going to be doing anyway, Dr Davidson,' said Dewar, matter-of-factly.

Davidson looked shell-shocked. 'Who is this . . .? What the . . .? Can he do this?' he appealed to Kelman.

Kelman shrugged his shoulders. 'I understand the Sci Med Inspectorate do have considerable powers should they choose to use them.'

'Look, it was obviously just a clerical error,' said Davidson, starting to back-pedal

You'll have to do better than that, thought Dewar.

'Perhaps we could go through the audit statement and you could point out just where the error occurred, Doctor?'

'I suppose I could try.'

And you'll have to do a lot better than that.

Davidson's lab was on the floor below. He led the way as if every step were an intrusion on his day and he wanted Dewar to know it. When they finally reached 'The Davidson Lab', as it was posted on the outside of the door, they were met by a tall blond man who was just exiting with a rack of tubes in his hand.

'Eric, I need the list of the smallpox fragments you made up for me,' snapped Davidson.

'OK, just give me a moment.'

'Now, Eric!'

The big Swede towering over Davidson gave an embarrassed shrug and retreated back into the lab. He put down his rack and went off to get the list. When he came back, Dewar gave him a smile of reassurance and it was returned. 'There is a problem?'

'We seem to have more fragments than the regulations allow.' Davidson endowed the word 'regulation' with distaste. 'This gentleman has come to check up on us.'

Dewar held out his hand and said, 'Adam Dewar, Sci Med Inspectorate.'

'Eric Larsen. I'm a postdoc here.'

The two tall men stood with Davidson in between them like the meat in an underfilled sandwich.

'You must have screwed up the paperwork, Eric,' said Davidson petulantly.

'I don't think so,' replied the Swede. 'I think you checked it yourself when I was finished.'

'I didn't *check* it: I signed it. God, do I have to do every little thing myself in this place?'

Larsen moved uncomfortably from one foot to the other. Dewar sympathised with the big man but decided to keep a stony countenance. It was always unwise to get involved in the politics of such a situation. He opened his briefcase and brought out his copy of the official fragment list for the department. 'Maybe you could read from yours and we can identify and agree the extra pieces.'

'Sure,' said Larsen. He started to go through the list.

Halfway through, Dewar said, 'No, I don't have that one.' Larsen read out the number again. 'No, definitely not.'

Davidson snatched the paper from Larsen and asked, 'Are you absolutely sure about this fragment?'

'Sure I'm sure. I went through the fridge, just like you asked. This one was there. I couldn't have made the number up,' said

Larsen, letting his anger show just a little.

Dewar suddenly sensed in Davidson the stirring of a memory that he would rather not have recalled. It was something to do with his eyes that gave him away. There was a slight pause while Dewar presumed Davidson was searching for some way out of his predicament. Eventually he just said, 'Oh dear.'

Humble-pie time, thought Dewar.

'I remember now,' Davidson announced, clearing his throat to cover embarrassment. 'Six months ago, I was talking to a French scientist I met at the Birmingham virus meeting. You remember, Eric?'

Larsen nodded. He was enjoying Davidson's discomfiture as much as Dewar was.

'He was working as a postdoc in Malloy's lab in Edinburgh. Maybe he still is. He was working on much the same thing as us and he'd obtained DNA for a couple of smallpox fragments that I thought would be useful to us too. He agreed to send some to me to save me going through the usual bureaucratic channels. I quite forgot about that.'

'Otherwise you wouldn't have declared them on your audit,' said Dewar. Davidson remained silent. 'As it is, you delegated the job to someone else who came up with the truth and declared it.'

'What happens now?' asked Davidson, coming as near to contrition as someone like him could.

'Six months ago, this sort of thing was little more than a paperwork offence,' said Dewar. 'But things have changed. There is an absolute ban on the movement of these fragments, official or unofficial, and the twenty-per-cent rule is being rigidly enforced. Decide what fragments you no longer need and I'll take them away with me to bring you under the twenty-per-cent mark. On this occasion this will be the last you hear of it. You will of course be subject to unannounced auditing from time to time in the future. I'll also have to ask you the name of the French scientist you mentioned.'

'Is that really necessary? He did it as a personal favour to me.'

'He knew the rules too.'

'Pierre Le Grice. He works at the Institute for Molecular Sciences in Edinburgh.'

As Dewar headed south again he looked around at his fellow passengers in First Class and wondered if any of them were carrying anything as bizarre as two fragments of smallpox virus DNA in their briefcases. It seemed unlikely but, there again, making predictions about human behaviour was something you could never do with absolute confidence.

What had happened in Manchester did not bode well for his current assignment. One institution had been caught out simply because someone had told the truth. How many others were holding illegal stocks and falsifying their returns so that officialdom would see what they wanted to see? From previous experience he knew that researchers were a competitive, self-centred breed. Rules were there for other people to obey unless it either suited or caused no inconvenience. Nothing would be allowed to get in the way of their pet projects if they could help it. There wasn't much he could do about that. Swimming against the tide of human nature was not an option for the intelligent. He had to be pragmatic in the circumstances. If he couldn't change the way things were in the scientific establishment he could at least be firm about stressing the consequences of not complying with the WHO/UN ruling. The prospect of having their labs closed down and their careers damaged should do the trick. If there was one thing researchers cared more about than their research it was their careers. Any good that came out of research was almost invariably a by-product of the competitive struggle for career advancement and personal glory.

He felt tired when he got into the flat. He kicked off his shoes and took a cold Stella Artois from the fridge, rejoicing in the first ice-cold swallow. After a second, he 'woke up' his IBM Aptiva computer and checked the message centre. There was one from Sci Med and one from Karen. He played that one first.

'Adam, I'm going to be tied up at the lab all evening. There's been a salmonella outbreak centred on Kensington. We're trying to find the source. Give me a call when you get back. Love you.'

Dewar permitted himself a small smile at the idea of salmonella in Kensington. He played back the Sci Med message. The voice said, 'Fax for you on code nine.'

Dewar frowned and sat down to bring up the fax centre on the machine and then prompt the unscrambling code with his password. The printer whirred into life and spawned a single-page message. It was an update on the institutions complying with the audit request. All had now reported and all had declared having only what they were supposed to have. There was, however, one addendum – the reason for the message coding. The Sci Med computer had come up with a piece of information that it had correlated as being relevant to his current assignment. A PhD student, working at the Institute of Molecular Sciences in Edinburgh, had recently committed suicide. He was Iraqi.

Dewar stared at the name, Ali Hammadi. 'Now, what were you working on, Ali? I wonder,' he muttered out loud.

He looked at his watch and called Karen at the lab before it got any later. 'How's it going?'

'Like a fairground. We've had seventeen confirmed cases over the last twenty-four hours and we've got another nine suspected ones to check out.'

'No idea where it's coming from?'

'Eight cases ate at the same Greek restaurant; the others didn't. So it must be something coming from a common supplier. It's just a question of which one and what product. How was Manchester?'

'Shit.'

'I'd rather you didn't mention that word at the moment.'

'Sorry. Are you going to come round later?'

'I think I may just go back to the flat. It's going to be late when I get away and I'm whacked.'

'Call you tomorrow?'

'You know where I'll be,' sighed Karen.

Dewar put down the phone and smiled affectionately. He and Karen, a down-to-earth Scottish girl from the East Lothian fishing village of North Berwick, had been together for nearly two years now. They had actually attended the same medical school but hadn't really got to know each other until they met up again some four years after graduating when Karen had already been with the Public Health Service for three years and Dewar had just joined Sci Med after deciding a career in research was not for him. He'd had an unhappy attempt at postgraduate research and finally decided he'd had enough of pretending to be a team player when he clearly wasn't. He was a loner by nature and wouldn't pretend any more. The fact the Earth went round the sun had not been discovered by 'a team' led by Copernicus. At Sci Med he'd found a job where he could do things his way.

He and Karen still had their own flats, an expensive arrange-ment but both were reluctant to risk damaging their relation-ship through fall-out from their jobs. Both had stressful, demanding occupations, even life-threatening on occasion in Dewar's case.

Dewar sat down by an open window where he could see the river. His flat wasn't actually on the waterside — he couldn't afford that — but was one street back on the first floor of a converted warehouse. It was very small but if he sat to the left of the main window he could see the river through a gap in the buildings across the street. He read through the fax from Sci Med again. If Hammadi was Iraqi he'd better find out as much as possible about him, starting with the police file on the incident – and then, of course, there was his research project. What exactly had he been studying? Although he'd been a student at the same institute where they had access to smallpox DNA fragments, it was, by all accounts, a very large institute. He could have been working on something completely different.

As a foreign student, Hammadi would have been on several official registers. The funding for his degree would presumably have come from abroad but the actual university registration would be British, unless, of course, he had been on some short-term exchange deal. Dewar opened up his dial-in connection to the Sci Med computer facility and used it to connect him to the Internet. He then used the Joint Academic Network (JANET) route to get to the computerised information services of the Institute of Molecular Sciences in Edinburgh. He accessed 'current research interests' from their home page and found seventeen research groups listed. Two were working on HIV virus and vaccine development. One of them, a group headed by Dr Steven Malloy, had Ali Hammadi listed as a postgraduate student.

'Shit,' said Dewar under his breath. Hammadi *had* been working in a group with a possible reason to use smallpox fragments. He swore again as he continued reading down the list of names. Pierre Le Grice was listed in the same group. He was the one who'd sent the fragments to Davidson at Manchester.

Dewar drank the remainder of his beer and threw the empty can into the bucket that sat beside the fireplace. It went in cleanly, keeping his average for this activity above eighty per cent, but tonight he could take little satisfaction from it. His 'paperwork assignment' did not seem so routine any more. In fact, he felt a distinct feeling of unease. Two research groups not playing by the rules and a dead Iraqi PhD student who'd had access to smallpox DNA meant he was going to be on a flight to Edinburgh in the morning. He left a message for Sci Med saying where he was going and asking them to inform the Edinburgh institute officially of his impending visit. He would also need the name of a police contact in the city.

# − *Six* −

The British Airways shuttle got into Edinburgh Airport only a few minutes late. Dewar made contact with Sci Med using the Executive Lounge facility on the first floor. He was told that the Institute of Molecular Sciences was expecting him and that the police had also been informed. An officer, Inspector Ian Grant, had been detailed to brief him at Fettes police headquarters. He was expected there at ten thirty.

The airport taxi made such good progress into town, despite the rush-hour traffic, that Dewar thought he might be too early for his meeting with Grant. He asked the driver to take him round by Princes Street. Being no stranger to the city − he'd come up with Karen on several occasions when she'd been visiting her mother − he always enjoyed the view of the castle.

'It's your money, pal,' replied the driver dourly.

Police headquarters in Fettes Avenue, Edinburgh, proved to be a large, white, modern, functional-looking building on the north side of the city, sitting opposite the striking and much older façade of Fettes College, the top Scottish public school that Prime Minister Tony Blair had attended.

Ian Grant turned out to be a burly man in his late thirties with a bushy black moustache that emphasised his dark eyes. He wore a sports jacket and dark trousers. He was wearing a tie but it was loosened, as was the top button of his shirt, making him look like Hollywood's idea of a journalist about to write up his story. Grant poured himself some coffee from a silver-coloured jug and waved it in Dewar's direction. Dewar shook his head.

'Foreign student tops himself. What's to say? Case closed as far as we're concerned,' said Grant as he sat back down at his desk.

'No suicide note?'

'Nothing.'

'Did you come up with any likely reason for him doing it?'

''Fraid not. We expected tales of exam pressure, fear of failure, the usual shit, but not in his case. His supervisor thought everything was going swimmingly. Shows how much he knew about the price of cheese.'

'University can be a pretty lonely place,' said Dewar. 'It can get to kids, particularly if they're from a different country.'

'Wouldn't know about that,' said Grant. 'A university of-life man, myself.'

'Are there any other Iraqi students in the city?'

'Quite a few as a matter of fact.' Grant brought out a sheet of paper and continued, 'They're all registered with us; they have to be. They have their own students' association; it's in Forest Road, near the Royal Infirmary. The address is on here. I guess a lot of them are medical students.'

Dewar nodded. 'Did you speak to any of them?'

'Went through the motions. Nobody knew anything. I got the impression they were all shit-scared to talk to the police about anything if you ask me.'

'Why's that?'

'Goes with their background, I suppose,' said Grant. 'If you live in a police state I suppose you think all police forces are the same.'

'Do you get the impression they were subject to scrutiny from home while they're here?' asked Dewar.

'Oh yes. There were a couple of blokes hanging around that I thought were a bit old to be students but I didn't bother asking. If you do, they nearly always turn out to be cultural advisers or some crap like that.'

Dewar nodded and got up. 'Thanks for your help. I'm going to have a word with the people he worked with, then maybe I'll pop into the place in Forest Road. Take a look around.'

'Right you are, I wish you joy. What's your interest in all this anyway?'

'Home Office routine,' shrugged Dewar. 'Foreign nationals always attract extra paperwork.'

'Tell me about it,' said Grant.

'Do you have a copy of the pathologist's report, by the way?'

'Not to hand,' replied Grant. 'But it was pretty straight-forward.' He looked to see if Dewar would be satisfied with this. Dewar remained impassive. 'Want me to send you a copy?'

'If you would.'


The Institute of Molecular Sciences was situated on a site just outside the city on the south side, or 'Science Park', as they preferred to call it. As he walked the final two hundred metres or so from the main gate, Dewar could see that academia was now working very much hand-in-glove with commerce. Many of the buildings seemed to be affiliated to pharmaceutical or chemical companies. He remembered being told by a colleague recently that these days you were as liable to find a patent lawyer in a lab as a scientist. Big money had moved in to exploit the promise of molecular biology in a big way.

Dewar had a brief meeting with Paul Hutton, the head of the institute, whom he found pretty much of the old school. A place for everyone and everyone in their place, the kind of public-school product who would show unswerving loyalty to a cardboard box as long as the cardboard box held an official position. This made him easy – by virtue of being predictable –

to deal with. He spoke briefly about the tragedy of Ali Hammadi's death in suitably muted tones and went on to tell Dewar of the proposed scholarship that Hammadi's parents had suggested.

'We're going to call it the Ali Hammadi Research Scholarship'.

Can't fault that, thought Dewar. He asked if he might speak with Ali's supervisor and colleagues.

'Dr Malloy is expecting you. He's been taking Ali's death rather badly, I'm afraid. He blames himself. Ridiculous of course. I'll have someone show you up.'

Dewar felt unsure about Malloy when he first saw him and took in the T-shirt and jeans. He was inclined to think he might be of the Mike Davidson school of pain-in-the-arses, another free spirit, untied by time, tide or geometry, tethered to this Earth only by his university tenure and comprehensive superannuation scheme. But he decided to withhold judgement.

Malloy for his part was equally unsure about Dewar, seeing the well-cut hair, the expensive dark suit, the polished shoes and the briefcase. A ministry pen-pusher was the initial thought, but he too decided to withhold judgement.

They talked in Malloy's office. Dewar picked up on a poster on the wall featuring the American tenor sax player, Stan Getz. 'You're a fan?' he asked.

'Certainly am.'

'Me too. I saw him live in Kansas City the year before he died. Played a lot of the Brazilian stuff from the early sixties. Wonderful.'

'I like that stuff too,' agreed Malloy. 'His guitarist, Charlie Byrd, came to Edinburgh a few years ago. I went along. Sounded just the same in real life. Little guy, looked like a bank manager, came on wearing a suit, did his thing and left after blowing all the would-be guitarists in the audience away.'

'You play yourself?'

'Not in that company I don't,' said Malloy. Dewar smiled. The ice had been broken. 'I understand you're here about Ali.'

'It's Ali's connection with smallpox fragments I'm concerned about,' said Dewar, putting his cards on the table.

Malloy seemed taken aback. 'I don't understand.'

'You know all about the ban on fragment movement at the moment?'

'It's a real bastard. It's stopped us in our tracks.'

'There's a reason.'

'But is it a good one?'

'The WHO and the UN think it is.'

'Not convincing enough in itself. It's always the safest course for bureaucrats to pull the plug on something. It's the best way to guard their own arses.'

'Be that as it may, the ruling's been made,' said Dewar, not wanting to get involved in that kind of discussion.

'Oh, don't get me wrong, we'll abide by it. Doesn't mean to say we have to agree with it.'

'Abiding by it will be enough.'

'So what's this got to do with Ali?'

'Nothing, I hope, but he was Iraqi,' said Dewar.

Malloy looked at him long and hard before saying, 'So you don't have to be Albert Einstein to work out that you think the Iraqis are fucking around with smallpox?'

'Let's say there's a suspicion and nobody's taking any chances.'

'If you think that Ali was involved in anything like that . . . well, it's just plain ridiculous,' said Malloy.

'I'm glad to hear it,' said Dewar. 'But he was Iraqi, he was a scientist, he did have access to the smallpox genome and . . . he did end up killing himself.'

'Point taken,' agreed Malloy reluctantly. 'But you're on the wrong trail. We've only got a few fragments of the virus here. You couldn't do anything crazy with that.'

'I saw your audit return,' said Dewar, maintaining eye contact.

'Oh, I see. You think we may have more than we're letting on.'

'Maybe not deliberately,' said Dewar. 'But that sort of thing does tend to happen in places like this. I've just been to a place where they had more than they should have. No criminal intent just . . . the university way.'

'You're welcome to carry out any inspection you like of the lab and its stocks,' said Malloy.

'Thanks,' said Dewar. 'It's always nice to have full co-operation. But first I'd like to get a feel for the group. How about telling me who you have working for you and what they're doing exactly?'

'I've got one postdoc, a Frenchman named Pierre Le Grice from the Institut Pasteur in Paris; he's been here two years, another one to go. I've got two PhD students, Sandra Macandrew — she's second-year supported by the Medical Research Council — and Peter Moore, he's first year, supported by the Wellcome Trust. Ali was my third student. He'd almost finished and was preparing to write up his thesis. He was on Iraqi government money.'

Dewar raised his eyebrows.

'Nothing unusual in that. Foreign students aren't entitled to British grants. They have to have their own money for tuition fees and subsistence and it usually comes from their own governments.'

'Anyone else?'

'George Ferguson, my senior technician. He's a medical lab technician. He came up to the university when they closed down the old City Hospital and they were looking to resettle the lab staff. He hadn't really found a niche and I needed someone who was used to handling viruses so I agreed to take him on until his resettlement period runs out. If I get another grant I'll keep him on.'

'Anyone else?'

'That's it.'

'Did Ali work alone?'

'No one was looking over his shoulder, if that's what you mean. He was a graduate student; he already had a good honours degree in his subject so he knew what he was doing. But you tend to know what the person next to you is doing and people talk all the time about their projects. Let's say if Ali was trying to create a complete smallpox virus, someone would have noticed,' said Malloy, making the notion seem ridiculous.

Dewar nodded. 'Seems reasonable.'

'Would you like to meet the team?'

'I've come all this way,' smiled Dewar.

'What reason would you like me to give them?'

'Routine Home Office procedure after the death of a student who was a foreign national, I think.'

Sandra Macandrew was first. Dewar found her pleasant and friendly. She couldn't understand Ali's death or the change that had come over him during the last few weeks of his life.

'You obviously noticed a change in his personality,' said Dewar. 'Did you notice a change in his work pattern?'

Sandra thought for a moment. 'He still came to the lab and seemed to be working on his project as usual. I suppose Steve would know from his notebooks whether things were working or not. By that time, he'd stopped talking to us.'

'But you didn't notice him doing anything different in the lab?'

'Different? No.'

'Thanks for your help, Miss Macandrew. If you think of anything else, you can leave a message for me here.' Dewar handed her a card with a Sci Med contact number on it.

Peter Moore was next. He couldn't tell him any more than

Sandra had. Hammadi's death was as big a mystery to him. Yes, he had liked Ali too.

Pierre Le Grice was a different kettle of fish. He was positively aggressive, complaining bitterly about the interruption to his research that the fragment ban was causing.

'To put a complete stop to circulation is ridiculous. OK, you impose the twenty-per-cent rule. Even that is stupid. What can you do with fifty that you can't with twenty? Tell me that.'

'Dr Le Grice, I don't make the rules. If you want to protest you'll have to do it through your government and the United Nations.'

'You people never accept responsibility for anything,' continued Le Grice. 'It's always someone else to blame.'

'I accept responsibility for what I have to do, Doctor. I say again, I don't make the rules but I am empowered and expected to enforce them.'

There was a pause, engineered by Dewar to allow what he'd said to sink in. He continued, 'So if I learn that someone here has been sending smallpox fragments to a research institute in Manchester without going through proper channels I just might nail his professional hide to the wall.'

Le Grice said simply, 'You know?'

Dewar nodded. 'I know it was some time ago and nothing is going to happen about it now but things have changed. Any more of that and you can kiss your career goodbye, monsieur.'

George Ferguson was not in the lab. Sandra explained that he and Malloy had been 'a right couple of heroes yesterday'. George was currently being thanked by 'the powers that be'. Dewar asked what had happened and was given a rundown on what Malloy and Ferguson had done.

'Better them than me.'

'Me too,' agreed Sandra. 'Would you like to see round the lab?'

'Sure would.'

The lab struck Dewar as being untidy. This was due in part

to a lack of space – people were vying with pieces of equipment for usable bench area. Rows of notebooks filled up the windowsills. Racks of test tubes were piled three high and electrophoresis photographs were hanging all along the wall from clips on wall hooks. 'How d'you ever find anything?' he asked, making it sound like a joke.

'It only *looks* a complete mess,' replied Sandra. 'We know where everything is. A tidy lab is a sterile lab – that's what Steve always says. If you're polishing benches it means you can't think of an experiment to do.'

'A point of view, I suppose,' said Dewar.

After Dewar had spent ten minutes or so passing the time of day with Sandra and Peter – Pierre Le Grice had decided to keep his own company and busied himself about the lab – George Ferguson returned to loud demands from the others to show them his medal.

Ferguson laughed. 'No medal,' he said. 'Only a few precious words from *Herr Direktor* to inspire me and make it all worthwhile.'

'George, this is Dr Dewar. He's enquiring into Ali's death,' said Steven Malloy.

Dewar shook hands with Ferguson and asked him the same questions as the others about the dead student. His reply was much the same. He, like everyone else in the lab, had liked Ali. His death had come as a complete shock.

'Did you know what Ali was working on?'

Ferguson shrugged and said, 'Only in the broadest of terms. I'm a hospital technician who had the hospital taken from under him. I look after the virus stocks and see to the culture media. This new molecular stuff is largely beyond me and you can't teach an old dog new tricks.'

'It must have been a bit of a change to come here.'

Ferguson smiled at what he saw as understatement. 'I'd been at the City for thirty-two years,' he said.

'Must have been tempting to call it a day and take early retirement.'

'The bank manager disagreed,' said Ferguson.

Dewar smiled. 'No golden handshake on offer, eh?'

'From the NHS? Pull the other one.'

'You seem to have settled in well with the group here.'

'It's a temporary thing. Steve had a vacancy but whether he'll get a new grant or not is another matter. If he doesn't I'll be out the door come Christmas. My face doesn't really fit in the institute anyway.'

'Why not?'

'Times change. These days science graduates outnumber jobs ten to one. You need at least an upper second to get a job that would have gone to an ONC ten years ago. If the job involves making the tea as well, we're talking about a PhD.'

Dewar smiled and said, 'I hope something works out for you.'

He had a last meeting with Paul Hutton to thank him formally for his cooperation.

'Does that mean you are finished with us?' asked Hutton.

'I should think so,' replied Dewar. 'Unless there are any more developments.'

'You're returning to London today?'

'I'm going to show my face at the Iraqi students' association. I'll take it from there.'

# ~ *Seven* ~

The Iraqi students' association was on the first floor of a Victorian building in a street largely taken up with restaurants offering cuisines of the world. The street was narrow, the buildings tall and traffic fumes hung in the air like a November fog. The smell of foreign food mingled with vague damp odours of plaster and cats as Dewar climbed the badly lit stairs and knocked on the door with the brass plaque and Arabic inscription on it.

A young man answered, obviously surprised to see a Westerner standing there. 'What do you want?' he asked in clipped but otherwise perfect English.

'My name's Dewar. I'd like to speak to any friends of Ali Hammadi.'

'He is dead.'

'I know he's dead. That's why I'd like to speak to them.'

'You are a policeman?'

'Not exactly.' Dewar showed him his Sci Med ID card.

The man seemed to compare the photograph on the card with the reality several times before deciding that it might be a reasonable likeness. 'Dr Adam Dewar,' he intoned.

'That's me,' Dewar agreed.

'Come inside,' said the man, suddenly turning on his heel and leaving Dewar to close the door behind them. They passed along a narrow hallway past a series of grey-painted doors leading off into badly lit rooms as far as Dewar could determine. Single, unshaded light bulbs seemed to be the preferred source of illumination and, in rooms with ceilings twelve feet high, there seemed to be more shadow than light.

There were about twelve people in the room Dewar was finally shown into; they sat separately in groups of three or four and all looked about the right age to be students. The furnishings in the room were old and the heavy curtains on the windows looked as if they hadn't been cleaned since the turn of the century. They hung behind several faded velvet-covered couches, each with one single wood-scrolled arm. The scene reminded Dewar of a Victorian illustration of an opium den. A few of the students had notebooks open and appeared to be discussing course work.

The man who had answered the door said something to them in Arabic. Dewar picked out the word Hammadi.

There was a prolonged silence while everyone looked at Dewar impassively. Then one student got up and came over. He smiled, showing perfect teeth. 'I am Tariq Saadi — Ali was my friend,' he said. 'Perhaps you'd like some coffee?'

Dewar sipped bitter coffee while Saadi, a postgraduate student in mathematics, told him what he knew of Ali. He and Ali had, in fact, come from villages in Iraq not more than twenty kilometres apart but had known each other only slightly before going to Baghdad to do their first degrees, meeting up properly and becoming firm friends. Both had been delighted when they managed to get on to the foreign study programme together.

'We didn't think it would be possible for us to travel abroad but science is above political difficulty,' said Tariq. 'The politicians may disagree but the universities continue to communicate.'

'Good,' said Dewar. 'How are your studies going?' he asked, hoping to gain the man's confidence.

Tariq shrugged and smiled. 'Sometimes I struggle.'

'Was it the same for Ali?'

'Oh no,' smiled Tariq. 'Ali was very clever and so . . .' – he searched for the word – 'about his science.'

'Enthusiastic?' suggested Dewar.

'Yes, thank you, enthusiastic but more . . . *dedicated* is the word. For Ali, science was everything. All he was interested in. The sky was the limit and one day he was going to do great things. He said it would be possible to have enough food for everyone on the planet. An end to starvation would be made possible through molecular biology and the cloning of the genes.'

Dewar smiled at the idealism of youth. Molecular biology might well enable scientists to do these things but it wasn't going to happen. It wasn't going to happen because no one invested money in things that didn't make a profit and feeding the hungry wasn't a paying proposition. Ali Hammadi would not now live to discover that awful truth. There was no point in pointing it out to Tariq.

'So why did Ali kill himself?' asked Dewar softly.

Tariq paused, his eyes misting over as he thought of his friend, then he said simply, 'It was so sad.'

Dewar needed more. 'Yes,' he said. 'But no one seems able to come up with any reason why he did it. There must have been one. Something must have gone terribly wrong in his life. Ali's colleagues at the institute tell me that he was obviously upset about something. They say he became very depressed during the weeks before he died. You were his friend; he must have confided in you, didn't he?'

The boy shrugged uncomfortably and Dewar got the impression that it wasn't just what he'd said that had produced the reaction. He glanced over his shoulder and saw that a new man had entered the room and was standing looking across at them. He seemed older than the others, an Arab, tall and

– 81 –

bearded with heavy, dark-rimmed spectacles. He remembered Inspector Grant saying something about older men being part of the setup.

'No, Ali told me nothing,' said Tariq, obviously unsettled at the appearance of the newcomer, even though he was out of earshot. 'I don't know why he did it. It's a mystery. Maybe he was ill. It can happen, you know.'

Dewar looked him straight in the eye and knew that he was lying. The presence of the bearded man was intimidating him.

'Look, Tariq, maybe this isn't the best place to talk,' he suggested quietly.

'I don't think there is any more to say,' replied the boy, but he spoke the words like an automaton.

'I think there is,' insisted Dewar, but keeping his voice low. 'Maybe you owe it to your friend to tell me exactly what you know. I understand how difficult things are for you so I'm going to leave now, but I'll leave my card on the seat. Call me when you feel it's safe. If I'm not there leave a message.' The boy nodded uncertainly. 'Well, thanks for your help, Tariq. I'm sorry about your friend's death. It was very sad,' said Dewar in a louder voice that invited overhearing.

He got up and was shown to the door by Tariq. To get there they had to pass the older man, who didn't acknowledge them as they passed, but Dewar took a good look at him anyway. Maybe Inspector Grant could come up with some pictures. It would be nice to know who and what he really was. As he walked out on to the street he decided that he would stay on in Edinburgh for the time being.

Dewar booked into a city-centre hotel and made his report to Sci Med using his laptop computer and a phone link from his mobile. There wasn't that much to report, just that he wasn't quite happy about the Edinburgh situation as it stood. He'd be staying on until he knew more. After he had shut down his laptop, he phoned Karen. She was at the lab.

'You're where?'

'Edinburgh,' Dewar told her again. 'I'm going to be here at least another day. How's Kensington? Is the world still falling out of its bottom?'

'People don't have that kind of problem in *Kensington*,' laughed Karen. 'They have "upset stomachs". I think we're on top of the outbreak. We've traced the problem to a cold-meat supplier and closed him down for the moment. In theory it's all over bar the sh— shouting.'

'I wish I could say the same,' said Dewar.

'That sounded like it came from the heart,' said Karen.

'I've got such a bad feeling about things here.'

'So there's no chance of you getting back by the weekend?'

'Shouldn't think so but there's no way of knowing for sure. I'm just playing it by ear. I'm convinced one of Ali Hammadi's friends knows more than he's letting on. That doesn't mean to say it's anything relevant but I'd really like to understand why this man Hammadi took his own life when he seemed to have so much to live for.'

'Maybe he didn't.'

'The police are convinced it was suicide and his behaviour had changed in the weeks leading up to his death.'

'While the balance of his mind was disturbed . . .' intoned Karen.

'It's what disturbed it,' said Dewar.

After a pause, Karen said tentatively, 'Why not pop down to North Berwick while you're up there, say hello to my mother? It'll take your mind off things for a wee while.'

'Could do,' agreed Dewar slowly.

'Not a good idea?'

The prospect of spending an evening with Karen's widowed mother did not fill Dewar with enthusiasm. A few drinks and a bit of light conversation in the hotel bar might have been a preferred option. However, he didn't want to offend Karen. 'OK,' he said. 'Could do.' He hoped he sounded more enthusiastic than he felt. 'Any messages?'

'I was actually hoping to get up to see her this weekend but I'm not sure how long the salmonella thing will take to resolve. In theory we should have seen the last of the new cases by tomorrow. Maybe I should plan for the week after next instead. I don't suppose you'll feel like a return trip to Edinburgh that soon.'

'Why not? It would be fun to spend some time together up here,' said Dewar. 'Maybe we could run off to the Highlands for a day or so.'

'That would be nice. Of course, you may still be there!' laughed Karen.

'If I am it means I've hit *big* trouble and *everyone* might be running off to the Highlands,' said Dewar.

'Give Mother my love and tell her I'll be up the week after next.'

Dewar's laptop bleeped as he reconnected it to the phone socket to put it on standby. There was a message waiting for him from Sci Med. A man named Tariq Saadi had called. He wanted to meet with him. The suggested place was James Thin's bookshop in South Bridge, the time, eight o'clock that same evening.

Dewar wondered why Saadi had called the Sci Med number. He deduced that he had probably tried his mobile number first and found it engaged with his call to Karen, so he had called the other number on the card rather than wait and try again. That implied a sense of urgency. A limited window of time in which to make a call.

Dewar looked at his watch. It was just after 7.30 p.m. Karen's mother would have to wait for another day.

\* \* \*

The taxi dropped him off in South Bridge outside the entrance to Edinburgh University's Old College building and opposite Thin's bookshop. He crossed the street, dodging the evening traffic, and entered the shop to find it pleasantly quiet. It was also deceptively large, occupying several floors of an old building that had seen many internal conversions in its time, leaving it a warren of rooms, corridors and staircases. Dewar moved slowly round the ground floor, getting a feel for the place and pausing occasionally to examine a book. At that time in the evening there were fewer than a dozen other customers browsing the shelves. Saadi was not one of them.

Dewar opted to try a lower floor and thought he was all alone there save for a member of staff — a student working part time, he guessed — reading a textbook by her till. He was suddenly startled to feel a tap on the shoulder and turned to find Saadi, who'd materialised from the shadows of an alcove. 'Thank you for coming,' he whispered nervously.

'So there *was* more to Ali's death?' said Dewar quietly.

Tariq nodded. 'I don't know everything but they wanted him to do something for them. Ali didn't want to have anything to do with it but they threatened him. They said it would be the worse for his family.'

'They?'

'Our . . . advisers.'

The man at the students' association?' Tariq nodded. 'They're government?' Another nod. 'How many are there?'

'Two. Professor Siddiqui and a man named Abbas, the man you saw.'

Dewar made a mental note of the names. 'Have you any idea at all what they wanted Ali to do?' he asked.

'He wouldn't say but he was very frightened. He said . . .'

'What did he say?' prompted Dewar.

'He was afraid many people would die.'

Dewar felt himself go cold. He could feel the pulse in his

temples start to beat harder. He was listening to a nightmare becoming a reality. 'Are you sure he told you nothing more than that?'

Tariq shook his head. 'Nothing. He said it was too awful but I know they gave him something.'

'Do you know what?'

'Pieces of something. I overheard a conversation one day. Ali was upset. He said something about not wanting the pieces. It was too dangerous.' Tariq shrugged to suggest it didn't mean anything to him. 'He said the pieces should be destroyed but Siddiqui said he had to do what they told him or it would be the worse for him and his family.'

'Pieces?'

'Yes . . .'

Tariq froze suddenly. Dewar watched him turn pale before his eyes and realised that he was looking past him, his eyes wide with fear. He turned round to see a face staring at them through a gap that had opened up in a row of books behind them. It was the man from the Iraqi students' association, his black beard brushing the shelf, his bespectacled eyes unblinking as they stared at Tariq. A shorter, more academic-looking Arab appeared at the end of the shelves.

Tariq looked as if he might pass out. 'I have to go,' he stammered.

'You don't have to go anywhere with them,' insisted Dewar in an urgent whisper. 'They can't do anything to you in this country. If you're afraid, I can help. We can sort it out. Stay here with me. Tell me what they wanted Ali to do.'

'You don't understand . . . my family . . .'

Tariq moved meekly towards the two Arabs and didn't look back. Dewar felt helpless but he had the feeling he'd only make things worse for Tariq by making a scene. He caught the eye of the bearded Arab and hoped he could suggest with a look that should anything happen to Tariq it might be bad-news day for him, but the man remained impassive. After a short, muted exchange in Arabic Tariq was ushered upstairs with the other Arab leading the way.

Dewar, filled with frustration, hit the palm of his hand against the end of a bookshelf causing the girl by the till to look up sharply. 'If we don't have what you're looking for, we can always order it,' she said helpfully.

Dewar looked at her, then realised what he'd done and apologised. He made for the stairs and left. He started to walk back to his hotel, knowing that he needed time to calm down and get his thoughts in order. He walked up Chambers Street and followed George IV Bridge up to the Royal Mile, which led from the castle down to the royal Palace of Holyrood. He crossed and paused at the head of the Mound, the steep thoroughfare that joined old Edinburgh to its so-called Georgian new town. The lights of Princes Street were strung out like pearls below him. To his left, the floodlit castle sat high on its ancient rock. Surely such a beautiful city could not really be host to a plot hatched in hell.

It was obvious to Dewar that Tariq had translated an Arabic word he'd heard as 'pieces' where 'fragments' would have been more correct, but Tariq wasn't a biologist. He'd had no idea what they'd been talking about. The 'pieces' just had to be DNA fragments of the smallpox virus. There was no other plausible explanation. The question now was, how many fragments did the Iraqi government men have access to and what had happened to them?

When Tariq had overheard Ali protesting that what they wanted him to do was too dangerous, had he been talking in general terms about the whole idea or specifically what they were asking him to do? Had Ali been approached as one of a number of people in a chain of events, each perhaps doing part of the virus assembly? Or had he been the final link in the chain, the scientist who would finally join up all the fragments?

Whatever it was, it had been enough to push him over the edge into suicide. Could the Iraqis really be at that stage? Was the resurrection of live smallpox really that close?

Another worrying question swam into Dewar's head. Had Ali committed suicide because he couldn't face doing something so heinous or because he'd already *done* it? The action could have been dictated by guilt. He tried convincing himself that someone in the Malloy lab would have been aware of what he was doing if he'd been working on it in the open lab, but the truth was that DNA in a test tube was a colourless liquid regardless of where it had come from. You couldn't really tell anything by looking at it. You had to establish its sequence to start to make sense of what it was. Even then the code would have to be fed into a computer and compared to the many known DNA sequences held in international scientific data-bases. Only then could its real identity be established.

Would Hammadi really have risked reconstructing live smallpox virus in the open lab beside his colleagues when he knew that it would have put them all at grave risk? On the other hand, if he had used the high-containment facilities in the institute for dealing with dangerous viruses, people would have been aware of it and asked questions about it. This might have forced him to take such a risk. It was not a comforting thought. It was, however, the worst possible scenario. Hammadi might have refused to do anything at all. The only thing for sure was that he had killed himself. Guilt, or a brave attempt to save his family from pressure?

Thinking back to what Tariq had said before they'd been interrupted, Dewar recalled his saying that Ali had not wanted to take the 'pieces'. He had not, however, suggested that he *refuse* to take them. If Ali had accepted them he must surely have taken them into the institute for storage if nothing else. There was a chance they were still there, sitting in some rack in some fridge, probably innocent-looking little plastic tubes.

There would have to be a proper examination of the storage space used by Ali Hammadi in Steve Malloy's lab and a detailed analysis of the contents.

Dewar's first instinct was to call a full-scale alert but then he reconsidered and thought better of it. As yet there was no proof of the existence of illegal virus fragments or how far the Iraqis had come along the way to reconstituting smallpox. Perhaps the fact that the Iraqi 'advisers' were still in the city suggested that they had not got what they wanted, otherwise they would surely have been long gone. That was a point: why were they still there? Surely they weren't hoping to recruit someone else for the job?

Dewar decided to make finding out more about these 'advisers' a priority. He'd see Grant about that. He would not push the alarm button just yet. He would wait to see what Grant, and Malloy for that matter, could come up with and continue to play it low-key for the moment. He called Karen at her flat when he got in and apologised for not having visited her mother, saying that something had come up.

'I'll believe you, thousands wouldn't,' said Karen.

'Believe me,' said Dewar. 'I would much rather have spent an evening with your mother, than the one I've just had.'

'Your fears are coming true?'

'It's not looking good,' said Dewar.

'So you won't be back tomorrow night, then?'

'I doubt it.'

# ~ *Eight* ~

Grant looked at Dewar long and hard before saying, 'Are you absolutely sure it's necessary to tangle with that lot?'

'I'm sure. What's the problem?'

'I know we don't have full diplomatic relations with Iraq these days but foreigners with any kind of diplomatic status are bad news and these two must have some kind of a deal going. I've been down that road before. Bastards can do just about anything they like and get away with it. Maybe one day we'll get a government who can at least figure out that not all countries fill up their diplomatic corps with gormless, public-school pillocks. We're the exception rather than the rule. There are some bad buggers out there hiding behind CD plates.'

'I agree. It's difficult, and I'm not sure what their status is either, but I need to find out as much as I can about them. Their names are Siddiqui and Abbas. The pair of them put pressure on Ali Hammadi to do something for them. I've an idea what it was but I need to know whether he did it or not.'

'And you can't tell me what it was. Right?'

'Not right now.'

Grant nodded and sucked his teeth slowly. 'And if I say no?'

'I'll have to go above your head.'

'Beats me why you didn't do that in the first place,' said Grant.

Dewar leaned towards him and said, 'I thought we could work together. I don't want to make waves right now in what is a very delicate situation. If I make a mistake and cry wolf where there isn't one there could be all sorts of unpleasant repercussions, international ones. I could end up being hard-pushed to find work washing dishes.'

'But you won't tell me what it's all about?'

'Officially I'm here to check that some routine regulations are being complied with. Ali Hammadi's death was a complicating factor which is leading me to suspect that they have not been complied with. To what extent I've yet to find out. Officially, you would be helping me with this.'

'Regulations,' said Grant. 'What sort of stakes are we talking about with these "regulations"?'

'On the one hand there could be nothing to worry about. On the other, we could be dealing with something that could affect the whole damned world, cause another war and wipe out millions.' Grant let out a low whistle. 'Are you up for it?'

'I'm in. Can't see me making superintendent any other way, the way I rub up folks the wrong way round here.'

'Good. See what you can come up with on Siddiqui and Abbas. I'll leave you my contact numbers. Get in touch as soon as you have anything. I'm going back to the Institute of Molecular Sciences.'

Dewar didn't bother going through official channels this time. He simply entered the building behind a group of students and walked past the man on the desk with an air of authority that defied challenge in the untrained. God, he thought to himself as the lift started to rise. My grandmother's coal cellar was more secure than this.

He knocked on the door of the Malloy lab and entered.

'Hello,' said Sandra Macandrew. She was alone. 'I didn't expect to see you again. Something you forgot?'

'Is Steve around?' asked Dewar, choosing to ignore her question.

'He's working at home this morning. He took his disks home. He had some paperwork to do for Professor Hutton and the gas board were coming to read his meter. Do you want me to call him?'

Dewar hesitated for a moment before saying, 'Maybe I'll go and visit him at home. Can you give me his address?'

Sandra hesitated for a moment and Dewar saw her dilemma. He said, 'If you'd rather, I'll go through the proper channels with Professor Hutton. I should have thought—'

Sandra smiled and insisted, 'No, really. I'm being silly. We know you and you're some kind of policeman anyway. Steve lives in a converted church building in a village to the south called Temple. Have you got a car?'

Dewar shook his head. 'I was planning on going by taxi. Is it far?'

'About eight miles from here. Not that far.'

'That's OK. Can you write it down?'

Sandra wrote down Malloy's address and asked, 'Would you like me to call you a cab from here?'

'Thanks.'

Sandra picked up the phone and called the admin section, asking for a taxi for a visitor to the lab who was just leaving. 'There'll be one here in seven minutes,' she said to Dewar. 'They always use the same company.'

'Much obliged,' said Dewar.

'Have you managed to find out any more about Ali's death?'

'Bits and pieces,' replied Dewar. 'Nothing that helps terribly much. I don't suppose you've remembered anything that might be useful?'

'Where does smallpox come into it?' asked Sandra, ignoring Dewar's question and establishing eye contact.

'Smallpox?' repeated Dewar, taken aback and stalling for

time.

'Steve started asking all sorts of questions about the smallpox DNA fragments we've been using after your last visit. I thought there must be some connection between you, Ali's death and the smallpox fragments.'

'I can see why you're doing a PhD,' said Dewar. 'What did Steve say exactly?'

'He impressed upon George just how important it was that our stocks of fragments should all be accounted for in case there was an impromptu inspection. We were told we had to obey all the rules to the letter and start keeping the place tidier. He got on to Pierre about clearing out Ali's stuff and creating more fridge space.'

Dewar stopped her with a raise of his hand. He asked, 'Are you saying that Ali's stuff wasn't checked before the audit return was made?'

Sandra moved uncomfortably. 'No, I'm not saying that at all. George checked it for listed smallpox DNA fragments; Steve asked him to,' she replied defensively. 'But naturally there were various tubes and bottles with labels he couldn't decipher and Ali is no longer around to ask. Steve asked Pierre to take a look before we got rid of it to see if he could decipher anything.'

'Shit,' said Dewar

'What difference does it make? Ali didn't have anything the rest of us didn't have access to.'

'How do you know that?' asked Dewar flatly.

'Surely you're not suggesting that Ali had some kind of secret project on the go?' Dewar didn't reply. 'Oh my God,' said Sandra. 'That is what you think, isn't it? It's not really Ali's suicide you're concerned with at all. That's not why you're here. It's something to do with this smallpox thing, something to do with the reason they banned movement of the fragments.'

There was no point in denying anything, Dewar concluded. He felt like a government spokesman acknowledging the appearance of new-variant CJD — it was all right to eat your words as long as they didn't contain beef. On the other hand he didn't want to enter conversation about it. Instead, he simply asked, 'Did Pierre Le Grice do what Steve asked him to do?'

'I've not had occasion to look.'

'Could you look now?'

Sandra looked surprised but she walked across the lab and opened the bottom door of a large fridge-freezer. 'Yes,' she said, getting down on her haunches to examine the contents. 'It's been cleared out.'

Dewar looked thoughtful.

The phone rang and broke the ensuing silence. 'Your taxi,' said Sandra.

'Here we are,' said the taxi driver over his shoulder as they drove into the small village of Temple in Midlothian. Dewar could see it was well cared for, pretty without being twee.

'Where is it you're looking for exactly?'

'A converted church.'

'Know it. They're a' goin' that way these days,' said the driver. 'Carpet warehouses, offices, health clubs. Sign o' the times.' He pulled up outside the church at the edge of the village and said, 'There you go.'

Dewar paid him and took a look at the building. There was very little from the outside to suggest that it wasn't a parish church any longer. The only giveaway was the fact that its front door had been altered and there was a letter box. He opened the iron gate and walked up the path between the gnarled yew trees on either side. He saw that autumn leaves had started to pile up against the wall exposed to the prevailing westerly wind. He knocked on the red door, wondering whether it would be loud enough. The wood seemed thick enough to absorb the sound but he couldn't see any bell-push. The sound of music reached him from inside. The door opened and Steve Malloy stood there.

Miles Davis was playing in the background.

'You?' exclaimed Malloy. 'I was expecting the gas man.'

'Maybe he'll come too,' said Dewar.

'Come in. This is a surprise.'

Dewar saw that the interior of the church had been altered extensively to provide an attractive, modern, open-plan living area. 'Did you do all this yourself?' he asked.

'Mostly. Not because I'm mad keen on DIY but because I couldn't afford to have anyone else do it by the time I'd bought the place.'

'Looks like you knew what you were doing,' said Dewar.

'Let's say I learned along the way. Coffee?'

'If it's not too much trouble. Thanks.'

Malloy went over to the kitchen area while Dewar continued to look around. All the major features of the original church had been retained, from the gallery to the stone pulpit – now used to house an array of spotlights, directed at key features. The pews had been removed and the floor area divided cleverly into what amounted to different rooms without there actually being partition walls. Malloy had obviously been working in the office area where the computer had gone on to screensaver mode with fish drifting across the screen and the sound of bubbles softly emanating from the speakers.

'It must be expensive to heat,' said Dewar, raising his voice to be heard.

'It would be if I tried to heat the whole place,' replied Malloy. 'But I've adopted a zone-heating policy, a bit like the days when houses were heated by coal fires. You had heat inside a radius of ten feet from the fire. Outside that semicircle you froze. I put heating where I'm going to need it and live within these areas.'

Malloy brought two mugs of coffee and handed one to Dewar. They both sat down. 'What's the problem?' asked Malloy.

'It's Ali,' replied Dewar. 'I've found out he was under pressure from Iraqi government officials to do something for them.'

'What?'

'Something concerned with smallpox.'

'Good God,' said Malloy. 'You're serious?'

'A friend of Ali's overheard an argument about "pieces" he was being given. I'm pretty sure they were talking about DNA fragments.'

Malloy shook his head as if not wanting to believe what he was hearing. 'But If Ali had been doing anything like that we would have known.'

'Would you?' asked Dewar.

'Of course. If you wanted to start assembling something like live smallpox you'd be using the high-containment lab all the time.'

'Or not,' said Dewar.

Malloy looked at him. 'You can't seriously be suggesting that he tried to do it in the open lab?'

'I'm not in the business of suggesting anything at the moment. I simply just don't know enough but we have to consider it as a possibility.'

'But we're all still alive,' offered Malloy as rebuttal.

'I agree that goes a long way towards saying that he didn't succeed in assembling live virus,' said Dewar. 'In fact it's my real hope that he didn't even try to do it. I think he may have refused and ended up killing himself in an attempt to protect his family from the consequences. But the fact remains that it's an outside possibility. What I think is much more certain is that he was given these DNA fragments and I'd like to know what happened to them.'

'I asked Pierre Le Grice to check out Ali's stuff,' said Malloy.

'I know. I've been to the lab. I spoke to Sandra.'

'Pierre didn't say he found anything unusual.'

'What would he have done with the stuff?'

'Depends what it was. Solutions and reagents that were clearly labelled and we could still use, he would have kept. Anything unlabelled or clearly finished with, he would have put out into the biological waste system to be sterilised and destroyed.'

'Supposing the fragments had been there.'

'They couldn't have been labelled, otherwise Pierre would have said something. If they were unlabelled, he wouldn't have known what they were; he probably destroyed them.'

Dewar looked thoughtful. Miles Davis played on in the background. 'Are the lab test tubes and containers used in the institute standard in all labs?' he asked.

'I suppose there might be some differences from one place to the next, depending on the supplier. Why?'

'The fragments Ali was given must have come from outside the institute. I just wondered whether or not Le Grice might have noticed containers that were foreign to the institute even if they hadn't been labelled.'

It was Malloy's turn to appear thoughtful. Eventually he said, 'I think we should go and ask him.'

As they prepared to leave for the institute there came a knock to the door. Malloy opened it to admit the gas man.

'A bit spooky living in a church,' said the man, making a note of the reading. 'Just think of all them funerals and that.'

'I concentrate on the christenings,' said Malloy.

The gas man left and they started out for the institute in Malloy's Ford Escort. The traffic was light and the journey took less that twenty minutes.

Sandra Macandrew raised her eyebrows when she saw Dewar appear in the lab yet again, but didn't say anything. Malloy called Le Grice into his office and closed the door without explaining anything to the others.

'Pierre, when you cleared out Ali's stuff did you come across anything unusual?'

Le Grice looked puzzled. 'Unusual in what way?' he replied.

'Did you find anything there that shouldn't have been there? Anything against the rules?'

'No.'

'Anything that looked as if it might have come from another lab — you know, different kind of container to the ones we use, that sort of thing.'

'No, nothing like that. There were lots of tubes with labels I didn't recognise, things that only Ali would have understood, but nothing out of the ordinary.'

'What did you do with the unlabelled tubes?'

'I put them into bio-disposal. There was no point in keeping them. No one else would have been able to decipher them either, I'm sure.'

Malloy held up his hand and reassured him. 'No one is suggesting anything else, Pierre. You did exactly what I asked you to do. There's no problem.'

'Can I go now? I'm very busy.'

'Of course.'

'Seems to work very hard,' said Dewar as Le Grice closed the door.

'He's very ambitious,' replied Malloy. 'Very bright too. Well, there we have it. If Ali had illegal fragments of the virus or even if he actually managed to reconstruct live smallpox, which I just can't believe, the whole lot went straight into the steriliser and I can't say I'm sorry.'

'Sounds good to me too,' agreed Dewar.

'From a purely selfish point of view I'm glad you came here,' said Malloy.

'How so?'

'You've given me a reason for Ali's suicide. I've been blaming myself ever since it happened for not recognising the symptoms of clinical depression. It sounds like he wasn't ill at all — he just got mixed up in a nightmare. The bastards who asked him to do it, I suppose they'll get away with it?'

'That's usually a fair bet where government-sponsored crime is involved. Anything goes, from genocide to blowing up an airliner.'

Dewar paused by Sandra's bench on the way out. 'I think I'm finished this time,' he said.

'No real problems?' she asked, her eyes asking more questions than the words.

'There might have been,' he replied.

'Will what you've been doing here help lift the ban on the movement of smallpox fragments for research?'

'It may go some way but it could take time. Anything involving the agreement of many countries takes time. You're worried about your degree?'

'Not just that. I think this lab had a real chance of coming up with a vaccine against AIDS. Without access to new fragments I'm not so sure. It would have been nice to have been associated with something like that, a paper in *Nature*, the whole bit.'

'If you're being slowed up, everyone else is too,' Dewar reminded her. 'I'm sure rival labs are feeling just as frustrated.'

'I suppose you're right,' agreed Sandra. 'We'll just have to make the best of things. Hope for a lucky break in another direction.'

'Well, I wish you the best of luck,' said Dewar.

'Thanks,' replied Sandra. 'Need a taxi?'

'I'm going to walk for a bit. Need the exercise.'

Dewar started to walk towards town. The sky was clear and autumn sunshine shone down on red-and-gold-leafed trees. There was a coolness in the air but it just made the conditions perfect for walking. He took out his mobile phone from his briefcase and switched it back on. There was one diverted call waiting for him. It was from Grant at police headquarters, asking him to call in when he had a moment. Dewar called him back.

'I've got something for you. Best if you came in,' said Grant.

Dewar flagged down the first taxi he saw. The journey took thirty-five minutes, largely because they had to cross town to get to police headquarters on the north side of the city. Dewar's impatience grew with every traffic-light halt, and when he finally arrived he felt as if he'd been released from prison.

'You're a hard man to track down,' said Grant.

'I turned off the phone earlier. I didn't want it ringing at awkward moments,' explained Dewar.

'I left messages at all the contact numbers you gave me,' said Grant.

'Thanks. That was the right thing to do. What have you got?'

'Recognise any of these bozos?' Grant pushed five computer-generated images across the desk.

'These two,' replied Grant. 'They're the Iraqis I saw at the bookshop, Siddiqui and Abbas. Well done. I'm impressed.'

'Aren't computers wonderful?' replied Grant.

'When they work. Find out anything about them?'

Grant leaned across the desk and tapped the end of his pen on the face of the bearded man. 'Abbas was straightforward, officially an educational liaison officer but thought by Special Branch to be triple "A".' Dewar raised his eyes. 'Iraqi secret police.'

'Fits.'

'The other bozo, however, was much more difficult because London didn't seem to know anything about anyone named Siddiqui being in the country. They checked their Iraqi picture album and cross-checked with intelligence and came up with three guys with that name known to them. The one you've picked is . . .' Grant checked the reference number on the back of the photo and read from his notes. 'Dr Ismail Siddiqui; he's on the faculty at Baghdad University and is credited with being a scientific adviser to the Iraqi government. He's also believed by the military to have been involved in Saddam's biological-weapons programme, although there's no proof. Make any sense?'

Dewar felt his limbs become heavy. He couldn't say this had come as a complete shock to him, or any kind of a shock at all, but it was just so enervating to have his worst fears confirmed. 'All too much,' he replied. 'You say Siddiqui's presence here is a surprise to London?'

'Apparently.'

'How?'

'That's for them to find out when I tell them who you've identified.'

'You know what really worries me?'

'What?' asked Grant.

'The fact he's still in Edinburgh. How long is it since Hammadi died?'

'Almost six weeks,' said Grant after checking his desk diary.

'Well, Dr Siddiqui,' said Dewar, picking up his photograph and holding it in both hands in front of him. 'Just what is it you're waiting for?'

# ~ Nine ~

'Anything else you'd like us to do?' asked Grant. 'Lots but you're going to say you don't have the manpower,' replied Dewar.

'Try me.'

'I'd like to know why Siddiqui is staying on in Edinburgh. I'd like to know what he does while he's here, what his movements are, where he goes when he goes out – if he goes out, who he sees, that sort of thing.'

'I don't think you'll need me or my manpower for that,' said Grant. 'The minute I tell London who it is you've identified, they're going to come quicker than a kid on his first date. You won't be able to move for surveillance officers on Siddiqui. That's my bet. Somebody screwed up at immigration so the others will be out for brownie points in recovering the situation.'

'He could have been smuggled in?' suggested Dewar.

'Possible, but he's not exactly been hiding himself away,' pointed out Grant. 'I'd say he's a man with the right paperwork.'

'Who'll be doing the job? Special Branch?'

'Special Branch, MI5, you name it. They're going to be tripping over each other. They don't get that much to do these days.'

'You're right. I should have thought,' said Dewar, trying to think how the involvement of other agencies might affect things and whether or not he should risk asking Grant to delay making his report. His first thought was that any obvious sign of surveillance might spook Siddiqui but he quickly changed his mind on that score.

If Grant was right and Siddiqui was here legally then he must have been prepared for it from the time he entered the country. Even if he hadn't been aware of people watching him – in reality because of some screw-up – he still would have had to assume that watching eyes were there and act accordingly.

'Anything else on your mind?' Grant asked.

'One of the Iraqi students using the centre in Forest Road, a friend of Ali Hammadi, gave me some information about Ali. Siddiqui and Abbas saw him with me; the kid seemed scared out of his wits. I couldn't persuade him to accept protection. They escorted him away. I'm worried about him.'

'Name?'

'Tariq Saadi. He's a postgraduate student in maths at Edinburgh University.'

Grant wrote down the details. 'No promises, but I'll see what we can find out. I take it you'll be staying on in town?'

'For the moment,' agreed Dewar, although, if he was honest with himself, he wasn't quite sure why. He'd been assured that anything Ali Hammadi had been working on had either been sterilised or destroyed so the spectre of smallpox virus emanating from Edinburgh had disappeared. But he still felt uneasy and it all seemed to stem from the fact that Siddiqui was still hanging around in the city, now some six weeks after Hammadi's death.

As he walked down the steps outside police headquarters he thought he'd enjoy the remainder of a perfect autumn afternoon with a walk in the nearby Royal Botanical Gardens. In the late afternoon the sunlight was the same rich gold colour that you found at ten at night in northern climes in high summer. It had a pleasant, mellow feel to it. It was even warm. He took off his jacket and walked with it slung over his shoulder.

He tried to think of reasons for Siddiqui's continuing presence as he strolled among beautiful trees, heavy with the sadness of a dying year. Could he, or more likely others, be planning some kind of operation to recover the fragments he gave to Hammadi? It seemed doubtful. Getting into the institute would be no problem – he'd already seen that for himself – but outsiders wouldn't know where to start looking once they were in. They'd quickly arouse suspicion and possibly create a major incident. Dewar took comfort from the fact that even if they were foolish enough to risk such an operation, there was nothing left for them to recover. Le Grice had destroyed all Hammadi's stocks. So why did he still feel so edgy?

He didn't find the answer growing in any of the huge Victorian hothouses or floating in the placid waters of the lily pond among reflections of weeping willows. It wasn't to be found in the tearoom where he had tea and chocolate cake to the muted sound of Scottish country dance music or in the small cottage gallery that hosted an exhibition of modern art – although it could have been in one of the pictures. He just didn't recognise it as the answer, or art for that matter.

He spent the evening writing up his report for Sci Med. In it he indicated that he believed there was an Iraqi intention to resurrect live smallpox virus. Ali Hammadi had been involved but it was not clear to what extent. A friend of Hammadi's had witnessed the handover of what were almost certainly illegal linear fragments of the virus DNA to Hammadi but it was unknown if Hammadi had actually done anything with these fragments before committing suicide.

Nothing untoward had been found among the solutions and reagents he'd left behind in the lab, suggesting that he might have refused to cooperate and had possibly taken his own life to protect his family back home. Everything belonging to Hammadi in the lab had been destroyed but the Iraqis, for some worrying reason, still showed no signs of leaving the city. It would be up to WHO and the UN to decide what steps they should take to prevent them making any more attempts to get their hands on live virus.

Dewar acknowledged the cooperation and excellent work by Inspector Grant of the Lothians and Borders police in identifying the Iraqis, Abbas and Siddiqui.

He read his report over twice and was satisfied after a few minor changes. He pressed the SEND button on the computer, then switched it off after confirmation of transmission. He picked up the phone and called Karen at her work number. She was there.

'Still got a bad feeling?' she asked.

'As a matter of fact, I have,' said Dewar. 'And it's getting worse by the day.'

'Want to talk about it?'

'Maybe not over the phone. How are the good folk of Kensington?'

'Getting back to normal,' said Karen. 'The figures are right on the graph line for a salmonella outbreak that's had its source removed so we got that right. I'm looking forward to having an evening off.'

'I'll probably fly back sometime tomorrow. We could go out to dinner.'

'I feel more like flopping out. Why don't you come round when you get back? I'll rustle up something simple for us and you can tell me all about your problems before we succumb to the lure of strong drink?'

'And sex?'

'Your honeyed words may win me over.'

'Sounds good.'

'Mmm,' said Karen. 'Sometimes I worry about the intellectual plane of our relationship.'

'Right now, horizontal sounds good to me.'

'And sometimes I wonder why I bother,' sighed Karen.

'Because I'm so lovable?' offered Dewar.

'There has to be something else,' groaned Karen.

Dewar had hardly put the phone down when it rang again. It was Grant at police headquarters. Dewar looked at his watch. 'Are you still on duty?' he exclaimed.

'I could say yes and make a good impression,' replied Grant. 'But there was a bit of a do for one of the blokes who's leaving. I just popped into the office on the way out and there was a message for me. Your friend Saadi.'

'What about him?' asked Dewar.

'He was on the seven o'clock shuttle to Heathrow. He's on his way home.'

'Shit,' said Dewar under his breath. 'It was my fault. I hope to God being sent home is the *only* thing that's going to happen to him.'

'They should have nuked these buggers while they had the chance in Desert Storm. Nukin' Norman would have sounded just as good as Stormin'. It even has . . . what d'you call it?'

'Alliteration,' said Dewar. 'It's just a case of one lousy regime that won't go away. The ordinary people are basically no different from any other nation.'

'I'll take your word for it,' said Grant sourly.

'Thanks for letting me know. Hear any more on Siddiqui?'

'Huge embarrassment all round. He entered the UK as a delegate to an international scientific conference in Birmingham. It was a pretty clever way to come into the country, using his academic credentials without any reference to diplomatic status. Story is he came through Cyprus, Schippol and into Birmingham as one of a large contingent of scientists bound for the meeting; they used a charter flight. I wouldn't like to be the guy who was on passport control that day. He's gonna finish up as a lollipop man in Caithness. Apparently Siddiqui came up to Edinburgh after the meeting ended, ostensibly to visit Iraqi science students and see how they were getting on. All quite legal and above board.'

During the night the weather changed. The wind got up and rain came in from the northwest in great heavy but intermittent downpours. It was the sound of rain being driven against the window at 3 a.m. that woke Dewar. He got up to look out at windswept, deserted streets bathed in yellow sodium light with water pouring down the gutters in fast-flowing streams. It collected in pools above storm drains that were blocked with autumn leaves, creating a series of mini lakes that the occasional car ploughed through with caution.

For some reason he started to think of Ali Hammadi and wondered where he had been buried. He supposed there must be a Muslim cemetery in Edinburgh. He seemed to remember that Muslims were traditionally buried as quickly as possible after death but couldn't remember anything about how the faith viewed suicide, if he'd ever known. He wondered if it had excluded Hammadi from some promise of afterlife or affected his right to the ritual and ceremony of a funeral. He felt sorry for Hammadi: as far as he could determine, the evidence pointed to his suicide having been an act of bravery rather than guilt. He had laid down his life rather than take part in something that might have caused the death of many millions. Maybe someday the full story would be told. For the moment the thought of rainwater gathering in puddles on Hammadi's grave as he lay in a strange land thousands of miles from home accentuated the fickleness of fate as it applied to all mortals.

He closed the curtains again and went back to bed but sleep was elusive as the rain kept up its tattoo on the window. He lay in the darkness thinking about what Grant had said about the involvement of other agencies in the watch on Siddiqui. He would contact Sci Med in the morning and ask that they make these agencies aware of Sci Med's interest in the man and his activities. This should be allied to a request that they keep their surveillance low-key. On the other hand Siddiqui and Abbas should most definitely be stopped when they left the country. The pretext didn't matter – it was a question of making sure they weren't carrying anything on them of a biological nature. They may not have handed over all their stocks of smallpox DNA fragments to Hammadi. If not, this would be a good opportunity to get hold of them and destroy them. If by any chance – and against all the odds – Hammadi had actually done what they'd asked of him and had delivered the goods before killing himself it would also be the moment to stop either viral DNA or even live virus leaving the country. He would feel a lot happier with such a safeguard in place.

Sci Med asked him to report in person when he contacted them in the morning. He caught a flight at lunchtime and was at the Home Office by two thirty. He went straight there; there was no time to go to the flat so he left his travel bag and computer case in Jean Roberts's office while he went in to see Macmillan.

'So you think there was something in this smallpox scare after all?' said Macmillan.

'I'm afraid so,' replied Dewar. 'Hammadi working with fragments of the virus and having the necessary skills, the presence of Siddiqui in the city, Hammadi's subsequent suicide. It all adds up.'

Macmillan nodded sagely. 'But you're convinced nothing came of it?'

'I'm as sure as I can be in the circumstances,' replied Dewar. 'I think if Hammadi had delivered the goods Siddiqui and his sidekick would have left immediately. As it is, they're still there.'

Macmillan raised his eyebrows and Dewar said, 'I know. That raises another question, but anything that Hammadi had been working with was either destroyed or reallocated after his death.'

'It's a pity they didn't find any incriminating evidence of what he'd been asked to do,' said Macmillan.

'The scientist who cleared out Hammadi's reagent bottles certainly didn't notice anything out of the ordinary,' said Dewar. 'But he concedes that there were unlabelled tubes and also tubes with labels that he couldn't decipher among Hammadi's stocks. In the circumstances I don't suppose Hammadi would have put warning signs and a skull and crossbones on them.'

'You mean he might have devised a code to disguise what they were?'

'I'm not suggesting anything elaborate. The staff there often use their own initials to label tubes along with sequential numbers, so AHI, AH2 et cetera would have meant something to Hammadi but not necessarily anything to anyone else.'

'I see. And you say they were all destroyed?'

'They all went into the bio-disposal system at the institute.'

'What does that entail?'

'Discarded glassware and their contents are steam-sterilised in an autoclave before washing and being put back into circulation. Plastic tubes are autoclaved too but they melt at that temperature so they're not reusable. The deformed plastic residue is destroyed later by incineration.'

Macmillan looked thoughtful. 'Why did the bastards have to try it in the UK?' he murmured. 'I fully expected to be reporting to WHO that there was no problem at our end.'

'Sorry about that,' said Dewar.

Macmillan smiled. 'You did well,' he said. 'As long as we're sure that the attempt failed?'

'We can't be one hundred per cent certain but all the signs are pointing to failure. Siddiqui didn't get what he wanted.' said Dewar.

'Good.'

'But he's still there.' said Dewar. 'And that worries me,' he confessed.

'You think it conceivable he could still do it?'

Dewar gave an uncomfortable shrug. 'I think it would be naive to assume that the Iraqis gave their entire stock of virus fragments to Hammadi so I think we should assume they probably still have the capacity.'

'Has Siddiqui any chance of persuading someone else in Edinburgh to take Hammadi's place?'

'There are no other Iraqi nationals in the institute. I checked.'

'If coercion isn't a possibility that leaves money as an incentive,' said Macmillan.

'I can't see any scientist being persuaded to do something like that for money. Far too risky and totally immoral.'

'But if the price were right . . .' mused Macmillan.

'I suppose so.' Dewar understood too much about human nature to argue the point. 'But even if such a person could be found there would be practical difficulties, he pointed out. They'd presumably want to live to spend the money. That would mean having to use the high-containment facilities at the institute and that would mean attracting attention. They would be noticed – even if they did it at night. Research isn't a nine-to-five job. There are always people around.'

'Nevertheless . . . if the money were right . . .' persisted Macmillan. 'I think you're right to be concerned about Siddiqui's continuing presence. He could be negotiating with someone or he could be past that stage and waiting for more fragments to arrive.'

'I take it security has been stepped up after the balls-up over his entrance to the country?' asked Dewar.

'Tighter than a gnat's rectum,' said Macmillan.

'What would you like me to do?'

Macmillan thought for a moment. 'Let's err on the safe side.

Go back to Edinburgh and wait it out with Siddiqui. You know the people at the institute. You know who's capable of doing what and who's not. That could prove invaluable. I'll have a word with the other agencies and request that they do nothing without running it past you first.'

'Let's hope they agree,' said Dewar.

Macmillan smiled at Dewar's reservations. 'I think they'll see it makes sense in this case,' he said. 'They won't know a damned thing about smallpox.'

'Do you want me back there tonight?'

'Tomorrow will do.'

Dewar got a taxi to take him and his stuff back to the flat. He hadn't expected to be going back north so he now had a clothes problem. There wouldn't be time to launder what he had in his travel bag and what was lying in the laundry basket; he'd have to buy some new stuff. He checked his watch: it was 4.30 p.m. Plenty of time: he'd said he'd be at Karen's at seven. He took a trip to a branch of Marks and Spencer and stocked up on what he needed. On the way back he stopped off at Oddbins and bought two bottles of wine to take round to Karen's. There was just time to take a shower, dress – using one of the new blue shirts he'd just bought and catch a cab to get him to Muswell Hill just before seven.

Karen lived in a ground-floor flat conversion of a terraced villa in north London. The flat's best feature was that it had a south-facing lounge with French windows, leading out into a pretty little walled garden. The upper part of the villa had been unoccupied for some time – the old lady who had lived there was dead and her estate was not yet settled.

This meant that the garden was not overlooked; it had been secluded and private throughout the summer. Karen and Dewar had used it, when the weather allowed, to do their paperwork and read up on background material for their jobs. Their relationship was good enough to sustain long periods of silence and they had spent many summer evenings there with only the sound of insects and the muted strains of Chopin drifting out from indoors. Tonight the doors to the garden were closed against a chill autumn wind that blew multicoloured leaves across the grass in mini whirlpools.

Karen was wearing a white T-shirt and jeans. Over this she wore a yellow apron with a large red wine bottle on it. The word 'Ciao' was scrawled across it diagonally. She was barefoot, which made her seem even shorter when Dewar took her in his arms and gave her a hug.

'I've missed you,' he said.

'Must be almost a week,' said Karen mockingly but not displeased at Dewar's show of affection.

'Eight days,' he said. 'How are you? Still knackered?'

'Tired but happy – as Enid Blyton used to say,' said Karen. 'I'm just so glad it's over. It's always the same with urban outbreaks: you know exactly what to do, you set up everything by the book, but after a couple of days without success you start to imagine that you're never going to able to pin it down. It's going to spread until it affects the whole population and you're not going to able to do a damned thing about it.'

'But you've never failed yet,' said Dewar.

'I know. And you tell yourself that, but it's no good: you still start to think that way and that's what really tires you. It's a sort of mental assault course. You've clambered over the wall before but this time it seems even bigger. You can see your bleeding fingertips scraping back down the stone as you fail to reach the top and slide back.'

Dewar took Karen's hands in his and kissed her fingertips. 'You did reach the top,' he said.

Karen smiled. 'And you?' she asked.

'I'm flying back to Edinburgh tomorrow.'

'I thought it was over,' said Karen, looking surprised.

'I suppose you could say it's a precaution. There's just an

outside chance the Iraqis might try something to recover their fortunes.'

'Like what?'

'Like persuade someone else to help them out.'

'You're serious?' exclaimed Karen.

'Like I say, it's just a precaution.'

'Why can't they just deport these damned people?' said Karen angrily. 'All this pussy-footing around.'

'That's not the way things are done in the diplomatic world,' said Dewar.

'Well it should be,' said Karen with a grin.

'What's for eating? All I've had today is a British Airways lunch.'

'Pasta, 'cos it's quick and easy,' said Karen, leading the way through to the kitchen with Dewar following along behind.

Dewar put his arms round Karen from behind as she stirred the sauce and brought up his hands to cup her breasts. He kissed the side of her neck.

Karen giggled and said with mock severity, 'Stop it, I need to concentrate or I'll burn the dinner.'

Dewar continued fondling her. He slipped his right hand down to the waist band of her jeans and undid the button.

'Adam!'

He slowly worked the zip down until he could slide his hand into her panties.

'Adam, you're . . . impossible,' she murmured, her resolve beginning to weaken as Dewar kept up his caress. 'Are we going to eat or am I going to turn the gas off?'

The gas was turned off, with Dewar still paying attention to the side of Karen's neck as they made their way slowly through to the bedroom.

Much later, Karen rolled over on to her front and pushed her tousled hair away from her forehead. She ran her finger lightly along Dewar's eyebrows as he lay with his eyes closed. 'Amazing what you can do on a British Airways lunch,' she said.

'You know what,' murmured Dewar.

'What?'

'I'm starving.'

# ~ Ten ~

The wind was so strong at Edinburgh Airport that Dewar had to lean into it as he stepped outside the terminal building and made his way along to the taxi rank. He hadn't quite reached it when a black Ford Scorpio pulled up at the kerb beside him and the passenger window slid down under smooth electric control.

'Dr Dewar?' enquired a male voice, competing with the sound of the wind.

Dewar bent down to look across to the driver. He didn't recognise him.

'Jump in. I'll give you a lift.'

'Who are you?' Dewar asked flatly.

The driver smiled and brought out an ID card from an inside pocket. He undid his seat belt to lean over and hold it up. 'Name's Barron, Simon Barron.'

At least it isn't Bond, thought Dewar, reading the Military Intelligence accreditation on the card. He opened a back door and put his travel bag on the seat before getting in the front to sit with his computer on his knee. He had to confess he was glad to be in out of the wind. He shook hands with Barron, saying, 'Is this part of a government strategy to save on taxi fares?'

'Not exactly,' smiled Barron. 'But it's an interesting idea. They told me you were coming in on this flight so I thought I'd meet you. Wretched day. We should talk, exchange business cards as it were.'

'Makes sense,' agreed Dewar. 'We don't want to be getting in each other's way. Are you on your own here?'

'No,' replied Barron without volunteering how many there were. 'Not that we're exactly being overtaxed. Siddiqui doesn't go anywhere apart from round the corner to visit a local coffee-cum-bookshop, the Bookstop Café. Just stays put in the Iraqi student centre.'

'How about the other one, the policeman, Abbas?'

'Much the same. A few visits to the local shops, that sort of thing. As far as we can determine he doesn't meet with anyone or go anywhere special and there's no timetable or regular pattern attached to his movements. That tells us something in itself, I think.'

'What?' asked Dewar.

'That they're just putting off time. They're waiting for something, something to happen.'

'That's my fear,' said Dewar. 'If they didn't have a reason to stay, they would have left the city before now.'

'And that something could be a virus, I understand,' said Barron.

'You're well informed. That's the worst-case scenario.'

'I'm also told you're in a position to give us a list of those who might be capable of supplying them with it,' said Barron.

'Not exactly,' corrected Dewar. 'I think it possible I can come up with a list of people who have the necessary expertise but I can't point you at anyone who would actually be liable to consider doing it.'

'The possibles will be fine,' said Barron. 'We'll take it from there, see what we can come up with.'

'I hope that doesn't mean staff harassment at the institute,' said Dewar. 'We're talking about an outside possibility here.'

'We're very discreet.'

Dewar glanced at Barron out of the corner of his eye. He was in his mid-thirties, tall, dark-haired, fit looking, well dressed, like himself, in an establishment sort of way. He exuded an air of confidence which extended to his driving. He moved in and out of gaps in the traffic quickly and surely. At the big roundabouts on the western outskirts of the city he accelerated quickly into the first available space without hesitation, seemingly knowing at all times what was inside of him, outside of him and coming up behind.

'I expected Special Branch to be doing the surveillance work,' said Dewar.

'That might still be true,' agreed Barron with just a hint of a smile.

'Are you saying you two don't talk to each other?' said Dewar, the surprise showing in his voice.

'You know how these things are,' said Barron. 'Professional jealousies and all that. The issues in this case aren't clearly defined. Some aspects say it's ours, others say theirs. It's all a bit awkward. I take it you're staying at the same hotel as last time?'

Dewar glanced at him, wondering how he knew but simply confirmed that he was.

They had reached the centre of the city. The words 'all a bit awkward' were going round in Dewar's head, and he didn't feel at all encouraged. This was a *prima facie* case of too many cooks about to spoil the broth, he feared. 'How do I get in touch with you when I've compiled this list?' he asked as Barron brought the car to a halt outside his hotel with a slight dip of the nose under braking.

'Don't bother. I'll get in touch with you,' said Barron. 'When d'you think you'll have it?'

Dewar shrugged. 'Tomorrow sometime.'

He got out of the car and opened the back door to retrieve his travel bag. 'Thanks for the lift.'

The Scorpio moved off with a slight squeal of protest from

the tyres, leaving Dewar standing on the pavement looking after its disappearing rear. 'Goodbye, Simon Barron, man of mystery,' he murmured. It was like watching the Lone Ranger gallop off at the end of every old TV show. If the job was finished, just where the hell was he going at that speed and why? If the Iraqis weren't doing anything, why the rush to keep station outside the student centre in Forest Road?

Dewar contacted Grant at police headquarters as soon as he'd unpacked and settled into his room. He swung his legs up on the bed and sat propped up against the headboard.

'Can't stay away, huh?' said Grant. 'Must be the Scottish air.'

'Something like that,' agreed Dewar. 'And there's plenty of it today. I was blown off my feet at the airport. It looks like I'm going to be here for the next week or so. Will you let me know of anything that happens at your end that looks like it might be relevant?'

'What sort of things?'

'I'll leave that to your judgement.'

'I'll keep you in mind.'

Next, Dewar phoned Steven Malloy at the Institute of Molecular Sciences.

'Didn't we just say goodbye?'

'I thought so too,' said Dewar. 'But my masters have decided not to take any chances with this one. They sent me back. It's a case of bolting the stable door *before* the horse has gone for a change. Can we talk? Somewhere other than the institute? I don't want to advertise the fact that I'm back.'

'You could come out to my place if you like,' suggested Malloy. 'Or I could meet you somewhere in town.'

'Your place will be fine. Eight o'clock this evening?'

'I'll expect you.'

Dewar called the reception desk and asked about renting a car now that he was staying for a while. A dark green Rover

600 was delivered in under twenty minutes. The interior was spotlessly clean but the previous driver had been a smoker: he could still smell the lingering stale legacy of tobacco smoke. He opened the sunroof and turned on the fan.

He drove up the Mound, then circled round past the Iraqi student centre in Forest Road trying to spot the surveillance. He couldn't. That pleased him. He'd been harbouring notions of rival surveillance teams squabbling outside the entrance after hearing what Barron had said about 'professional jealousies'. Maybe his fears had been groundless.

He drove slowly down the Royal Mile in the shadow of the old tenements, eventually turning right to pass in front of Holyrood Palace and enter the Queen's Park, a large green area open to the public with an extinct volcano, Arthur's Seat, as its centrepiece. He followed the road running through the park, then turned off to the right to drive up round the hill and pull into a lay-by on the south side. He got out to take in the view and stood with his right foot resting on the first bar of the railings separating the road from a sheer drop. To the east he could see the sea. In the distance an oil tanker was making its way out of the Firth of Forth into the North Sea. To the south he could just make out the white tower block of the Institute of Molecular Sciences. He shivered slightly as a cool breeze caught his cheek.

It was a couple of minutes after eight when he drew up outside Malloy's church home. It had been daylight the last time he'd been here so this time he stopped at the gate to take in the atmosphere of the place in the dark. Yellow light was spilling out from the windows where the stained glass had been replaced with ordinary clear glass. He thought it unusual to see a church building exuding light. It made him think of Christmas.

'Come in,' said Malloy. He was wearing jeans and an Aran

sweater and holding a glass of red wine in his hand. 'Can I get you anything?'

'A glass of that would be very nice,' replied Dewar, nodding to the wine.

'A precocious little bugger I picked up from Safeway's,' said Malloy, pouring Dewar a glass. 'Rich in ambition but modest in price.' He exaggerated a Scottish accent for the last few words. 'What's the problem?'

'The men who tried to coerce Hammadi into working on smallpox are still in the city. I don't know why but I have to consider all possibilities.'

'Why doesn't someone arrest them?'

'No evidence,' said Dewar. 'We couldn't even prove they met Hammadi, let alone what they asked him to do.'

'So why do you think they're still here?'

'At worst I have to consider that they might be trying to persuade someone else to help them to get what they want.'

Malloy looked aghast. 'You've got to be joking,' he said in a shocked whisper. 'No one in their right mind would even dream of it.'

'I take it no one's approached you?'

'No. They'd get short shrift if they did.'

'How about if they were to offer you half a million pounds to do it?'

'Half a mil— No, absolutely not.'

'A million?'

'I—'

'Two million?'

'All right, I take your point,' said Malloy. 'We've started to haggle about the price. But I still hope I would say no. It would be sheer madness to attempt it. And how could you live with yourself, knowing you'd resurrected one of the worst killers the world's ever known? You wouldn't be able to sleep at night, assuming you survived at all after playing around with something like that.'

'I sincerely hope everyone feels like that,' said Dewar. 'But I have to ask you who at the institute might be put to the test.'

'You're serious?'

Dewar nodded. 'I need you to tell me who has the necessary expertise to do the job without, of course, suggesting in any way that they would.'

'Assuming they were supplied with everything they needed?' Another nod. 'There are lots of people with DNA skills but not that many with practical experience of working with high-risk microorganisms. Basically it would come down to the people in my lab and those in Malcolm Cairns's lab. We work with HIV so we're used to handling dangerous material.'

'Point taken.'

'We could leave out first-year grad students. Second-year? Possible. Postdocs, yes, and of course, Malcolm Cairns and me, I suppose.'

'Technical staff?'

Malloy thought for a moment. 'Andrea in Cairns's lab would be a possibility. She has the right background and she's been here a while. She might be able to do it at a pinch.'

'George Ferguson?'

'No experience of DNA manipulation, technically able and well used to handling dangerous organisms but wrong background for this sort of thing.'

'So how many are we talking about?'

Malloy brought his shoulders up to his ears and made shaking gestures with both hands. 'I'd go for eight,' he said.

'I need their names,' said Dewar.

'This is giving me a bad feeling,' said Malloy, as he got up. 'It feels like I'm betraying my colleagues.' He fetched pen and paper from his desk.

'You're not,' Dewar assured him. 'You're simply appraising their competence and expertise.'

Malloy wrote down the eight names and handed it over. 'Mind you, I'd bet my life savings against any of these people being involved in anything like this,' he said.

'And I wouldn't dream of betting against you,' said Dewar. 'If only our Iraqi friends would get the hell out of the city then we could all stop being so paranoid and rest easy.' He declined the offer of a second glass of wine and was escorted to the door. 'I'd be grateful if you didn't tell anyone else about our meeting.'

'It's hardly something I'm likely to brag about,' said Malloy.

Dewar drove back to the city, taking his time on the narrow roads in the dark. In many places they had acquired a coating of wet leaves, and it would be all too easy to come to grief under heavy braking and finish up among the trees whose tall, dark presence blotted out the sky. He felt better when he'd got back on to the main road and had a clear run back into the city.

Once back in his hotel room he phoned Karen to exchange notes about the day and make arrangements for the weekend.

'You won't think of an excuse not to come down and see my mother, will you?' asked Karen.

'Of course not,' Dewar assured her, his spirits falling at the thought of an evening in the company of Karen's mother. He found her hard to take.

'Good, so why don't we say that you'll be down for supper on Saturday and you'll stay over till Sunday?'

'Fine,' said Dewar. 'I take it I'll be on the couch downstairs?'

'You know how Mother feels about that sort of thing,' said Karen.

'I know,' agreed Dewar.

'Besides . . . she goes out to her church social on Sunday afternoon – that'll give us plenty of time . . .'

'Here's to Sunday afternoon,' said Dewar.

Dewar entered the names of the eight people Malloy had given him into his laptop as part of his next report for Sci Med. He looked at them, white letters on a blue screen. He hadn't been quite honest with Malloy. It wasn't just a matter of compiling a list of people with the right know-how. Once Barron had the names, all the people on that list would be subject to round-the-clock surveillance just like the two Iraqis. To imagine anything else would be naive.

Steven Malloy and Malcolm Cairns headed it, Pierre Le Grice and Simone Clary were next, then Sandra Macandrew and Kurt Vogel, finally Andrea Bowman and Josh Phelps. He assumed the names he didn't recognise were people working in the Cairns lab. It might be worth running the names through the police computer. He'd bet on eight zeros coming up but it would be a sensible, routine thing to do and Sci Med liked him to do sensible, routine things from time to time. You never know, he assured himself, one of them might turn out to be a mad axe-killer.

He called Grant at police headquarters on the off chance he might be there, although it was now after ten. He wasn't there but the man who answered from Grant's office – Sergeant Nick Johnstone – said that he was still on duty.

'There was a nasty hit-and-run incident over in Marchmont,' said the sergeant. 'A lassie got knocked off her bike; I think she was killed. He went over to the hospital about an hour ago. Anything I can help with? The inspector said if you called at any time we were to play ball, to use his expression.'

'I was going to ask him to run some names through the computer for me,' said Dewar.

'Fire away,' said Johnstone.

Dewar read out the list and Johnstone wrote them down with Dewar providing spelling where necessary.

'Wait a minute . . .' said Johnstone.

'What's the matter?'

'Just a minute . . .'

Dewar heard the phone being put down. The wait started to

seem endless when Johnstone finally returned, and the receiver was fumbled before being picked up successfully.

'I thought so,' said Johnstone. 'The lassie in Marchmont, she's on your list, if it's the same one. Sandra Macandrew. Student at the Institute of something or other?'

'That's her,' said Dewar, feeling as if a heavy weight had suddenly descended on his shoulders. 'You said she was dead?'

'The report from the attending officers said she was a goner.'

'I see.'

'When Inspector Grant heard she was a student at the institute he said he was going up to the hospital. That was the last I heard. That was about an hour ago.'

'Where did they take her?'

'The Royal Infirmary.'

'Thanks,' said Dewar, feeling numb.

'Do you want me to call you back when the computer's had a look through your names?' asked Johnstone.

'No, I'll get back to you later. I'm going to see if I can catch Grant at the hospital.'

Dewar felt sick in his stomach. He hadn't known Sandra Macandrew well but well enough to like her as a person and see that she was a bright student with a promising future. Now she was dead. Hit-and-run, Johnstone had said, the second person from Malloy's lab to die in the space of a month. The uneasy feeling he'd been carrying around with him had just multiplied tenfold.

Mounting frustration at the slowness of the traffic was pushed to even higher levels at his not being able to find a parking place near the hospital. He tried reminding himself there was no hurry, that Sandra was dead, but his instincts overruled his reason. His gut feeling was that somehow Sandra's death must have had something to do with the smallpox thing and the sooner he got to the hospital and talked to Grant about it the better.

He saw a Ford Fiesta start to vacate a place by the kerb, so he braked abruptly, to the annoyance of the driver behind. He ignored the angry tooting and waited until the Fiesta had pulled away before putting the Rover in nose first and abandoning it with its tail sticking out untidily.

'Arsehole!' shouted the driver who'd been held up. Dewar ignored him and headed for the hospital. He had eyes only for the infirmary, which loomed in front of him against the night sky. It was an old-fashioned hospital, all towers and turrets on the outside – like a Disney castle – with endless corridors and peeling ceilings on the inside. Light spilled out from the A&E entrance, lighting up the ambulance apron where two vehicles stood waiting for fate to play its next card. Dewar entered through the automatic doors and approached the desk.

'Sandra Macandrew,' he said to the clerk. 'Hit-and-run victim, brought in dead about an hour ago. Are the police still here? I'm looking for Inspector Grant in particular.'

The clerk looked at him over his glasses. 'And you are?' Dewar showed him his ID. 'Are you Ms Macandrew's own doctor?' asked the man.

'No,' answered Dewar, wondering why the question was asked in the first place and what the politically correct term was these days for mental defective. Differently intelligent, he supposed. Right now he didn't feel like going to war with obstructive officialdom.

'Are you a relative?'

'No,' replied Dewar, now having difficulty keeping his temper. 'Is Inspector Grant still here or not?' he asked again in level tones devoid of social nicety.

'Ms Macandrew's not dead,' said the man, trumping Dewar's card.

Dewar felt stunned. He felt his mouth drop open. 'Not dead,' he repeated in a bewildered voice.

'She's in a bad way; she's in intensive care but she's not dead.

The police are still here. I'm not sure if your Inspector Grant is one of them.'

Dewar asked for directions and followed them quickly without actually running, a memory from his early medical training. Nurses and doctors don't run inside the hospital. They can walk fast but they don't run. He found Grant, who had just been briefed on Sandra Macandrew's injuries by a young-looking doctor who'd then disappeared into a side room in the intensive-care unit.

'How is she?'

'How did you know?' Grant asked him.

Dewar told him about his phone call to headquarters. 'What happened to her?' he asked.

'She was cycling home from work and some drunken bozo ran into her and didn't stop. The street was well lit. Her bike had serviceable lights and her jacket had fluorescent tape on it so there was no excuse for not seeing her. He must have been pissed out his mind.'

'I hope you get the bastard,' said Dewar looking through the glass panel to the room where Sandra was lying. Two nurses were busy with her. With so much bandaging and intubation it could have been anyone lying there, he thought. 'What did the doctor say?'

'Fractured skull, multiple fractures to both arms and legs, her collarbone's smashed and her pelvis is damaged. I think the bottom line is touch and go, poor lassie. Malloy's not going have much of a research group left at this rate. I'm beginning to think that place is jinxed.'

'Were there any witnesses?' asked Dewar.

'Nothing useful. A couple of people said they saw the car speeding off after they heard the crash. They couldn't tell us the make, not even the colour under the street lights. A light one, they thought. There were lots of people about but their eyes automatically went to the victim and stayed there. By the time they thought to look for the car it had gone.'

'But you'll get paint scrapings from her bike?'

Grant shrugged. 'For whatever good that'll do, unless it was a white Rolls-Royce or a yellow Ferrari. If it's from a blue Ford I don't fancy our chances.'

'Have you considered it wasn't an accident?' asked Dewar, still looking through the glass panel.

'What d'you mean?'

'Supposing it was attempted murder.'

Grant came over to join Dewar in looking through the glass partition. 'Have you any reason to believe that?' he asked.

'No,' admitted Dewar. 'No good reason but gut feeling tells me it was. I think someone deliberately tried to kill her.'

'Why?'

Dewar decided to trust Grant completely. 'The Iraqis have been trying to get their hands on smallpox virus,' he said.

'Christ! I thought that was a thing of the past.'

'It involves reconstructing it from fragments of the viral DNA that are used in research, but it's difficult. I think they tried forcing Ali Hammadi to do it for them, but he killed himself so they need someone else. I think Sandra Macandrew might have been approached; we suspected they might try something like this. That's why I'm back here. If they did and Sandra turned them down they might consider she knew too much. If she were to report them to the authorities we'd have the evidence we need to nail them to the wall. We might still get it if and when she regains consciousness. Are your men planning to stay with her?'

'An officer will be stationed here throughout the night in case she comes round, although the medics don't think that's too likely.'

'No one can ever be sure in a case like this,' said Dewar. 'It's always hard to define or quantify brain damage. I think it would be a good idea if there was more than one officer with

— 127 —

her,' said Dewar. 'And they should be made aware of a possible further attempt on her life.'

'OK,' said Grant. 'But I take it there's no proof of this?'

'No,' agreed Dewar. 'But I'll take responsibility, and I want to be the first to talk to her when she comes round.'

'By rights a serious crime has been committed and we should speak to the victim before—'

Dewar interrupted and held up his hand. 'I understand that,' he said. 'But millions of lives could depend on what she has to say. If the Iraqis asked her to do something, I have to know exactly what it was so we can find out what stage they're at in the reconstruction. I know the right questions to ask. You don't.'

'I thought the glamour boys were sitting on the Iraqis,' said Grant, changing the subject.

'So did I,' said Dewar, taking Grant's point. If MI5 and Special Branch were watching the Iraqis' every move, how come they could mount an attempt on Sandra Macandrew's life?

# ~ Eleven ~

When Dewar opened his eyes in the morning, the first thing he considered was the fact that no one had called him during the night. He threw back the covers, swung his legs round and dialled the hospital, to ask about Sandra Macandrew's condition.

No change, still critical and deeply unconscious, was the report from the intensive-care unit. The policemen outside her room had had an uneventful night too, without any other kind of problem. No one had attempted to visit Sandra.

Dewar was having breakfast in the hotel dining room when he was joined by Simon Barron. Without saying so, Barron gave the impression that he had been up for hours. Probably run ten miles and swum across the Forth to pick up his morning paper, thought Dewar uncharitably.

'Hoped I might catch you,' said Barron. 'Have you got the list?'

'It's ready,' replied Dewar. 'Coffee?'

'Never touch the stuff.'

Probably impedes performance, thought Dewar, refilling his own cup. 'Did any of your lot slip up yesterday?' he asked.

'In what way?'

'Could the Iraqis have got out to play without you knowing about it?'

'Which ones? We're just watching Siddiqui and Abbas,' replied Barron. 'The students come and go as they please. Why d'you ask?'

Dewar thought for a moment before replying. He was considering what Barron had said about the students, in particular the possibility that one or more of them might have been recruited to Siddiqui's cause.

'One of the graduate students from the Institute of Molecular Sciences was involved in a hit-and-run incident last night. She was knocked off her bike as she was cycling home from the lab; she's critically ill. It could have been an accident – the police thought some drunk might have hit her – but her name's Sandra Macandrew and she's on the list.'

After a moment of blankness, realisation dawned on Barron's face. 'You think it wasn't an accident? It had something to do with her being on that list?'

'If she's on the list we have to consider that she may have been approached by the Iraqis. For the sake of argument let's assume she was and she turned them down, probably even threatened to go to the police. What d'you think would happen then?'

'Point taken,' agreed Barron. 'That's quite a thought. Turning down the Iraqi offer would be like signing your own death warrant.'

'On the other hand, the Iraqis must know that most scientists would be outraged at being asked to do what they suggest. They can't be planning to kill them all so they must have some way of deciding what individuals might be amenable to a business arrangement.'

'They'd have to do their homework,' said Barron. 'Make discreet enquiries, find out who's disgruntled, who has financial problems, who has secrets they'd rather not have made public, that sort of thing.'

'So what made them think Sandra Macandrew might be a possibility?' Dewar wondered aloud. 'When I met her she struck me as a normal graduate student, doing exactly what she wants to do in life. Not many of us can say that. Her thesis work was going well according to Malloy, although the ban on smallpox fragments will cause some interruption. She lives in a flat with other students, she's vegetarian, a member of Friends of the Earth, cycles to and from the lab, has occasional nights in the pub, Chinese meal at the weekend with her friends, not much money but no money worries either. If you're looking for Ms Typical Grad Student, Sandra Macandrew gets my vote.'

'Then maybe you're jumping the gun here. Maybe it really was an accident,' suggested Barron.

Dewar shrugged, unconvinced. Both men fell silent for a while, then Dewar said, 'There's another possibility.' Barron raised his eyebrows. 'Sandra wasn't approached by the Iraqis . . . but she knows who was.'

'And they tried to kill her to keep her quiet? Yes, that's a starter,' agreed Barron.'

'It would also imply that the one they approached has actually agreed to do it,' said Dewar. 'Otherwise the Iraqis would be more interested in killing the one who'd turned them down than Sandra.'

'It's hard to believe they'd use students as hit men,' said Barron. 'And my people are good at their job. Their report for yesterday says that Siddiqui and Abbas left the student centre in the afternoon, accompanied by two of the students, but they just went round the corner to the Bookstop Café in Teviot Place. They stayed there for about forty minutes, talking, then returned to the centre. Neither went out again.'

'So we're either looking for a hit man we know nothing at all about . . . or maybe the police were right and it was some drunk.'

'I take it you told the police about your suspicions?'

Dewar nodded. 'I wanted them to mount a guard on her last night.'

'Her being alive really is the trump card in this game. It could make all this speculation academic if she pulls through. Her evidence could be absolutely crucial.'

'I've asked that I be the first to speak to her when she comes round. Right now, finding out what she knows about the smallpox business is more important than finding out who did this to her.'

'Right,' agreed Barron. 'If you give me that list, the sooner we start keeping tabs on the others the safer it might be for them.'

Dewar suddenly didn't feel so bad about not warning Steven Malloy that he would be put under surveillance. It didn't seem so bad if it was for his own good. He went upstairs to his room and returned with the list.

'No addresses,' said Barron.

'I asked my informant for the names of people who were competent to do this sort of thing. He wasn't happy about it, felt like he was letting down his colleagues. If I'd gone on to ask for their addresses he would have seen there was more to it and clammed up altogether. I'm sure Her Majesty's Secret Service can take it from here.'

'Fair enough,' said Barron. 'You'll let me know if there's any change on the injured girl?'

'I would if I had some way of contacting you,' said Dewar flatly. 'You didn't give me a number.'

Barron brought out a pen from his inside pocket and wrote down a phone number on the card Dewar handed him.

'Out of interest, why didn't you?'

'Never on a first date,' said Barron.

Ye gods, the man has a sense of humour, thought Dewar, but he kept looking at Barron as if waiting for a proper answer.

'I showed you my ID at the airport,' said Barron. 'You didn't show me yours. Simple as that.'

My God, different world, thought Dewar as Barron left. He

must have run checks on me to make sure I was Adam Dewar and not an impostor. He supposed this level of suspicion and security-consciousness was a comfort. It just left him feeling bemused.

It occurred to him that Steven Malloy might not yet actually know about Sandra Macandrew. He checked his watch: it was just after eight thirty. He'd probably still be at home.

Malloy sounded as if his mouth were full. 'Sorry, I'm just finishing my breakfast,' he apologised.

Dewar pictured toast crumbs on the receiver and imagined the incongruous smell of coffee in church. He told him about Sandra.

'God, that's awful,' exclaimed Malloy, sounding distressed. 'How is she? Can I see her? Is there something I can do?'

'I'm afraid she's critical,' said Dewar. 'She's in Intensive Care at the Royal Infirmary. She has multiple injuries and nobody's committing themselves about her chances.'

'Have her parents been told?'

'I'm sure the police will have done that.'

'This is an absolute tragedy,' said Malloy. 'I must go there. I'll go into the lab first and tell the others, then I'll come straight to the hospital.'

Dewar was about to warn him about the police guard but he stopped himself; he didn't want to explain why. He would do it the other way around. He would warn the police to expect Malloy. 'I'll probably see you there,' he said.


Grant was there by the time Dewar arrived at Intensive Care. He was talking to two uniformed policeman stationed at the doors.

'Any improvement?' asked Dewar as he joined them.

'They say nothing much has changed,' replied Grant. 'Her parents are sitting with her. They've come down from Elgin.'

The two uniformed men sat down again on their chairs on

either side of the door as Grant and Dewar entered the unit and looked in through the glass panel. They saw a scene played out every day in hospitals across the country as Sandra's mother, tears running down her face, sat holding her daughter's hand. Her father, equally stricken but barred from emotion by male custom, sat on the other side of the bed with granite features. Only his eyes showed the pain he felt.

Sandra slept on, her broken body ventilated and monitored by machinery. Green lights, gentle bleeps and clicking relays said that it was doing its job. It would continue until Sandra's brain was ready to take over from it or until such time as a decision was made that said it never would and a switch would be turned off.

Malloy arrived in an agitated state. 'How is she? Has there been any improvement?' he asked as the policemen on the door let him through.

Dewar put a finger to his lips and said quietly, 'Her parents are with her.'

Malloy nodded and spoke in a whisper. 'Oh God, this is awful. You didn't say when it happened.'

'Just after eight last night. She was cycling home,' said Grant.

Malloy shook his head. 'It could only have been about twenty minutes after I spoke to her.'

Dewar and Grant looked at each other. 'You spoke to her?' exclaimed Dewar.

'She phoned me about half past seven.'

'Why?'

'She said she'd discovered something we should talk about.'

'What?' asked Dewar, trying to keep the excitement out of his voice.

'I don't know.'

'You don't know?' exclaimed Grant.

Malloy seemed puzzled at the effect what he was saying was having on Dewar and Grant. 'No, I suggested it could wait till morning. I was going out last night.' The accusing stares he was getting prompted Malloy to continue. 'Graduate students are always making "discoveries". It's a fact of life. They nearly always turn out to be red herrings or some kind of artefact in the experimental system. I saw no reason to drive into the lab at that time.'

'So you assumed that Sandra's discovery had something to do with her research work,' said Dewar, suddenly understanding Malloy's attitude.

'Of course,' replied Malloy, looking surprised. 'What else?'

Grant and Dewar ignored the question. 'Did she seem upset at all when you said it could wait till morning?' asked Grant.

'Upset? No, I don't think so, although . . .'

'Go on.'

'She did sound a little . . .'

'Yes?'

'It's hard to say. She sounded a bit reserved, if you know what I mean. That's the wrong word but I don't know the right one. Inhibited maybe.'

'Could that have been because she wasn't alone?'

'I suppose,' agreed Malloy with a shrug. 'I just thought she was a bit disappointed I wasn't going to come in straight away.'

A commotion outside the door interrupted them. Grant went to investigate. The words 'Why won't you let me speak to someone?' spoken with a French accent announced the arrival of Pierre Le Grice. The policemen on the door had turned him away. Grant calmed things down and brought Le Grice back in with him.

'The others told me at the lab when I got in,' Le Grice explained to Malloy. 'I came straight here. How is she?'

'Not good, I'm afraid,' said Malloy.

'And you. Why are you here?' Le Grice asked Dewar.

'I was concerned, just like you,' Dewar replied, avoiding the real question.

Le Grice looked through the glass. 'God, I hope you get the bastard who did this to her,' he exclaimed.

'We'll do our best,' said Grant not best impressed by the fiery Frenchman.

Sandra's parents came out with their arms wrapped around each other in a search for comfort in their pain. Her mother kept a handkerchief pressed to her face as a nurse guided them gently through the door.

Malloy approached them saying, 'Mr and Mrs Macandrew, I'm Sandra's research supervisor. I think we met once before when Sandra came for interview.' The conversation trailed off as Malloy went outside with the couple to offer his sympathy. Dewar and Grant moved to a corner to discuss the implications of Sandra's phone call to Malloy before she was run down. Le Grice, finding himself alone, took the opportunity to go through and sit beside Sandra. He held her hand gently and spoke to her as if she were conscious and awake. The nurse with her smiled her approval and busied herself elsewhere in the room.

On the other side of the glass partition Grant said, 'So all we have to do now is find out who was with her in the institute last night when she phoned Malloy and we have our man.'

'Or woman,' agreed Dewar, recalling that there were two women on the list apart from Sandra. 'That's about the size of it.'

The two men lapsed into silence as they considered different things. Grant was thinking about arresting Sandra's attacker. Dewar was considering the implications of someone having agreed to work for the Iraqis and wondering how far had they got.

'A doctor wearing surgical greens came into the room and said rather angrily, 'Look, I've been very patient. I know you all have good reasons for being here but if I see another official ID I'm going to throw up. This is my unit and I want you all out of here. You're getting in the way of my staff. You'll have to wait somewhere else. We'll let you know if there's any change.'

'You're quite right, we're sorry,' said Dewar. 'It's just that she's a very important young lady at the moment.'

Predictably, thought Dewar, the doctor replied that all his patients were important.

Grant said, 'Sorry, Doc, but my men outside will have to stay.'

'I accept that, but we must have room to move in here.'

Le Grice was called back from Sandra's bedside and everyone was ushered out of the unit. Malloy rejoined them as Sandra's parents went off with a nurse for tea and sympathy. 'They're in an awful state,' said Malloy. 'She's their only child.'

As they moved away from the entrance to IC they heard the sound of an electronic alarm come from inside.

'What's that?' said Malloy.

Dewar didn't wait to discuss the possibilities: he rushed back into the unit to see feverish activity around Sandra's bed.

'What's happened?' he demanded, knowing that if he sounded officious enough someone would tell him.

'Ventilation's failed,' said a nurse bustling past him.

'Hurry up with that other unit,' demanded the doctor who'd asked them all to leave a few minutes earlier.

Dewar moved round to where the ventilation unit that had been breathing for Sandra had been moved back out of the way. The doctor in charge was now administering mouth-to-mouth through the plastic airway tube already inserted in her throat.

Dewar idly examined the detached flexible tubing leading from the unit, not knowing what he was looking for or even what exactly the fault had been. The machine seemed to have been running normally before he'd left the unit. He distinctly remembered seeing the bellows moving up and down and hearing the unit's distinctive clicking noise when Le Grice opened the door to come out of Sandra's room.

Something caught his eye where the tube was attached to the

metal outlet pipe on the side of the machine. His blood ran cold as he examined it more closely. The plastic tube had been cut cleanly at two places on its circumference. There was no danger of its falling apart or even of appearing abnormal but at least half the air being pumped out the machine would escape to the atmosphere rather than go into Sandra's lungs. Someone had tried to kill her right under their noses and that someone had to be the Frenchman, Pierre Le Grice. He was the last person to have been with Sandra.

Dewar took a moment to calm himself. Le Grice was standing outside in the corridor with the others. If he had the arrogance to do what he'd done in the circumstances he probably had the nerve to gamble that no one would work out what had gone wrong just yet. And when they did there would be a good chance that it would be construed simply as a leaking hose. None of the medical or nursing staff would be looking for deliberate sabotage

The absolute priority now was to arrest Le Grice quietly and efficiently without any fuss or dramatics in a hospital. He stood back out of the way for a moment as a new respiratory unit was wheeled into place and connected to the electricity supply.

'We're losing her,' came a voice from the ordered scrum round Sandra. 'Please hurry.'

For a moment Dewar found himself mesmerised by the scene. He was seemingly invisible to the others in the room as they concentrated on the job. He could feel Sandra Macandrew's life hanging in the balance and he was filled with anger and frustration as he had the awful feeling he was about to witness the moment of her death. The background bleeps became a monotone, the oscilloscope spikes became a featureless plane, but the team kept working on.

A single bleep, a single spike on the scope, then nothing. Two beeps. A surge of optimism, a few more irregular bleeps, then rhythmic harmony.

'We've got her back. Thank you, everyone.'

Never had electronic sound seemed so sweet, thought Dewar as the bleeps from the heart monitor became even and regular again, the hiss and click of the ventilator music to his ears.

Dewar joined the others outside. 'Touch and go for a moment there,' he said. 'But she's OK again.'

'Thank God,' said Malloy. This was echoed by the others.

Dewar caught Le Grice's eye and in that one moment the game was lost. Dewar's own eyes gave him away. The two men held eye contact for a moment, then Le Grice turned on his heel and started running along the corridor.

'Quick! After him!' shouted Dewar, all hope of a quiet civilised arrest gone to be replaced by the urgency of the situation. 'He tried to kill Sandra!'

The two uniformed men from the door took off after Le Grice. Grant barked into his radio that backup was required urgently at the hospital. He gave a description of Le Grice and ordered that the exits should be covered first.

Dewar took Malloy aside and said, 'You've got to get back to the institute and close down your lab. Quarantine all Le Grice's stuff. Above all else, make the place secure even if it means shutting the whole institute down.'

Malloy seemed stunned. 'I just can't believe this is all happening,' he complained.

'Just do it!' insisted Dewar. He turned to Grant and said, 'Maybe it would be an idea to get some men to the institute just in case Le Grice gets away and tries to go back there. He's blown it; he's got nothing to lose now.'

Grant nodded his agreement and radioed for a patrol to get to the institute and guard the doors. 'I'd better let hospital security know what's going on,' he said, going off in search of an internal phone.

Dewar stood, looking down from a corridor window to the busy streets below. Would Le Grice have made it to the outside in time? he wondered. And, if he had, what then? The police already had details of his car obtained from Malloy and relayed by Grant, his description would be circulating faster than a rumour. He was trapped in the middle of the city — surely he couldn't get far before they picked him up.

All the exits were now covered, Grant reported. There had been no sightings of Le Grice in the vicinity of any of them. 'I think maybe we were too late,' he said. 'But he won't get far.'

Dewar nodded at the confirmation of what he'd just been thinking but didn't reply. He was thinking ahead: he knew that Le Grice couldn't get far; Grant knew he couldn't get far, but Le Grice was a clever man. He'd probably worked that out too. So what would a clever man do in the circumstances? he asked himself. Stay put, was the answer.

'What's on your mind?' asked Grant.

'I think he's still in the hospital,' replied Dewar.

'What makes you think that?'

'He's clever and he's got nerve. Coming here today and doing what he did shows that. It's my guess he's found somewhere to lie low. He's going to tough it out until the rest of us start believing he's got clean away. Then getting out will be a whole lot easier.'

'I don't fancy trying to search the whole hospital,' said Grant. 'This place probably has rooms the staff don't even know about.'

Dewar nodded and agreed. 'It's not feasible. But if you keep men on all the exits we'll at least pen him inside until he's forced to do something rash.'

'Like take a patient hostage,' said Grant.

'I wish you hadn't said that,' said Dewar. He hadn't considered the possibility.

'Like you said, he's got nothing left to lose. His career's over and he's looking at life if the girl dies. Not much less if she doesn't.'

'I think that situation might arise if you send in teams of uniforms to scour the place,' said Dewar. 'If we leave him alone he's going to be happy biding his time. That gives us a window of a few hours while he thinks his plan is working.'

'So what do *we* do with this window?'

'We get plans of the hospital and see if we can figure out where he might be holed up. We know where he started out from. Let's see if we can think like him.'

The clerk of works for the hospital came up with plans after ten minutes, during which Grant managed to negotiate an office to work from down on the ground floor. Dewar examined them on his own until Grant returned from briefing the men on the doors to be doubly vigilant. Le Grice wasn't going to try to run past them after all this time — twenty minutes had passed. They should be on guard for some sort of disguise.

'Any thoughts?' asked Grant on his return.

Dewar traced his finger along a line on the paper. 'This is the corridor we were in. Le Grice took off along here and disappeared from sight at this corner.'

Grant leaned closer, his forefinger edging towards Dewar's. 'Gotcha,' he said. 'So he had two choices. He either came down these stairs or he turned right through this door. But that leads to nowhere — a circular staircase by the look of it inside a round tower. No way out at ground level.'

'Which would you have taken?' asked Dewar.

'Down these stairs, without a doubt,' said Grant. 'He'd just started to make a run for it. His adrenaline would be pumping and he'd be making for the outside. Coming downstairs gives him several choices: three corridors to choose from and several exit points.'

'But maybe he was smart enough to work out that he still wasn't going to make it even at that early point in the proceedings.'

'If he worked all that out in the few seconds it took him to reach this turn in the corridor then we are dealing with one smart cookie,' said Grant. 'And if he's that smart it sure scares the shit out of me.'

'He is and we are,' said Dewar.

# ~ Twelve ~

'So what do you want to do?' asked Grant.

'I want to check out the round tower,' said Dewar. 'Just in case.'

Grant grimaced and said, 'You're certainly one for playing your hunches. I'm prepared to bet you that the door to the tower is locked. The place's not been used for years.'

'I wouldn't bet against you,' said Dewar. 'But I'd be happier in my mind just giving it the once over.'

'Suit yourself,' said Grant with a shrug that said, Waste of time. 'I'll check out the rooms in this corridor one floor down. I'll meet you on the stairs when you're through.' Dewar nodded his agreement. 'And before we start let's agree on something,' added Grant. 'No heroics. We call for backup before we do anything.'

'Agreed,' said Dewar.

Dewar climbed back up to the corridor where he'd last seen Le Grice disappear from view, jacket flying open as he made a bid for freedom. He followed in his footsteps to the turn where, just as the plans promised, he found a choice. There was a double door to the left leading to the main staircase; there was also a door to the right. His first thought on looking at it was that Grant had been right. There was something about the door that suggested that it had not been in use for many a long year.

It had a glass panel but it had been boarded over on the inside. The handle seemed dirty and unused. He tried it and found it locked.

Conceding wryly to Grant, he turned to go downstairs when something made him stop. The resistance he'd felt in the door when he'd turned the handle had been lower down than it should have been. It had not quite been behind where the handle was. He went back and tried it again. This time he was sure. He looked up and saw the door move slightly inward at the top. The door wasn't locked: it was being held shut by something placed behind it on the floor. This didn't automatically mean that someone had recently blocked it — entrance to the tower at this level could have been closed off at some time in the past by someone coming down or up from another level inside the tower. On the other hand, it was worth checking out.

He turned the handle and held it while he put his shoulder to the door frame to apply mounting pressure. The door started to edge open as what sounded like a large cardboard box was inched back out of the way. The opening was now big enough to allow Dewar to squeeze through. He closed the door behind him softly and took a look at the box that had been blocking entry; it was full of heavy rubber sheeting. The cracks on the visible folds told him that the rubber had perished a long time ago.

The air around him smelled stale and musty — there was obviously no ventilation in the tower. A thick layer of dust covered all the flat surfaces he could see and there was junk everywhere; there was a premature-baby incubator lying on the floor, one of its glass panels broken and paint peeling off its other surfaces. Dewar guessed that it had been dumped in the tower when the glass had broken and it had been deemed to have come to the end of its useful life. There were plastic chairs in various states of disrepair stacked one on top of the other in threes, planks of wood propped up against one wall, several red metal pails with the word FIRE faded but still visible on their sides, relics of the days when pails of water were placed at intervals along corridors as the sole method of firefighting should the need arise.

The tower room itself was half tiled, the tiles crazed and cracked so they resembled unlettered road maps. They were clearly from another age, an age that might have known gas light and the sluice of carbolic as Joseph Lister and his colleagues introduced the then new concept of antisepsis to this very hospital. An old operating table was propped on its side under the window, its pedestal nowhere to be seen. This and various other bits and pieces led Dewar to conclude that the room had once been an operating theatre for minor surgery, perhaps the draining of wounds, the lancing of septic cysts and the like, but that had all been a very long time ago. It had clearly been a junk store for many years.

What was more important was that there was no sign of Le Grice having been in the room, no telltale foot or hand prints in the dirt and dust. Dewar came out on to the landing and started to climb up to the next level, the spiral stone steps inducing vague feelings of claustrophobia as he lost the daylight of one level and entered almost complete darkness before emerging into the light of the next. There were no working lights on the stair walls or in the ceiling — the electricity to this part of the building had been cut off when occupancy had ceased.

Dewar stood for a moment at the head of the stairs, just listening. There was no sound save for the distant background rumble of the traffic outside the hospital gates. Standing perfectly still and listening, however, had heightened his other senses. The air still smelled musty and unpleasant but there was something else in it, a vague suggestion of cologne. He recognised it. Le Grice was somewhere up here.

Dewar's heart rate rose until he was physically aware of it

beating in his chest. He supposed he should start back down the stairs and tell Grant so that they could summon assistance, but, if at all possible, he would prefer to speak to Le Grice alone about the smallpox virus and how far he'd gone with it. Once the police were involved with handcuffs and the attendant trauma of arrest he feared that Le Grice might just clam up and say nothing. If he could persuade him to talk before officialdom stepped in he might just have a better chance of getting at the truth. He'd have to be careful but if the worse came to the worst he was as big and as strong as the Frenchman. If he kept his wits about him and didn't walk into any kind of trap or ambush, he should be all right.

He took a step towards the tower room on this level; the door was almost closed but not quite. He looked above it to see if anything had been mounted there to fall on unwary heads; there was nothing. There was, of course, the possibility that Le Grice could be waiting just inside, his body pressed to the wall ready to jump him as he walked through. He pushed the door open gently but didn't enter. The door hinges creaked in protest at having their slumber disturbed.

To his surprise, Dewar found Le Grice sitting there facing him. He was directly opposite the door and sitting on the floor with his legs stretched out in front of him, his back propped up against the circular wall. It was as if he'd been waiting for him to arrive. Although Le Grice could hardly have been deemed to have adopted an aggressive stance, Dewar was still wary of the man. He wasn't dealing with an idiot.

'Hello, Pierre,' he said quietly.

Le Grice nodded. 'I 'ad a feeling it might be you,' he said, his accent seemingly more pronounced than on past occasions. 'I misjudged you.'

'I hoped you might tell me all about it before the police join us.'

Le Grice shrugged. 'What's to tell? If it hadn't been for that stupid, interfering girl everything would 'ave been all right. She just didn't understand. She would have benefited too from access to more fragments, so would Peter, but no, the silly bitch decided to – 'ow you say? Cut off her nose to spite her face.'

'Sandra?'

'Bloody Sandra.'

Not exactly filled with remorse, thought Dewar, steeling himself to keep his cool in the interests of learning as much as possible. 'How much did they pay you to do it?'

'What are you talking about?'

'The Iraqis.'

'What Iraqis?'

Dewar sighed and said, 'What's the point of denying it now? If you've any decency in you at all you'd make a clean breast of things and tell me everything. We've got to make a start on minimising the damage. Christ, man, don't you care at all? Don't you realise what you've done?'

'I broke the rules, the holy rules, the sacred bloody rules and that little bitch decided to ruin my career. 'Ow long will I get?'

'If Sandra dies, thirty years. If she doesn't maybe a bit less. But if you've reconstructed that virus and handed it over they're going to bring back hanging specially for you and I'll be cheering in the front row. So tell me, how far did you get?'

'I don't know what the hell you're talking about,' said Le Grice.

Dewar shrugged and said, 'If you really want to play it that way it's time we were going.'

Le Grice shook his head slowly. 'I think not,' he said.

Dewar felt the hairs on the back of his neck rise; he became very wary. Although Le Grice was still sitting on the floor and there was no way he could mount an attack, the words made him feel uneasy. The feeling heightened when he saw Le Grice take out a surgical scalpel from his inside pocket and take off the blade protector.

'That's what you cut the ventilator with,' he said, remembering the clean, sharp incisions in the plastic tubing.

Le Grice smiled and moved to bring his legs round. 'I really did underestimate you,' he said.

'Don't do anything stupid,' cautioned Dewar, as Le Grice started to move into a kneeling position. 'You're not going anywhere. You must see that. There's no way out. The police are downstairs.'

Le Grice nodded slowly and said, 'Oui, all over. My hopes for the vaccine . . . my career . . . my ambitions . . . my freedom . . . all over. You don't 'ave to tell me that. I know.' He smiled wanly and with a sudden darting movement of his hand he brought the scalpel blade cleanly and deeply across his own throat.

Dewar stepped back as a fountain of crimson splashed into the dust at his feet. Le Grice tipped over on to his face and lay in a crumpled heap.

'Oh, my God,' whispered Dewar.

'Hello! Anyone up there?' came Grant's voice from the stairs.

'Here,' answered Dewar. He waited, motionless until Grant joined him.

'Christ almighty,' said Grant. 'I hope you didn't do that.' Dewar shook his head. 'Bloody considerate of him, I'd say,' said Grant. 'Saves us a great deal of time and trouble, not to mention the cost of a trial and legal aid to fund some smart-arsed lawyer to claim he was actually halfway up the bloody Eiffel Tower at the time of the incident. Why'd he do it?'

'Like we said, he was a very bright man. He saw the future and it didn't work for him.'

'Did he tell you what you wanted to know?'

Dewar shook his head. 'Not a thing.'

'So where does that leave us?'

'With something unpleasant to do. I'm going to close down Steven Malloy's lab and have everything in it taken away.'

'Christ, he'll love that.'

'There's no alternative. The place is full of bottles and tubes with labels that mean nothing to anyone except their originator. Trying to pick out Le Grice's stuff from the rest in the absence of Ali Hammadi and now Sandra Macandrew is a nonstarter. The only way we can be sure we've destroyed whatever Le Grice was working on is to put the whole damned lot into the steriliser. We'll analyse what we can but the main priority is safety.'

'I'm glad you're the one going to be telling Malloy,' said Grant. 'This is going to put an end to his research career.'

'It might also destroy two PhD theses and what's left of a technician's working life.'

Dewar waited until Le Grice's body had been bagged and taken away before driving over to the Institute of Molecular Sciences. He showed his ID to the two uniformed policemen on the door but didn't tell them that Le Grice wouldn't be coming after all. He found Steven Malloy going through racks of tubes that he'd removed from a lab fridge. George Ferguson and Peter Moore were removing the contents of a chest freezer and stacking them on an adjacent bench. There was a large wire basket sitting on a table in the centre of the room. Dewar guessed that this was for Le Grice's stuff.

'Have they caught him?' asked Malloy as soon as he saw Dewar.

'In a manner of speaking.'

'Something's happened,' said Malloy, reading Dewar's expression.

'Pierre Le Grice is dead. He took his own life when he saw there was no way out.'

'My God,' whispered Malloy. Ferguson and Peter Moore exchanged shocked glances.

Dewar gave them a moment to come to terms with the news,

then Malloy asked, 'Did you get a chance to speak to him before he did it?'

Dewar nodded. 'He wouldn't tell me anything. He didn't deny trying to kill Sandra but he wouldn't admit to anything else.'

'I still can't believe he did it,' said Malloy. 'Christ! What's happened to us all. A few short weeks ago we were on the verge of making the biggest breakthrough in years and suddenly all this happens. Ali dead, Pierre dead. Sandra lying at death's door.'

'I'm afraid there's more,' said Dewar. Malloy looked unwilling to believe that there could possibly be any more bad news. 'I'm going to have to seal off this lab. A special team will be brought in to remove everything from it.'

'Pierre's stuff, yes, we're getting it together now.'

'Everyone's stuff,' said Dewar.

Malloy's face registered disbelief but he saw that Dewar was serious. He sank down on a stool and stared down at the floor, shaking his head.

'I'm sorry,' said Dewar. 'But it's the only way to be sure that there's no possibility of live smallpox virus being left around.'

'This is crazy,' said Malloy. 'I just don't believe for a moment that Pierre Le Grice tried to reconstruct live smallpox virus in the open lab. That would have been just plain crazy.'

'I agree. But you wouldn't have believed he would have tried to kill Sandra Macandrew either.'

Malloy couldn't argue.

'This means my PhD goes down the tubes,' said Peter Moore, suddenly seeing the implications for himself. 'Sandra's too.'

'I'm sorry, there's no other way.'

'Christ,' muttered Peter Moore. 'Talk about shit happening!'

'It means the end of the lab, doesn't it?' said George Ferguson. 'No grant-funding body is going to come up with money to support a line of research that no longer exists.'

'It means starting over again,' agreed Dewar. 'But you'll have all your experimental notes to work from.'

'Forget it,' said Malloy. 'By the time we got back up to speed, the opposition would be out of sight. It's not feasible. It's all over. When d'you want us out?'

'I'd like you to leave the lab now. The sooner I seal it off the better.'

Malloy smiled without humour. 'Don't trust us, eh?'

'Nothing like that,' said Dewar. 'Just procedure.'

'And these Iraqi fuckers, the ones behind it all, the movers and shakers, they'll get away I take it?'

'There's no evidence against them as yet.'

'Christ! Half my group are dead or dying. My entire research programme is going down the Swanee and "there's no evidence against them as yet",' mimicked Malloy.

'I can understand your bitterness,' said Dewar.

'Jesus, Dewar! You sound like a Californian — "Thank you for sharing your anger with me".' With that, Malloy stormed out of the room.

'Well, I suppose I'd better think about getting my arse down the job centre,' said Peter Moore. 'See if they need any double-glazing salesmen. The Medical Research Council aren't going to give me another grant to start over again.' He, too, left the room with a black look in Dewar's direction.

'Your turn,' said Dewar to George Ferguson, the only one left. 'I feel like the grim reaper.'

Ferguson gave a half-hearted smile. 'You're only doing your job,' he said. 'But you must see how these guys feel.'

Dewar nodded. 'Of course.'

'This lab is Steve Malloy's life. His research is the only thing he cares about unlike half the wankers in this place who spend most of their time sitting on their arse talking about research rather than doing it. It takes more than knowledge to be a researcher,' Ferguson continued. 'You can know every fact in the damned world and still not know what to do next. Steve's different. He's a natural. He knows the questions, the experiments to do, the paths to follow. It's a bloody shame.'

Dewar nodded sympathetically. 'And you? What'll you do now?' he asked.

Ferguson shrugged. 'I'll survive.'

'You're married?'

Ferguson nodded. 'Yes, we've got one boy.'

'Still living at home?'

'A veil came over Ferguson's eyes. 'He's not right,' he said. 'Brain damage when he was a kid.'

'Bad luck. I'm sorry.'

Ferguson shrugged. 'That's the way it goes. Anyway, I think I'll go find the others, leave you to your business.'

'I really am sorry,' said Dewar.

'Yeah.'

Dewar called Macmillan at Sci Med from Malloy's office and told him what had happened.

'Did this man, Le Grice, admit it before he took his life?' asked Macmillan.

'He didn't deny the attempt on Sandra Macandrew's life and he mentioned extra smallpox fragments but he didn't actually acknowledge any dealings with the Iraqis.'

'Damn,' said Macmillan. 'But there seems little doubt?'

'He had extra smallpox fragments and he tried to kill Sandra,' replied Dewar. 'It sounded to me like he'd tried to convince Sandra that the extra fragments would have helped with her research but she decided to blow the whistle on him anyway.'

'That still leaves us with nothing against these damned people. You don't think he actually managed to supply them with the virus, do you?' asked Macmillan.

'I don't think so. I don't think there was time and the Iraqis haven't looked like they're ready to leave, according to the secret service.'

'What are you doing about the lab where Le Grice worked?'

'I've just told the research group leader that everything in his lab will have to be removed. I'd like a team from Porton Down called in to take it away. We can't afford to take chances. They can analyse anything they think looks promising under conditions of maximum containment and destroy everything when they're finished.'

'You're right – the last thing we need is someone contracting smallpox because it was left lying around and nobody knew about it.'

'I'm going to lock and seal the lab. Would you arrange for the Porton team to be called in to do their stuff? I'll tell the head of the institute here to expect them.'

'Are you planning to come back to London?'

'I'll hang on for a couple of days if that's all right. I'll brief the Porton team when they arrive and I'd also like to see the back of Siddiqui and his pal before I return. Presumably they'll leave when word about Le Grice gets out.'

'I've done what you requested about arranging to have them stopped and searched on the way out.'

'Good, the more thorough and unpleasantly the better. Siddiqui can't play the diplomatic card because he entered the country as an academic, not a diplomat. God knows what Abbas's status is but I'm sure a "misunderstanding" could arise.'

'I think the immigration people have got the message,' said Macmillan. 'They're still smarting from having let Siddiqui in unnoticed.'

'Good.'

'I'll get on to Porton. I'll give them your number to contact when they get there.'

'Any idea how long?'

'I'm going to make this top priority. They have a rapid-response squad. With the help of the military I should think four to five hours.'

'I'll be waiting.'

Dewar found that Hutton, the head of institute, already knew what was happening by the time he got to his office.

'Dr Malloy told me,' said Hutton. 'He's devastated. He sees it as the end of his career.'

'He's still a brilliant scientist,' said Dewar. 'Surely there will be a place for him somewhere.'

'Unfortunately that's not the way research works,' said Hutton. 'Research groups are a bit like Italian city states in the middle ages. There's no question of the leader of one being able to join the forces of another. His rivals in the vaccine race will see his misfortune as one less runner in the race to worry about.'

'Not exactly a Walt Disney world, is it,' said Dewar.

'What is these days?' replied Hutton.

That old excuse, thought Dewar.

'These people who're coming,' said Hutton. 'What exactly are they going to do?'

'They will take away absolutely everything from Steven Malloy's lab in sealed containers and fumigate the lab itself when it's empty. The contents of the containers will be subject to analysis under secure conditions when they get back to Porton, then everything will be destroyed, just in case anything has been missed.'

Hutton nodded. 'This all seems like a bad dream.'

'For all of us,' Dewar assured him.

'Is there anything you'd like me to do?'

'Just make sure that the Malloy lab is kept locked.'

'I'll put the whole corridor out of bounds until your people arrive. I'll have one of the porters sit by the door.'

'That might be best.'

Dewar returned to his hotel and asked for beer and sandwiches. He hadn't eaten since breakfast time and it was now four in the afternoon. He called Grant rather than the hospital to ask about

Sandra Macandrew's condition.

'They say she's improving,' replied Grant. ''Becoming stable'' I think was the expression. Do you still want the guard left on her?'

'Yes,' replied Dewar after a moment's thought. 'It's just possible that Le Grice admitted to her what he was doing for the Iraqis. Let's keep her safe.'

'You're the man.'

Dewar wondered what film Grant had picked up that expression from.

Next he called Simon Barron on his mobile number. 'Anything happening?' he asked.

'Nothing, but I hear you've been having a lot of fun and games,' replied Barron. Dewar filled him in on the details. 'So panic over. We can expect our friends to pack their bags shortly?'

'Let's hope so.'

'Can we be sure that this Le Grice character didn't succeed in reconstructing the virus?'

'All the signs are that he didn't. Porton Down are going to investigate the entire contents of the lab he worked in to see if they can get an idea about what stage he was at and if Sandra Macandrew comes round she can probably tell us a good deal.'

'Let's hope she does,' said Barron. 'In the meantime we go on watching while you have all the fun.'

'I think I've had quite enough ''fun'' as you put it. I just want to see the back of these two up in Forest Road.

Dewar received a call from the Porton team after they landed at Edinburgh Airport just after eight. He arranged to meet them outside the institute and found them already waiting when he got there. He had not taken into account a police escort, which cut down their town travel time considerably. The small convoy comprised two police cars and an unlettered black

Transit van. Dewar presumed that this also had been supplied by the local police.

He introduced himself to the leader of the team, Dr Robert Smillie, and briefed him on events.

'That's more or less what we've been told,' said Smillie when he'd finished. 'If you'll just show us to the lab in question we'll take over from there. Any special problems? Do we need respirators?'

'No,' Dewar assured him. 'The man involved in this affair was a highly trained scientist. If there's anything to be found it will be in an appropriate container. The question is, which one? There could be several; alternatively, there may be none. This is a precaution but a very necessary one.'

The team of three changed into coverall suits and put on gloves before entering Malloy's lab, carrying a number of sealable plastic containers. They took less than sixty minutes to remove every single tube and bottle in the place, even moving all the furniture to examine the floor underneath for anything that had fallen and rolled.

'I'm impressed,' said Dewar to Smillie when his team had finished and were setting the sterilising 'bombs' in place.

'I think this is where I say, all in a day's work,' said Smillie.

Dewar grinned and said, 'But I don't envy you the next bit.'

Smillie nodded his agreement. 'There's no question of analysing the contents of every single container,' he said. 'But we'll do a DNA scan and concentrate on those that come up positive. Can't say how long it's going to take. We'll be using the high-containment suite. That always slows things up. It's like picking your nose with boxing gloves on.'

# ~ Thirteen ~

Dewar watched the lights of the small convoy disappear into the night as they headed off back to the airport. Hutton, who had seen it as his duty to be present throughout, looked at his watch and said that he'd have to rush, muttering something about dinner with friends. Dewar wished him good night and suddenly wondered what he himself was going to do with the rest of the evening. He felt a distinct sense of anticlimax.

So much seemed to have happened since he'd got up that morning but, he asked himself, did he really know that much more at the end of the day? True, Le Grice had been identified as Sandra Macandrew's attacker and it seemed almost certain that he must be the Iraqis' man on the inside, but he still didn't know exactly what the Iraqis had asked him to do or how much of it had been achieved, any more than with Ali Hammadi. These were still the key questions in the whole affair.

Maybe he knew even less about them, was Dewar's next depressing thought. Up until now he'd believed that Hammadi had refused to do anything at all for Siddiqui but that conclusion had been partially based on Le Grice's report that he'd found nothing out of the ordinary when he'd cleared out Hammadi's stuff in the lab. That was possibly a lie. If only Le Grice had owned up before he'd taken his life instead of saying nothing. What had been the point of that? he wondered. It was hard to believe that any man about to die would not take the chance to redress the balance of good and evil in his life even if he hadn't been any kind of believer.

Another man to whom this day had been pivotal was Steven Malloy. It was the day his career had effectively come to an end. Despite having every right to do what he'd done in the circumstances — indeed, he'd had no real option — Dewar felt something approaching guilt. He liked Malloy and believed the good things Ferguson had said about him. Good research scientists weren't that thick on the ground — much less so than Joe Public imagined. One such person tended to make a university department a good one, two made it a centre of excellence.

He wondered what Malloy was doing tonight. Would he be with friends, or was he brooding at home alone? Almost on impulse, Dewar decided to drive out to Temple and find out for himself but, before doing that, he stopped at an off-licence and bought a bottle of good malt whisky.

The drive out to Temple took longer than last time because of heavy rain that started on the way. By the time he left the main road, the wipers were struggling to cope, forcing him to slow right down on the dark winding roads where water quickly gathered into pools in the dips and made estimating their depth a gamble each time before he ploughed through. He was relieved when the lights of the village began to flicker through the needles of the pine trees.

When he stopped outside Malloy's place he could see that the lights were on. He sat in the car for a moment listening to a small voice inside his head that told him this was not a very good idea, but eventually it was overridden by his conscience telling him that this was the right thing to do. People automatically said sorry often when they didn't mean it. He hoped that driving out here to say it again would convince Malloy that at least *he* did. He got out the car and hurried up the path, pulling up his jacket collar against the rain and hugging the whisky to his chest.

Just before he reached the door he had the thought that Malloy might not be alone. He could hear music coming from inside and recognised it as Stan Getz playing 'These Foolish Things'. He sidestepped into the garden so that he could take a peek in through the window. As far as he could tell, Malloy was alone. He could see him slumped in a chair with his back to him, glass in hand, feet up on a stool.

Dewar knocked gently on the arched door at first but had to rap progressively louder as he failed to get an answer.

'All right,' complained Malloy's voice as he finally responded to Dewar's insistence. 'Who is it?'

'Adam Dewar.'

There was a long silence before the door finally opened. 'What the f—'

Malloy looked at Dewar as if he still didn't believe it was him. He was obviously the last person on Earth he expected to see standing there, or wanted to see for that matter.

'Hello. How are you doing?'

'I don't think I believe this,' said Malloy, his voice slightly slurred. He scratched his head.

'I just came to say that I really meant it when I said I was sorry about your research.'

Malloy regarded Dewar for a long moment through screwed-up eyes. 'And now you'd like forgiveness,' he said. '*Te absolvo*. Feel any better?'

'I didn't come to ask for forgiveness,' said Dewar evenly. 'I did what I had to do and I think you know that if you're honest with yourself. I don't regret it but I am genuinely sorry. I thought we might have a drink together.' He held up the whisky.

Malloy looked as if he were running through a series of options inside his head, ranging from bursting out laughing to slamming the door in Dewar's face. Eventually he shrugged and said, 'You'd better come in.' He accepted the bottle from Dewar and splashed whisky into two tumblers.

'What shall we drink to?' he asked, handing one to Dewar.

'The future,' replied Dewar evenly. 'Whatever it holds. May it be kinder than the present.'

'The future,' repeated Malloy, without adding the cynical rider Dewar had been half expecting. That pleased him, for, although Malloy was drinking, he was not wallowing in self-pity. Both men took a large swallow.

'Sit down.'

'I thought you might be with Peter Moore and George Ferguson this evening,' said Dewar.

Malloy shook his head. 'No, Peter will be at the postgrad union, playing the tragic role to the hilt, I should think. Always a more successful gambit with the ladies than Mr Happy, I seem to remember.'

'You don't see his predicament as serious, then?'

'He's first-year. He's not lost much. Most of them take a year learning to pick their noses without poking their eye out. He's a good student. I'll have a word with Cairns about him. I'm sure he'll take him over. Maybe a change of research project but no real harm done.'

'Good,' said Dewar. 'And Sandra?'

Malloy grimaced. 'She's different. She's going into her third year, too late to change I'm afraid. Assuming she survives her present predicament she won't have enough for a PhD but she could write up for an MPhil.'

'Let's hope she gets the chance,' said Dewar.

'Amen to that,' agreed Malloy, raising his glass to the notion.

'That just leaves George Ferguson.'

'Poor George. He's not having the best couple of years, poor bugger. They pull his hospital down after thirty years, transfer him all around the university and now this. He's got a wife with cancer and a mentally retarded boy, you know.'

'I knew about the boy,' said Dewar. 'I didn't know about his wife. I was speaking to him before I left, or should I say he was the only one left speaking to me by that time!'

Malloy gave a lopsided grin. 'I can imagine.'

'He seemed to be taking it philosophically,' said Dewar.

'Good,' said Malloy. 'He usually imagines that life is waging a personal vendetta against him.'

Dewar smiled. 'He has a point by the sound of it. And you? What will you do now?'

'I've had a couple of offers from drug companies in the last year. I turned them down but maybe it's time for a slice of humble pie. Maybe mammon and me'll get along just fine.'

'Academics often talk a lot of nonsense about working in industry,' said Dewar. 'If you're good, there's no problem. It's half-arses industry's not so keen on and most of the university luvvies throwing up their hands in horror at the very idea of industry are exactly that. They know they'd be rumbled in that world within ten minutes and be shown the door.'

'Maybe you're right.'

Malloy got out of his chair and replenished their glasses. Dewar was about to decline but thought better of it. He could always get a taxi back to town and pick up his car tomorrow. Malloy needed company; it seemed the least he could do in the circumstances.

The Getz record had come to an end. 'Other side?' asked Malloy.

'Why not?'


Dewar woke with a splitting headache to find that he still had all his clothes on and was still in the church at Temple. Malloy was asleep in the chair opposite, snoring quietly, his glass lying on its side on the carpet at his feet. He looked for his own and found it standing on the table beside an empty whisky bottle.

'Strewth,' he muttered as he rubbed at the stiffness in his neck from having slept in a chair. He stood up at the second attempt and went over to the window to look out. The rain had stopped but the sky didn't look too promising. The grass was speckled with wet autumn leaves, themselves spattered with mud after the downpour of last night. He went off to the bathroom and felt better when he'd sluiced some hot water up into his face, then rinsed out his mouth.

When he returned, Malloy was coming to with groans of protest at the stiffness in his limbs. 'God, what time is it?' he asked.

Dewar looked at his watch. 'Seven thirty.'

'Coffee, I need coffee.'

Dewar grinned and switched on the kettle.

Malloy didn't speak again until he had taken a second mouthful of black coffee. Then he said suddenly, 'You know, I still don't believe that Le Grice agreed to do what you think he did.'

'Everything points to it.'

Another long pause while Malloy, coffee mug cupped in two hands, considered. 'I knew the man well,' he said. 'I didn't like him much but we got on and I respected him as an able scientist. He was a lot of other things too — ambitious, insensitive, intolerant, obstinate: I wouldn't have wanted my sister to marry him but he was anything but a fool and only a fool would have contemplated playing around with smallpox.'

'I hear what you say,' said Dewar. 'But I have to go on the facts and they say he was up to no good.'

'Oh, I accept that,' said Malloy. 'I just don't think live smallpox was involved in the no-good he was up to.'

'I can honestly say I hope to God you're right about that,' said Dewar with feeling. 'Let's look forward to Sandra being able to tell us what really happened before too long.'

'Thanks for coming over last night,' said Malloy. 'I appreciate it.'

Dewar got up and started to put on his jacket. 'It's been a while since I drank myself to sleep.'

'Me too,' said Malloy.

The two men shook hands and Dewar started back for the city. The journey was uneventful and he got a knowing look from the desk clerk at his hotel when he asked for his key. He answered it with a stony stare before going upstairs to shower and change. He checked with the hospital: Sandra was still unconscious. He checked with Barron: the Iraqis still hadn't shown any signs of leaving. He reported in to Sci Med and was told that the contents of Malloy's lab had reached Porton Down safely and were now being examined as a matter of urgency. There was nothing to do now but wait.

By Friday morning Dewar was starting to worry, not because Sandra was still in a coma but because the Iraqis were still not preparing to leave the city. This was not in the script. The fact that they were still there even started to cast doubt over Le Grice's role.

'We're bored stiff,' complained Barron when Dewar spoke to him in the afternoon. 'What the hell are they waiting for?'

'I'm damned if I know,' replied Dewar. 'But it sure isn't going to come from the institute now. The Porton mob took away the lot.'

'Maybe they're just sitting tight to make us think we were wrong all along,' suggested Barron.

'Or maybe they're waiting until a new target institute's been identified and then they'll move on.'

'As long as it isn't in the UK,' said Barron.

'Self, self, self,' said Dewar.

Karen phoned just after five to say that she had arrived at her mother's. When would he be joining them?

'About seven?' replied Dewar tentatively.

'No excuses,' replied Karen *sotto voce*, suggesting her mother was listening in.

'Would I?' said Dewar.

'Hmmm.'

As good as his word, Dewar turned up at the house in North Berwick just before seven and kissed Karen lightly on the cheek before doing the same to her mother and saying, 'Good to see you again, Jean.'

'I understand you're working in Edinburgh just now, Adam. What brings you up here?'

'A problem at one of the research institutes,' replied Dewar, accepting the glass of sherry that Karen held out to him.

'Nothing to do with that foreign student who hanged himself a few weeks ago by any chance?'

'He was a student at the same institute,' conceded Dewar.

'Foreigners,' snorted Jean. 'Intrinsically unstable.'

Dewar looked at Karen, who shot him a warning glance.

Dewar said nothing. He had prepared himself for an evening of reactionary nonsense from the woman in tweeds. He was not to be disappointed as Jean put forth her views on the absolute necessity of arming the police, using the handle of her knife to emphasise important points by banging it down on the table. She followed up with a treatise on repatriation of coloureds and the introduction of more stringent immigration laws. Finally she outlined her master plan of imposing curfews on all UK streets after ten in the evening. She was, of course, willing to relax regulations on certain days like New Year's Eve – 'I'm not a monster, Adam' – and certain other festive dates. Naturally some people would have to be exempted from the rules.

Dewar couldn't help but feel that among those would almost certainly be certain elderly women, wearing tweeds, body warmers and substantial stockings who lived in large comfortable houses in North Berwick on money left to them by their late husbands.

Karen, suspecting that Dewar's patience was running thin, suggested that he and she should have a walk round the harbour before doing the dishes. Dewar leapt at the chance.

'How come you turned out normal?' he asked Karen as they walked down the cobbled street leading to the harbour.

'She's not as awful as she sounds,' said Karen. 'She has a good heart really.'

'I'll take your word for that,' said Dewar ruefully.

'Granddad — Mum's father — was a colonel in the army like Dad. She's always been used to standards influenced by the ruling classes. She didn't like it when the world changed so she and her friends built a little world for themselves. They stick together and pretend nothing's changed. They all have money so it's not difficult to find tradesmen and professional people who will pander to them and maintain the illusion.'

'That still doesn't answer my question. You're not like her.'

'I might have been had I not gone to university and learned to think for myself. Then I did voluntary service overseas and saw just how little some people had to live on. Working in public health has been a bit of an eye opener too, seeing just how little some people in this country have. Unlike my mother, I know what the real world's like; I'm not afraid of it like she is. I have no illusions about it but I don't feel threatened all the time. I feel OK.'

Dewar put his hand on Karen's buttock and squeezed lightly. 'Yup, you do,' he agreed.

'Trust you to lower the tone.'

'Now you're sounding like your mother.'

Karen gave him an elbow in the ribs and said, 'You haven't told me how your investigation's going.'

Dewar told her what he could.

Karen shivered slightly and Dewar suggested they start back. 'You are going to stay over?' she asked.

'If you want me too.'

'Of course I want you to. Mother would take it as a personal slight if you didn't.'

'Even though she can't stand the sight of me?' said Dewar.

'Don't be silly. Being slightly to the right of Mussolini herself, she sees you as an incipient red menace because you care about people and tend to say so.'

'So do you in your job,' said Dewar.

'Ah, but she sees that differently. She thinks of me as doing charity work. People like her have always done that. You know, the knitting-socks-for-soldiers bit, the WVS tea van, driving ambulances and the like.'

Dewar took a deep breath before they entered the house and Karen smiled. 'I'm proud of you,' she said. 'Keep it up. She's an early bedder.'

Karen's mother asked if they'd noticed the graffiti down by the harbour. They hadn't.

'Young thugs with nothing better to do with themselves,' declared Jean, using this as a starting point to expound her views on the shortcomings of the young and how they should be tackled. 'And what do they get if they're caught? Probation,' she snorted. 'As if that's going to stop them. They're laughing at authority, that's what they're doing.'

'I think I know how to stop recidivism,' said Dewar.

Karen shot him a warning glance but it was too late.

'Really, Adam?'

'Hang first offenders,' said Dewar with a straight face.

'Well, you know my views about hanging, dear . . .' Jean began, then she realised she was being mocked. 'That's silly, Adam,' she said with a sour expression.

Karen closed her eyes momentarily then said, 'It's about time we did the dishes, Adam.'

'Right.'

'I think I'll go up to bed dear,' said Jean. 'I think I've got a migraine coming on.' She kissed Karen on the cheek and said a frosty good night to Dewar.

'And you were doing so well,' said Karen, making a start to the washing up.

Dewar came up behind her and slipped his arms around her waist. 'Sorry,' he said, nuzzling her neck.

Karen moved her head to one side and held up her rubber-gloved hands. 'Don't think you're going to get round me that way,' she said, but she was smiling.

'Are you going to let me come to your room?'

'No, we agreed – it's right next to Mother's.'

'Well, you can come to mine.'

'You're on the other side of her,' said Karen.

'I bet she planned it that way,' complained Dewar. 'With all that military background in the family, I bet she's a tactical genius.'

'A little exercise in self-restraint won't do you any harm at all,' said Karen.

'On the other hand . . .' said Dewar sliding his hands down on to Karen's hips.

'What?'

'I could have you right here over the kitchen sink.' He slid his hands down further to grip Karen's skirt and start hitching it up.

'Adam!' protested Karen in a stage whisper.

Dewar continued to nuzzle the side of her neck as he brought her skirt right up over her bottom and drew her back into him.

'I don't really . . . think this . . . is a very . . . good idea,' moaned Karen in a voice that suggested it wasn't entirely a bad one. 'You randy b——'

'Karen, darling, I should have said, you really must use up the——' Jean's voice behind them faded away. Dewar closed his eyes and prayed for the ground to open up. Karen just froze.

'Well, really!'

'Oh God, tell me that didn't happen,' prayed Dewar aloud.

'It did,' said Karen, who was now taking the situation better than Dewar. She even found the look on Dewar's face amusing. 'Well, that cured your randiness, didn't it?'

'Damned right,' replied Dewar, still stricken with embarrassment. 'I may never rise again.'

'It's not the end of the world,' said Karen. 'I'm sure after all this time even my mother has worked out that we don't spend all our time together playing Scrabble.'

'Even though . . .'

The telephone rang and Karen left the kitchen to answer it. She returned saying, 'It's for you.'

'I had to leave a number,' Dewar apologised.

The call was from Ian Grant. 'I'm at the hospital. Sandra Macandrew is showing signs of regaining consciousness. I thought you'd want to know.'

'I'm on my way.'

Dewar explained to Karen that he'd have to go.

'Saved by the bell,' said Karen.

Dewar still looked embarrassed. 'What should I do about your mother?' he asked. 'Apologise?'

Karen shook her head. 'If I know my mother, she'll pretend nothing ever happened. It'll probably never be mentioned. Let's just do the same.'

'I'm sorry,' said Dewar putting on his jacket.

'I'm not,' said Karen. 'It's rather nice to be wanted. Long may it continue.'


Dewar gunned the Rover up the thirty-odd miles to Edinburgh in a little over thirty minutes. He found Grant seemingly having an argument with one of the medical staff. Both men were speaking in whispers but the fact that it was an argument was pumping up the volume. Grant caught sight of Dewar and looked relieved. 'Good to see you,' he said. 'I've been trying to explain to Dr Sellars here that you must speak to Miss Macandrew first.'

'What's the problem?' asked Dewar.

Sellars, looking harassed, said, 'I'm under pressure from her parents. They know she's coming round and they want to be with her. It's only natural.'

Dewar nodded his understanding. 'Maybe I should have a word with them.'

'Worth a try,' said Sellars, happy to pass the buck to anyone in the circumstances.

Dewar was shown into the room, where a nurse was attempting to pacify Sandra's parents.

'This is outrageous,' her father was complaining.

'I'm sorry. I'm the cause of all this trouble,' said Dewar, announcing his presence. He held out his hand and shook hands with both of Sandra's parents. 'I know this must all seem totally unreasonable but it's vital I speak to Sandra first. She knows something that could conceivably affect the lives of millions of people.'

'Our Sandra?'

Dewar nodded. 'I think you can take it as a good sign that she's coming out of her coma and you have my assurance that you'll be allowed to sit with her as soon as possible. Please, just bear with me a little longer.'

The couple seemed satisfied, if more than a little taken aback, at what Dewar had told them. They sat down and Dewar left them alone with the nurse again.

'OK?' asked Sellars.

'For the moment,' replied Dewar. 'Can I see her now?'

Sellars led the way.

'Sandra! Can you hear me?' asked Sellars loudly.

Sandra moved her head on the pillow as if annoyed at the insistence in Sellars' voice. 'Go away,' she murmured.

'Come on now, Sandra. Open your eyes.'

Sandra's eyes opened like those of a toy doll that had been moved into an upright position. 'How many fingers, Sandra?' asked Sellars, holding up three fingers.

'Three,' replied Sandra.

'How many now?' Sellars held up four.

Sandra moved her head from side to side again in a gesture of annoyance. 'Four,' she mumbled.

'Good. Who's the prime minister?'

'Leave me alone.'

'Come on now, Sandra. Tell me who the prime minister is.'

'Blair,' mumbled Sandra.

'Who? Louder.'

'Blair. Tony bloody Blair.'

'All yours,' said Sellars to Dewar.

# ~ *Fourteen* ~

Sellars left Dewar alone with Sandra and the machines that monitored her every breath, their gentle bleeps and clicks creating a soothing background, the coloured LEDs complementing the subdued night-lighting in the room. He moved a chair up to side of the bed and sat down facing Sandra with his elbows resting on the edge.

'Sandra, do you remember me?' he asked. Unlike Sellars, he didn't raise his voice; his face was very close to hers.

Sandra's eyes flicked open then closed again. A good ten seconds passed before she replied, 'Dewar.'

Dewar felt elated. There was nothing wrong with Sandra's long-term memory. There was, of course, still the possibility that accident trauma had wiped out memory of the incident with the car and possibly for some time before it. This was very common.

'Sandra, do you remember what happened to you?'

Again Sandra's eyes flickered open momentarily, then closed again as if she'd found her eyelids too heavy. 'Hospital,' she said slowly.

'Do you know why you're in hospital?'

Sandra made a sound as if she were about to answer, then stopped and exhaled. She did the same twice more then uttered, 'No.'

So there was memory loss. This was bad news. If she couldn't remember anything about the accident right now, there was no guarantee she ever would. It was impossible to predict what might happen in cases like this. She might remember everything within a couple of days or nothing at all for the rest of her life. The big question now was, how much of what had gone on before the accident could she remember?

'You had an accident on your bicycle, Sandra.'

'Bike,' repeated Sandra. The word did not seem to trigger any special memory for her.

'You don't remember?'

'Bike. No.'

'Do you remember Pierre, Sandra? Pierre in the lab.'

'Pierre, know Pierre . . . French.'

'That's right. He's French. Tell me what else you remember about him.'

'In the lab. He was in the lab.' Sandra moved her head uncomfortably. Dewar felt encouraged. He'd pushed the right button.

'When was he in the lab, Sandra? The last time you were there?'

'Last time . . . yes.'

'I think you came across him doing something wrong in the lab, Sandra. Is that right? What was he doing?'

'The sequence,' replied Sandra as if she was recalling some-thing unpleasant. She frowned and tried opening her eyes again. This time she managed a few seconds before closing them again.

'What sequence?'

'DNA . . . Smallpox DNA. Not ours.'

Dewar felt his throat tighten a little with excitement. 'Not yours?' he said gently. He desperately didn't want to upset Sandra's train of thought.

'Not our fragments.'

'How did you know that, Sandra?' he asked. 'How did you

find that out?'

'Computer . . . Pierre left sequence in computer. I ran . . . database check. Not our smallpox.'

'Let me see. You found a DNA sequence in the computer. It had been entered by Pierre and it was the sequence of a smallpox fragment that your lab was not supposed to have. Have I got that right?'

Sandra nodded her head on the pillow. She seemed pleased and relieved to have got it across successfully.

Dewar had understood what she'd said but he didn't quite understand the implications. He frowned and said, 'But the sequence of the smallpox virus is available to all scientists. Anyone can access it in the DNA database. What was odd about finding a bit of it on the computer?'

This time Sandra shook her head as if to signify a misunder-standing. 'Pierre's sequence,' she said. 'Not from database.'

Suddenly Dewar realised what she meant. 'Oh, I see,' he said. 'It wasn't a sequence he'd taken *from* the database, it was a DNA sequence that he'd *put in*. Something he'd got from an experiment he'd done in the lab. It was *you* who checked it against the database to find out what it was?' A relieved nod from Sandra. 'So Pierre was working in the lab with smallpox fragments that he shouldn't have had access to?'

'Yes.'

'And you confronted him about it?'

'Yes.'

'What did he say?'

'Angry . . . told me . . . keep mouth shut.'

'He wanted you to keep quiet about what he was doing?'

A nod.

Dewar could sense from Sandra's restlessness that unpleasant memories were starting to flow back at an unwelcome rate. The bleep rate on the heart monitor had started to increase but he had to keep questioning her before she tried to shut them out.

'What was he doing with the fragments, Sandra? Where did he get them from?'

'Ali's.'

'They were Ali Hammadi's fragments?'

'Pierre found illegal fragments when . . . he cleaned out Ali's fridge . . . lied to Steve . . . said nothing there. Pierre wanted . . . to use them.'

'Was Pierre trying to make live smallpox virus, Sandra?'

Sandra opened her eyes wide as if shocked by the idea. She looked directly at Dewar. 'Nooooo,' she replied in along sigh. Even in her debilitated state she managed to convey that she thought this a ridiculous notion.

'Are you absolutely sure about that?'

A nod. 'Pierre found . . . the fragments he needed for his research . . . the ones you wouldn't let him have. Said I could have them too but I said it was wrong and I was going . . . to tell Steve.'

Dewar thought for a moment before asking any more. If what he was hearing was true, then there was no connection between Le Grice and the Iraqis. Le Grice had simply stumbled across the fragments given to Ali Hammadi and, being the ambitious sod he undoubtedly was, he had decided to say nothing and use them to further his research in breach of regulations. Le Grice hadn't been feigning ignorance of the Iraqis: he'd really had nothing to do with them. He must have panicked when Sandra said she was going to tell Steve and tried to save his career by running her down.

'Were there any other smallpox DNA fragments apart from the ones he used?'

'Pierre said . . . a lot.'

'What happened to them, Sandra? The other fragments Ali left behind?'

'Pierre destroyed them . . . too dangerous to keep.'

'That's what he told you?' A nod. 'And you believed him?'

'Didn't know what . . . to believe . . .'

Dewar could sympathise. He didn't know what to believe either. 'Did you try telling Steve?' he asked.

'I tried . . . phoning but it was difficult . . . couldn't make him understand with Pierre . . . there.'

'Did Pierre threaten you at all?'

'Tried to persuade me . . . not to tell Steve. Very angry. Called me stupid. Said I was . . . ruining my career before it had even started . . . I said I would think about it overnight but I just wanted away from him . . . I was going to tell Steve in the morning anyway.'

But Le Grice knew that, thought Dewar. 'So you set off for home on your bicycle?'

'Yes . . .' said Sandra as if unsure.

'On your bicycle.'

'Dark.'

'Yes, it was dark but you had your lights on.'

'Dark.'

Dewar knew he'd reached the limit of Sandra's recollection. He got up from the chair and drew it back from the bed.

'I'm going to let your mum and dad come in now, Sandra, and then you must get some sleep,' said Dewar. 'I'll see you again soon.' Dewar gave the back of her hand a little rub and left the room.

'Well?' asked Grant.

'I don't know,' replied Dewar, thoughtfully.

'She couldn't tell you anything?' exclaimed Grant.

'Oh yes, she said quite a lot. It was pretty much as we thought. Le Grice *was* working with smallpox fragments that he shouldn't have had but he told Sandra they belonged to Hammadi. According to him, he found them in a fridge he was clearing out after Hammadi died. He was using a couple of them to help with his research on an AIDS vaccine, not to make live smallpox with. He told Sandra he had destroyed the ones he didn't need. He never had any direct connection with the Iraqis at all.'

'D'you believe it?'

'Don't know. Mind you, a lot of it would fit. Le Grice didn't seem to know what I was talking about when I tackled him about working for the Iraqis. I thought he was feigning ignorance but maybe not. Then there's Malloy. He insisted Le Grice would never be so stupid as to try making live virus. Maybe he was right.'

'So why have the Iraqis stayed on? Why are they still here?'

'Back to square one,' said Dewar. 'I don't know.'

'So that's it,' said Grant. 'We're not going to get any more information from Ms Macandrew, I take it?'

'I think she told me everything she knew,' said Dewar.

'Where does that leave us?'

'The Iraqis obviously gave smallpox fragments to Hammadi but I don't think he did anything with them. I think I'm inclined to believe that Le Grice wasn't trying to make live virus either. He just took the opportunity to steal a couple of DNA fragments for his own ambitious ends. That stopped him reporting the finding and blinded him to the consequences should he be found out — and he was — but I think he probably did destroy the fragments he didn't need.'

'So there's no danger to anyone?'

'Maybe we should reserve judgement on that until we see what Porton comes up with, but I'd bet a month's salary against them finding live smallpox virus in any of the tubes.'

'Call off the police guard on Sandra?'

'I think so,' said Dewar.

'All right if we question her tomorrow about the accident?'

'Sure.'

'And the Iraqis?'

'MI5 are calling the shots on that one.'

* * *

Dewar checked his watch. It was 3 a.m. The streets were quiet and the wind had dropped. He left the infirmary and crossed the top of Forest Road on his way back to the car. As he did so he caught sight of someone about fifty metres to his left stepping back into the shadows. He smiled; it would be one of Barron's people keeping watch on the Iraqi students' association. At least it wasn't raining.

Dewar paused as he reached the car. He still had to decide whether he should drive back to North Berwick or stay the night at his hotel instead. If he went back to Karen's mother's place it would mean waking up Karen – or, worse still, Karen's mother. That and the earlier embarrassing scene swung him in favour of the hotel. It was the easy way out but he was too tired to take on any other.

Dewar called Karen first thing in the morning. 'It was after three when I left the hospital,' he explained. 'I didn't want to wake anyone up.'

'Very thoughtful,' said Karen coolly. 'And now you're going to tell me you're going to be tied up all day?'

'Certainly not,' replied Dewar, sounding aggrieved.

'I thought we might take Mother out to lunch.'

'Good idea,' said Dewar, trying to sound convincing.'

'Good. And we are going to be on our best behaviour, aren't we?'

'Yes, dear.'


As Karen had predicted, her mother said no more about the events of the previous evening. Dewar was so relieved that he allowed her to rant without interruption all through lunch at the Grey Walls Hotel in nearby Gullane. He permitted himself only a slight raise of the eyebrows occasionally in Karen's direction, so that she would raise her napkin to her mouth, covering a smile with a pretended cough.

Dewar stayed overnight and went for a walk along the beach

with Karen on the following morning. Despite a blustery wind and white horses on the waves they stayed out for nearly two hours, during which they decided they would travel back to London together after Dewar had been up to the hospital in Edinburgh to see Sandra Macandrew one last time.

'So the danger's past?' said Karen.

'For the moment,' agreed Dewar. 'But it does seem likely that the Iraqis have managed to get their hands on most — maybe even all — of the DNA fragments they'd need to make live virus.'

'Presumably that would be much harder now with everyone on their guard,' said Karen.

'Let's hope so,' said Dewar.

On the following Wednesday, Dewar saw a copy of the report from Porton Down. He had been called into the offices of Sci Med to discuss it with Macmillan. The people at Porton had been working round the clock and had succeeded in identifying several tubes containing DNA from the smallpox virus. Only two tubes were found to contain DNA not registered to be held by the Institute of Molecular Sciences. Dewar checked their identity. They were the exact two fragments that the people in Malloy's lab had wanted to continue their research on an AIDS vaccine, the two that Le Grice said he'd taken from those left by Hammadi.

'This more or less confirms what Le Grice told Sandra Macandrew,' said Dewar. 'He really must have destroyed the other fragments as he said. All he was interested in were the ones he needed for his research.'

'Good,' said Macmillan. 'There's an end to it.'

'Have you heard anything from MI5 about Siddiqui and Abbas?' asked Dewar.

Macmillan frowned. 'Nothing, apart from the fact they're still there,' he said.

'Still a worry,' said Dewar.

'Maybe you're reading too much into it,' suggested Macmillan.

'I'd feel a whole lot better if they'd just get the hell out of there.'

'MI5 will continue to monitor their every move and, if they're carrying any of these damned fragments when they do finally leave, we'll be destroying the lot and bringing their actions to the attention of the UN as well as WHO.'

Dewar nodded. He had hoped he'd feel better about the whole affair when Porton came up with their report but somehow, in spite of the fact that they seemed to have confirmed what Le Grice had told Sandra, he didn't. He was in danger of becoming paranoid about the continuing presence of the Iraqis in Edinburgh, but part of that paranoia at least was due to Simon Barron, who'd said at the outset that their behaviour suggested that they were waiting for something. As to what it was, the question remained, and it still haunted him.

Dewar was given the following week off as terminal leave. This was usual when Sci Med staff completed assignments. Although Karen still had to work, they made the most of their evenings together, eating out and seeing shows and generally just being together rather than communicating by telephone.

'I could learn to like this life,' said Karen when they returned to Dewar's flat on Thursday evening after a concert. 'This must be what normal people do.'

'No, they watch television and go to bed early,' said Dewar.

'One of these sounds all right,' said Karen.

'Good to hear it.'

'I was talking about television,' teased Karen. 'Anything on?'

'Nothing at all,' said Dewar, taking her in his arms. 'But I'm afraid we can't have an early night.'

'Why not?'

'It's already gone midnight.'

The phone rang at half past three. Telephones always

seemed louder at that time in the morning, fracturing dreams and silence like an alarm. Dewar fumbled the receiver off the bedside table and brought it clumsily to his ear, half expecting a wrong-number apology. Macmillan was on the other end. 'I'm in my office. I want you over here right now.'

The phone went dead before Dewar had had a chance to say anything at all in reply. He looked at the phone as if *it* were responsible for the incident.

'Something wrong?' asked Karen, who'd rolled over on to her front and was sleepily rubbing her eyes.

'I think that's a safe yes,' replied Dewar. 'But God knows what. That was Macmillan. He wants me over there.'

'I thought it was too good to last,' said Karen pushing her hair back from her face. 'They've got another assignment for you. I knew it.'

Dewar wasn't so sure. 'I've never known one start off with middle-of-the-night dramatics,' he said. 'Something must be awfully wrong if they got Macmillan out of bed at this time in the morning. I don't think I've ever heard him sound so rattled.' He dressed hurriedly and kissed Karen goodbye while checking his pockets for keys and wallet.

He raced through quiet streets, anxiously turning over the conversation with Macmillan in his mind and searching for reasons. A barge was approaching the bridge as he crossed the Thames; its lights seemed friendly in the darkness and the dull monotonous thump of its engine contrasted with the rasp of his own as he accelerated away when the lights changed. He was at the Home Office in under fifteen minutes.

There were four other men in Macmillan's office when he entered: Frobisher, Macmillan's deputy, looking grave, two he didn't recognise but who were introduced as being from the Department of Health and the Public Health Service respectively, and another man he did recognise. It was Hector Wright from the London School of Hygiene and Tropical Medicine, the man who'd briefed him on smallpox at the outset. It was Wright's presence that alarmed Dewar most. His first thought was that there had been some mistake in the report from Porton on the contents of Steven Malloy's lab; they must have come up with something really alarming.

'We've had some very bad news,' said Macmillan.

'About the contents of the tubes?' asked Dewar.

Macmillan looked puzzled, then he understood Dewar's train of thought. 'If only! Worse than that, a lot worse than that,' he said. 'There's a case of smallpox in Edinburgh.'

Dewar felt as if he'd been hit in the stomach. Then he started to feel stupid and finally angry. In spite of all the protests he'd heard about no one being irresponsible enough to attempt reconstruction of live smallpox virus, it now appeared that one of them had actually done it.

'Are you absolutely sure?' he asked.

'There's no doubt,' continued Macmillan. 'A twenty-six-year-old man. He's been in the city's Western General for over a week; they didn't know what was wrong with him at first but they do now. They've done all the tests and they're positive; he's been moved to the hospital's isolation suite.'

Dewar tried to think who at the institute might fit the patient's description but his mind was doing cartwheels. He couldn't concentrate. 'Which one of them's gone down with it?' he asked.

'It gets worse,' said Macmillan. 'The patient is not one of the institute staff. As far as we can ascertain, he has no connection with the institute at all.'

Dewar couldn't believe his ears. 'But there must be a connection,' he protested.

'You'd think so,' agreed Macmillan. 'Common sense demands it but if it's there, we can't find it.'

'Our people have drawn a complete blank,' said the Public Health official.

'So who is this man?'

Macmillan read from the sheet of paper in front of him. 'Michael Patrick Kelly, aged twenty-six, currently unemployed, last job, site labourer for J.M. Holt and Sons, known to the police, one conviction for theft, two more for drugs-related offences. Divorced four years ago, current partner, Denise Banyon, also known to the police, drugs offences. They live in the Muirhouse district of the city, an area of high unemployment and drug problems.'

'But there just has to be a connection with the institute,' insisted Dewar, although he had to admit that it wasn't blindingly obvious.

'Can you see it?'

'Not at first glance,' conceded Dewar. 'Maybe he has friends at the institute.' The doubting glances became infectious. 'All right, I agree, doesn't seem likely. Maybe he carried out some work there. What does this firm, Holt and Sons, do?'

'The people on the ground up there looked at that,' said the man from the DOH. 'They're house builders. That's all they do. They've never done any kind of contract work for the university.'

'Well you said he's unemployed at the moment. Maybe he's been working as a window cleaner,' suggested Dewar, clutching at straws.

'They're looking into that sort of thing at the moment,' said Macmillan. 'Getting information from the circle of people he moves in isn't proving easy.'

'I can imagine,' said Dewar.

'You don't know the half of it. This is going to be a public-health nightmare. Can you imagine what isolating the contacts is going to be like when most of them are antisocial drug addicts?'

'It's got to be done,' said Wright, speaking for the first time.

'Easier said than done,' said the DOH man.

'You've got to get these contacts off the street,' said Wright. 'You've got to isolate them and then vaccinate everyone else for miles around.'

'I think we have to leave the logistics of the operation up to the people on the spot,' said the DOH man.

'Christ, I hope they know what they're doing,' said Wright, whose intensity was making everyone else in the room feel uncomfortable. This included Dewar, but he felt uncomfortable for a different reason. He understood that Wright knew what he was talking about. If he was afraid of the consequences of screwing up the public-health operation, there was every good reason for everyone else to feel the same way, if only they knew it.

'Have these people ever been involved in something like this before?' asked Wright.

'They were involved in the *E. coli* outbreak last year.'

'There's no comparison!' exploded Wright. 'Most people could sprinkle *E. coli* on their cornflakes and neither be up nor down. It's only the old and infirm it's a major problem for. It's not in the same league as smallpox when it comes to killing people.'

'I don't think there's any need to overdramatise the situation, Dr Wright,' said the man from the ministry.

'Over dra—' exploded Wright. 'Sonny, we are talking about the most deadly disease the world has ever known.'

'We've put in a request for vaccine,' said Macmillan, attempting to defuse the situation.

'You mean they don't have any up there?' asked Dewar.

'Or anywhere else, apparently,' replied Macmillan. 'Large stocks haven't been kept routinely for some years.'

Wright shook his head and cursed under his breath. 'The WHO hold the only substantial stocks of it. It'll have to come from Geneva. More time wasted. Shit!'

'Do we know what strain of smallpox it is?' asked Dewar.

Macmillan looked down at his desk before saying, 'I understand it's been typed as variola major.

'The worst kind,' said Wright. Fifty per cent mortality.'

'So we'll have to isolate all Kelly's contacts and establish the link between Kelly and the institute,' said Dewar. 'Anything else would be an unbelievable coincidence.'

'I'm glad you see it that way,' said Macmillan. 'Because that's what you're going back up there to establish.'

# — *Fifteen* —

'**D**o I work alone?' asked Dewar. He had a hollow feeling in his stomach. Wright's presence had brought back to him all the man had said about smallpox.

'You'll have your usual autonomy in terms of independence of action,' said Macmillan, 'but you'll be attached to the major-incident team that's being set up to handle the problem. The team will be based at a command centre in the Scottish Office building in Leith, the so-called Port of Edinburgh. Conveniently, it's in the north of the city and just to the east of Muirhouse, where the problem is centred. It's also quite near to where the Western General Hospital is. The team will comprise medical experts, public-health people, police and government represent-atives. More experts will be co-opted as necessary. It's very much a hands-on team. Politicians will be taking a back seat. I need hardly add that time is against us in all of this.'

Dewar turned to Wright and asked, 'Are you going to be involved?' Wright shook his head and looked down at the table in front of him. 'Why not? You are the leading expert on this disease by all accounts and one of the few people who've actually worked with it.'

'I haven't been asked,' replied Wright flatly, but there was no mistaking the resentment in his body language.

The DOH man moved uncomfortably in his seat. 'No slight

was intended to Dr Wright, I assure you, but we have what we feel is an excellent team in place.'

Dewar recognised this as ministry doublespeak for 'Wright's not one of us'.

He disagreed that any team could be described as excellent when the leading expert in the field had been deliberately excluded. He turned to Macmillan and said, 'You did say more experts could be co-opted as required.'

Macmillan, seeing what was coming, shrugged his cautious agreement.

'I'd like to request that Dr Wright be invited to join if he's agreeable. As a Sci Med associate if that makes things easier for the paperwork.'

'It's all right with me,' said Macmillan.

'I can think of nicer things to happen to me,' said Wright. 'But all right, count me in.'

'Any other requests?' asked Macmillan.

'I'd like to request the attachment of two more people,' said Dewar.

'Before you even start?'

'You said time was against us. I'd like Dr Steven Malloy's help in establishing the institute connection. He doesn't have a lab any more, thanks to me, so he's got time on his hands and he's an insider. I'd also like to use the same police contact as before, Inspector Ian Grant. We get on.'

'I'll see to it,' said Macmillan. 'You're on the first shuttle up to Edinburgh.'

'I'll have to join you later,' said Wright. 'I'll have to square things with my wife. It's our anniversary tomorrow.'

'How long?'

'Eighteen years.'

Dewar turned to Macmillan. 'I take it the press haven't cottoned on to this yet or we would have heard?'

'It's a case of so far so good,' replied Macmillan. 'Kelly

leading the life he does, not having a GP or any regular family, has made it easier to keep his condition under wraps, but, let's face it, sooner or later they're going to smell a rat. The use of the isolation suite at the hospital begs its own questions.'

'Do we know anything about Kelly's condition at the moment?'

'It's grave,' replied Macmillan. 'He was pretty ill by the time he was admitted, not that even modern medicine can do anything about the progress of the disease. But one of the major problems is that he's beyond answering questions about his movements before he caught the disease.'

'What about his partner? I've forgotten her name.'

'Denise Banyon. She thought he'd fallen ill because of a bad fix, as she put it.'

'She thought his condition was a reaction to drugs?' exclaimed Dewar.

'Apparently.'

'That was a bit of luck, but what did they tell her when they put her into isolation too?' asked Dewar.

'No information,' said Macmillan. He looked to the others, who shook their heads. 'But illness isn't at all uncommon among drug addicts; it goes with the territory, particularly in Edinburgh, AIDS capital of Europe and all that.'

'Maybe it could be made to work in our favour,' suggested Dewar. 'We can probably get away with calling it hepatitis for a while. Then there's the social factor on our side too.'

Eyebrows were raised.

'Nobody gives a damn what happens to drug addicts anyway,' Dewar explained. 'There's a largely unspoken belief among the general public that they're getting exactly what they deserve. The paparazzi aren't liable to be queuing up at the door and the hospital won't be required to post daily bulletins on the gates.'

'Be that as it may, this is likely to be a very temporary

window,' said Wright. 'The disease may have started in the drug-taking community but it's unlikely to stay there. Small-pox has no sense of social order; it's no respecter of persons; it'll kill anybody and everybody.'

'Then let's do our best to see that it doesn't get the chance, gentlemen,' said Macmillan. With that, the meeting ended.

Dewar lingered for a few minutes outside on the pavement with Hector Wright. 'What d'you think of the chances of containing it as an isolated case?' asked Dewar.

'Nil,' replied Wright without hesitation. 'In these circum-stances, not a snowball's chance in hell.'

Dewar drove back slowly to his apartment through drizzly rain. Milk floats were already on the move. There wouldn't be time to crawl back into bed with Karen and seek a last loving cuddle before the night ended. He wouldn't be able to accuse her of stealing all the covers in his absence and she wouldn't get a chance to complain about his cold feet. To his, almost poignant, regret, a new day had already begun.

He had packed his bag and checked the contents of his pockets for the second time before Karen stirred and realised he was up and dressed.

She sat up in bed, looking alarmed. 'What is it?' she asked. 'Where are you going?'

'Smallpox has broken out in Edinburgh. Just one case at the moment. I'm going back.'

'God, that's awful, but why you?'

'They want me to establish the link between the patient and that damned institute.'

'You mean it's not obvious? It's not one of the staff?'

'It's some unemployed junkie who lives on the other side of the city from the institute, would you believe?'

'You're kidding.'

'I wish.' Dewar shook his head and told her about Kelly.

'What a nightmare,' said Karen.

'It's all too easy to draw pictures, isn't it?' agreed Dewar.

'Oh my God, you will be careful, won't you?'

'Of course,' Dewar assured her. 'I've been vaccinated.'

'They can't vaccinate you against a knife in the ribs, or HIV or Hep C. Addicts are bad news.

'I'll be fine.' Dewar sat down on the edge of the bed and cuddled Karen tightly, suddenly very conscious of the softness of her hair. 'I'll call you later.'


DAY ONE

Dewar had to admit he was impressed with the coordination centre at the Scottish Office. It had been designed as a command centre for times of national emergency without being specific over what kind was envisaged. It was sited in the basement of the building, and not only were its conference rooms and communications facilities the best he'd come across, but living quarters had been prepared on the floor above for those members of the team who wanted to use them. He was going to be one of them; he put Hector Wright down for a room as well.

He expressed his admiration to the government official who had been showing him around and who was in charge of seeing the team had everything they needed.

'They're pulling out all the stops on this one,' confided the official. 'They see this affair as a huge potential embarrassment. They want it cleared up as quickly as possible. Between you and me that's why I suspect they're not putting politicians in charge.'

Dewar smiled but he could see another reason why politicians were not going to be running the show. They'd be more keen on distancing themselves from it. If and when the public realised that smallpox had returned to stalk the community, the embarrassing question of where it had come from would be raised and the press would not be slow in pointing out that for once, this could not be dismissed as 'just one of those things'. Mother Nature would not be conveniently shouldering the blame as she had so often in the past. If smallpox didn't officially exist any more, it had to have escaped from some laboratory. There would be no way of passing the buck. Britain would be held responsible for reintroducing the disease to the world.

Dewar was told that there would be a meeting of the team at 2.30 in the afternoon. The medics and public-health people were currently out, doing their thing, and, as it was still only 10.15, Dewar got settled into his room and called Steven Malloy.

'I've just been talking to a man named, Macmillan,' said Malloy.

'Then you know what this is all about. I need your help. How about it?'

'In the circumstances I can hardly say no,' said Malloy. 'But it sounds positively bizarre.'

'Macmillan told you about Kelly?'

'An unemployed smack-head living in Muirhouse. It's crazy.'

'Crazy, it might be but I just can't believe it's any kind of coincidence. There just has to be a connection with what's been going on at the institute and your lab in particular. Hammadi and Le Grice are both dead, so what's your best guess?'

'There's still no evidence that anyone at all tried to resurrect smallpox here, so how could anyone catch it if it doesn't exist?'

'But it does exist,' said Dewar. 'A man's dying from it, so, for the moment, let's work on the assumption that it did come from the institute.'

'Assuming for the sake of argument that it did,' said Malloy, 'I think the first thing we have to work out is how this guy from Muirhouse got his hands on it.'

'Agreed.'

Malloy came up with the same sort of suggestions that Dewar

had made earlier in London about Kelly's possible employment in some kind of casual way at the institute – cleaner, porter, messenger.

'It's going to be difficult to check without being able to ask him personally,' said Dewar.

'I'll have a look at what records the institute keeps.'

Dewar told him about the meeting at two thirty. They arranged to meet for lunch first in a pub in Rose Street at Malloy's suggestion.

Dewar called Grant at police headquarters. Macmillan had already been in touch with him too.

'I heard last night the shit had hit the fan,' said Grant. 'I was half expecting you to call. The division has been put on full alert – ostensibly for possible trouble in the Muirhouse area. For the moment we're operating a need-to-know policy. Officers selected for duty are being screened discreetly for vaccination history. Only those with recorded smallpox protection are being deployed in the area.'

'Doing what?'

'Riding shotgun on the public-health people as they go about their business.'

'Tell me about the area. Bad?'

'The pits. Officially we wouldn't admit it but we've settled for the status quo. As long the smack-heads stay put we don't interfere too much. Some parts of that estate make Bosnia look like Disneyland. If you folks are thinking of appealing to the druggie denizens' better nature, don't. It isn't an option; they don't have one. They're either stoned out their heads or doing whatever's necessary to get the stuff to get themselves stoned out their heads. Nothing else matters. Take my word for it. Don't ever get yourself in a position where you have to rely on a junkie, don't believe them and don't ever trust them. Leave it to the bleeding hearts; they never seem to learn. Bloody place is crawling with initiatives for this and initiatives for that, Euromoney, schemes, projects, cooperatives, support groups. Waste of bloody time as far as I'm concerned. Situation's getting worse every day.'

'You're not big on remedial initiatives then?' said Dewar, tongue in cheek.

'Only if they involve napalm,' replied Grant.

'Thanks for the cameo,' said Dewar.

'Why couldn't it have been a responsible church elder from Marchmont who got this fucking thing?' asked Grant from the heart.

'I think getting the answer to that might be down to me,' replied Dewar.

'Some guys get all the good jobs.'

'I don't suppose you've got any idea how this man Kelly could have a connection with the Institute of Molecular Science, have you?' asked Dewar.

'The only way Kelly and his mates could get near a university involves a back window and a crowbar,' replied Grant.

'That's a thought,' said Dewar. 'I hadn't considered burglary. That's a possibility.'

'I was joking.'

'I know but it *is* a possibility. Kelly is a drug addict and he's unemployed. He has to get money for drugs from somewhere so presumably stealing's an option?'

'Option numero uno,' said Grant sourly. 'Do you know how much crime is drug-related these days?'

'My point exactly,' said Dewar. 'So maybe Kelly broke into the institute at some point and contaminated himself in the process?'

'But I thought you told me they didn't have live virus there,' protested Grant. 'Apart from that, what would Kelly have been after? Why cross to the other side of town to break into a place that probably contained nothing he could sell? The only things that go missing from that sort of place are bicycles!

They're pinched from outside. And, last but not least, we've had no report of any break-in at the institute anyway.'

Dewar had to admit that Grant had made a pretty good job of shooting him down in flames. 'Just a thought,' he said.

Dewar met Malloy in the Auld Hundred pub in Rose Street at 12 noon. It was still quiet at that time before the offices started to break for lunch.

'I hope you're going to tell me you've thought of the connection,' said Dewar as he shook Malloy's hand.

'Unfortunately no,' replied Malloy. 'There's no record of Kelly being employed at any time on the portering, cleaning or maintenance staffs. That still leaves window cleaning as a possibility; we contract that out but I really think this idea of contaminating himself accidentally in the institute labs is a non starter.'

'Why?'

'Firstly because it implies that there was something there to contaminate himself with and secondly that it was accessible to a casual intruder. If the people from Porton Down failed to find it and they were highly skilled people actively looking for it, what chance has a casual intruder? I'm convinced the guy got it somewhere else.'

'For me, coincidences don't stretch that far,' said Dewar. 'There's an institute connection somewhere along the line but I take your point. Unfortunately I don't think we're going to get the chance to question Kelly: he's too far gone. We'll have to talk to his friends and associates. See if something strikes a chord.'

'Sounds fun,' said Malloy drily.

'The public-health people should be able to tell us something about that at the meeting this afternoon.'

The chair of the Crisis Management Team was a consultant in infectious diseases from the Western General Hospital named

George Finlay. He was a man in his late forties, grey-haired and thinning on top, wearing a suit that seemed too large for him, particularly at the shoulders. This gave him a slightly lopsided appearance when he leaned on the table with one hand, which he was prone to do while speaking. He introduced the head of Public Health Services for the city, Dr Mary Martin, a woman about ten years younger than Finlay, slim, well-dressed and with the 'big' hair of a much younger woman. She in turn introduced two junior colleagues before handing back to Finlay to introduce Malcolm Rankin, the senior Scottish Office official, assigned to the team to smooth the administrative way.

Rankin's suit fitted perfectly, as did his shirt and tie and everything else about him. He was a man who clearly believed that image was important, thought Dewar as he heard him assure everyone present that he would be available to help in whatever way he could at any time. He introduced two equally charming colleagues who would be dealing with communications and public-relations issues. A silver-haired man wearing the uniform of a police superintendent introduced himself as Cameron Tulloch. Finally Finlay welcomed Dewar and Malloy to the team, telling the others that their particular interest would be in identifying the cause of the outbreak.

'I'll just bring everyone up to date and then we can say what we have to say,' said Finlay. 'Kelly's condition has deteriorated markedly over the past twenty-four hours. His whole body is pustulated and I think we can expect him to die within the next few days. Denise Banyon, his partner, is as yet showing no signs of the disease.'

'It's early days,' said Mary Martin.

'In the normal run of things,' agreed Finlay. 'But when Kelly was brought into hospital his rash was already becoming pustular. This suggested that he'd had the disease for well over a week but Banyon, who had been with him throughout, insists that he developed the disease quite suddenly and that he'd only been ill for a short time when he was admitted.'

'That's possible,' said a voice behind Dewar's shoulder. It was Hector Wright. He was still wearing his overcoat and carrying a travel bag. 'Sorry I'm late.'

Dewar did the introduction and Wright took his seat.

'I'm familiar with your work through your papers, Dr Wright,' said Finlay. 'We're fortunate to have your expertise at our disposal.'

Dewar thought the welcome for Wright formal and polite. It lacked genuine warmth but wasn't outside the normal coolness expected between academics and medical practitioners.'

'You have the better of me,' said Finlay. 'You say there's a way this man could have developed the disease this quickly? Much faster than any of the textbooks suggest?'

'If by any chance he received a massive dose of the virus at the outset, he could have skipped the flu-like stage and pustulated within twenty-four hours,' said Wright.

'And just how would he have done that?' asked Finlay.

'Direct contact with a pure culture of the virus.'

'A pure culture of smallpox virus?' repeated Finlay with a question mark in every syllable.

Dewar looked at Malloy, mutely suggesting that the ball had just landed in his court. Malloy moved his shoulders uneasily but didn't say anything.

Finlay noticed the look that had passed between the two of them and asked of Dewar, 'Would that be an avenue you and your colleagues might be considering, Doctor?'

'One of several,' replied Dewar, unwilling to volunteer more.

Finlay looked as if he might pursue the matter but then decided against it. He said, 'Perhaps before we go any further this would be a good time to define our roles and objectives as team members,' he said.

'Good idea,' said Tulloch.

'Dr Martin and her public-health team are in charge of finding and isolating contacts of Kelly and Banyon. Superintendent Tulloch's men are currently being deployed to see that she can carry out this task without hindrance. A secondary team comprising health workers from surrounding areas, and again supervised by Dr Martin and aided by police where necessary, will carry out a comprehensive vaccination programme in an attempt to contain the disease.

'The isolation and medical treatment of victims of the disease will be my responsibility and that of my people at the Western's high-risk containment unit. Dr Dewar and his colleagues will try to find out just how this situation arose, that is to say, they'll be tracing the source of the outbreak and eliminating it. Mr Rankin and his colleagues will oil the wheels and act as a buffer between ourselves and outside interests.

'I think it's important that we don't step on each other's toes; we should communicate with each other as much as possible. I say this because I suspect there are certain factors connected with this outbreak that I know nothing about and no one has seen fit to tell me as yet. I can only guess that the reappearance of a virus I and my colleagues believed to be extinct may have something to do with some scientific accident or other, although I was given to believe that no live smallpox existed outside certain secure establishments, none of which were in this country.'

There was a short silence in the room before Dewar, understanding Finlay's resentment, said, 'The escape of an unlicensed source of virus is a possibility, Doctor, but we don't know yet if that's the case. I assure you, I'm holding nothing back. That's as much as we know at the moment.'

'Very well,' said Finlay. 'We'll leave it at that for now. Are there any questions so far?'

Dewar said, 'As it sounds like interviewing Kelly is not going to be possible, I'd like to talk to Denise Banyon on the grounds that I've got to start looking for the source somewhere.'

'We've already talked to her at length,' said Mary Martin.

'Frankly, she was uncooperative. No help at all.'

'Uncooperative?'

'She has an inherent dislike of authority and doesn't hesitate to show it but she genuinely didn't seem to know anything about Kelly's movements. The life they lead is like that. He'd apparently be out with his friends all day, leaving her behind. She'd no idea what they were up to and didn't really care as long as he had enough money for her drugs at the end of it.'

'Did she come up with the names of any of these friends he spent his days with?'

'A few but they're vague: Eddie, Jimmy, that sort of thing.'

'Addresses?'

'I think the term "no fixed abode" was the bottom line for many. Pubs and snooker clubs are a better bet.'

'How are you managing to keep her in isolation, by the way?' Dewar asked Finlay. 'She's a drug addict herself, isn't she?'

Finlay nodded. 'She's on methadone – a prescribed substitute for heroin. I think with Kelly out of the running she saw a regular supply of this and free board and lodgings as her best option for the moment.'

'I think I'd still like to speak to her,' said Dewar.

'All right with me,' said Mary Martin. 'I wish you luck.'

'You can come back with me to the hospital if you like,' said Finlay. 'Any more questions?'

Hector Wright asked, 'How many people can your high-risk unit cope with?'

'Eight, maybe ten at a push.'

'Then what?'

'We're rather hoping it doesn't come to that,' said Finlay. Mary Martin nodded her agreement.

'I think you should give it some thought,' said Wright.

His comment made people feel uncomfortable. Finlay had been promoting a positive outlook. Wright had introduced a negative note.

'The irony is they've just closed our infectious-disease hospital here in Edinburgh,' said Finlay. 'The powers that be decided we didn't need it any more. Suddenly we're a bit pushed for that kind of accommodation. If necessary we could open up a couple of wards that have been shut down to save money in the Western, but they wouldn't exactly be tailor-made for the job.'

'Totally unsuitable, I would have thought,' said Wright, speaking his mind but making no friends in the process. 'If you're talking about old-style Nightingale wards. Barns with beds in them.'

'No one envisaged smallpox returning,' was Finlay's barbed reply.

'How about nursing staff trained in barrier nursing and ID techniques?'

'We have a few. Mainly those who moved down to the Western when the City Hospital closed. But they stopped the fever training register many years ago.'

'Medical staff experienced in infectious diseases?' asked Wright.

'The City always dealt with that sort of thing. Two of their consultants took early retirement when it closed down. A third went abroad. My people here have had training, of course.'

Wright didn't say anything but his silence irked Finlay. 'Good God, man, how many doctors these days have ever come across smallpox?' he snapped. 'We'll all just have to do our best and get on with it.'

Wright nodded, as if taking the point. He said, 'I'm just trying to make sure that no one's underestimating what we're up against. I think we should be looking ahead and planning accordingly. If we wait for things to happen first it'll be too late.'

'Too late?'

'Deaths in the city could run into five figures.'

It was suddenly clear that people at the table thought Wright had flipped. Whereas before they had been listening in silence with serious expressions, they now broke into smiles and shakes of the head.

'Come, come, Doctor, don't you think you're being a little melodramatic?' said Finlay. 'I appreciate you're an expert on the disease but we've had a few smallpox outbreaks in the past in this country in the last sixty years and they've passed without anything like the numbers you're suggesting.'

'That's because the vast majority of the population at the time had been vaccinated against the disease almost as soon as they were born. Things are different now. Mass vaccination stopped in the seventies, well over a quarter of a century ago. The people of this city are as vulnerable to smallpox as any community in the middle ages.'

The laughter stopped.

'How is your vaccination programme coming along, Dr Martin?' Finlay asked.

'We've not been able to start it,' replied Mary Martin. 'We haven't received any vaccine yet.'

# ~ *Sixteen* ~

'Any idea what the hold-up with the vaccine is?' asked Finlay as he drove back to the hospital, taking Dewar with him.

'It has to come from the WHO stores in Geneva,' replied Dewar. 'But all the same, I thought it would have been sent by now as a priority. I take it you had enough for key workers?'

'They've all been done,' Finlay confirmed. 'But the sooner we get public vaccination under way the better.'

'Amen to that,' said Dewar.

The drive from the Scottish Office in Leith to the Western General in Finlay's Range Rover took less than ten minutes. Finlay parked his car in a spot that Dewar noticed had his name on it, one of the perks of being a consultant in a profession that regarded feudalism as a virtue, he thought.

The high-risk containment unit was not advertised as such on any of the direction boards they passed on foot, but through a process of elimination Dewar worked out that they were making for something called, the 'Wellcome Trust Suite'.

'Age of the sponsor,' said Finlay. 'The Wellcome Trust put up the money.'

The Wellcome Trust Suite turned out to be a long, low, modern building, standing on its own near the western perimeter of the hospital. At first glance, Dewar thought it could have been anything from a physiotherapy unit to an admin block, but as they got closer he saw that it was fitted with windows that did not open and a door with an electronic lock and entryphone system. There was also an absence of pipework on the outside of the building and a further visual inspection of the roof showed that the ventilators were rather more complicated than an office block might require. Dewar knew that they would contain a comprehensive filter system to ensure that nothing from inside the building escaped to the outside. All air inside would be sterilised and filtered before venting.

Finlay opened the door with an electronic card and said, 'The changing area is along here.' He led the way to a room where Dewar was handed a white coverall suit. Both men changed in silence.

'Perhaps you'd like to take a look at Kelly before you meet Miss Banyon?' Finlay asked.

'Might as well,' replied Dewar after a moment's thought. 'If only to see what we're dealing with.'

He did up the top flap of his suit and followed Finlay along the corridor and through a negative-pressure airlock. Finlay opened a door to his left and said, 'There's an observation window in here.'

The room was small and quite dark. Finlay did not put on the light. There was a glass panel in the back wall. Light from the adjoining room was coming in through it. Dewar joined Finlay in looking through to where the patient, Kelly, was lying on his back, motionless. He had been expecting the worst but the sight that met his eyes still made him gasp slightly. Kelly's skin was covered in rough pustules to such an extent that skin itself was scarcely visible. Against the white of the sheets he looked like an unwrapped Egyptian mummy.

'Not a pretty sight,' said Finlay.

Dewar looked on in silence as a nurse, dressed in a Racal 'spacesuit', tended to the man. Her visor and gloves made fluid motion difficult but she was obviously adapting well to the problems and had slowed the speed of her hand movements to match the limitations of the suit. She was doing her best to clean up the pustulation round the man's eyes with cotton wool swabs and saline. Her biggest problem was that the pustulation wasn't only around the eyes: it was actually *in* them. He remembered what Wright had said about patients who recovered from the disease often being blind. 'Poor bastard,' he whispered.

'Seen enough?'

Dewar nodded.

Denise Banyon was not in bed. She was sitting in a chair watching television and smoking a cigarette. She turned away from the children's programme she was engrossed in when Finlay entered.

'Denise, this is Dr Dewar. He'd like to ask you a few questions.'

'I'm fed up answering bloody questions. I've been here long enough. I want out this bloody rabbit hutch. I wanna see my friends.'

Dewar smiled politely. He was looking at a woman in her twenties who could have passed for early forties. She was painfully thin and markedly roundshouldered with straight, lank hair that rested on bony shoulders, exposed unselfconsciously in the nightdress she was wearing. She tucked her bare feet underneath her on the chair and went back to watching television.

Finlay looked at Dewar and shrugged.

'I won't keep you long, Miss Banyon,' said Dewar, taking over. 'It really is rather important I talk to you. I'd be very grateful for your help.'

Denise looked at him balefully then, pleased at being treated like a lady, she said, 'Five minutes. No more.'

Finlay smiled and backed out of the room, leaving Dewar

alone with Denise.

'How are you feeling?' Dewar asked.

'Bored bloody stiff.'

'At least if you're bored, you're not ill,' said Dewar. 'And that's the main thing.'

'Course I'm not ill. Mike's the one who's bloody ill. Have they found out what's wrong with 'im yet?'

'They're not quite sure,' lied Dewar. 'What d'you think's wrong with him?'

'I keep telling them. He took some bad stuff. It happens.'

'Tell me about it. What happened exactly?'

Denise shrugged and took a final drag from her cigarette before stubbing it out nervously. The process seemed to go on for longer than it needed.

'He was OK when he came home at teatime but about nine o'clock he went all pale and started sweating, said he was feeling like shit. He went to bed but when I went through later he was shivering like he was cold but he wasn't; he was burning up and he couldn't speak and he had this rash on his face like he'd grazed it or somethin'.'

'Had he taken drugs between teatime and then?' Denise nodded. 'He'd injected?' Another nod. 'You'd taken something too?'

'Sure.'

'But you didn't share the needle?'

'I'm on methadone. You take it by mouth.'

'Where did Mike get the stuff you think was bad?'

Denise's eyes hardened. 'You're some kind of cop!' she spat.

Dewar tried reassuring her that he wasn't but to no avail. Her demeanour had changed in an instant.

'Oh yes, you bloody are. Yer all the fucking same, think you can con us with a few soft words, then bang, in comes the question about what you're really after. Well you're getting fuck all out o' me so fuck off, you English prick!'

'Denise, I might be an English prick but I'm not a cop. Promise.'

'Fuck off.'

Dewar gave it one last try. 'Denise, I'm a doctor, not a policeman. I work at the university . . . in the Institute of Molecular Sciences,' he lied, hoping to salvage at least something from the interview and see if there was a response to the name.

Denise looked at him blankly. 'Are you deaf?' she said. 'Fuck off!'

Dewar left the room and went off in search of Finlay.

'How'd you get on?'

'Not brilliantly,' confessed Dewar. 'She seemed to think I was a policeman out to trap her.'

'Paranoia's all part of the game when you're dealing with addicts,' said Finlay. 'If Jesus Christ himself were to give them a kind word they'd think he had an angle. Don't take it personally.'

'That's not what's worrying me. I didn't even get to the first question I wanted to ask her. I thought I was passing the time of day with her, trying to gain her confidence when she flew off the handle. I knew she thought Kelly's illness had something to do with drugs so I thought she'd be keen to let off steam about the supplier. How wrong can you be?'

'Maybe you'll have better luck with some of the contacts Mary Martin's team have been coming up with.'

'Let's hope so.'

'Want me to call you a taxi?'

Dewar shook his head. 'I'll walk for a bit first.'

The light was already fading fast as Dewar left the grounds of the hospital and crossed the road. Sea fog was rolling in from the Forth about a mile to the north and traffic was already building in the run-up to rush hour.

He felt depressed about his failure to establish any kind of meaningful contact with Denise Banyon and tried to analyse it, feeling that it was important to understand what had gone wrong. He was unused to dealing with drug addicts yet it looked as if he was going to be dependent on them for information. His start with Denise did not bode well.

Despite Finlay's dismissal of her behaviour as par-for-the-course paranoia, he wasn't so sure. Maybe he had accidentally touched a raw nerve when he asked who had supplied Kelly with the drugs she imagined were to blame for Kelly's condition. Come to think of it, why did she believe that anyway? he wondered. She was an addict herself. She must have seen a lot of bad trips in her time, seen a lot of her friends go down with AIDS and hepatitis and septicaemia and infected needle sites. What made her think in this instance that Kelly's illness was drugs-related? No answer was forthcoming as he reached a busy intersection.

To his left, the concrete blocks of the Muirhouse housing estate sprawled out to the west where the last light of the day was now a narrow band in the sky. A bus shelter across the road had graffiti on its one remaining glass panel. It said FUCK EVERYBODY. For a moment Dewar thought about the virus at large in the estate. 'It just might,' he murmured before turning away to the right.

He was now in Ferry Road, the main thoroughfare that ran along Edinburgh's northern edge. He flagged down the first taxi with its sign lit up and returned to the Scottish Office.

Dewar found Hector Wright poring over a map of the Muirhouse area in one of the basement rooms. He looked like a general planning a campaign. He was drawing a circle on the map using as its centre a flag marker that sat on the flats where Kelly and Denise Banyon lived.

'Any luck?' asked Wright.

'I blew it,' said Dewar. 'She told me to fuck off.'

Wright smiled and said, 'Women have been telling me that all my life.'

Dewar smiled at the sympathetic comment and asked what Wright was up to.

'Working out vaccination schedules, primary, secondary, tertiary. It's a bit like digging ditches round a forest fire. You hope the first ditch will hold it but you never rely on one alone. If we can vaccinate everyone in this inner circle within three days we might just manage to contain it in the area with only limited spread outside the line. Vaccinating everyone in the secondary area should slow it further and doing people in the tertiary area should confine the spread to travellers.'

'I suppose that's the one plus to having the outbreak in this area,' said Dewar. 'People tend not to travel much. They stay put.'

Wright nodded but added, 'That's only true right now. Once the cat's out of the bag and the shit really hits the fan we could be looking at several thousand people who've just discovered they've got the gypsy in their soul.'

'What a thought,' said Dewar, imagining scenes of mass panic.

'It's all going to hang on how many people we can get vaccinated before the truth gets out. We need that damned vaccine soon.' Dewar nodded. 'And we have to get more contacts off the streets!'

'It's finding them that seems to be the problem,' said Dewar. 'You heard what Mary Martin said. Vague information involving first names and pubs. It's like trying to trace the origin of things that fell off the back of a lorry.'

'That reminds me: Mary Martin left this for you. One of her people says that Kelly was a regular in this pub. They didn't have much luck. She thought you might like to try yours.'

Dewar took the piece of paper. It said, 'The Bell Tavern, Salamander Street'. 'I'll give it a try.'

'Want some company?'

Dewar considered for a moment. 'A kind thought,' he said.

'But two men asking questions smacks of officialdom. I'll go alone.'

'Please yourself. Are we going to eat first?'

'Sure. I just have a couple of calls to make first.'

Dewar went up to his room and called Simon Barron on his mobile number. 'What's happening?' he asked.

'Zilch,' replied Barron. 'All the action seems to be at your end. All our boys ever do is nip round the corner to have coffee at the Bookstop Café and then it's back to the student centre.'

'So they're still there?'

'Still waiting by the look of it.'

'You have seen both of them? Not just Abbas?'

'Siddiqui and Abbas and two students were at the café this afternoon. They stayed for about forty minutes. The girl who runs the place treats them like regulars now.'

'I know this must be bloody boring for you and your men but it's absolutely vital that they keep tabs on Siddiqui and his pal over the coming week. All hell could break loose.'

'So I understand. If it's any comfort, there's a contingency plan for dealing with the Iraqis should they threaten the containment of the incident.'

Dewar chose not to ask what this meant in practice but he could guess. When he'd finished speaking to Barron he called Karen.

'How are things?' she asked.

'Not good. Still only one confirmed case but they've only managed to isolate one contact — Kelly's partner, Denise Banyon. Worst of all, no vaccine has turned up yet. The words "knife" and "edge" spring to mind.'

'Let's hope Kelly and Denise were a couple of stay-at-homes,' said Karen.

Dewar and Wright ate in one of the many waterfront bistros that had sprung up in the last five years in Leith. The area was undergoing a transformation: the run-down tenements and warehouses of yesteryear — the typical environs of any docks area of a major city — were giving way to trendy new apartment blocks and chic cafés and shops. The transformation, however, was not as yet complete. Old Leith and its inhabitants were still there, eyeing the designer-clad newcomers with unease and suspicion and disguising it as wry amusement. This in itself gave the area a certain exciting ambience. Pleasure was always heightened when a dash of uncertainty was added.

The Bell Tavern was located in a street which had so far escaped the attentions of the developers. It was as it had been since the early part of the century and before. One side of the street comprised bonded warehouses, their blackened stone-work and iron-barred windows preventing views of the docks themselves, the other side, lines of dark stone tenement buildings. The Bell Tavern was on the corner of one of these buildings.

Dewar's first impression was that it was lit by a candle, his second that the air inside had been replaced by tobacco smoke. He asked for a large whisky.

'Kind?' asked the barman. His minimum wording matched his expression. It wasn't hostile, it wasn't friendly. It wasn't anything.

Dewar glanced at the gantry. 'Laphroaig.'

The glass was placed down in front of him, the money taken and change returned, all without expression or comment from the barman, who went back to his conversation with two customers at the other end of the bar.

Dewar added a little water to his whisky from the jug on the bar top and looked around him. He supposed that this might once have been called 'a working man's pub' but his guess now was that it was more of an unemployed or old man's pub.

He was very much aware of the lack of colour in the place, an impression heightened by the bad lighting. The walls were beige and brown and the ceiling a dirty yellow from years of nicotine attack. The clientele almost universally wore dark clothes. The overall effect was of an old photograph, a sepia-tint picture of the past.

'You've got good taste in whisky,' said a voice at his elbow.

Dewar turned to find a smiling man in his sixties, about a foot shorter than he, dressed in a coarse black suit and wearing a cap at an angle to the side. His complexion suggested a heart problem but he seemed cheerful enough as he put his empty half-pint glass on the bar.

'You drink it yourself, then?' asked Dewar.

'The days when I could afford malt whisky have long gone, Jimmy,' laughed the man.

'Then you must have one with me,' said Dewar.

The man seemed slightly offended. 'Now dinnae get me wrong. I wisnae suggesting for one minute that—'

'And I didn't think for one minute that you were,' interrupted Dewar. 'I'm a stranger; I'd be glad of the company.'

'In that case then . . .' the man conceded. 'Thanks very much. Name's Bruce, Jackie Bruce.'

Dewar bought Bruce a drink and asked, 'You're local then?'

'And you're not,' said Bruce. 'English?'

'Yes, I'm looking for someone.'

'A relative?'

'Not exactly, his name's Michael Kelly.'

'What's someone like you wantin' with a waster like Kelly?'

'You know him?'

'He comes in here aften enough, him and his mate, Hannan, but the word is, Kelly's in hospital. Drug overdose, somethin' like that. As if these nurse lassies didnae have enough to do without numpties like Kelly adding to it. Junkies! Christ, when I was young, drugs were something you saw the Chinese taking at the pictures. Now you're trippin' over the buggers on every street corner.'

'It's a big problem,' Dewar agreed, taking a sip of his drink. He didn't want to push things along too obviously. 'You mentioned someone called Hannan?'

'Tommy Hannan. Come to think of it, I've no' seen him for a few days either.'

'Is he local?'

'Aye, that's why Kelly comes along here. Tommy stays just round the corner in Jutland Street.'

'Maybe he could tell me how Mike is,' said Dewar.

'If anyone can, Tommy can. These two are thicker than thieves . . . come to think of it, they are thieves!' He let out a cackle of chesty laughter that Dewar joined in. 'You'll have another one?' he asked, seeing that the whisky had disappeared.

'That's very nice of you. It's no' often I can have an intelligent conversation in this place.'

Dewar ordered the drinks and went for the final hurdle. 'You wouldn't happen to know which number in Jutland Street, would you?'

'Sure, he stays in the stair next to my brother. Number thirty-seven.'

'Thanks,' said Dewar, feeling well pleased with himself. He lingered on for a bit, talking about this and that so that Bruce wouldn't be too conscious of the fact he'd been pumped for information. He left shortly after nine thirty.

The air was cool and damp on his face when he emerged from the Bell. but after all the tobacco inside it seemed sweeter than a mountain breeze. The street lights were reflected in puddles on the ground. He hadn't realised it had been raining while he was inside. Now he had to find out what 'round the corner' meant in real geographical terms.

He walked along Salamander Street looking at the street names off to his left but stopped after four hundred yards, feeling he was out of 'round the corner' range. He retraced his steps and started out in the other direction. Jutland Street was the first opening he came to.

There were no names or entryphone tags outside the common entrance to number 37 but, on the other hand, there was no lock on the front door either. It was propped open with a wooden wedge. Dewar entered and found that there was no lighting. He figured this was why the door had been jammed open – to let some light from the lamppost outside filter into the passageway. There was enough light to see that neither of the names on the two ground floor doors was the one he was looking for so he climbed the stairs to the first landing. 'Hannan' was on the second door. It was written in biro pen on a piece of white card and Sellotaped to the wood. Dewar pushed the buzzer.

'Who is it?' asked a female voice from inside.

'My name's Dr Dewar. I'm from the hospital. It's about Michael Kelly,' he lied although it was only a white lie.

The rattle of a chain guard gave way to a creak as the door opened against hinges that needed some attention. 'Mike? What about him. What's the problem?' asked a short woman with spiky hair, wearing jeans and a tight white top.

'Can I speak to Tommy?' said Dewar.

'He's ill. Tell me instead.'

'Ill? What's wrong with him?'

'None o' your bloody business. Now, what the hell do you want?' retorted the woman angrily.

'If Tommy has the same problem as Mike, he's in serious trouble. He could die. Is he here?'

'Who wants to know? Here, are you polis?'

'No, I'm a doctor. All I'm interested in is saving his life,' insisted Dewar.

'It's just a bad trip, that's all,' said the woman. 'He'll get over it. It's no' the first.'

'Can I see him?'

The woman considered for a moment, then stood back

slightly to allow Dewar inside. The flat smelled of onions.

'He's in here.'

Dewar entered a small bedroom where the bed, an old-fashioned double bed with polished wood headboard and bottom panel, took up ninety per cent of the floor space. The woman clicked on the light. It got a groan of protest from the man lying there. His well-muscled upper body was naked white and had a film of sweat on it even though the room was cold. He put up his hand to shield his eyes from the light but Dewar could see enough of the eruption on his face to recognise the rash.

'He's very ill,' he said. 'He's got to go to hospital right now. You may be in danger too.'

'Danger?' exclaimed the woman. 'I don't even take the bloody stuff. As for this silly bugger, he promised me he was coming off too and then what does he go and do to himself? Stupid bastard!'

Dewar called the hospital on his mobile phone and arranged for one of the special ambulances assigned to the Wellcome Trust Suite to come for Hannan.

'Is he going to die?' asked the woman, suddenly regretting her outburst of temper.

'Are you his wife?' Dewar asked.

'Aye, God help me. Three years.'

'Mrs Hannan . . .'

'Don't remind me. My name's Sharon.'

'Sharon, this isn't a drug reaction. Tommy's very ill. You might be affected too. The people at the Western will do their best for him but we need your cooperation. Will you come with us?'

The woman fetched a jacket and put it on without saying anything.

'Maybe you could pack a few things for yourself? Nightdress, toothbrush, that sort of thing.'

Sharon looked at Dewar directly and suddenly he saw the fear and vulnerability in her eyes. All earlier feistiness and bravado had gone.

'Right.'

As they waited for the ambulance to come, Dewar noticed that Sharon's hands were shaking. 'It shouldn't be much longer. Are you OK?' he asked kindly.

Tears welled up in her eyes as she put both hands between clenched knees and hung her head. 'God, I'm scared,' she murmured. 'I don't know what I'm going to do if Tommy dies.'

Dewar put his hand on her shoulder as, somewhere outside, the wail of a siren started to get louder.

'Well done,' said George Finlay to Dewar as they met up in Finlay's office after admitting Tommy Hannan and seeing Sharon settled for the night.

'A bit of luck,' said Dewar. 'And a few whiskies. Apparently Kelly and Hannan were great friends.'

'Why did you want to keep Sharon and Denise apart?' asked Finlay. Dewar had made this request when he arrived in the ambulance with Tommy and Sharon.

'I think Sharon trusts me. I hope she might tell us more about the movements of Kelly and her husband. She might not if Denise Banyon gets to work on her.'

'Good point,' said Finlay.

'You know, it's interesting, said Dewar thoughtfully. 'Sharon Hannan thought her husband's condition was some kind of drug reaction too.'

'Bizarre,' said Finlay.

'But interesting.'

# — *Seventeen* —

DAY THREE

Dewar was wakened at four in the morning. It took him a few
moments to register the phone ringing and adjust to his
surroundings. He'd forgotten where he was. Finlay's voice
brought him quickly back to reality.

'Bad news. It looks like yesterday's lull is over. We've had
seven admissions to the unit during the night. I'm pretty certain
they've all got it.'

'Shit,' murmured Dewar. 'All from Muirhouse?'

'Yes.'

'That's something I suppose.'

'Not unless we get the vaccine very soon. Mary says there's
still no sign of it. She thinks she's being fobbed off every time
she enquires. What are these people playing at?'

'I'll try again to find out,' Dewar assured him.

Dewar went next door to wake Hector Wright and tell him the
news. Wright sat up in bed and rubbed the sleep from his eyes. He
cursed, 'God damn it, I was hoping we might have got through
one more day before this happened. We're now too far behind on
vaccination schedules. Chances are we could completely lose any
possibility of control unless the vaccine comes today.'

'I've told Finlay I'll try and find out what the problem is.

Mary Martin feels she's being given the runaround.'

Wright got out of bed to get dressed while Dewar returned to his room and called Sci Med in London. He spoke to the duty officer on the night desk. 'Any idea why the WHO vaccine hasn't reached Edinburgh yet?' he asked.

'I don't have details but I know Mr Macmillan spoke to Geneva earlier this evening. He was worried about that himself.'

'What did they say?'

'Mr Macmillan didn't say exactly but he was in a foul mood after he'd finished the call — something about being fobbed off with an office boy.'

Dewar looked at his watch and said, 'I'll call him when he comes in at nine.'

'I'll leave a note for him,' said the man.

Dewar found Hector Wright downstairs. He was sitting at a table with his city street map spread out in front of him, tapping his pen nervously on the table while apparently deep in thought.

'Seven more means things have changed,' he said. 'I think we may be forced to admit that it's smallpox we're dealing with. If one gets you seven, seven will get you forty-nine.'

'Actually, one got us eight,' said Dewar. 'You're forgetting about Tommy Hannan.'

'We're going to have to open up a second centre before the end of the week and come clean with the relatives. I don't see how we can avoid it.'

'I've got an awful feeling the vaccine isn't going to be here today,' Dewar confided. 'I haven't spoken to Macmillan yet but something's wrong, I know it is. We can't tell people anything if we haven't anything to offer them. They'll panic. Contacts could spread faster than bad news.'

'If you're really serious about the vaccine not coming then we'll have to go for physical containment,' said Wright. 'There's no other way.'

'You mean seal the whole area off?' asked Dewar almost agog

at the notion of isolating an entire housing estate with thousands of residents.

Wright nodded slowly. 'I can't see any other way of stopping it spreading if we don't have the vaccine. And stop it we must. If we just admit that it's smallpox that people have been going down with there will be a pause of about two days while people talk about it and come to terms with the news. Then they'll start moving out of the affected area. Trains, planes and automobiles will do the rest. Smallpox will be back to roam the planet just like the old times when it regularly killed two million a year.'

'Well, you can try putting that to the team,' said Dewar sounding less than confident of a positive outcome.

'Will you back me up?'

'Yes,' replied Dewar. 'Not because I think it's an attractive idea but because I think you're right: there's no other way. The big question will be, can the police manage it on their own or are we talking military help here?'

'We'll see what Tulloch has to say.'

'What time's the meeting this morning?'

'Finlay said he'd try to get everyone here for nine thirty.'

There was no point in going back to bed. Sleep would be impossible and the dawn wasn't that far away. Dewar decided he would go over to the isolation unit at the Western General at eight. He wanted to talk to Sharon Hannan. He called a taxi at seven thirty.

George Finlay looked exhausted. He'd been up all night with the new admissions. Grey stubble showed on his chin and he was struggling to keep his eyes open.

'There were too many relatives and close contacts to put up in the unit so the public-health people sent out decontamination teams to their houses and apartments; they've taken them back there and given them strict instructions that they are to remain indoors until further notice.'

'Sounds sensible,' said Dewar. 'But will it work?'

'There will be problems,' conceded Finlay. 'Social Services are going to contact them today to provide help and support during a period equal to the incubation time of the disease.'

'Do they know what the disease is?' asked Dewar.

Finlay shook his head and said, 'I thought up a suitably complicated medical term for the condition which, so far, people have been accepting. They're assuming it's some awful new disease.'

'You need sleep,' said Dewar.

'I'll get my head down for a few hours after the meeting,' said Finlay. 'What are you doing here anyway at this time?'

Dewar told him about wanting to speak to Sharon Hannan. 'How's her husband doing?'

'On a downhill slide,' said Finlay. 'Kelly 'll die soon and Hannan won't be that far behind by the look of h. :.'

Sharon was eating cornflakes when Dewar knocked on her door and entered.

She smiled, pleased to see a familiar face, albeit one that had only recently become familiar. 'How's Tommy?' she asked. 'You won't bullshit me like the nurses.'

'He's pretty ill,' admitted Dewar. 'But at least he's in the right place. The doctors and nurses will do all they can for him.'

'Can I see him?'

'Maybe later. Could I ask you some questions, Sharon? It won't take long and it might help a lot.'

'What sort of questions?' Sharon replied, looking suspicious.

'First let me say my only interest is in stopping this awful thing happening to anyone else. I'm not concerned with guilt or blame or criminal charges. I really don't give a damn if any laws have been broken. I just have to get at the truth. I have to understand what happened. OK?' Sharon nodded. 'I promise you that anything you tell me will go no further than this room. Have you ever heard of a place called the Institute of Molecular Sciences?'

Sharon shook her head. 'No, never.'

'It's part of the university.' Another shake of the head. 'Tommy never mentioned it? Or anything about being at the university with Michael Kelly?'

'Never.'

'I know they're no angels. Have either of them broken into any place in the last month?' Sharon's eyes grew sharp. 'I meant what I said,' Dewar reminded her. 'This is between you and me, nobody else.'

'A newsagent's shop. They did it about three weeks ago. Do you want to know where?'

'No,' replied Dewar quickly. 'Tommy told you about this?'

'He had lots of fags in the flat. He was getting rid of them down the pub. I asked him about it. He told me.'

'Anything else?'

Sharon hesitated. Dewar suspected there was more to come. He waited patiently, not wishing to pressurise her.

'Before he got the sack from his job, Mike Kelly helped some guy recover drugs from a stash he had hidden away somewhere. He stole some from the guy when his back was turned. He gave Tommy some.'

'Kelly stole drugs from a dealer?'

'I don't know if the guy was a dealer; I suppose he was but that's what Tommy told me anyway.'

Dewar thought for a moment. Maybe that was why Denise Banyon had jumped down his throat when he'd asked where Kelly had got his drugs. Stealing from a dealer could be a fatal mistake. 'Anything else I should know about, Sharon?'

'Nothing big. The pair of them have been doing odd straight jobs, like, and not telling the Social Security, but everybody does round here.'

'What sort of things?'

'The usual. House removals, bit of rubbish clearance. Tommy painted a fence for a woman along Trinity way, that sort of thing.'

Dewar nodded and said, 'I want you to think carefully again about the university. Are you absolutely certain that it never came up in conversation at any time between Tommy and Michael Kelly.'

'I'm positive,' replied Sharon. I'm sure I would've remembered.'

Dewar smiled and called a halt to the proceedings. 'OK, Sharon. If you do remember anything else, tell one of the nurses to contact me and I'll come and see you,' said Dewar. 'In the meantime, enjoy your breakfast.'

Dewar returned to the Scottish Office and called London. It was ten past nine. He drummed his fingertips on the desk while he waited for Macmillan to come on line.

'Sorry about that. I've just been talking to Geneva on another line,' said Macmillan. This was followed by a pause that made Dewar expect the worst. He wasn't disappointed.

'The vaccine's not coming,' said Macmillan.

Dewar felt as if time had suddenly stopped. He tried convincing himself he had misheard what Macmillan had said but it had been plain enough. 'You can't be serious,' he said.

'I'm afraid I am,' confessed Macmillan quietly. 'The WHO acted on your earlier report that the Iraqis were making serious attempts to get their hands on live smallpox virus. At a joint meeting with a UN advisory body, they acceded to an Israeli request for stocks of vaccine to be administered as a precaution. It's all been used.'

'Jesus Christ, where does that leave us?'

'They've been frantically trying to locate other stocks; that's why they've been playing hard to get.'

'How'd they get on?' asked Dewar sourly.

'They've come up with some but it's in the United States. It's going to take three, maybe four, days to reach you.'

'We don't have that; there were seven new cases last night. We can expect many times that today.'

'I'm sorry. Everyone's doing their best. WHO have instructed the National Institute at Bilthoven in the Netherlands to
recommence vaccine production. They hold the vaccinia seed
virus. They'll be up and running within two weeks.'

Dewar's impulse was to say something rude but he stopped
himself. It wouldn't have done any good and his silence proved
just as eloquent.

'I know, Adam, it's a bloody mess, but we'll just have to get
on with it. Any luck with the source of the outbreak?'

'None at all.'

'Keep trying.'

People had arrived for the meeting when Dewar went
downstairs. Mary Martin congratulated him on his success at
the Bell. 'We didn't have any luck there at all.'

'I just bumped into the right person,' said Dewar. He still felt
numb at the news from London.

Wright read the worried look on his face and came over.
'Something wrong?' he asked in a whisper.

'There won't be any vaccine for three, maybe four, more
days, maybe even longer the way our luck's going,' Dewar
whispered.

'Christ Almighty. What the fuck are they playing at?' hissed
Wright.

Dewar told him about the stocks being used. Wright rubbed
his forehead as if completely bemused by the fickleness of fate.

'I think we're all here,' announced Finlay, bringing the
meeting to order. 'I think everyone knows we now have nine
cases in total and can expect more today; the fear is, many more.
We'll be admitting new cases to one of the unused wards at the
Western and a second is being prepared. As Dr Wright pointed
out earlier, they're not ideal but needs must when the devil
drives. The works department have done their best to partition
them and install extra sinks and drainage and we've managed to
find enough vaccinated nurses to staff them.'

'What about medical equipment?' asked Cameron Tulloch.

'Truth is, we don't need much in the way of equipment for this disease. There's very little we can do except keep the patients as comfortable as possible and hope for the best.'

'What about the contacts? Are they staying there too?'

'There are too many. Contacts will be traced as quickly as Mary and her people can find them and confined to their homes with Social Services support. I think we have to be realistic in recognising that not all of them are going to comply but, if the majority do, that's probably as much as we can hope for.'

'As of this morning, the vaccine still hasn't arrived,' announced Mary Martin, her voice filled with exasperation. 'I can't get any sense out of London. We're trying to fight the spread of this disease with our hands tied behind our backs.'

'The WHO vaccine isn't coming, Mary,' said Dewar quietly and evenly.

The comment brought an instant silence to the room. People looked at each other and then to Dewar for an explanation.

'The WHO have used up their stocks,' he said. 'They've been trying to find an alternative source for us; that's what the hold-up's been. They've found one in the States but it won't be here for another three days at least. That, ladies and gentlemen, is the plain awful truth of the matter.'

Wright took advantage of the fact that most people were stunned by what Dewar had announced. He said, 'That being the case, we now have only one chance of containing the disease and that is to physically isolate it. We must act now to close off Muirhouse from the rest of the city.'

'I agree,' said Dewar emphatically. 'We can't let smallpox go on the rampage in a largely unvaccinated community.'

'But sealing off the area would be an enormous undertaking,' protested Rankin, the Scottish Office man.

'Do you know how many people live there? How many streets in and out there are?' asked Mary Martin. 'People living there already feel a sense of injustice. There would be a revolt.'

'It's either that or a full scale smallpox epidemic,' said Wright. 'And, believe me, everything you've said is preferable to that. If it means calling in the army then do it. If it means putting down riots with guns, do it, but we must contain the outbreak.'

'I don't think it need come to that,' said Cameron Tulloch. 'If things are handled properly.'

'What the hell did the WHO do with the vaccine?' asked a stunned and angry Finlay.

'They sent it to the Middle East. There was a scare,' said Dewar, without volunteering any more information.

'There must be another way of dealing with this,' said Finlay.

'There isn't,' said Wright.

'But what would we tell the people concerned?' said Finlay.

'The truth,' said Dewar, who'd been thinking about that very question. 'We use the media to come clean and tell the citizens there's been an outbreak of smallpox and that we're trying to contain it. We ask for their help and cooperation.'

'I agree with that,' said Tulloch. 'It would be lunacy to even contemplate sealing off the area without giving people a reason. They would start making up their own reasons and the rumours would be worse than the reality.'

'We'd be kidding ourselves if we imagined that no one was going to try to leave but with a bit of luck we might persuade the majority to stay put,' said Dewar.

'You probably don't have the manpower to supervise such an operation, Superintendent?' said Finlay.

Tulloch bristled. 'I've been highly trained in civil-unrest situations,' he said. 'I think my men and I will manage.'

'In that case it might be a good idea to start off with a minimal police presence to get a feeling for the mood,' said Wright.

Dewar nodded his agreement. 'The police are accepted as

part of the community, whether they're liked or not, but when they appear in large numbers with helmets and shields it's a different matter. They could be invaders from a different planet.'

'I also think we should call in the military if there should be any sign of general unrest,' said Wright. 'We don't want a slowly escalating series of running battles on the streets with police. We just want to contain the population within the confines of the area until they're vaccinated.'

'That may be *your* priority,' said Tulloch. 'It's our responsibility as a police force to maintain law and order within the area whatever the circumstances. I've no intention of sitting back and watching the yobs take over. We owe it to the law-abiding citizens.'

'There's always been tremendous resentment in the past when the army have been used in civilian situations,' said Mary Martin. 'Surely, if it became necessary, police could be drafted in from other areas so they can control the situation through sheer weight of numbers rather than involve the army?'

Tulloch shrugged in a negative way. 'I don't think it will come to that,' he said. 'I'm confident my men and I can maintain law and order.'

'The truth is, we just don't know what's going to happen, either with the disease or with public reaction,' said Dewar. 'I suggest a compromise should it come to it. We agree to call the military in sooner rather than later but we use them solely to secure the perimeter allowing the superintendent and his men to carry out normal police duties within the estate.'

'Oh God,' said Finlay, sounding weary. 'This is all beginning to sound nightmarish.'

Wright and Dewar were the only two at the table who were convinced of what was right in their own minds. The others were still trying to think of alternatives to sealing off the estate. There was silence for a full minute.

Wright broke it. 'Doing nothing is not an option,' he said. 'Neither is waiting and seeing. We're already running out of time.'

'I'd feel happier about physical containment if we had vaccine to offer the people affected,' said Finlay.

'But we don't and we can't afford to wait until it arrives,' said Dewar flatly. 'As I see it, the majority of people living in Muirhouse will be ordinary, decent citizens who'll be stunned by the announcement. They'll accept the situation, at least for the first day or two, by which time the vaccine will be here. It's the junkies and yobs we have to worry about. They'll probably put up resistance from the word go. They'll see it as a licence to cause mayhem under the banner of fighting for individual civil liberty or some such high-sounding ideal.'

'In my experience, fighting for individual civil liberty usually involves smashing Dixons' window and walking off with a television set,' said Tulloch sourly.

'The shops will have to be closed, the schools too,' said Wright. 'Local businesses shut down, public transport suspended.'

Finlay, already suffering from the effects of lack of sleep, supported his head in his hands as the administrative nightmare unfolded. 'What d'you think, Mr Rankin?' he asked.

'It'll take a couple of days to set up but if that's what the team wants, sir, I'll make arrangements.' replied Rankin without a trace of personal opinion.

'I don't think Social Services will be able to cope,' said Mary Martin. 'And my people are going to be run off their feet.'

'We can put out an appeal for volunteer help from the rest of the country,' said Wright. 'There should be enough vaccine floating around the various health authorities to offer them protection.'

People lapsed into silence again for a short time before Dewar said, 'I think we need a decision.'

All eyes fell on George Finlay, who looked haunted. 'Well, if there's no other way,' he said, 'so be it. I'll draft an announcement and the Scottish Office people can make the necessary arrangements.'

Wright closed his eyes and gave silent thanks. Everyone else bustled into action. Dewar phoned Inspector Grant and told him what had been decided.

'Did I hear you right? You're going to seal off Muirhouse?' said an astonished Grant.

'It's our only chance of containing it,' said Dewar.

'And Cameron Tulloch agreed to this?'

'He said it would be difficult but he could do it. Chances are, the military will be called in to maintain the perimeter if the going gets tough.'

'I hope it's 2 Para and the Foreign Legion,' said Grant. 'They might have a chance.'

Dewar ignored Grant's pessimism. He had expected nothing better. It wasn't in Grant's nature to see the bright side of anything, not that there was much of a bright side to isolating a whole community. 'Right now I need a computer check on a Thomas Hannan,' he said.

'Tommy Hannan? Known associate of Michael Patrick Kelly. What d'you want to know?'

'His past form. I take it you know him?'

'I've done him a couple of times, breaking and entering, the usual stuff, videos, hi-fis, cameras. Sells them down the pub to feed his habit. Him and the rest.'

'Nothing more ambitious?'

'Still working on a university break-in, eh? Hannan's not your man. Kelly pulls the strings in that pair. How did you meet up with Hannan anyway?'

'I was looking for contacts of Michael Kelly. Somebody put me on to Hannan. The bottom line is that Hannan was admitted to the Western General with smallpox.'

'So both of them have gone down, then,' sighed Grant. 'Did one give it to the other?'

'That would be the obvious explanation,' said Dewar. 'But I'm not sure it's the right one. It all depends on when Hannan last saw Kelly. If the incubation period is wrong for that sort of transfer it would mean that Kelly and Hannan were infected independently but around the same time.'

'While on a job together, you mean?'

'That's the line I was working on,' said Dewar.

'They're just a couple of prats,' said Grant. 'I think you're barking up the wrong tree with the university break-in idea. They wouldn't know where to begin fencing anything more complicated than a telly or a video recorder.'

'Trouble is, it's the only tree I've got,' confessed Dewar. 'But thanks for the local knowledge.'

'Any time. When are you pulling the plug on Muirhouse?'

'Day after tomorrow.'

DAY FIVE

Twenty-four new cases were admitted by the end of the morning. The total reached forty by four in the afternoon and forty-seven by the end of the office day, when it was decided not to go ahead with the containment plan until the following morning. The Scottish Office officials who had been working feverishly for the past two days had failed to achieve some of their objectives in correlating press and media announcements with police movement and Social Services' response. It was important that things should happen in an orderly sequence, otherwise the whole operation would be compromised and could turn into a shambles. It had simply turned out to be more difficult than they had anticipated; they had been forced to ask for more time.

In the circumstances, the police were more than happy with this, pointing out that it would be much easier to put everything in place in the early hours of the morning than in the evening. The operation was rescheduled to commence at four the following morning.

# ~ *Eighteen* ~

The team took advantage of the postponement to meet at seven in the evening and assess the overall situation. It was bad; no one pretended otherwise but there were still some positive aspects to take heart from, as Finlay pointed out. The heads of newspapers, both local and national, and of radio and television stations had had to be informed of the true situation prior to the containment operation and yet there had been no leak.

Radio and television did report the outbreak in their evening programmes but obviously without information from above. They labelled it a 'mystery virus currently affecting an Edinburgh housing estate'. The cause was currently said to be under laboratory investigation. Local newspapers, adding 'width' to the story, had obligingly contributed neighbourhood red herrings citing, variously, an old gas works, a nearby sewage treatment plant and a local chemical-waste-disposal firm as being possible candidates for blame.

'First things first,' said Finlay. 'From tomorrow we're going to need more space. I'm going to open up the second ward at the Western.'

'Have you thought beyond that?' asked Hector Wright.

'I have,' replied Finlay. 'I've asked Mr Rankin to look into the prospects of using the currently unoccupied Wester Drylaw

Primary School should it prove necessary. I feel this would be preferable to using hospitals outside the immediate area.'

Wright nodded his agreement.

'The school will be available if you need it,' said Rankin. 'There were no objections. I've asked that furniture be moved out tomorrow just in case and I've warned central supplies about an imminent request for fifty beds.'

'Good,' said Finlay. 'What's the position with contacts, Mary?'

'Better than we feared. Most are staying put as requested. In fact, they're rather enjoying being run after by Social Services. We've had one or two awkward customers who are adamant that no one is going to tell them what they can and cannot do, but, generally, it's been fine. It can't last, of course. Social services will be stretched to the very limit by the end of to-morrow — maybe the next day if we're lucky.'

'By which time, the vaccine will be here,' said Finlay. He held up crossed fingers on both hands. 'Vaccination clinics will provide a diversion for everyone.'

'But will the vaccine help people who've already been exposed to the disease?' asked Cameron Tulloch.

'Yes,' replied Hector Wright. 'Vaccinating people during the incubation period can help a lot although it itself takes about seven days to become fully effective. The bottom line is, the sooner after exposure it's given, the better.'

'I've been asked to point out that the lab feels it's being stretched to the limit,' said Mary Martin. 'The technicians have been working flat out and things can only get worse. Maybe we could enlist the assistance of other labs or maybe bring in extra staff from somewhere?'

'I suggest we stop the lab work entirely,' countered Wright bluntly. 'There's no need to send specimens to the lab from every patient and contact we come across. To all intents and purposes, we're in the middle of an epidemic; we *know* what's wrong with people. It isn't necessary any more to have the lab confirm it.'

'Or even desirable,' added Dewar, thinking that the less infected material there was moving around the city the better.

Finlay looked tentatively around the table. 'I think we might really consider that option,' he said cautiously.

'We have a duty of care to these people,' insisted Mary Martin 'They are entitled to be treated just like any other patients with regard to a full range of lab tests and status monitoring.' Her cheeks were flushed with annoyance at what Wright had said, or more correctly at the way he'd said it.

Wright didn't relent. 'For God's sake, woman, it's smallpox we're dealing with. Once it's broken out, it's not exactly difficult to diagnose. A blind man on a foggy night could do it. We don't need lab confirmation and, believe me, confirmation is the only thing a lab can give us. There's nothing medical science can do for these people once they've succumbed to the disease. No monitoring or strain typing or drug-sensitivity testing. Nothing. The disease will run its course and that's all there is to it. Medical staff are largely redundant too. Nursing care is the thing that matters to the patients; it's the only thing that can make a difference. Old-fashioned TLC, tender loving care, is the one thing that can swing a borderline case. Forget about modern medicine: it has no role to play. If they were brought in today, Florence Nightingale's nurses from the Crimean War could do the job just as well. If we're asking for the whole gamut of modern lab tests on these people, we're giving our minds a treat. All we're really doing is creating more work for lab technicians, so much so that we're thinking of spreading it out to other labs. If we're honest with ourselves, it doesn't make sense.'

'I still think we should do things by the book,' said Mary Martin, digging in her heels. 'Medical routine is important. It helps maintain discipline and order. That will be essential if we're to keep control of the situation.'

Wright took a deep breath and stared down at the table in silence. For him, it was the supreme effort in self-control.

Dewar knew that Wright had made an excellent point. It was just unfortunate that he didn't have the diplomatic skills necessary to make it without offending anyone. He wouldn't be getting a Christmas card from Mary Martin.

Finlay did his best to pour oil on troubled waters. 'I think exceptional circumstances may call for exceptional measures,' he said. 'Let's stop sending samples to the lab and make the diagnosis on clinical grounds alone.'

It was Mary Martin's turn to look down at the table in silence.

'Is there anything else we should consider?' asked Finlay, anxious that a bad moment should pass.

'Corpse disposal,' said Wright, now with the bit between his teeth. 'We'll have to burn them. This means alerting the crematoria as soon as the announcement is made. They'll have to start making special provision.'

Mary Martin screwed up her face in an expression of distaste. Others visibly winced.

'I think it's a bit early to be thinking along these lines,' said Finlay, now anxious to protect Mary Martin's sensibilities after siding with Wright on the last issue. 'I'm sure that'll be a matter for the families concerned, if and when it comes to it.'

'There's no "if and when it comes to it",' insisted Wright. 'We've got forty-odd cases already — that means twenty-odd deaths in the pipeline. We can't have smallpox-ridden corpses lying around while relatives ponder over what kind of box they're going to have. We've got to get rid of the bodies as quickly and cleanly as possible. That means quick cremation.'

'For God's sake, we're human beings,' stormed Mary Martin, finally losing her composure. 'We have to consider the feelings of the families, their wishes, their religious beliefs. Have you no sense of common decency?'

When he saw Finlay nodding his agreement, Dewar decided it was time to wade in on Wright's side.

'I know it sounds awful but I think Hector's right,' he said softly. 'What we're up against here has no conscience or weakness. Viruses have no sense of decency or fair play. However much it goes against the grain, we'll have to be equally ruthless if we're to stand any chance of winning the war. I know it's going to be difficult but we must steel ourselves to do what all of us at any other time might feel unthinkable. It's not a case of being callous or unfeeling: it's just the way it is. We can't give the virus an inch.'

'Just how would I go about explaining this to the relatives?' asked Finlay.

'You present them with a *fait accompli*,' said Dewar, who'd anticipated the question. 'We have the bodies removed and cremated as soon as they die; we don't tell the relatives until it's all over.'

'Ye gods,' said Finlay quietly.

'I hope we're talking about some worst possible scenario here,' said Cameron Tulloch. 'We'll have people painting crosses on their door next and throwing out their dead on to handcarts.'

Wright looked at him without smiling. He said, 'The situation right now in Muirhouse is exactly as it would have been in seventeenth-century Edinburgh. The only thing that can make a difference to the outcome is the vaccine and, in case you haven't noticed, we don't have any.'

Everyone considered this in silence for a few moments.

'But we will have,' said Finlay, wanting to end the pause and trying to bring a positive note to the proceedings.

The others smiled but the meeting broke up with people feeling very subdued. Dewar felt he wanted to be alone for a bit so he took himself off for a walk by the shore. It had been raining recently, leaving everything sparkling wet under the street lights. The air smelled of seaweed but not unpleasantly, just enough to remind him he was close to the sea. For him, that had always been a good place to be and an excellent place to think.

He crossed the road and rested one foot on the wall to look down at the placid, slightly oily water as it undulated ever so slightly with the swell, distorting otherwise perfect reflections. He picked up a stone and threw it in. The spreading rings had an unmistakable symbolism.

He started to think about why he was there and what he was really there to do. In the current state of uncertainty, he felt it would be all too easy to submerge himself in the fight against the epidemic. After all, he was a trained doctor and there would be plenty for him to do even if it was only, as Wright had pointed out, administering basic patient care. But this really wasn't why he was here. It was still his job to find out how and why this nightmare had come about. He hadn't been giving that much of his attention.

He acknowledged a tendency in himself to dismiss the question now as being academic. Someone had reconstructed live smallpox in the institute and it had escaped. It was too late to do anything about it. Filling in details about how and why this had happened must be secondary to preventing the spread of the disease at all costs. *But*, he reminded himself uncomfortably, he had proved none of it. He was still proceeding on an assumption.

There was still no proof that the virus had come from the institute. It just seemed so overwhelmingly likely, so much so that he didn't have any alternative ideas. He couldn't bring himself to believe that Michael Kelly could have contracted the disease from a source other than the Institute of Molecular Sciences. Officially, there simply *weren't* any other sources. In addition to that, the events in Steven Malloy's lab conspired to make this the favoured explanation. This was even further fuelled by Wright's explanation for the rapid progress of the disease in Kelly. He had come into contact with a massive infecting dose of virus, the amount you'd be exposed to if you contaminated yourself with a pure culture of the virus, the sort of thing you could find only in a laboratory.

If only he'd had the chance to question Kelly at the outset, but Kelly, the potential star witness in all of this, was too far gone when he'd arrived in the city and now he was dead. Hannan, his partner in crime, was going downhill too. If he died before coming up with something useful, that would just leave the two women, Denise Banyon and Sharon Hannan, to throw light on the real chain of events.

Sharon had been cooperative. She'd told him all she knew but it simply hadn't been enough. There was a slight chance that she might still remember something but that seemed doubtful. That just left Denise Banyon who didn't trust him an inch. If he couldn't get anything more from Sharon Hannan, he would be faced with having to gain her confidence somehow. Maybe if she and Sharon were allowed to associate now it might help matters. Perhaps even if he talked to them together, Sharon's presence might mellow Denise.

His walk was over; he started back. He would call Steven Malloy, find out if he'd had any thoughts. If not, he would go straight over to the Western and talk to Tommy Hannan, then he'd tackle the two women.

'I'm sorry,' said Malloy. 'I really have been doing my best to find some institute connection and I agree, on the face of it there must be one, but it must be so tortuous that I'm not going to find it. I've drawn a complete blank. There's just no evidence that Kelly was ever at the institute in any capacity, legal or otherwise. There's also still no evidence that live smallpox was ever created here either.'

Dewar sighed but was not really surprised. He said he'd be in touch. The words 'no evidence', as applied to Kelly, stayed with him as he drove over to the hospital, this time in a pool car supplied by the Scottish Office. When considered dispassionately, that could mean one of two things. Either there *was* evidence but Malloy hadn't found it yet or there never could be any evidence because Kelly really never had been there ⸻

If the latter were true but the institute was still the source of the virus, then he must have come into contact with a pure culture of the virus somewhere *outside* the institute. That was the simple conclusion. He was back to wondering about Kelly possibly having known Ali Hammadi or Pierre Le Grice. He'd been down that road before but maybe Kelly had been employed as some kind of go-between somewhere along the line. But then, who would use a drug addict, with all that that implied in terms of unpredictability and unreliability, on any kind of an errand involving a deadly virus? He was back to square one.

George Finlay wasn't in the Wellcome Unit: he was up in the ward they were using. Dewar spoke to the doctor left in charge; he'd seen her on his last visit but hadn't spoken to her.

'Anne McGowan,' she smiled as she shook his hand.

'How are things?'

'It's going to get worse before it gets better. 'We're full; the ward upstairs has been filling up and there are still more coming in. Dr Finlay is supervising the commissioning of the second ward. Anyway, what can I do for you?'

'I need to speak to Tommy Hannan.'

'I don't think you'll get much sense. He's been deteriorating rapidly since he came in.'

Dewar grimaced and said, 'I should have interviewed him when he was first admitted but he seemed at an early stage of the disease and I thought it would be more productive if I let him settle in first, get over the disorientation of being admitted, that sort of thing.'

'I could say I'd never seen anything like it, but that wouldn't mean much. None of us have seen smallpox before. What I really mean is that it wasn't like the textbooks say it should be. The disease in Tommy Hannan's case developed much faster than it should.'

'As fast as Kelly?' asked Dewar, suddenly excited and seeing a very good question to ask.

Anne McGowan thought for a moment. 'Yes, I think so,' she said. 'The other cases have been more textbook in terms of development time. Only Hannan and Kelly had the rapid form.'

This was progress, thought Dewar. If the 'rapid form', as the doctor called it, was really down to a much higher infecting dose, as Wright had proposed, then Hannan had not caught the disease from Kelly. He too must have been in contact with a pure culture. That was worth knowing. It meant that Hannan, in theory, might be able to tell him everything that Kelly might have.

'What about Hannan's wife, Sharon?' he asked. 'Is she still OK?'

'She's been complaining of feeling unwell. She's developed flu-like symptoms. I think she may be coming down with it.'

'Damn,' said Dewar quietly. 'And Denise Banyon?'

'Still well and still as obnoxious as ever.'

Dewar smiled but he recognised it would no longer be possible to put Sharon and Denise together if Sharon was coming down with the disease. He'd have to see them individually if he couldn't get any sense from Hannan.

'I think I'd like to see Tommy Hannan anyway,' he said.

'If you get suited up, you'll find him in number six. I'll tell the nurses to expect you.'

Dewar put on his protective clothing, checking all the points listed on the wall of the changing room before venturing into the airlock leading through to the corridor that in turn led to the isolation suites. It was quiet, the only sound coming from the hum of the electric air filters. He knocked and entered Suite 6.

He was shocked at the appearance of Hannan. The slight

papular rash he'd had on his face when he'd first seen him had progressed incredibly quickly into full pustular smallpox. His breathing sounded rasping and laboured; the mucosa of his throat was obviously affected. The sound made Dewar ponder on just how much faith he and the people working here and up in the ward were putting in the vaccine that protected them. The breath that Hannan was expelling with so much difficulty would be loaded with tiny moisture droplets containing thousands of live virus particles.

'Tommy, can you hear me?' he asked.

Hannan stopped staring at the ceiling and turned his head slightly, as if it were painful to do so. 'Who . . .?' he croaked.

'Adam Dewar. I brought you in. Remember? With Sharon in the ambulance?'

Hannan closed his eyes and gave a slight nod and a croak.

'Tommy, I need to know how you got this disease. Will you help me? I have to ask you some questions.' No response. 'It's important, Tommy.'

'Bastard,' croaked Hannan.

Dewar wondered about the abuse, then realised it wasn't directed at him. 'Who, Tommy? Who's a bastard?'

'Mike . . . took . . . stuff from this guy . . . Bastard!'

Dewar hadn't realised that Hannan still thought his condition was down to bad drugs. The hospital obviously hadn't sought to disillusion him as yet.

'Tommy, your illness is a disease. It's got nothing to do with drugs. Do you understand?'

'Bastard . . . when I get . . . out of here . . . I'm gonna cut . . . that bas—'

A rasping sigh came from Hannan's throat and his head rolled on the pillow. For a moment Dewar thought he was dead but he could still hear his breathing like a saw cutting soft wood. He was exhausted; he had lapsed into the margins that lay between sleep and unconsciousness. Dewar stood there watching him for a few moments before he heard the nurse come in. He nodded and moved away, wondering if he would get another chance to talk to Hannan. It was something he wouldn't bet on.

As he straightened up, he noticed the light in the room catch the tiny drops of moisture on his visor. For the first time in a long time he felt a pang of genuine fear. It lasted only a moment or so but to feel his throat tighten and his stomach go hollow while goose bumps rose on his neck was something that made him feel slightly ashamed before he started to rationalise it. Maybe it was no bad thing to be afraid of the virus. If nothing else, it meant you had respect for it. More importantly, it made damn sure you wouldn't underestimate it.

Dewar returned to the changing room and went through the routine of primary disinfection of his protective suiting and visor before taking a shower. He had decided to tackle Denise Banyon again.

Denise was slumped in a chair, watching television as she had been the last time he'd seen her. This time she was watching something involving wailing police sirens. She greeted his entrance with, 'I thought I told you to fuck off.'

'I hoped we might clear up the misunderstanding and start over,' said Dewar calmly.

'There's no fucking misunderstanding, pal. Just get your arse out of here.'

'Denise, I desperately need your help. I have to know how Mike caught the disease.'

'Mike's dead.'

'I know and I'm sorry but I still have to know how he got it. It could save many other lives.'

Denise sneered at the notion. 'Not that old one. Other lives my arse. You just want to know where he got the stuff. Well, you're not getting it from me. Right? Now, for the last time, fuck off!'

'For Christ's sake woman, I don't want to know anything about drugs! Can't you get that through your thick head? Mike died of smallpox, not bad drugs!'

Dewar immediately regretted having lost his temper. He saw the look of triumph appear on Denise's face. 'Dearie me,' she sneered. 'Whatever happened to Mr Nice Guy?'

'I'm sorry, but it's true.'

'Bollocks! You lot are always so full of shite. You think I don't know what you're really thinking but I do. You think the likes of me and Mike are rubbish, little pieces of shit for you to smarm up to when it suits you, just until you get what you want. Treat her like a lady and she'll think Prince Charming's arrived on his bloody horse. The silly cow'll tell you every-thing, shop her mates, drop them in it, drop her drawers for you too if you fancy a bit of rough. Dead easy. Well, you've picked the wrong one here, pal. Now for the last time, *fuck off*!' The look of loathing in Denise's eyes made Dewar accept defeat and leave the room.

The drive back to the Scottish Office was a time for facing facts. The wipers cleared away light rain as he recognised he wasn't going to get any more out of Hannan or Denise Banyon – Hannan because he'd be too ill or even dead by the morrow and Denise because she was absolutely determined not to tell him anything. He doubted that Sharon Hannan would have any more to add to what she'd already said so that meant he had all the information he was going to get. It wasn't much.

Two drug-addicted petty criminals had come into contact with a live culture of smallpox virus. God knew how. Both men had ascribed their illness to bad drugs. Neither man had any known connection with the Institute of Molecular Sciences or any of the staff there. It definitely wasn't much.

Dewar phoned Karen when he got back.

'You don't sound too happy,' she said.

'I've got nothing to be happy about. Things are going from

bad to worse up here.'

'I caught the news,' said Karen. 'Your "mystery illness" seems to be getting a hold.'

'It looks like it,' agreed Dewar.

'I had a vaccination today,' said Karen.

'What for?' asked Dewar, sounding alarmed.

'We had an internal request for Public Health Service volunteers to come to Edinburgh. I volunteered.'

'Jesus,' said Dewar.

'That's it? That's all you have to say?'

'God, I don't know what to say . . . I'm proud, I'm pleased . . . I'm scared stiff and I wish to God you hadn't done it.'

'Well, I have. I'll be up the day after tomorrow. I'll stay at Mum's until they tell me where I'll be most useful. My briefing also said you lot were going for physical containment of the disease.'

'We don't have an alternative. Starts tomorrow before daybreak.'

'The sort of thing that could go very wrong,' said Karen.

'We won't know until we try it.'

'I'll be thinking of you.'

'Karen, I love you.'

'I love you too. Take care. I'll see you soon.'

Dewar put down the phone and walked over to the window. It was raining heavily now. There was no wind; it was falling like stair rods.

DAY SIX

The rain persisted throughout the night and was still falling heavily when the police, wearing their yellow, wet weather gear, put up the first of the barriers at 3 a.m. and started stopping traffic. At the same time, twenty-four-hour news channels and all-night radio gave out first news of the smallpox outbreak, thereafter at fifteen-minute intervals.

As the barrier system was completed, buses were stopped from entering Muirhouse and turned round to return to the city. Their passengers, mainly shift workers returning home, were allowed to continue home on foot after being told to tune in to their radios and televisions as soon as they got in. At 6 a.m., police cars equipped with loudspeakers started touring the streets, giving out details of the containment order and advising people to tune in to local radio stations for more information. The radio stations carried the Scottish Office press release, announcing that the mystery illness affecting people in Muirhouse had been identified as smallpox. To ensure that the disease did not spread people would not be allowed to leave Muirhouse for the next week or so. This was regretted but the authorities felt sure that citizens would understand. Vaccine for everyone was on its way but in the meantime everyone should remain indoors as much as possible and keep tuned to their radios and televisions for updates on the situation.

The Scottish Office had set up special phone lines for people with particular problems. The numbers would be given out in later broadcasts but people were urged to use them as little as possible to prevent jamming and to cooperate fully with the medical and social-work teams operating in the area. If everyone displayed good sense, as the authorities were confident they would, the outbreak would be contained quickly and life would be back to normal in no time.

The special phone lines were jammed from eight o'clock onwards. Crowds of people gathered at police barriers to argue their case for being allowed to go to work. The police remained polite but firm using their extensive pre-duty briefing to deal with the more common points. No one was going to be sacked because they didn't turn up for work because of the order. Those who maintained they had sick relatives to visit and care for were instructed to give details to the social-work teams, who would see that the situation was covered for them. The awkward questions – like, Why isn't the vaccine here right now? – were fielded with, 'The medical people know what they're doing.'

Crowds built up throughout the morning and there was apprehension at police headquarters when it was thought that the duty officers might not be able to hold the barrier lines, but the heavy rain which had streamed down their waterproofs from the word go, seeking out weaknesses and sneaking in through collars and zips, proved to be their greatest ally. The crowds might have been even bigger had the weather been better, and the people who were arguing tended to drift off after a couple of hours of getting soaked to the skin. By mid-afternoon, the crisis time had passed and people were staying indoors.

# ~ *Nineteen* ~

Dewar decided to call Ian Grant at police headquarters at a quarter to seven. There was going to be a meeting of the team at seven and he was interested to hear Grant's assessment of the police role so far.

'The honeymoon period,' said Grant when Dewar said he'd heard things were going well. 'People are confused, a little bit afraid. They don't understand what's going on yet so they're watching television to find out. Tomorrow if it's dry they're going to go out and start talking to each other in earnest. They'll fuel off each other's dissatisfaction. They'll complain about being kept in the dark. Leaders will emerge and we can expect some concerted opposition.'

'You don't expect trouble tonight then?'

'Oh, yes,' countered Grant, 'but just from the yobs not the ordinary folks. As long as Tulloch realises that and doesn't get too heavy, they should be able to head off trouble where and when it looks like happening, although there's no denying it could get a bit unpleasant. There's nothing nastier than a bunch of yobs who think they've come up with a good reason for behaving like they usually do anyway. Piece of trash to urban hero in one easy step. It's important not to fuel their self-delusion by taking them on head to head. You've got to play it by ear, back off when it seems right, be prepared to lose a little face even.'

'And the superintendent knows this?'

'He's read the book and done the course,' said Grant.

'What does that mean?'

'There's a big ravine between book learning and reality in most situations.'

Dewar knew what he meant.

Cameron Tulloch was the last to arrive for the meeting at eight minutes past seven. Rainwater formed a puddle round his feet as he took off his waterproofs in the hallway and hung them up on a peg. He entered the room, rubbing his hands but exuding confidence. 'Sorry I'm a bit late.'

George Finlay smiled and said, 'How are things, Superintendent?'

'Everything's been going very smoothly, thank you. I think we're on top of the situation. We've made our presence felt and I think people have accepted that law and order will prevail.'

'Good,' George Finlay said. 'I wish I could be as upbeat with my news. We've had twenty-seven new cases today.'

People sighed and exchanged worried looks, except for Hector Wright, who held up a broad sheet of graph paper. 'I know that seems a lot,' he said. 'But by my reckoning that's a good few less than expected from the earlier figures. This is the predicted course of the epidemic. You can see the numbers fall below the line just here.'

'If it's good news, don't knock it,' said Finlay, showing no real inclination to examine the graph for himself.

'How's the contact tracing going?' asked Finlay of Mary Martin.

'I hesitate to say it but I think we've been lucky there too. The very fact that most of Kelly's contacts were unemployed addicts like him has meant that they didn't wander far from the area most days. The contacts and disease are still confined to a relatively small area. It hasn't had a chance to spread out into other parts of the city.'

Hector Wright, who had been puzzling over his graph and was deep in thought, said, 'I think I know why the numbers were a bit lower today than expected.' He turned to Dewar and said, 'Adam, you told me last night that the man Hannan had gone downhill as fast as Kelly.'

'The change in him was quite dramatic.'

'He'll die soon,' said Finlay.

'But, you said that the other cases were developing in a more textbook fashion.'

'That's what Dr McGowan told me last night when I spoke to her,' said Dewar.

Finlay nodded his agreement. 'That's quite true. The others are running to form, starting with a macular rash, progressing through papular, finally becoming pustular after seven days or so.'

'I think this would argue that both Kelly and Hannan contracted the disease through an abnormal route,' said Wright.

'Agreed,' said Dewar.

Wright said, 'It would therefore seem certain they were the cause of the original outbreak in Muirhouse, but they infected people they came into contact with in the normal way so that these people would develop the disease over a more usual timescale.'

'But how does this explain the dip in numbers?' asked Finlay.

'Being infected with a high initial dose not only meant that Kelly and Hannan succumbed much faster to the disease, but also that they had less time to infect people around them before being admitted to hospital. The number of people they infected was therefore less than we and the book might otherwise have expected. It worked in our favour.'

'Makes sense,' agreed Finlay, nodding his head. 'So we've been lucky in having fewer primary-contact cases arising from Kelly and Hannan.'

'But we won't be so lucky with the fallout from the secondary cases,' said Dewar. 'They've had the normal incubation period and therefore much more time to spread the disease before they fell ill,' said Dewar.

'Lap of the gods,' said Finlay. 'On the other hand, Dr Martin and her people have been doing their best to minimise that through confining the contacts to their homes.'

'With mixed success, I have to say,' said Mary Martin. 'Social Services have been struggling to cope with the demands of some of them today; a few have been getting very restless. We've done our best to persuade them to stay indoors but it's an uphill struggle. People miss not being out and about.'

'That was only to be expected,' said Finlay.'

'I take it you've been supplying addicts with drugs where necessary?' said Dewar.

'As the lesser of two evils,' replied Mary Martin. 'We thought if we supplied the addicts it would act as an incentive to keep them indoors. The trouble is, we don't know who's really an addict and who's not. The junkies have been persuading the others to say they're hooked so that they can get their hands on some extra stuff to sell. On top of that, everyone lies about how much they're taking in order to get as much as possible. There's constant cause for friction and argument.'

'Nothing's ever easy,' sighed Wright.

'Are we any closer to understanding how Kelly and Hannan came to get the disease in the first place?' asked Finlay.

'I think we do know,' said Dewar. 'But proving it is quite another matter. Kelly's dead and Hannan is out of the reckoning as far as being a source of information is concerned. Denise Banyon won't say anything on principle and Sharon Hannan hasn't got anything useful to tell.'

'I suppose, as long as the primary source isn't still out there somewhere, we don't have to worry too much about it right now,' said Finlay.

It was an unsettling thought all the same, thought Dewar, and one he hadn't dwelled on too much. He took comfort from the fact there had been no further cases of the rapid form of the disease. If that were to happen it would mean there was a source of the virus outside of the institute and outside of anyone's control. Surely fate just couldn't be that malevolent?

As the meeting broke up, Dewar asked George Finlay about Sharon Hannan's condition.

'She wasn't very well this morning when I looked in,' replied Finlay. 'I'd say she's entering the final stages of incubation. The virus will be well into her bloodstream by now. We can expect to see the rash break out tomorrow or the next day.'

Dewar went up to his room to phone Karen and tell her of the day's events.

'Any gut feelings?' asked Karen.

'Still too early,' replied Dewar. 'Could go either way.'

'Wright's point about there being fewer contact cases arising from the first two was a good thought,' said Karen.

'A candle in the dark,' said Dewar.

'Cheer up.'

'Sorry, I'm trying to come to terms with the distinct possibility that I'm not going to be able to forge the link between the institute and the outbreak and it's getting me down.'

'Maybe absolute proof isn't needed,' said Karen. 'The circumstantial evidence is just so strong that it just about precludes anything else.'

'I was brought up watching films where strong circumstantial evidence was nearly always proved wrong in the end. Circumstantial was a dirty word.'

'Maybe in films,' said Karen. 'But in life it's different. If it looks like a rat and it smells like a rat, it almost invariably turns out to *be* a rat.'

Dewar called Malloy, only to be told that Malloy had run the same checks on Hannan that he had on Kelly and again drawn a blank. There was no obvious link between Hannan and the institute either. A final call to Barron confirmed that there had been no change in the position with the Iraqis. Abbas and Siddiqui were still there and they were still just waiting.

'Just like us,' Dewar whispered to himself as he put down the phone and crossed to the window. 'For that damned vaccine to come.'

There was a red glow in the sky to the west. He thought at first it was down to street lighting — the 'light pollution' from cities that astronomers complained so much about — but then he decided its source was more sinister. He went downstairs and asked the Scottish Office people in the communications room.

'They're rioting in Muirhouse,' said the one liaising with the police operations room at Fettes headquarters. 'Situation's getting out of hand. Three major fires and they won't let the fire brigade get near them.'

Dewar listened in to the radio traffic for a few minutes before deciding to drive up to police headquarters to see if Grant was there. He found him in his office, eating cheese-and-pickle sandwiches and monitoring the situation on police radio. His feet were up on his desk. He waved a welcome with his sand-wich and indicated a chair.

'What d'you think?' asked Dewar.

'The commancheros are coming,' replied Grant between mouthfuls. 'See the glow in the sky? That's Tulloch's career going up in flames. Live by the book, die by the book.'

'You don't think he'll contain it?'

'Not a chance now the yobs have scented power. He thought he could outmanoeuvre them, show them who's boss, but they know what they're doing. Look here.' He got up out of his chair and approached the map on his office wall. 'They started fires here, here and here.' Grant used his forefinger, leaving three greasy prints on the plastic. 'They set fire to cars in the middle of the road, stopping police access, then they set fire to this building.' Another greasy print. 'The building was empty but they were making a point. The fire brigade couldn't get near because of the blazing cars in the road and the fact that their officers were stoned when they tried to pull them out of the way.'

'You said they were making a point?' said Dewar.

'They were showing Tulloch who was really in control,' replied Grant. 'They've taken over this whole area now and it won't be easy to get them out.'

'But why?' asked Dewar.

'God, they don't need a reason. Their natural loathing for any kind of authority is enough. When you combine that with instinctive animal cunning and a situation like they've got down there, it's a recipe for disaster. Evil rules OK.'

'But the ordinary people living in this area,' said Dewar. 'What about them?'

'They've just had a change of government,' said Grant. 'Fear is now the ruling currency. They'll do what the yobs tell them or they'll be taking flying lessons from the balconies in the flats.'

'What a mess,' said Dewar.

'I think it was always going to be that,' said Grant.

DAY SEVEN

The army was called in at 3 a.m. to take over manning the barriers so that more police officers would be available to patrol the streets. The soldiers — infantry from Redford Barracks on the southwest side of the city — had been on full alert since the decision to go for physical containment had been taken. Their officers, now familiar with the street layout of the area after several days studying maps supplied by the local authorities, had impressed upon their men the delicacy of the operation. Their role was to maintain the integrity of the line, nothing more. Their presence was to be kept as low-key as possible.

They moved quietly and efficiently into position when called upon and took over manning of the barriers with a minimum of fuss. One police officer was retained at each barrier site to liaise between civilians and the military should this prove necessary. In the event, the barriers were not challenged to any significant degree during the night.

In the estate itself, sporadic outbursts of violence continued into the small hours with stolen cars being set alight and police vehicles attacked with bottles and stones. Windows were broken, street lighting damaged and an electricity substation put out of action so that two tower blocks were plunged into darkness with no prospect of repair until order had been restored. Two policemen were injured by flying glass and four youths taken into custody. It should have been many more but police confidence had taken a pounding.

Things quietened down around six in the morning when the first streaks of daylight in the eastern sky signalled an end to the night and called a natural halt to the proceedings. As with so many things in life, a new day heralded a new beginning.

Tulloch looked as if he had aged ten years overnight when he arrived at the Scottish Office. There were dark circles under his eyes and such an air of weariness about him that Dewar thought he might well be ill or injured. Pride made him insist he was just tired but his eyes showed signs of defeat. He had badly misjudged the situation. His earlier success had encouraged him to think that he'd established a natural respect for law and order and he could come down hard on any troublemakers. Zero tolerance had been the wrong option to go for. The yobs hadn't read the same textbook he had. They'd just been waiting for night to fall.

The team was joined this morning by Major Tim Hardy, the officer commanding the troops from Redford Barracks. Although it had been left to the team to decide when troops should be called in, they had been briefed at the outset of the outbreak and their 'terms of engagement' decided by Scottish Office ministers. Hardy reported that his orders were to hold the line using minimum force at all times. His men were to remain strictly outside the affected area, leaving matters of civilian law and order to the police. He looked towards Tulloch, who avoided his gaze.

'What exactly *is* the position this morning?' Finlay asked Tulloch, who was now gratefully nursing a mug of black coffee, using it to warm his hands as well as his insides.

'We've had to concede control of about one-third of the containment area.' There was a stunned silence in the room. Tulloch continued, 'There came a point when I thought it best, in the interests of keeping casualties to a minimum, that my men retreat and set up lines of containment outside the epicentre of the trouble.'

Finlay asked, 'Are you saying that we now have a containment area within the containment area?'

'If you want to put it that way.'

'You're saying we now have a no-go area within Muirhouse?' said Dewar.

Tulloch nodded. 'You'd think the bastards had been planning this for years,' he said bitterly.

Mary Martin looked puzzled. She seemed to have difficulty formulating her question. 'Am I being stupid or are you saying that, with things as they are, none of us can reach the population inside this area?' she asked, making a sweeping gesture over part of the map on the table.

'I'm saying that my officers cannot guarantee the safety of anyone entering this part of the estate. In fact we'd have to advise strongly against it.'

'So the yobs are running the show,' stated Martin. Tulloch looked down at the table. 'And the contacts? How do my people reach them? And the Social Services teams? And the vaccine when it arrives? How do we set up vaccination centres in an area controlled by a mob? What exactly do we do now, Superintendent?'

Tulloch took a deep breath. 'I fully understand your concern but regaining control of the area would mean a full frontal assault involving hundreds of officers in full riot gear. Flushing out the opposition on home ground would almost certainly be very costly in terms of police and possibly innocent civilian casualties.'

'It has to be done,' said Wright. 'The people in there must be vaccinated as soon as it becomes available.'

'Perhaps the army?' suggested Mary Martin tentatively.

'Only as a last resort,' said Finlay. 'The Scottish Office wasn't that keen on bringing troops in to man the barriers this morning but the situation was such that we just had to. But I think that's as far as it goes unless something really awful happens.'

'Couldn't you send in snatch squads to arrest the ringleaders?' George Finlay asked Tulloch. 'If you know who they are, that is?'

'Oh yes,' replied Tulloch. 'They're known all right. The same trash are running things just like they seem to run everything else in that godforsaken place from drug dealing to money lending, but proving it is always quite another matter. Asking people to stand up in court and testify against them is like asking the tide to go out on Royston beach. As for sending in a snatch squad, we're talking about the heart of drug-land here. Steel-reinforced doors and blocked stairways, broken lifts and prams suddenly appearing across your path, teenage mothers yelping about police brutality. Pieces of concrete falling from the flats and more knives than you'd find in the Swiss Army.'

'My God, as if we didn't have enough to contend with,' said Finlay. 'A riot on top of an epidemic.'

'The vaccine's not here yet,' said Dewar. 'So we've probably got another day to wait. I suggest we leave the police, the politicians and the military to work on the problem of regaining control. When the vaccine finally comes – probably this evening

— we can decide then what we do next.' There were no dissenting voices. 'By the way, Major, are your men armed?'

'Plastic bullets, and only then as a last resort.'

As they rose from the table, George Finlay came over to Dewar and said, 'I almost forgot, Sharon Hannan was asking for you. She seemed agitated about something. Maybe you could come over to the hospital? Have a word with her?'

'Of course,' replied Dewar, suddenly excited at the prospect of hearing something useful from her. Maybe this was the break he'd been hoping for. Maybe she'd remembered something important. 'How is she?'

'The rash appeared this morning; she definitely has smallpox; she's putting on a brave face but she's really quite ill.'

Dewar drove over to the Western General, slowing down at the Crew Toll roundabout just to the north of the hospital to look at a gaggle of military vehicles and police panda cars parked across the main road on the eastern perimeter of Muirhouse. There was something sinister about seeing soldiers with automatic weapons hanging from their shoulders on the streets of the city. Something inside him said their weapons should be up on their shoulders and they should be in dress uniform, marching behind a band on their way to some ceremonial duty at the palace or up on the castle esplanade, entertaining tourists. That's what soldiers did in the city. Seeing them stand beside a striped lifting bar, spanning the width of the road, looked like old newsreel footage from Northern Ireland.

Beyond the barrier, the road was absolutely empty of people or traffic, a dark ribbon of tarmac leading to the concrete skyline of Muirhouse with a pall of smoke still hanging over it from last night.

Dewar turned away and drove up to the hospital, where he found parking a lot easier than last time. All clinic and day patients, whether surgical or medical, had had their appointments cancelled. Any patient who could possibly go home had been discharged. All non essential surgery had been rescheduled for some unstated time in the future. Plastic hips and knees would have to wait. Benign cysts would stay where they were for the moment. The hospital was purely for emergencies only

Dewar changed quickly; he was anxious to hear what Sharon had to say. The room was in semidarkness when he entered. One of the nurses had told him this was because Sharon's eyes were hurting. He shuddered as he remembered Michael Kelly's eyes when he'd first seen him.

'Hello, Sharon. I hear you're not so well,' said Dewar gently as he sat down at her bedside.

Sharon had been facing the wall; the rash was clearly visible on her cheek. She turned her head, smiling slightly at the voice she recognised, but the smile faded when she saw Dewar's visor. She seemed to recoil slightly and stare at it as if its use were some kind of betrayal. But it was what the nurses wore, thought Dewar. All the same, he didn't want anything to alarm or alienate her. He needed to keep her trust if she were to tell him anything. He took his visor off and said, 'This damned thing is far too hot. How are you feeling?'

There was no denying the rise in his pulse rate once the visor had gone. He felt exposed and vulnerable. Once again he was trusting his life to a vaccination. The thought made the site on his arm itch slightly, but maybe that was imagination, the power of suggestion as Harry Hill might have put it, he thought stupidly. He wasn't big on bravado but he felt it was necessary in this case. He hoped he looked calm because it didn't feel like that on the inside.

'I feel like I've been run over by a bus,' complained Sharon weakly. 'I hurt all over.'

'You've got to hang in there,' Dewar encouraged. 'Think of nice things. What you're going to do when you get out of here. Sunshine, beaches, swimming pools, Pina Coladas.'

'I drink Bacardi,' replied Sharon.

'All right, Bacardi,' smiled Dewar. He reached out his hand and smoothed the hair on Sharon's forehead and felt a warm dampness there. The hairs rose on the back of his neck. 'Dr Finlay said you wanted to speak to me.'

'There was no one else I could tell,' said Sharon. 'You said I could call on you if there was anything . . .'

'Of course, Sharon.'

'It's Puss.'

'Did you say Puss?'

'My cat. She's in the flat. She's not been fed for days. There was no one else I could ask. Could you possibly go along and feed her, maybe? I'd be ever so grateful. I don't think I'm going to get better for a few days yet.'

Feed the cat? That's what she wanted to see him about? She wasn't going to provide the missing link? Jesus, Mary and Joseph, he couldn't believe it. He'd really been up for this. He'd really believed that Sharon had remembered something important, something that might enable him to identify the source of the outbreak, and all she'd wanted was someone to feed her cat! He took a few moments to compose himself, then he swallowed his disappointment and said, 'Of course, Sharon. Where will I find a key?'

'The nurses have my clothes. You'll find my key in the leather jacket, left-hand pocket.'

'I'll see to it,' he assured her.

'Thanks very much,' said Sharon. 'I'm really obliged. Will you come back and see me?'

Dewar suddenly saw the fear in her eyes. There was no mistaking it. She was behaving bravely but of all human emotions perhaps fear was the most naked and exposed when it appeared in someone's eyes. His sense of frustration evaporated.

'Of course I will,' he said softly. 'I'll come back and tell you how Puss is getting on.

Dewar went through the disinfecting procedure with a heavy heart, then went in search of a nurse who could help him with Sharon's key. He found two nurses sitting together in the duty room having a cup of tea. They looked exhausted. Dewar said so.

'We've been working twelve-hour shifts since the outbreak started,' said the elder of the two.

'And no day off,' added the other.

'I guess that's what angels do,' smiled Dewar, tongue in cheek. 'Florence has a lot to answer for.'

'Florence my bottom,' said the older nurse. 'In my case, the building society insists. What can we do for you?' Dewar told them about the key. 'Sharon's clothes were sent off for disinfection but the contents of her pockets would remain here.' She got up and went over to a wall cupboard. She swung it open to reveal a number of plastic boxes, each with a shallow layer of red fluid in it and a label on the front. She brought down one and said, 'Here we are.'

Dewar looked into the box and saw some change and a keyring with two keys on it lying in the fluid.

'Everything gets disinfected,' said the nurse. She removed the keys and held them under a tap in the sink for a few seconds before drying them in a paper towel and handing them to Dewar.

'The cat needs feeding,' explained Dewar.

'And he called us angels,' said the younger of the nurses.

Two buzzers went off at the same time sending the two nurses scurrying into action.

Halfway to Leith, Dewar started wondering whether there would be cat food in the Hannans' flat. He decided to play safe and take some with him. Half a mile further on, he stopped at an Asian-owned corner shop that seemed to be a cross between a mini supermarket and Aladdin's cave and bought four tins of assorted cat food and some dry biscuits. He felt sure if he'd wanted a gas boiler he would simply have been asked, 'What colour?'

Dewar paid and the proprietor, a plump Indian man with an engaging smile, who offered him a sweet from his own bag he kept by the till. Dewar accepted and popped the striped candy into his mouth. 'Thanks.'

For some reason the simple kindness made him feel a whole lot better about life.

# ~ Twenty ~

Jutland Place did not look any better in daylight than it had done in the darkness of his last visit. There was an air of quiet decay about the street that suggested the tenements had outlived their time. Like the sprawling docks nearby, they were an anachronism, a reminder of the time when families were traditionally large, cramped conditions were the norm and unskilled jobs were plentiful. The bulldozers of progress were lurking just to the west, inching ever nearer, just waiting for the chance to clear the way for luxury apartments, waterside bistros and chic galleries, many of which would ironically chronicle in painting what had just been knocked down.

Dewar remembered the unpleasant smell of the common entrance to the building. He recalled thinking last time that it could have done with a good sluice-out with disinfectant. This time, however, the same thought stopped him in his tracks. He brought his hand to his forehead and cursed his stupidity. 'What an idiot!' he berated himself. He had been assuming that the flat had been lying empty since the night he and Sharon Hannan had left it to take her husband, Tommy, to hospital but this wasn't so. The public-health people would have been here in the interim! They would have carried out a full fumigation of the place immediately after the couple's admission to the Western General!

Dewar cursed as he saw the implication of just what that meant. The team would have taken the cat away and most likely had it put down. The cat itself couldn't get smallpox but its fur would have been seen in the same light as contaminated bedding or clothes – a potential vector for spreading the disease. How could he go back and tell Sharon that? A dead pet at a time like this was all she needed!

He looked down at the keys in his hand, feeling stupid and thinking about turning away, but at the same time trying to think of some way the cat might have survived. It was just conceivable that the public-health people had decided to attempt cleaning it up but that would have meant going to a lot of trouble and it would still have left a risk, albeit a small one. On balance, he felt it more likely they had decided to put it down and take no risks at all. They would have put it to sleep and burned the corpse.

On the other hand, he argued with himself, this had happened at an early stage in the outbreak – before any real pressure had been put on the Public Health Service. Hannan was only their second case. They just might have gone for the difficult option. He took out his mobile phone and called the switchboard at the Scottish Office, asking to be patched through to Mary Martin.

Reception on the phone was a bit poor because of the high tenements. He walked slowly towards the corner of the street as he waited for an answer, watching the strength of signal pick up on the meter.

'Hello, Adam. What can I do for you?' said Mary Martin's voice.

'You can confirm my worst fears, Mary. This is going to sound silly, but when your people carried out the decontamination of the Hannans' place did they have the cat put down?'

'The cat, did you say?'

'Yes. Sharon Hannan had a cat.'

'Hold on.'

Two young boys, kicking a plastic football backwards and forwards between them, came past. One spat at regular intervals as he'd seen his heroes do on TV. Perhaps he thought it aided ball control, Dewar thought idly. The other boy, wearing baggy jeans and baseball cap fashionably reversed, looked up at him and saw the mobile phone. 'Prat!' he said on the way past.

Dewar digested the social comment without response and ignored the itch in his right foot. He watched as a huge lorry, laden with beer, according to the markings on its side, came labouring past, heading for the docks. The noise it made drowned out the first part of Mary Martin's reply. 'Sorry, can you say again?'

'I said, I've spoken to the team leader. He doesn't actually remember a cat being in the flat. He certainly didn't have one put down. If there was one there, of course . . .'

'Quite so,' said Dewar, filling in the details for himself. The gas used in the fumigation procedure would have killed it.

'Thanks, Mary. I'm obliged.'

Dewar looked at the keys in his hand again and decided to take a look at the flat anyway. He'd better know the worst. It could have been hiding. Cats did have a habit of finding obscure hiding places for themselves, under beds, in cupboards, on top of high shelves, so it was quite possible that the decontamination team had overlooked its presence if they'd had no prior warning.

The flat felt cold and damp and still smelled strongly of the disinfecting gas. Dewar examined the windows and saw that the seals applied during the sterilising procedure had been broken. So the team had returned after the fumigation to air the flat. Nevertheless, the smell remained. He suspected it might for a very long time. He imagined some future tenants wondering what it was.

He put the plastic bag containing the cat food on the kitchen table and took off his coat, hanging it on the back of a chair. Starting with the kitchen itself, he walked slowly round each room, expecting, at every turn, to find the corpse of a poisoned cat lying there. The bathroom door was difficult to open and he feared the worst, but it was a scrunched-up bath mat rather than a feline corpse causing the trouble. He completed a tour of the premises without finding a body.

He then started on the airing cupboard, patting the lagging on the hot-water tank to make sure the cat had not slipped inside. He continued his search in the bedroom wardrobe, which was empty but for a few cardboard boxes containing photographs and memorabilia of Sharon and Tommy's life together. He searched through the boxes briefly, sadly contemplating a framed wedding portrait showing the couple smiling at each other.

Now the marriage was over, one way or the other. If Sharon survived she would be a widow, badly scarred and maybe even blind. If she didn't, the Hannans would just be two more people who'd briefly passed through the tenement in its long life. Dewar put the boxes back and stepped down from the chair to stand there, wondering where to look next.

As he shivered slightly in the cold of the bedroom, he became aware of a scratching sound. His eyes darted to the skirting board, where he thought the sound had come from. He waited for movement. Had mice or, worse still, rats moved in to replace the Hannans as tenants? The noise came again but still he saw nothing move despite being sure that the sound was coming from inside this room. Another scratch and his gaze finally settled on the fireplace in an unblinking stare.

Before the decontamination team had set off the gas 'bomb' to fumigate the flat they would have sealed up all the doors and windows to make sure that the gas could not escape before it had done its job. The bedroom fireplace would have been seen as a route to the outside; they had sealed it up with plywood secured by adhesive tape. The scratching was coming from behind the seal that the team had obviously forgotten to remove when they returned to air the flat.

Could it be that the cat was behind it? Had it been hiding in the chimney when the team arrived? Maybe it had fled there out of fear when strangers had walked in?

Dewar stood in front of the fireplace, regarding it with a mixture of hope and apprehension. It could still be a mouse or a rat, and angry rats came pretty high up the list of things Dewar would rather not have fly at his face when he removed the plywood seal. He looked around for some kind of protection, quickly deciding that the black-wire fireguard standing beside the fireplace should suffice.

Before he did anything else he went back to the kitchen and opened one of the tins of the cat food he'd brought and tipped it out into a plastic dish, filling a second dish with water. He brought them both back to the bedroom and placed them under the window. This might be tempting fate, he thought, but he needed a positive thought to work on. He really wanted it to be the cat but common sense demanded that he make another trip to the kitchen and return with a heavy soup ladle just in case.

He closed the bedroom door and positioned the fireguard in front of him with one hand while he started to strip away the adhesive tape with the other. The scratching noise stopped instantly. He couldn't help but imagine the animal preparing its next move, crouching, tensing its limbs, preparing to spring, ready to fight for its freedom. A frightened cat or an angry rat?

He paused for a moment, then repositioned the fireguard for maximum protection before taking a deep breath and pulling away the last piece of tape holding the seal.

Cautiously, he slid the board away and recoiled slightly in anticipation before looking into the maw of the grate. There was nothing to be seen. He was looking at an empty black grate that hadn't been used in years. Once again silence reigned supreme in the room. Dewar shivered with the cold and a sense of anticlimax. He waited for what seemed an eternity for the scratching noise to come again but, instead, he saw something appear at the top of the fireplace. It was a furry nose, a cat's nose. He watched, fascinated, as more of it appeared until finally a cat's head emerged to look him in the eye. It was a ginger cat but covered in soot.

'Hello, Puss,' said Dewar, suddenly filled with relief. 'Fancy something to eat?' He lowered the protective fireguard and stepped back to let the cat make its exit in its own time. The smell of food ensured this did not take long. Dewar watched the cat pad quickly over to the dish and tear into the meat.

As he watched it, he started to wonder where exactly it had been hiding. Still curious, he knelt down in front of the fireplace to look up the chimney. He could see nothing but blackness. Then he remembered that chimneys in countries where it rained a lot did not rise up in a straight line. They had to have a kink in them to stop rainwater dowsing the fire.

He rolled up his sleeve and reached up inside the fireplace to find a narrow shelf leading off to the left. This was where the cat had been sitting. He smiled. 'Now that was one smart place to hide, Puss,' he said, reflecting that it was the only place in the flat where she could have survived the gas. The decontamination team had unknowingly protected her by installing an airtight seal in front of her and, of course, she'd had a supply of fresh air from above.

'One down, eight to go, Puss,' he muttered.

As he investigated just how far the shelf stretched before the chimney turned upward again, Dewar's fingers touched something else lying there. It felt like some kind of smooth plastic container. Carefully, he coaxed it round into a position where he could grip it firmly between his fingers, then brought it slowly down. It was a small plastic box about eight inches by four. He wiped the dirt off the top and removed the lid. Inside were a number of sealed glass vials, but it was a syringe that took Dewar's attention and, in particular, the long needle still mounted on the end. He'd just stumbled on Tommy Hannan's drug stash and fixing gear.

His blood ran cold as he realised he should have known better than to reach into blind corners in a drug addict's flat. He'd been careful enough when looking into the boxes on top of the wardrobe, appraising what was there before touching anything, but the excitement of finding the cat and then the box on the ledge had made him careless. If the syringe hadn't been in a box but inside a plastic bag, for instance, he might have stuck himself on the needle and given himself hepatitis or even AIDS for his trouble. Many addicts were HIV-positive through needle sharing. He'd got away with it this time with nothing more than a dry mouth and a hollow feeling in his stomach.

The sound of the cat lapping water made him turn round and see that the food bowl was empty. He took the plastic box with him when he went through to the kitchen and put it down on the draining board by the sink while he opened a second tin of cat food and added some dry biscuits to the mix on the plate. He gave it to the cat before coming back and taking a closer look at the contents of the box. The glass vials were a puzzle. Drugs off the street didn't come this way and the vials had no manufacturer's label on them. It wasn't just that they'd had the label stripped off, he felt. They seemed far too small and narrow ever to have had one. Something told him they hadn't come from a pharmaceutical company at all. The sealing on their ends seemed strange, too. Irregular taper, uneven in size, as if they'd been sealed individually instead of by a machine, as if someone had manually melted the ends in a flame.

Very carefully, he picked up one of the vials and examined it more closely. There was a white crystalline powder inside and a narrow little strip of paper with something written on it in pencil by the look of it. He held it up to catch the light from the window. He could make out the initials VM and the numbers 4 and 9. It didn't mean anything. He couldn't recall seeing drugs being supplied like this before. Sealed glass ampoules usually contained sterile liquid substances for injection and had a weakened area on their stem so that it could be snapped open cleanly. These vials contained a crystalline solid and there was no weakened area. They weren't meant to be opened easily. All the same, there was something vaguely familiar about them and it disturbed him. For the moment, he put the vial back in the box and went back to see how the cat was getting on.

There was a gas water heater in the bathroom that provided instant hot water. Dewar prepared a shallow bath for the cat. He was idly watching the water level rise – painfully slowly because of the narrowness of the instant supply pipe, when he suddenly realised why the glass vials in the box seemed familiar. Beads of sweat broke out on his forehead and his fingers tightened on the rim of the bath. These vials didn't contain drugs at all and they hadn't been supplied by a pharmaceutical company. He'd seen vials just like them before; he'd come across them at medical school. They were used for the long-term storage of freeze-dried cultures of viruses and bacteria! Liquid cultures of laboratory-grown micro-organisms were aliquotted into small volumes in thin-bore glass tubes and subjected to vacuum drying. When all the liquid had evaporated the dried culture would be sealed inside the glass tube by melting the end. In that form, viruses could stay viable for many years.

The letters on the paper strip inside were the key to what the vial contained. In this instance, it didn't take a rocket scientist to work out that VM must stand for variola major, the most dangerous form of smallpox virus. No wonder Denise Banyon and Sharon Hannan had thought bad drugs to blame for their men's condition. Kelly and Hannan had injected themselves with live smallpox virus!

Exposure to a large dose of virus now seemed like a gross understatement.

Thanks to the cat-rescue operation, Dewar had just solved part of the puzzle. This, of course, led to more questions. How many of these vials did Kelly have? Where had they come from? If these really were the 'bad drugs' then, according to Sharon Hannan, it had been Kelly who had stolen them from a man who had asked him to help in their recovery. She hadn't known any more than that. There was only one person who could perhaps tell him about the man and where the vials had been recovered from and that was Denise Banyon. She had to talk now. The nightmare had come true. There *was* a source of live smallpox outside the institute and, right now, he didn't know where the hell it was!

Dewar went through the process of cleaning up the cat, which had fortunately decided that he was a friend – or at least a provider of food – and should be tolerated as such. This was fortunate because his mind was on other things and dealing with a reluctant snarling moggie wouldn't have helped either of them. This was particularly true of the last part of the clean-up when Dewar had to immerse the cat completely for a few seconds in warm water containing disinfectant.

He turned on the gas fire in the living room because there was no towelling in the flat to help dry the animal. The decontamination team had taken away all clothes and linen for destruction. The cat would have to see to her own rehabilitation while he thought about what to do next. It wasn't enough to raise the alarm about the virus source, maybe not even desirable. There was nothing anyone else could do about it. It was going to be up to him. He needed a positive plan of action and it unfortunately had to centre on Denise Banyon. He took out his phone and called George Finlay.

'How is Denise Banyon today?'

'Still no problem,' replied Finlay. 'She must be one of these lucky people with natural immunity.'

'George, I need a favour. An unethical favour.'

'What?' replied Finlay uncertainly.

'I want you to give her a TAB shot.'

'An anti-typhoid injection?' exclaimed Finlay. 'What on earth for?'

'I want her to feel ill. I want her to feel achy all over. I want her to think she's going down with smallpox. She's the key to this whole damned outbreak. I've got to make her talk.'

'Making someone believe they've got a deadly disease is just not on,' protested Finlay.

'Remember you said something about it being all right not to know the details of how all this started as long as the source of the epidemic wasn't still out there?' interrupted Dewar. 'Well, it is.'

'Good God.'

'Denise Banyon can help me get to it.'

There was a pause before Finlay finally said, 'All right, I'll do it.'

'As soon as you can, please. I'll give her a few hours and then come in. With a bit of luck she'll be feeling ill.'

Dewar phoned Steve Malloy next.

'Nothing new to report, I'm afraid,' said Malloy. 'And I've just about exhausted every avenue.'

'I've found several cultures of the virus.'

'What?' exclaimed Malloy. 'Where?'

'In Tommy Hannan's flat. Freeze-dried cultures in glass vials. He and Kelly must have thought the vials contained heroin.'

'Jesus Christ,' whispered Malloy, painting the picture for himself. 'They injected themselves?'

'Looks that way. I'd like you to take a look at the vials,' said Dewar. 'Maybe you could confirm their origin?'

'Of course,' replied Malloy. 'When? Where?'

'If you could come over to the Scottish Office? I'm going back there right now. My first priority is going to be trying to get my hands on all the vials that Kelly had in his possession. I think I've got all the ones he gave to Hannan. I'll have to talk to the team who decontaminated Kelly's flat. They may have taken possession of them without realising what they were or maybe even the police have them, believing, like Kelly, that they contained drugs.'

'Jesus, but where did Kelly get the damned things from?'

'The story, as I know it, is that some man approached Kelly and asked him to help him recover a stash of drugs and at some point, maybe when his back was turned or whatever, Kelly stole some from him. I haven't been able to find out anything about this man or where the stuff was hidden — or why he needed help in the first place — but I'm assuming that Pierre Le Grice must be involved somewhere along the line.'

'I suppose you're right, but God knows how he came to make it without anyone suspecting,' said Malloy. 'And, as you say, why would he need help in recovering the vials? Where had he hidden them that they needed "recovering"?' he asked.

'Can't think,' admitted Dewar, although he had just remembered that Sharon Hannan had happened to say that this had taken place before Kelly had lost his job. Maybe this was relevant.

'I'm going to have another go at getting Denise Banyon to talk,' said Dewar. 'She knows far more than she's let on so far.'

'Anything you'd like me to do?'

'There is one thing you might be able to help me with.'

'Oh yes?'

'I need a home for a cat.'

'You're serious?'

''Fraid so.'

# ~ Twenty-One ~

Dewar drove back to the Scottish Office, very conscious of what was in the vials sitting in the box on the floor behind him. He'd gone to considerable trouble to individually wrap them using toilet roll from the pack he'd found in a cupboard to provide protection from any sort of impact. The whole box was then wrapped up in the plastic bag that had held the cat food. The last thing in the world he – or indeed the city – needed was for him to be involved in any kind of accident. In the event, he reached the Scottish Office without incident.

He took the box with the vials up to his room and put them safely away in a drawer to await Malloy's arrival. It seemed such a mundane thing to do with enough virus to wipe out the city and more, but there was no call for drama, he reasoned. A convoy of police cars, sirens wailing and lights flashing, could be summoned to take the vials for safekeeping at the university, but right now that wasn't necessary. The vials were perfectly safe as long as the glass didn't break.

He called Mary Martin to say that he had to speak with the team who had dealt with the decontamination of Kelly's flat. She promised to ask them to get in touch when they returned from their current assignment. 'Is it urgent?'

'Very.'

Dewar sat down and embraced a few minutes' silence while

he got his thoughts in order. He still couldn't make much sense of a putative link between Kelly and Pierre Le Grice. It was very much a case of the old question: why on earth would Le Grice involve someone like Kelly? But, as far as he could see, the alternative to that scenario was even more unattractive. It would involve the virus not having come from Le Grice at all. He'd have to consider that there might be another source of virus out there, a completely different one, one that he hadn't even imagined.

The phone rang. It was Karen.

'I'm in Edinburgh,' she said.

'Whereabouts?'

'I've just come in from the airport. I'm going to take my stuff down to Mum's and then I'll come back up. Maybe we could meet? I've to report with the other volunteers to Dr Martin at the Public Health Service at six this evening.'

'I'm going to be tied up this afternoon. I've made some progress at last. I'm not sure where it's going to lead me but you'll be carrying your phone?'

'Yes.'

'I'll get in touch the minute I'm free.'

'Take care, Adam.'

'Nobody's hero, that's me.'

'If only that were true,' said Karen. 'Please be careful.'

Dewar went down to the communications room to see how things were in the estate. He left instructions that he be called as soon as Malloy arrived.

'The police have been touring with loudspeaker vans telling the people that the vaccine will be here tomorrow and where they should go to get it,' said the official currently in charge of the room.

'Please God they're right,' said Dewar.

'Superintendent Tulloch was adamant that good news was needed to head off any more trouble. It's his responsibility.'

Dewar reflected that it wasn't going to matter a damn whose responsibility it was if the vaccine didn't come soon. 'What about the no-go area?' he asked. 'Anything happening?'

'The yobs are still in control. There's been no attempt to retake it. The police are keeping a low profile. I think they're hoping that the broadcasts about the vaccine will tip the balance in their favour and the ordinary people inside the area will stage their own revolt.'

'Has anything at all been getting in or out?'

'They've let in ambulances to remove sick people and they allowed a doctor and nurse in this morning to see a sick child.'

Dewar nodded.

'Dr Malloy is here,' said a woman's voice behind him.

Dewar returned upstairs and greeted Steven Malloy. 'The vials are in my room,' he said.

Malloy raised his eyebrows but didn't say anything. He followed Dewar upstairs and stood by while Dewar carefully removed one of the vials from the drawer and then from its wrapping to hand it gingerly to him.

Holding it carefully in two hands, Malloy took it over to the window and examined it. After a few moments he sighed. Strangely, there was an element of relief in the sound. He looked at Dewar. 'These didn't come from the institute,' he said. 'They're very old. Nobody's used FD capsules like these for years.'

'Maybe Le Grice used old equipment to avoid detection. Something he found in a basement maybe?' said Dewar.

Malloy shook his head. 'I'm afraid not,' he said. 'What's good news for the institute is bad news for you.' He looked at the vial in his hand again. 'This vial is really old . . . in fact, I'd even suggest that these numbers on the strip inside the vial . . . four and nine, forty-nine, stand for 1949, well before the institute was even built and certainly before Pierre Le Grice was born.'

Dewar closed his eyes and said in a flat monotone, 'That means there is another source of the virus out there and we've no idea where it is.'

'Bloody hell,' said Malloy.

'Sweet Jesus Christ,' muttered Dewar.

'We could be sailing up shit creek here. Government secrets and all that.'

'What d'you mean?'

'It was before my time, of course, but you hear these stories about so-called defence initiatives at the time of the Second World War when the government experimented with all sorts of disease-carrying bombs. I suppose I'm thinking of Gruinard Island off the west coast of Scotland, the one they infected with anthrax and consequently put the island out of commission for over half a century.'

Dewar nodded. 'I think there was some kind of accident with plague, too, on Salisbury Plain if I remember rightly,' he said.

'That sort of thing,' said Malloy. 'A lot of it went on in the forties and fifties.'

'So now we have to consider that somebody has stumbled across a stash of secret wartime biological weapons,' said Dewar.

'Just an idea,' said Malloy.

'But at exactly the same time the Iraqis come to Edinburgh, trying to persuade people to make smallpox for them? I don't think I buy that.'

'I agree it's stretching coincidence a bit far,' conceded Malloy.

'Even so, I'll get Sci Med to check out your idea but getting any information out of the ministry of defence can break your heart. They've turned stonewalling into an art form. But whatever they say, there's still a linking factor in all of this,' said Dewar. 'One that involves the institute.'

'If you say so,' said Malloy.

'As for getting more information right now . . .' Dewar took a deep breath and said, 'I guess it's going to be all down to Denise Banyon now, bless her little cotton socks.'

'Anything I can do?'

'If you're still willing to take the cat, I'll give you the address. Maybe you can go over and pick her up. Her name's Puss.'

Malloy left to drive over to Jutland Place and Dewar called George Finlay at the Western.

'She's complaining of a sore arm at the moment; the flu-like symptoms shouldn't be far behind.'

'Good. I don't want anyone reassuring her, not you, not the nurses, not anyone. I want her to dwell on things. I want her to think about it and worry.'

'Understood.'

Two black Bedford vans were leaving the hospital grounds when Dewar arrived a couple of hours later. He suspected they would be taking bodies of smallpox victims to the crematorium and mentioned this to George Finlay who confirmed it.

'We've lost seven patients today,' said Finlay. 'I'm expecting twice that number tomorrow, but thankfully we've not been having the trouble I anticipated over disposal of the bodies. I think people are just too frightened to make a fuss. You said you thought the source was still out there?'

'I'm afraid so. All along I thought the virus had escaped from one of the university labs; I even thought I knew which one, but it turns out it didn't. I need Denise Banyon to tell me where her man, Kelly, stole what he thought were drug capsules when, in fact, they were freeze-dried cultures of smallpox virus.'

'My God.'

Dewar told Finlay about Kelly and Hannan injecting reconstituted virus, believing it to be heroin. Finlay screwed up his face in horror. 'What a thought.'

'Denise is probably our last chance of finding out where they got them in the first place,' said Dewar.

'Good luck and God help us all,' murmured Finlay.

'I think he could do with some help from a vaccine right now,' said Dewar. 'Any word of it?'

'Nothing yet.'

A nurse came into the room and said, 'Sorry to interrupt, Doctors, but Dr Dewar is wanted on the telephone.'

Dewar followed the young woman to the unit's main duty room and picked up the phone.

'Malcolm Ross here, public health laboratory service. Dr Martin said you wanted to speak to me urgently. I was in charge of the squad who did the decontamination on Kelly's flat. Is there a problem?'

'No problem,' said Dewar. 'But I wanted to know if you came across a number of glass vials in the flat, small, round capsules about four centimetres long and half a centimetre in diameter; they contained a crystalline white powder.'

'No, we didn't,' replied Ross without hesitation.

'You're quite sure?'

'Absolutely certain. What is this?'

Dewar could understand Ross becoming defensive. He was bound to think he was being questioned about drugs that had gone astray. He didn't want to tell him what was really in the vials so he simply said, 'Thanks, that's all I wanted to know.'

'Bad news?' asked Finlay, who had followed him along to the duty room and had heard the one word expletive Dewar had used when he'd put down the phone.

'Not good,' said Dewar. 'It makes Miss Banyon's contribution more important than ever.'

'Anything you need?'

'Protective clothing, including visor, an injection-site swab, some pyrogen-free, sterile saline and a ten-millilitre syringe,' replied Dewar.

A second nurse came into the room and Finlay said to Dewar, 'Staff nurse Flynn has just been in to see Denise. How is she?'

'Feeling sorry for herself. She's convinced people are keeping something from her. Says there's a conspiracy and we're all the same. Stuck-up shitheads, to use her exact words.'

'So, no change there,' said Dewar. 'Good. Couldn't be better.' He went along to the changing room and donned full protective gear before proceeding to Denise Banyon's room. Outside the door he stopped and listened. The television was on as usual but it wasn't too loud. Dewar had hoped her headache might persuade her to turn the volume down. For once, things were going his way. He started to have a loud, false conversation outside Denise's door.

'No, I'm sorry nurse,' he said firmly. 'There simply isn't enough American vaccine to go round. Some patients will just have to take their chance with the disease. I'm sorry. I know how you and your colleagues must feel. I know it's rough but that's what difficult choices are all about.'

Dewar waited a few seconds, then entered Denise Banyon's room.

Denise's eyes opened wide when she saw the protective gear Dewar was wearing. He had the visor down.

'Who the fuck are you?' she exclaimed, holding her sore arm and shrinking back into the chair she was sitting in.

'I've just come to see how you are, Denise,' said Dewar. 'Any problems with headaches? Stiff limbs?'

'I've got it, haven't I? I've got this bloody disease. That's why they wouldn't tell me anything. Bastards!'

'Tell me about the headache. Is it bad? Is your neck stiff and sore?'

'Yes,' bleated Denise. 'Oh, Christ, I've got it. I'm going to die!'

'If I can just take your pulse,' continued Dewar without contradicting her.

'Wait a minute, I know you. You're the bugger who came before.'

'I told you at the time I was a doctor, not a policeman,' said Dewar evenly. 'But if you're declining medical help I'll go now and leave you alone. You have the right.' He made to back away.

'No, wait. I don't want to die. I want this American vaccine stuff. I need it. I've got the disease!'

'The American vaccine? No, I'm afraid that won't be possible, Denise, but if you take it easy and do what the doctors and the nurses tell you I'm sure you'll have more than a fighting chance.'

'A figh— I don't want a fucking fighting chance, I want the vaccine. Why won't you give me the vaccine, you bastard? It's because you think I'm rubbish, isn't it? Fucking is.'

'Don't be silly, Denise. There just isn't enough vaccine to go round. Some of us have to make difficult decisions, hard choices. It isn't easy, you know. But you're young and fit.'

'You sound like that Tory bastard Blair. Difficult decisions my arse. I want the vaccine!'

'Don't be silly, Denise. Behaving like that isn't going to get you anywhere. I suggest you get into bed and take it easy. Stop upsetting yourself. You're going to need all your strength to fight the disease.'

Dewar saw fear replace the raw aggression he was used to seeing in Denise Banyon's eyes. He was well pleased.

'Wait! Wait!' said Denise as she thought Dewar was about to leave. 'You wanted to know things?'

'What things?'

'You know, about the drugs Mike stole. Where he got them. You remember. You asked me often enough.'

'Oh, yes,' said Dewar vaguely. 'What about them?'

A look of cunning came back to Denise's eyes despite Dewar pretending to be offhand. 'First the vaccine,' she said.

'No deal,' said Dewar, making to turn away, but his eyes were wide and his pulse was racing. He mustn't blow this. On the other hand he couldn't trust Denise to keep her part of any bargain.

'All right!' said Denise, putting both her hands to her cheeks. 'I'll tell you everything you want to know. Just say that you'll give me some of the American vaccine.'

'I can't make deals like that,' said Dewar. 'It wouldn't be fair but I will give your case . . . further consideration.'

Denise's face lit up. That was as good as you got from these bastards, she seemed to be thinking. They'd never make a bargain with you. They always had to dress it up as something else. 'What did you want to know?'

Dewar took off his visor and turned off the television. He sat down facing Denise. 'Tell me about the man who asked Michael help him recover the drugs he later stole from him.'

'Some guy approached Mike at the building site where he was working and asked if he'd do a wee job for him.'

'Why Mike? Did he know him?'

'Mike was driving the bloody digger,' said Denise. She said it as if Dewar was some kind of idiot.

'So it was a digger driver he was after, not Michael in particular?'

'Well done,' said Denise sarcastically.

'The drugs were buried?'

'Give the man a prize.'

'But presumably Mike couldn't just drive off in his employer's digger when he felt like it?' asked Dewar.

'The job was at the building site,' said Denise.

Dewar paused to digest that. He leaned forward and said, 'You're saying that this man wanted Michael to dig up part of the site he was already working on?'

Denise nodded. 'Mike said it was nearby. He did it at night. Gave the watchman a few bob to turn a blind eye.'

'The man that Mike agreed to help. Did he have a name?'

'No.' Dewar looked at her doubtingly. 'Straight up.'

'You never met him?'

'Never. Mike just met him twice. Once when he approached him and the second time when he did the job.'

'When did Michael steal the drugs from him?'

'Mike went back later that night and helped himself.'

'You mean the man left some behind after Michael opened up the stash?' Dewar sounded incredulous.

'Mike said there were lots of the things. The guy just picked some and then asked Mike to help him partially cover up the hole again, saying he would be back. Mike beat him to it.'

'You mean he emptied it out?'

'Christ, no, he didn't want the guy to even know he'd been there just in case he'd get in deep shit with a supplier and have the heavies after him. He just took a handful hoping the guy wouldn't notice.'

'Did he?'

'Mike never saw the guy again.'

'Did Mike go back to the stash?'

'Yeah, he thought he'd go back the next night and push his luck. There was nothing left.'

'It had been emptied out?'

'Not exactly,' replied Denise with a bitter grin. 'The guy had been back, right enough; he'd burned everything. Mike said he must have used petrol or paraffin. All that was left was a black hole in the ground. Mike just about went spare, said it must have been worth thousands. Then he tried some and found out why the guy torched the stuff.'

'The drugs were in glass vials, weren't they?' Denise nodded. 'Did Michael know this man as a pusher in the city?'

Denise shook her head. 'He said he'd never seen him before in his life.'

'Didn't he think that odd?'

Denise shrugged. 'Dunno. Never thought about it. These days there are probably more pushers than postmen.'

'Where was this building site?'

'Dunno.'

'You never asked Mike?'

Denise shrugged and said sourly, 'South side somewhere, didn't exactly matter. We weren't thinking of buying one.'

'You said Michael took a handful. How many was that exactly?'

Another shrug. 'Dunno. Twenty maybe, hard to say.'

'Did he sell any?'

'Never had the chance. Fell ill after the first one he took, didn't he?'

'But he gave some away.'

'To who?' snapped Denise.

'Tommy Hannan.'

Denise's aggression evaporated. 'Oh, yeah. Tommy came round the night Mike came home with the gear. He gave him five, I think.'

The number matched Dewar's thinking. There had been four in the box in the chimney. Hannan had mainlined the other one and killed himself.

'So where are they now, Denise?'

Denise looked at him suspiciously. 'Have you "reconsidered" my case?' she asked.

'I've reconsidered,' said Dewar. 'I'll give you an injection.'

'They're in the flat.'

'Where in the flat?'

Denise paused as if giving away this secret was still something that was difficult to do despite the circumstances. 'Under the sink.'

'In the cupboard under the sink?'

'Not just in the cupboard. There's a board at the back that hides the pipes. Mike fixed it so it lifts out. There's a space behind it. You'll find what you're looking for there.'

'They're still there?'

'Unless any of you bastards have had them away.'

'Thanks, Denise.'

'Don't thank me, you shit. Just give me the vaccine.'

'Roll up your sleeve.'

Denise did as she was told. Dewar brought out his little bottle of sterile saline and charged a syringe. He swabbed the skin on her upper arm and injected a little of the solution, something that would do her neither good nor harm. 'There you go,' he said. 'All done.'

'Good. Now fuck off and leave me alone.'

'Another satisfied customer,' murmured Dewar as he left the room. He called George Finlay on an internal phone in the hallway. He didn't want to get out of protective gear just yet.

'He was called away,' said the nurse who answered. 'Some problem up in the wards. He said to ask you when you came out if we were to treat Denise any differently.'

'Yes,' Dewar replied. 'Be very positive. Tell her she's looking better each time you go in. Tell her you think she's got away with it. She's not going down with the disease after all.'

'Understood. Are you coming out now?'

'I'd like to see Sharon Hannan first.'

'She's in number seven.'

Sharon Hannan was obviously in a bad way but she recog-nised Dewar when he entered. The rash on her face was now well developed and she was shivering despite suffering an obvious fever showing in the sweat on her skin. 'Did you go?' she croaked.

'I did. Puss is fine. She sends her love.'

Despite the fact that Denise's eyes were almost hidden in small slits due to the swelling of the tissue around them, Dewar saw relief appear in them.

'Thanks. Thanks a lot,' she said.

'She's quite a cat.'

'She's all I've got.'

# ~ Twenty-Two ~

Dewar called Karen's mobile number on the way back. 'Where are you just now?' he asked.

'I've just come back up to town.'

Dewar glanced at his watch. It was coming up to five o'clock. 'What d'you say we meet for coffee? Then I'll run you over to Public Health in time for your meeting.'

'What about the café in the Royal Mile?'

'Fifteen minutes.'

They met up in a small coffee shop which they'd frequented on previous visits to Edinburgh, usually on Sunday mornings after walking in the old town and before returning to London after spending the weekend with Karen's mother.

There was only one other couple sitting there when Dewar arrived five minutes late. Karen was sitting in the opposite corner nursing a cappuccino. She got up and he hugged her. 'Good to see you but I still wish you hadn't come. More coffee?'

'No, I'm fine and no lectures, please.'

Dewar smiled. There was no point in arguing.

'The city seems remarkably calm,' said Karen, when Dewar returned from ordering black coffee at the counter.

'The Scots aren't big on panic,' said Dewar with a smile.

'I know we're not but I did expect people to be a little less laid back over something like smallpox.'

'So far, we've been lucky,' said Dewar.' The problem's remained confined to the Muirhouse estate.'

'You mean things might be different if it broke out in Morningside or Comely Bank?'

'Call me cynical.'

Karen smiled. 'You look tired,' she said.

'I'm OK.'

'You said you'd made progress?'

Dewar nodded. 'I more or less stumbled over the reason for the outbreak. I found the virus cultures that started the whole thing off.' He told Karen the story of the cat rescue. 'Trouble is, I only found the vials Kelly gave to Hannan. The others are still hidden in Kelly's flat.'

'So you were right about a laboratory source. Well done. What's the institute saying about the egg on its face?'

'The virus didn't come from the institute,' said Dewar.

'You're kidding!' exclaimed Karen.

'I know, it's almost unbelievable but it didn't.'

'So where . . .'

'The vials contain freeze-dried virus from forty or fifty years ago.'

'Freeze-dried?'

'One of the best ways of storing viruses long-term.'

'I know. I went to medical school too,' said Karen. 'I was just trying to think who would want to do that.'

'Steven Malloy suggested the Ministry of Defence. I've asked Sci Med to check out any interest the MOD might have had in smallpox in these parts in the past.'

'As if they'd admit it,' said Karen.

'Macmillan carries a lot of weight in Whitehall. If anyone can get it out of them, he can.'

'But at the moment, you've no idea where these vials came from?'

'In a local sense, yes. Kelly was working as a digger driver on a new housing development when some man approached him and asked him to do a bit of private digging on the side. According to Kelly's girlfriend, he unearthed a store of these vials for this character. Kelly, being Kelly, assumed they contained drugs. He went back later and helped himself. You can fill in the rest.'

'My God. He injected . . .?'

'Both he and his pal, Tommy Hannan.'

'God, what a nightmare! So where was this place? And the man? Who was he?'

'I'm trying to find that out.'

Karen looked at the clock on the wall. 'I'm sorry. It's time I was making a move.'

Dewar paid the bill and drove Karen over to Public Health headquarters. The pavement outside was crowded with volunteers – about thirty in all – who'd come in from all over the country and were converging for their introductory briefing from Mary Martin. Karen saw some people she knew and, kissing Dewar on the cheek, she went off to join them. Dewar was about to drive off when he saw Mary Martin in the rear-view mirror pull up behind him in her Volkswagen Passat. He got out to exchange a few words.

'Did Malcolm Ross get in touch?' she asked, locking her car door – a task made difficult by the fact she was carrying a briefcase and a number of files tucked under one arm. She seemed harassed, an impression heightened by her hair blowing over her face in the wind.

'He did but unfortunately he didn't come across what I hoped he might. I'm going to have to go to Kelly's flat myself.'

'You can't,' said Mary flatly. 'It's in the no-go area.'

Dewar stood there, stock still, as she brushed past him, greeting the volunteers and apologising for being late. Karen, who, like the others, had turned to witness Mary Martin's arrival, noticed the look on Dewar's face and came back over to him as the crowd filed inside.

'Something wrong?' she asked.

'I've just been told the yobs have control of the virus.'

'You're serious?'

'I didn't realise Kelly's flat was in the no-go area. I'd been assuming it had been left safe and secure after the public-health people had dealt with it. Now it's under threat from any yob who cares to break into it. With a bit of luck, they won't realise what's in there but this changes everything.'

'What are you going to do?'

Dewar looked at her distantly. 'I'll have to find some way of getting in there to recover the vials.'

For once, heavy town traffic was welcome as Dewar drove back to the Scottish Office. He needed time to think. He hadn't even considered that Kelly's flat might be in the area controlled by the yobs. He tried convincing himself that there was no reason for them to break into it but, on the other hand, Kelly was a known addict; he associated with known addicts. Someone might just have reasoned that he might have had drugs hidden away there and, as he wouldn't be needing them any more . . . It was too risky to leave to chance. He'd have to recover the vials as soon as possible. But how?

Instead of driving straight back to the Scottish Office he took a detour to Fettes police headquarters and sought out Grant. 'I've got a problem,' he said.

'Join the club,' replied Grant.

'I've got to get into the no-go area in Muirhouse. I've got to get into Michael Kelly's flat.'

'Then you want the Brigade of Gurkhas,' said Grant sourly.

'I'm serious.'

'I can see that,' said Grant. 'Are you sure this is absolutely necessary? I mean a matter of life and death. Absolutely no alternative?'

Dewar shook his head. 'Believe me, there must be a million

things on this Earth I'd rather do,' he said. 'Kelly left some glass vials in the flat. They contain pure, concentrated smallpox virus.'

Grant's eyes widened. 'How the f—'

'Don't ask. But you can see why I've got to get them back.'

'Bloody hell,' murmured Grant. 'Have you told old Cammy Tulloch about this?'

Dewar shook his head. 'No, I wanted to hear what you had to say first.'

Grant sighed and swung his feet up on the desk. He thought for a moment before saying, 'Tulloch would go by the book; he knows no other way. In the circumstances that would probably mean a full-scale assault on the block using armed officers. He'd figure that something as big as this would warrant it. We could be talking big-time casualties here. World War Three maybe. The trash maybe don't have guns but, by God, they'll make up for it with bricks, bottles and Molotov cocktails. They'll burn the flats down rather than surrender them.'

'Paradoxically that would be an acceptable outcome,' said Dewar. 'At least fire would destroy the virus.'

'Maybe one problem solved,' said Grant. 'But, as I see it, the trouble would spill out into other areas and there's a real chance we'd have widespread anarchy by morning. No law and order at all.'

'We've got to keep what order we have,' said Dewar. 'It's vital that the vaccine programme goes ahead or we can kiss goodbye to the city.'

'Then you're talking an undercover operation with just a few people,' said Grant.

'I suppose I am,' agreed Dewar. 'In fact, I'm thinking just two. What d'you say?'

Grant looked at Dewar without expression. He said, 'You're asking me to engage in a covert operation without my superior officer's knowledge, knowing that he'd be totally opposed to it?'

'You know the flats; you know the people; you know the

good guys from the bad guys and, most importantly, you know how they think,' said Dewar.

'That still doesn't get me in there in the first place.'

'I've been thinking about that on the way over. I heard earlier the yobs were letting in ambulance crews. There was also a report about a doctor and a nurse being allowed in to visit a sick child.'

Grant smiled cynically. 'Sounds like them,' he said. 'They all like to think they're Robin Hood at heart.'

'Be that as it may, I thought we might borrow an ambulance and answer an emergency call.'

'Might work,' agreed Grant.

'Well?'

Grant sighed and shook his head as if to show it was against his better judgement. 'I don't know,' he said. 'It's been a while since I worked the area but some people might just remember me. That could be bad news.'

'I take your point,' said Dewar. 'But maybe with a cap on and a change of uniform . . .'

'I must be crazy but, OK, I'll do it,' said Grant. 'I'll organise an ambulance and some uniforms.'

'We'll have to choose our time,' said Dewar. 'That means waiting until we see how the night's going.'

'If the yobs come out to play again tonight it might not be possible at all,' said Grant. 'They may use fire barriers again to stop any invasion of what they see as their territory.'

'If you monitor things here, I'll do the same. It won't take us long to meet up if the moment seems right.'

Dewar drove on down to the Scottish Office. There was a message waiting for him from Sci Med in London. The Ministry of Defence hadn't stonewalled this time. They had stated categorically that smallpox had never been used in any experimental programme instigated by them and had at no time been seriously mooted as a potential biological weapon either during the Second World War or afterwards in the Cold War period. They cited the existence of a highly effective vaccine as sufficient reason to rule out its use as a potential agent.

'Well, well,' muttered Dewar. 'Where does that leave us?' He looked for the other message he was expecting but found nothing. There was still no reply to his enquiry about the location of Michael Kelly's last job.

Dewar found Hector Wright down in the operations room updating his epidemic map with the day's figures coming in from the hospital.

'How's it looking?'

'See for yourself,' replied Wright.

Dewar took a closer look at the map of the Muirhouse estate with each red-flagged pin indicating a confirmed smallpox case. He asked what the blue markers were.

'Schools and church halls to be used as vaccination centres. Many of Mary Martin's team have spent the day preparing them. All we need now is the vaccine.'

'And the black ones?'

'Temporary morgues, should we need them. At the moment the crematorium is coping.'

'Gut feelings?' asked Dewar.

'The vaccine has to come tonight, not just for practical reasons but for psychological ones too. If we don't have some good news soon all that fear and uncertainty out there is going to change to anger and resentment.'

'I understand the police have been telling the people the vaccine will be available from tomorrow,' said Dewar.

'I think Tulloch was trying to stave off another night like last night. It's a big gamble. If the vaccine doesn't come and all hell breaks loose tomorrow, I suspect the superintendent's going to be spending a lot more time with his family.'

'I hope he's successful for personal reasons apart from anything else,' said Dewar. Wright looked at him quizzically. 'I've got to go in there tonight.'

'What the hell for?' Dewar told him. 'Bloody hell, that's all we need,' exclaimed Wright. 'The loonies in charge of the asylum.'

'Maybe you can show me on the map exactly where Aberdour Court is.'

Wright turned back to the map and traced a curving pattern in the air with his pen. He homed in on one spot and then looked at Dewar over his glasses. 'Right in the middle of the no-go area. You must be mad. Surely the police, if they knew what was at stake, would—'

'I've already been down that road,' interrupted Dewar. 'I've been talking to Grant at police headquarters. The likely backlash from a mob-handed police raid might make things infinitely worse in the long run than they are at the moment. The vaccination programme would be hopelessly disrupted and the epidemic would almost certainly spill over into the rest of the city.'

Wright shook his head but he saw the sense in what Dewar was saying. 'Need company?' he asked.

Dewar smiled. 'That was a kind thought, and a brave one,' he said but Grant and I have worked out a plan we think will work, providing the streets aren't blocked off.' He told Wright about using an ambulance.

Wright looked dubious. 'As I understand it, the yobs have been letting ambulances through in the daytime. No one's tried it at night yet.'

The same thought had occurred to Dewar. He shrugged and said, 'If we don't try it we'll never know.'

A meeting of the crisis-management team was scheduled for seven but it was nearer half past before enough people had arrived. Tulloch sent his apologies but the night had already started as far as he was concerned. He was needed elsewhere. Mary Martin was late through welcoming the new volunteers and assigning them tasks for tomorrow.

'Do you have enough people?' asked Wright.

'I think so. The response has been good. I'm going to continue using my own people for new patients and contacts because they have local knowledge. The new people will be used mainly to man the vaccination centres. They are all qualified so little or no training will be required. They can get straight into it.'

George Finlay was the last to arrive. He didn't bother with apologies. He simply smiled and said, 'I've just heard. The vaccine is on its way.'

The relief round the table was palpable. People just hadn't realised how tense they had become over the delay with the vaccine. It was like having a dull, nagging headache suddenly disappear.

'The first shipment is due in at the airport at around eleven tonight', said Finlay. 'If the vaccination centres are functional we'll take it directly to them. What d'you think?'

'Fine by me,' said Martin. 'They're all set up and ready to go. Just as long as Superintendent Tulloch manages to keep the trouble confined to the no-go area. I don't want my people being stoned or fire-bombed.'

'I'd better put the superintendent's mind at rest about the vaccine and tell him his gamble paid off,' said Finlay. 'Maybe he can continue with the street broadcasts throughout this evening. Might help to keep things calm.'

'Good idea,' said Dewar without declaring an interest.

'When shall we open the centres for business?' asked Finlay.

'The sooner the better, I would have thought,' said Rankin.

'First thing tomorrow,' countered Wright. 'If we open the centres through the night we'll just be ensuring a large number of people on the streets during the hours of darkness. I don't think Superintendent Tulloch would welcome that.'

There was no real dissent after Wright had pointed this out.

'Very well, seven thirty tomorrow morning,' said Finlay. 'I'll relay the information to Superintendent Tulloch. Mary, you'll probably want to deploy your people to the centres to get ready for the arrival of the vaccine.'

'Gladly,' said Martin, smiling for the first time in many days. 'I'll just have to go and find some of the people I've just said good night to! Tell them they won't be going to bed after all. Luckily they're all being put up at the same hotel.'

Finlay reported that there had been no surprises that day in terms of numbers of new cases, adding, most importantly, that the disease was still confined to the estate. 'We're coping' was the bottom line.

'Maybe someone's smiling on us at last,' said Wright.

Dewar called Sci Med in London to ask why there had been no answer as yet to his enquiry over the location of Michael Kelly's last job.

The duty officer answered. 'Mr Macmillan thought you'd be calling,' he said, sounding slightly embarrassed. 'Apparently the building company are having a little trouble with their records . . .'

'You mean Kelly's employment didn't go through their books,' said Dewar with world-weary cynicism. 'He was taken on as casual labour, a day at a time, cash in hand and they've no idea where.'

'Something like that. They say they're going to make their own enquiries. Ask their squad leaders if they remember him. That sort of thing.'

'Jesus,' murmured Dewar. 'I hope somebody told them they're about to have the Inland Revenue going through their financial trousers like a ferret with attitude if they don't get their finger out.'

'I believe Mr Macmillan did mention something along those

lines,' said the duty officer.

'Get back to me as soon as you hear.'

Dewar went downstairs to the operations room. Hector Wright was there. 'Everything's OK at the moment,' he said.

Dewar looked at his watch. It was eight thirty. He called Grant. 'Seems quiet enough. What d'you think?'

'If this was a western I'd say it was too quiet. I don't like it,' replied Grant. 'The bastards could be up to something.'

'Maybe it's just the good news about the vaccine taking the edge off things,' said Dewar.

'You wish. Let's give it another half-hour, then we'll chance it if it's still quiet. I've got the ambulance outside.'

Dewar stayed down in the operations room, familiarising himself with the surroundings of Aberdour Court on Wright's map while he listened in for any change in the situation. At eight fifty reports of a stone-throwing confrontation started to come in from police patrolling the northern edge of the no-go area.

'Just kids' was the phrase Dewar latched on to. The estimated age of the stone-throwers was fourteen. There was no response from the police. Grant called just after nine. 'I'm game if you are.'

Dewar drove over to police headquarters and changed into the green overalls of an ambulance crew man. Grant had already changed. He was carrying a clipboard and looked the part. The vehicle was parked in shadow round the back.

'Harry Field, my mate at ambulance HQ, says if we break it, we pay for it,' said Grant. 'Who's going to drive?'

'You'd better. You know the streets. I'll do the talking.'

They climbed into the ambulance and put on their forage caps. Grant familiarised himself with the controls before starting the engine. Before driving away, he turned to Dewar and said, 'I hope you feel better about this than I do.'

'The words "scared" and "shitless" spring to mind,' replied Dewar.

'Let's do it.'

'*Son et lumière*?' asked Grant as they pulled out on to Crew Road.

'Why not?'

With lights flashing and siren wailing, they accelerated down Crew Road until they could see the barrier at the Crew Toll roundabout. 'Are they going to stop us?' Grant wondered out loud.

'No reason to,' said Dewar. 'Might be different coming out.'

They were within two hundred metres of the striped bar across the road when it rose and they were waved on through. Dewar lifted his arm casually in thanks as they sped past into the estate. 'So far so good,' he said. As he himself had said, there was no reason for the soldiers to stop them but it was still nice to have it confirmed that they weren't carrying a huge sign on the front saying, 'This ambulance is not for real.'

They turned off the siren and slowed down as they navigated the narrower streets of the estate, passing occasional police cars touring the area with their loudspeaker messages about the vaccine's imminent arrival. Dewar looked to see if he could see Karen when they passed a church hall with a Health Board minibus parked outside and people carrying equipment inside. She wasn't among them.

'Here we go,' said Grant as they came to an open space and saw the police cars up ahead. They were blocking the road about two hundred metres from the start of the no-go area. 'I just hope Cammy Tulloch isn't slumming it with them or I'll have some explaining to do.'

Grant slowed the vehicle right down, leaving twenty-five metres between them and the patrol cars in the road, hoping to avoid an interview. He stopped at fifteen metres, letting the engine idle and their blue lights continue to flash silently in the dark. The gambit worked. The police, watched by the posse of journalists and cameramen who had moved into residence beside the barrier, moved their vehicles aside and waved the ambu-lance through. One officer stepped up to Dewar's side as they eased their way past. Dewar opened the window.

'You'll be stopped up ahead. If they say you can't go in, don't argue and don't try to. Just turn around and leave. It isn't worth it.'

'Understood,' said Dewar.

They moved on slowly across no man's land until a group of five men materialised out of the blackness. Two, wearing leather jackets and jeans, held up their hands.

'Just like wood lice creeping out of a tree,' murmured Grant.

'Where d'you think you're going?' asked a thin youth with spiky black hair. He was carrying a baseball bat. He smacked the end of it in his palm as he spoke and smiled at the look on Grant's face. Most of his front teeth were missing, leaving a dark gap when he parted his thin lips.

'We've had an emergency call from Aberdour Court,' said Grant. 'A sick kid, sounds like appendicitis. Stand back please.' He made to wind up the window.

'Just a minute, pal,' threatened gap teeth. 'You don't go anywhere withoot oor say-so.'

Dewar could sense Grant's anger straining at the leash. He recognised that Grant's diplomacy threshold wasn't ideal for the job in hand. He leaned across to intervene and said, 'So what's the problem?' he asked pleasantly.

'Open up the back.'

'Look, a kid's life is in danger,' said Grant.

'Open the fuckin' back or *your* fuckin' life's in danger,' said the gap-toothed yob, his features exploding into snarling anger.

'I'll do it,' said Dewar, putting a restraining arm on Grant. He got out, feeling suddenly very vulnerable as the night engulfed him and the men moved in closer. Three of them had baseball bats resting on their shoulders. All chewed gum. He had the ridiculous thought that they looked like dairy cows chewing the cud. He walked round the back of the vehicle and opened up the doors. Gap tooth climbed inside to inspect the interior. Dewar could see he was enjoying his moment. He didn't look the part but he was behaving like a German officer looking for a suspected escape tunnel in an old war film. He tapped the walls and floor of the vehicle while Dewar stood by, outwardly respectful but inside thinking if the yob had a second brain it would rattle.

Having established that the ambulance was not a Trojan horse full of policemen, hiding in the wheel arches, the yob stepped out on to the road and asked. 'What gear are you carryin'?'

'Gear?'

'Drugs, ya bampot.'

'Not much,' shrugged Dewar.

'See's a look.'

Dewar opened up the scene-of-incident case and the yob had a rummage. He stuffed what he fancied into his pockets.

'We might need that,' said Dewar.

'C'mon, Durie, the guy's right, the kid might need it,' said one of the watching band.'

'Shut yer hole!' snapped gap tooth.

The speaker lapsed into sheepish silence while gap tooth finished taking what he wanted, then got out. 'Right, you,' he said to Dewar. On you go. And don't talk to any strangers.'

He seemed to think this was enormously witty. He burst into laughter and turned, encouraging the others to join him. They all obliged.

Dewar smiled. He didn't need a second invitation. He closed up the back and climbed in beside Grant.

'Fifteen million years of human evolution and we reach that,' said Grant with disgust as they moved off.

'Maybe he had a deprived childhood,' said Dewar, tongue in cheek.

'I know what I'd like to deprive the little bastard of,' said Grant, slowing the vehicle again to manoeuvre round a burned-out Ford Cortina that had been dragged off to the side but not quite off the road. 'That's Aberdour Court up ahead.'

Dewar looked at the huge tower block, standing tall against the night sky, its front elevation pockmarked with lights, many of its balconies still draped with washing that had been soaked earlier in the sudden heavy rain and been allowed to remain there, as optimists looked to a drier tomorrow.

'Seems quiet enough,' said Grant as they came to a halt on the broad tarmac apron outside the front entrance.

'With a bit of luck it's going to be in, out and away,' said Dewar.

'Providing they leave the wheels,' said Grant, as he locked the vehicle and pocketed the keys before joining Dewar. They took a stretcher with them to make their visit seem plausible to anyone watching.

'Where you goin', mister?' asked a ten-year-old by the entrance. He held a lit cigarette in his hand, quite unself-consciously. He could have been Humphrey Bogart in *Casablanca*.'

'What? Aren't you in bed?' retorted Grant. 'You've got school tomorrow.'

'Nae school,' replied the boy. 'It's closed.'

'So it is,' agreed Grant. 'I forgot. If you want to make fifty pence, keep an eye on the ambulance, will you?'

'Make it a quid and you're on.'

'All right, a quid it is.'

'In advance.'

'D'you think I came up the Clyde on roller-blades?' exclaimed Grant. 'When we come back, providing you're still standing beside it and it's still got wheels and an engine, you'll get your money.'

'Nae problem. Any shit and I'll get my brother to them.'

The boy ran off to stand by the ambulance. Grant and Dewar took the lift to the eighth floor and walked along the gangway to Kelly's flat. Grant brought out a bunch of keys and said, 'Just as well Kelly wasn't a dealer. Some of these guys put on steel doors that withstand cruise missiles.'

The door opened with the third key he tried. 'We're in business,' said Grant.

# — Twenty-Three —

The electricity supply to the flat had been turned off — something they had anticipated; they were using torches they'd brought up from the ambulance. Grant stood by while Dewar knelt down in front of the kitchen sink and opened up the small cupboard below it. He emptied out the cupboard of various bottles of cleaning agents and accumulated a smelly pile of rags, scouring pads, dusters and old newspapers at his side. He stretched out and positioned himself on the floor to reach in and around the plastic trap in the sink drain to touch the plywood backboard. It felt encouragingly loose.

He laid down his torch so that he could reach inside with both hands and begin manoeuvring it upward with his palms. He did it a centimetre at a time in case it should suddenly give way and slip backwards. He didn't want it breaking any glass vials that might be lying directly behind it.

'How's it going?' asked Grant, who was becoming impatient at standing doing nothing in the cold darkness of the room as time ticked by.

'Nearly there.'

Dewar felt the board suddenly become free of its improvised side channels. He tried unsuccessfully to turn it round to pull it out on the left side of the sink trap, but it stuck fast. He tried again to the right, and this time let out a sigh of relief as the board slid out past the drainpipe. He handed it to Grant, who propped it up at the side of the cupboard. Dewar started to feel his way round the cavity at the back of the pipes. For one awful moment he thought there was nothing there but then his hand met a plastic-wrapped package. He gripped it gently and pulled it out slowly. He could not have been more careful had it contained unstable nitroglycerine.

'Is that what you were after?' asked Grant as Dewar turned to sit on the floor and shine his torch on the wrapping. He could see through the clear plastic that it contained about fifteen of the vials he'd first seen at the Hannans' flat.

'It's them, all right,' said Dewar. 'We've got them back.'

'Good. Let's get out of here.'

Dewar put the board back behind the pipes and loaded the vials carefully into the metal paramedic equipment case he'd brought up from the ambulance. He used surgical dressing material to add extra padding and make sure they were well protected from any vibration or buffeting they were liable to encounter.

'All ready,' he said.

Dewar walked out on to the gangway and paused to look over the guard rail while Grant locked up the flat. Things still seemed very quiet. He could see the Great Bear in the clear northern sky and he could see the ambulance far below with the small figure of the boy standing beside it. Despite the fact that the boy was the only other living soul in evidence, he still had the uneasy feeling that their every move was being watched.

'Like clockwork,' said Grant enthusiastically as they made their way along to the lifts. 'God, I wish all operations went like this. If I had a quid for every cock-up I'd been out on I'd be a rich man.'

Dewar wasn't ready to relax just yet and Grant sensed the tension in him. Neither man spoke as they descended in the lift. Dewar watched the floor indicator; Grant read the graffiti which covered every inch of wall space despite the use of corrugated metal in an attempt to prevent this. The doors slid open and they stepped out into what appeared to be a deserted hallway. They had almost reached the front doors when several figures suddenly emerged from the darkness to surround them.

'Haven't you guys forgotten something?' asked a swarthy, thickset man with greasy brushed-back black hair and a slight speech impediment which introduced a sibilant hiss to his voice. 'A patient, maybe?'

'Hoax call,' said Dewar, gathering his wits quickly. 'Happens all the time. Kids I suppose. Pain in the bloody arse. Don't their parents teach them anything these days?'

'Little buggers,' added Grant.

'But you went into one of the flats. You were in there quite a long time,' said the soft hissing voice.

They had been watched, thought Dewar. They were in real trouble. 'We have to do that sometimes,' he said. 'The caller was specific about the flat number so we had to check it out just in case someone was lying there unconscious or unable to get to the door.'

'Are you telling us they give you pass keys these days?' asked the man who was doing all the talking. His voice held a mixture of amusement and disbelief.

Dewar didn't like the man. His voice was a bit too even, a bit too controlled, intelligent and, in his opinion, belonged to someone who was downright evil.

'If they're council flats,' said Grant, also thinking quickly and taking over. 'It's a council initiative; there are simply so many old people living on their own these days.'

'Bullshit!' snapped the man with the hissing voice.

'I beg your pardon?'

'Bullshit,' repeated hissing voice, but he sounded even and controlled again. 'You're coppers. I've seen you before.' He moved round to take a better look at them. 'Grant, isn't it? Inspector bloody Grant.'

'You're mistaken,' growled Grant. 'Now just stand aside and we'll be on our way. We've got more to do than stand around here all day.'

'Hold it!'

Three men moved in front of Dewar and Grant to bar their way.

'Now what would the polis be wantin' in Mike Kelly's flat, d'you reckon, guys?' continued the ringleader. 'It would have to be something important enough for them to dress up for . . . Naughty substances maybe? We'd have to be talking a substantial amount if they put a police inspector into fancy dress for it . . . Or was that your idea, Grant? Fancied some glory? Fancied seeing your name in the papers. "Police undercover squad in major drugs snatch"? I think we'd better have a wee look in that case you're carrying, pal . . .'

As one of the men stepped forward to take the case from Dewar, Grant moved in between. 'All right, I am the law and you are interfering with the police in the execution of their duty. Stand aside or I'll do the lot of you for obstruction.'

'My my, we are in trouble,' said the hissing voice to the amusement of the others, then more harshly, 'Right now you don't mean jack shit in this neck of the woods any more, Grant. Hand over the case!'

Dewar knew there was no question of tacitly handing over the virus. The chips were down. It was five against two but there was no choice in the matter. In the event, it was Grant who opened the proceedings. He had been holding the stretcher in a vertical position while they spoke. Now he suddenly slid his hands down to the bottom and swung it round in a scything arc to catch two of the opposition in the face before they could move out the road.

Adrenaline flowed in a violent flurry of swinging feet and

fists. Dewar was forced to put his careful packing of the vials to the test by using the metal case as a two-handed battering ram to break through the two-man barrier in front of him. For a moment there was nothing between him and the doors as the two fell like skittles.

'Go!' shouted Grant. 'Get the fuck out of here!' He threw Dewar the keys to the ambulance. Dewar caught them one-handed.

Dewar hesitated but only for a second. Grant was right. He had to get the virus out of this place but he hated to leave Grant on his own. He forced his way out through the glass doors, opening them with his shoulder as he held the case close to his body with both hands to avoid contact with the glass or precipitate any kind of fumble. He sprinted across the tarmac apron to the ambulance, knowing that there were running feet behind him but not turning to look as it would only slow him down.

He tried to unlock the door with fingers that had suddenly become all thumbs as haste cancelled dexterity. He finally found the right key and had succeeded in half pulling the door open when the boy who'd been guarding the vehicle cried out, 'Behind you, mister!'

Dewar instinctively dropped to the ground and the body of the man pursuing him crashed straight over him slamming the door shut with his momentum as he fought to regain balance. Dewar got to his feet first and swung his fist several times into the body of the man, hoping to disable him before he could recover, but recover he did in a testament to formidable strength. He suddenly whipped his hamlike fist back-handedly across Dewar's face, sending him to the ground with pain exploding inside his head like a starshell. Dewar just managed to get out of the way of the follow-up kick and get to his feet. There was little or no time to get his breath, however, as his opponent came hurtling in again to grab him in a vicelike grip and send both of them back to the ground.

Dewar felt the man's hands grip his throat, obliging him to grasp his attacker's wrists in a desperate attempt to free himself. To his dismay he found the man's grip too strong to break. The pressure on his throat was increasing despite his using all his strength to force his hands apart. He had to concede there was no use in continuing with this and went for a desperate gamble. He let go the man's wrists and sought out his fingers.

Despite the sudden increase in pressure on his throat, which he'd anticipated and which threatened him with unconsciousness, he managed to find his attacker's little fingers and succeeded in getting real purchase on one of them. Focusing all his remaining strength, he bent it violently backwards against the joint as hard as he could and heard it snap. The man let out a scream of pain and let go of Dewar's throat.

Dewar took in a huge lungful of night air. He knew he had only as long as the man was concentrating on his broken finger to take the initiative. He rolled over on the ground and sprang to his feet to aim a vicious kick at the man's head. Right now the human consequences didn't matter. This was a fight he had to win. The man tried to duck but Dewar's foot still connected with his cheekbone and it shattered under the blow. The man slumped into unconsciousness, suddenly no longer a problem.

Dewar looked up to see another of the men starting to run out from the flats. He recovered the metal case from where he'd left it at the side of the vehicle and got into the cab to turn the key. He revved the engine hard and flung the gear stick forward into first but froze with his foot on the clutch. He knew exactly what he had to do. His clear priority was to get the virus out of this godforsaken hell hole and into safe hands as quickly as possible, but he'd just found that he couldn't do it. He couldn't leave Grant there to suffer the consequences.

Grant was a powerful man, an experienced streetwise copper who knew how to handle himself, but the odds against him were overwhelming. The bastards would probably kill him. Dewar let out the clutch and swung the vehicle round to race over the tarmac back towards the flats. The man running towards him had to dive out of the way as Dewar drove straight at him without varying his line. He could see three figures through the glass; they were kicking at something on the ground.

'Bastards!' He turned the headlights on full beam and crashed the vehicle straight through the doors to enter the hallway. The armoured glass frontage exploded into a million fragments, showering the yobs in clouds of glass shards as they sprang back from Grant's prostrate body. They split into two and one. Dewar drove the vehicle at the pair who presented a bigger target and caught the legs of one as he failed to get out of the way quickly enough. Two down, three to go. In a crunching of gears Dewar turned the vehicle and raced it over the floor to have a go at the other man before finally swinging it round and screeching to a halt beside Grant's still body.

He got out of the vehicle and ran round the front to pull Grant up by his shoulders and feed him into the cab as quickly as he could, but it still took time: Grant was heavy. He felt as if life had gone into slow motion. It seemed to take an eternity before he finally tucked Grant's feet inside and slammed the door shut. He ran round to get in the driver's side just as one of the yobs – the man who'd dived out of the way on the tarmac outside, came hurtling towards him. Dewar grabbed the cab's fire extinguisher and swung it round to smash the base of it into the new arrival's face. The man fell backwards, teeth and blood spilling from his mouth, his screams stifled into a liquid gurgle. Dewar revved the engine to screaming point and burst out of the hallway to race across the tarmac apron and up on to the road. He turned on the blue lights and set the siren wailing as he jammed the accelerator pedal to the floor and kept it there.

He was now running on pure adrenaline. He had to get help

for Grant but the truth was that he wasn't at all sure if the policeman was still alive. He glanced to the side and saw that his face was practically unrecognisable. Nausea was added to his anger. He swerved round the burned-out Escort without taking his foot off the pedal and raced up to the hill leading down to where gap tooth and his friends had their barrier. As before, figures moved out into the road, signalling him to stop.

'That'll be right,' muttered Dewar as he headed towards them at full pelt with all the fired-up zeal of a Japanese kamikaze pilot

One of the yobs realised he wasn't going to stop and lit something he'd been holding in his hand. Dewar saw the arc of flame against the night sky as the yob threw the Molotov cocktail. The bottle smashed on the road in front of him allowing the lit paraffin rag in its neck to ignite the spilling petrol and sending up a yellow wall of flame. Dewar was going so fast it scarcely mattered. What mattered more was the half-brick that came crashing in through the windscreen and hit him on the left temple.

The windscreen had taken the brunt of the impact and most of the momentum out of the throw, but Dewar still felt himself go woozy as he fought to find vision through the shattered glass by punching at it with his fist until he had a hole big enough to see out through. He hadn't taken his foot off the accelerator throughout. The ambulance was swinging madly from side to side as he fought to control it until, finally, he hurtled out of the no-go area into the relative safety of beyond.

Dewar put his hand to his head as he slowed the vehicle. Blood was trickling down his face and he felt dizzy. He looked at Grant's unconscious body and shattered face and recognised that he was still the lucky one. 'Please God you're alive, old son,' he muttered as he caught sight of Health Board vehicles parked outside one of the schools they were going to be using as a vaccination centre. He pulled in behind them, slightly misjudging the distance and hitting the rear bumper of the last one in line. He got out to find help.

Dewar felt himself become even more dizzy as he entered through the swing doors of the main hall and sought support from the wall at the side as a blurred figure came towards him and a female voice said, 'Adam! My God, what's happened to you? You're hurt!' It was Karen.

Karen helped Dewar to a seat and made him put his head between his legs for a few moments until proper blood circulation to his brain had been restored.

'Grant . . . He's outside in the ambulance,' he stammered. 'You've got to help him . . . He's badly hurt.'

Karen organised help for Grant and returned to Dewar. 'You've had a nasty blow on the head,' she said. 'I take it you two have been out recovering the something that was lost?' Dewar agreed. 'Successfully?'

'We got the virus . . . The case in the ambulance. It has the vials in it . . . Don't leave them there. Got to get them . . .'

Karen put a restraining hand on his shoulder and said, 'It's all right, I'll do it. Just sit still for a few minutes.' She returned in under half a minute with the case and put it down at Dewar's side. 'Feel better?' she asked with a smile.

Dewar nodded. 'How's Grant?' he asked in trepidation.

'He's in a bit of a mess. His nose and cheekbones have been smashed; his jaw is broken in three places and several ribs have gone. They can't be sure about damage to internal organs at the moment but an ambulance is on its way to take him up to the Royal Infirmary.'

'Is he going to pull through?'

'I wouldn't bet my salary on it, but I'd say yes. Superintendent Tulloch is on his way over.'

'Tulloch? Just what we need.'

'One of the others called him when they saw the state of Inspector Grant. It's right he should know,' said Karen.

I suppose so,' agreed Dewar. 'But maybe I can be out of here by the time he comes.'

He made to get up but Karen stopped him. 'You're not going anywhere for the moment,' she said. 'You're concussed.'

'I was never actually unconscious,' argued Dewar.

'You soon will be if you don't do what you're told. You're in no fit state to go anywhere. What d'you have to do that's so important?'

'I'll feel happier when the vials are a long way from here,' said Dewar.

'Someone else can take care of them. I strongly suggest you go up to the hospital for a check-up with Inspector Grant in the ambulance.'

Tulloch and the ambulance for Grant arrived almost together. Tulloch watched mutely while Grant's broken and unconscious body was loaded into the back and the doors were closed. Dewar declined to go with him. He decided to face Tulloch instead.

'What the hell happened?' stormed Tulloch. What were you doing in the no-go area? Of all the irresponsible—'

Dewar's head hurt but he was in no mood to roll over. 'There was nothing irresponsible about it!' he retorted. 'Do you honestly think we wanted to go in there? Do you think we did it for a laugh? A dare? Use your brain, man. We had to go in.'

'For God's sake, why?'

'Because there was enough smallpox virus hidden in Aberdour Court to wipe out the entire city and most of the county besides. Grant and I went in to recover it and we succeeded.'

Tulloch looked at Dewar, unsure of what to say. 'This is all incredible. I'll wait until I hear what Inspector Grant has to say before I take this further but, as I see it, disciplinary measures will be inevitable.'

Dewar said coldly, 'Assuming Inspector Grant lives, the only measures you will be taking with respect to him will comprise a strong commendation for a bravery award. He's the real reason the virus is currently sitting in that case instead of a flat half-way up a concrete tower in the middle of a no-go area controlled by yobs. As to why there should be a no-go area at all . . .'

Dewar sensed that Tulloch had taken the point. He continued, 'Right now there are some shitheads out there who're pretty miffed that two policemen, as they saw it, broke in and took something – they know not what – from the flats, and that's only made them look foolish in front of the others. They're not going to be able to start a war on the back of that whereas a full-scale operation with police riot squads might have had a very different outcome.'

Tulloch did not choose to argue with the logic.

'All the same, I think you'd do well to strengthen the area round the road leading up to Aberdour Court. It could be bonfire night again. They'll probably block off the road, too, to make sure no one else tries to gate-crash them, but, with a bit of luck, that's as far as it'll go.'

'And the virus?'

'I'll make arrangements for it but I'll need transport. My car's sitting at police headquarters.'

'Where do you want to go?'

'Back to the Scottish Office. Maybe one of your people could contact Dr Malloy and ask him to meet me there.'

Tulloch nodded. 'I'll arrange a suitable escort.'

As Tulloch turned away, Karen returned to remonstrate with Dewar again. He held up both hands, saying, 'Honestly, I'm fine and I'm getting a lift back to the Scottish Office so there's no driving involved. I'll see that all the vials are handed over to Steven Malloy and then I can sleep easy.'

'I really wish you'd stay here tonight where I can keep an eye on you if I can't persuade you to go to hospital, where you really should be.'

'I'll be fine.'

Karen looked for a moment as if she was going to continue the argument, then her expression softened and she said, 'Go straight to bed after you've handed over the vials?'

'I promise.'

They kissed but the sound of a large truck pulling up outside interrupted them.

'It's the vaccine!' said a voice by the door. Karen and Dewar resumed their hug.

'Thank God,' said Karen.

'He usually gets the credit,' muttered Dewar. 'Pity no one questions his creation of smallpox in the first place.'

A powerful police traffic-division car with four motorcycle outriders took Dewar back to the Scottish Office. He sat in the back with the case containing the vials on his knee deep in thought. The only advantage offered by this 'parade' — as he saw it — was that neither officer in the front asked him anything about the case or its contents. Presumably they had been instructed not to by Tulloch. This was fine: he didn't feel like talking. The silence, however, did allow him to consider another aspect of the package he was carrying. It was not only very dangerous, it was also very valuable. There were people, already in this city, who might pay as much as a million pounds for it and he was about to hand it over to an unemployed scientist named Steven Malloy.

Dewar trusted Malloy but he remembered having an earlier conversation with him about what people would and would not do where large sums of money were concerned. He remembered Malloy 'hoping' that he would have the resolve to turn down the offer of a huge sum if it involved his doing something against principle. Was hope good enough in this instance?

Halfway through the journey, Dewar began to see his accompanying police officers as the solution to his problem. He leaned forward and said he'd like to speak to Tulloch. The officer in the passenger seat made radio contact and gave the handset to Dewar.

'Superintendent? I'd like to requisition your officers for another assignment. I'd like them to accompany the case to its final destination and oversee its destruction.'

'Won't these vials be required as evidence?'

'We can sterilise them without destroying them physically. No one's going to check what they contain is still alive.'

'I'm not sure that tampering with evidence is—'

'My responsibility,' interrupted Dewar.

'As you say.'

'Square it with your men, will you?' Dewar handed back the handset to the front seat officer and listened in while Tulloch told him that they should take their orders from him.'

'Are you armed?' Dewar asked.

'This is an armed response vehicle, sir.'

'Good. I'm going to hand over a package to Dr Steven Malloy when we get to the Scottish Office. You are going to accompany Dr Malloy to the Institute of Molecular Sciences at the university and watch him sterilise this package in a steam steriliser. Although this is a formality, at no time is the package to leave your sight. Understood?'

'Sir.'

'There will be a temperature gauge on the steriliser. Watch the needle climb over a hundred and twenty degrees centigrade and watch it stay there for at least fifteen minutes. After that you can relax and return to normal duty.'

'Does this mean there's a chance Dr Malloy won't comply with the sterilising procedure, sir?' asked the officer.

'A very slight one.'

'What then?'

'You inform him that you're armed; show him your gun and tell him to hand over the package. Bring it back here.'

'And if he argues?'

'Shoot him and recover the package. Stay where you are and telephone me.'

'Bloody hell.'

'"Bloody hell" is what could happen if the package escapes. Is that all clear?'

'Sir.'

The rest of the journey was completed in silence and one officer held the door for Dewar when he got out at the end. He was escorted inside. Hector Wright was there to meet him.

'Well done, Adam,' said Wright. 'Looks as though you've taken a bit of a knock.'

'I'll survive,' said Dewar, anxious to avoid embarrassment. 'Is Malloy here yet?'

'Not yet, but the vaccine is. It arrived half an hour ago.'

'I know, I stopped at one of the centres in the estate.'

Dewar took the case upstairs and opened it up to add the vials he'd brought back from Tommy Hannan's flat to the padded bundle. He added yet more padding and several layers of adhesive tape round the outside. He emptied the case of everything else and put the vials back to bring it downstairs, where Malloy was now waiting.

'Hello, Steve,' he said. 'We got all of them back.'

'Well done. What do want me for?'

'We want the vials sterilised but not destroyed: they might be required as evidence. I thought you could autoclave them at the institute.'

'Sure, if that's what you want. Right now?'

'Is that a problem?'

'No,' replied Malloy.

'These police officers will take you over and bring you back when it's done.'

'There's no need for that,' said Malloy. 'I've got my car outside.'

'We'll have to do this by the book, I'm afraid,' said Dewar.

'Still, it's not often you get an armed escort to work.' He opened up the case and showed Malloy and the two police officers the contents. 'It can go straight into the steriliser,' he said.

Dewar could tell by the look on Malloy's face that he'd taken all the key points on board. The police weren't letting him out of their sight; they were armed and there was no reason for him to open up the package.

Malloy looked Dewar in the eye and said accusingly, 'I've no problem with that, Adam. Still looking for a bogey man at the institute?'

'Just procedure, Steve,' said Dewar, but he felt bad.

# ⁓ Twenty-Four ⁓

Dewar sat alone in his room until he was informed by the police that the vials had been put through the steriliser without incident. The feeling of relief that the news brought him, and the knowledge that the actual source of the outbreak had now been destroyed, increased his feelings of tiredness until he found it difficult to keep his eyes open. Despite that, he knew the affair was still a long way from over. He'd accounted for the stolen vials but the others were still out there, taken by an unknown man from an unknown location to an unknown location. Staring out of the window didn't help. It had just started to rain.

He checked the message centre on his laptop. There was still no word from Sci Med about Kelly. What were they playing at? He punched in a memo reminding them of the urgency of his request and sent it off down the line with an impatient stab of his finger on the SEND button. The message disappeared from the screen and left him feeling empty. There was nothing to do now but wait. He considered ringing Steven Malloy and trying to make things right between them but decided it was perhaps too soon. He checked his watch and called to the hospital to ask about Ian Grant's condition. Grant was in Intensive Care but he was stable.

Dewar put down the phone and let out a long sigh. He gazed unseeingly at the wall for a moment, concentrating on the word 'stable' and trying not to think of 'Intensive Care'. 'Stable' had a nicer ring to it.

It was late. Dewar was exhausted. He knew he must rest but he felt guilty about sleeping when there was still so much to be done. He compromised by making one last call of the day. It was to Simon Barron. Nothing had changed. The Iraqis still seemed to be waiting. As usual, the only place they'd been out to was the Bookstop Café round the corner. They were now on friendly terms with both the staff there and other regular customers.

'Frankly, we're all bored out of our skulls,' complained Barron. 'Maybe we should just join them in the café. It's hard to motivate people to be vigilant when they're seeing less action than a museum attendant. Are you really sure these guys are after smallpox?'

'Yes,' replied Dewar, 'I am.'

Still fully clothed, Dewar lay down on the bed and fell into a deep sleep.

## DAY EIGHT

The phone rang at seven and Dewar wished it hadn't. He rubbed at the stiffness in his neck as he put the receiver to his ear.

'How are you this morning?' asked Karen.

'I'm OK,' Dewar assured her. 'You're up early,' he added, glancing at the clock.

'We're just about to leave for the vaccination centre. I thought I'd call first and see how you were. I probably won't get much of a chance later on.'

'That's a fair bet. You can't have had much sleep. What time did you finish last night?'

'It was just after one o'clock when we got the last of the vaccine unloaded. We're opening the doors at seven thirty. They're waiting for me outside. I'd better go. I hope you're going to take it easy today.'

'I might just do that. Take care. Talk to you later.'

Dewar was caught in two minds. One half of him was saying that he should get back into bed, the other was saying that as he'd already got up he might as well stay up. He probably wouldn't sleep much if he went back to bed. The second option won. He turned on the shower and examined the bruising on his forehead in the bathroom mirror while the water temperature settled. The discoloration didn't seem too bad, although the spot where the brick had hit him was very tender to the touch. 'Bastards,' he muttered, although he was thinking more about Grant's condition when he said it. He'd call the hospital as soon as he had showered and dressed.

He felt better after a long soak in the shower, which got rid of a lot of the stiffness in him. He put on clean clothes and called the infirmary. Grant had had an uncomfortable night but his condition was still stable. He'd be undergoing a series of tests throughout the morning.

Dewar went downstairs in search of coffee. He found Hector Wright had beaten him to it. Wright was already examining the incoming case figures for the previous night, glasses on the end of his nose, calculator in hand. Dewar helped himself to a mug of strong black coffee from the flask and joined him. 'How's it looking?'

'I didn't expect to see you up and about this morning,' said Wright. 'You looked like death last night.'

'I'm OK. What's been happening?'

'Mercifully, nothing that we wouldn't have predicted. The numbers of admissions and the numbers of deaths are statistically about right. There's no sign of any secondary source appearing. The police report a fairly quiet night by all accounts. A few fires in the no-go area but no big problems.' Wright looked at his watch. 'Vaccination's due to start about now.'

Dewar nodded. 'Let's just hope it all goes smoothly. Is there a meeting this morning?'

Wright shook his head. 'The early start to the vaccination programme means that everyone's going to be busy with that.'

'Jab jab is better than jaw jaw.'

'If you like,' smiled Wright.

Just after 9.30 Dewar's laptop beeped to herald an incoming message. It was the one he had been waiting for. The building company, Holt, who had employed Michael Kelly, had traced a ganger who remembered having Kelly on his squad. It appeared that Kelly had worked on a development of executive housing at the top end of the market on the southwest side of the city. The estate, named the Pines, had been completed and was now fully occupied. It lay half a mile to the east of Redford Barracks between Firhill High School and the Morningside area of the city.

Dewar felt an adrenaline surge. He grabbed his jacket and ran downstairs, pausing only briefly to tell Hector Wright where he was going.

Dewar entered the Pines from the west and stopped the car to take a look from the slightly higher ground he was on. The estate looked pleasant enough in the way that many such estates did. Large, comfortable villas predominated but, as yet, without the benefit of mature gardens to provide any semblance of privacy. They sat in bare earth, open to scrutiny from all angles, separated from their neighbours by stretches of minimal boundary fencing.

Dewar watched as one young mother come out from her back door and tiptoed over a temporary path of flat stones to pin out her washing on a rotary drier. A toddler tried unsuccessfully to follow her on her tricycle but came to a halt at the start of the second stone. She tried an even more unsuccessful route across clods of earth before tumbling over on to her side. Her cries, more due to frustration than any injury, carried upward in the morning air.

Dewar decided it was time to get out and look around. He opened his briefcase and took out the clipboard he'd brought with him. It had no real function: he'd brought it as a prop. People carrying clipboards were usually presumed by the rest of society to be doing something legal and above board. They could mooch around in the strangest of places, making little notes, where people without clipboards might attract police attention. Dewar would readily admit that he wasn't the first to realise the potential of the clipboard. He'd known people in universities and the civil service who'd made a career out of walking around with them, pencil at the ready, questions to be asked, lists to be made, results to be filed and forgotten.

Denise Banyon had not been able to give him any information about where on the building site Kelly had been asked to dig, only that it was quite near to the houses. But on which side? Dewar started walking. There were trees to the south, mainly pine trees, which he presumed had suggested the name. To the north was a road with yet more new housing on the far side of it. He couldn't see the east side properly as yet because the Pines stretched a good quarter of a mile east from where he was at the moment. He decided a good start would be to walk round the perimeter of the whole estate, starting with a sweep round the north side.

He left the pavement and crossed to an area of rough ground lying between the Pines and the road to the north, a strip about twenty-five metres wide but extending for most of the length of the estate with breaks for road entrances. There was just too much ground for one man to cover, Dewar concluded as he wove his way to and fro across the strip moving slowly eastwards. He kept referring to his clipboard just in case anyone was watching but what he was really looking for was signs of a recently filled-in hole in the ground with scorch marks around it.

As time went on and he seemed to be making very little progress, he started to question why he was doing this anyway. Finding the hole would only confirm what Denise had told him and he didn't think she'd had any reason to lie about it. It wasn't going to bring him any nearer to finding the man who'd asked for Kelly's assistance and who had the vials. He stopped and glanced at his clipboard again as he admitted he was doing this because he didn't know what else to do in the circumstances.

Dewar became aware that he had come under scrutiny. A man, wearing a Sherlock Holmes style of hat and turning over the earth in the early stages of garden creation, had stopped to watch him. Dewar carried on with his crisscross search hoping the man would lose interest, but he didn't. He put down his spade and crossed the road.

'Trouble?' he asked in a plummy voice.

'Not really,' smiled Dewar. 'Cable television. I'm just looking for the best access routes.'

'Wouldn't it have been more sensible to put these things in when the estate was being built?' demanded the man with a frown.

'Not up to me, I'm afraid,' replied Dewar, making his role in the great scheme of things a very minor one.

'Well my wife and I won't be wanting the damned thing. We hardly watch the box as it is.'

'Apart from David Attenborough and documentaries,' whispered Dewar under his breath.

'Save for David Attenborough and the occasional documentary.'

Dewar made a little note on his clipboard. 'And the name is, sir?'

'Pennel-Brown'

'With a hyphen?'

'Yes.'

Dewar put a hyphen between 'pompous' and 'twerp' on his clipboard. 'Right you are, Mr Pennel-Brown, I'll see our people don't bother you.'

Pennel-Brown returned to his digging and Dewar continued his survey of the ground. His back was aching by the time he reached the end of the northern stretch and it was time to turn south along the eastern perimeter. He paused to take a look at what lay to the east of the estate, although it was still hard to see because of shrubbery which had been allowed to grow wild there. Here and there he caught a glimpse of chain-link fencing beyond the shrubbery. It had a strand of barbed wire running along the top.

He was about to start out along the eastern edge of the estate when he saw a chimney through a gap in the greenery. It was a round, redbrick chimney, the sort you'd find on an old industrial boiler house. Could this have something to do with what he was looking for? A building behind barbed wire and close to the Pines estate?

Dewar was about to enter the shrubbery when he caught sight of a postman coming round the corner. He saw that the postman had seen him.

'Good morning,' he said with a friendly smile and a half-raised hand.

The postman stopped in his tracks but didn't smile back.

Dewar crossed over to him. 'I wonder if you can tell me what's over there,' he asked, nodding in the direction of shrubbery and the chimney.

The postman gave him a suspicious look.

Dewar held up his clipboard. 'I'm a surveyor. My client is interested in buying the house that's for sale just over there.' Dewar nodded vaguely in the direction of the Pines. 'I'm just checking there are no awful secret neighbours before I make my report.'

'A house for sale? In the Pines? Already? The buggers have just moved in,' exclaimed the postman.

'The busy, ever-changing life of an executive, I suppose,' sighed Dewar.

'Bunch of greedy gits more like. Probably sell it for ten grand more than they paid.'

Dewar wasn't sure of the validity of the economic analysis but he nodded in agreement. 'You're probably right. About this place . . . ?'

'No idea, pal. It's been derelict since I started delivering here.'

'No nasty smells, then,' said Dewar, making a little note. 'Thanks a lot.' He waited until the postman had gone before sidling into the shrubbery and making his way up to the fence. He could now see that the buildings were in a bad state, a cluster of small redbrick outhouses surrounding a larger building with a tall central chimney. Weeds were growing up through concrete paving that was strewn with broken glass and rusty iron.

Dewar's initial impression that the chimney belonged to a boiler house still seemed right, but for what? There were no signs or name boards to give a clue to what the compound had once been. After looking at the site for a few minutes, Dewar knew he would have to get closer. He started looking for a gap in the fencing. There was no question of going over the top because the barbed wire, although rusty, still looked as if it could inflict damage on anyone foolish enough to try. The chain-link fencing underneath, however, was suspect in several places, particularly along the bottom where post fixings had rusted away. Dewar found a particularly bad one and pulled the mesh away from the post. Three strong tugs and it separated.

Once free of the post, the wire allowed enough movement for him to bend it upward. With a final look behind him to ensure he'd still be hidden from view, he got down on the ground and wriggled underneath the wire on his back. He let out a gasp of pain as a free strand of wire caught the bruise on his head. He had to pause for a moment until the red mist in front of his eyes abated.

Once through the wire, he got to his feet and did what he could to stop the bleeding that had resumed from his head wound. He brushed the dirt from his clothes and approached the buildings.

He was right: the place had been a boiler house. Two large rusting pressure-vessel hulks testified to that, but there was still no clue as to what they had provided heating for. Dewar started to trace piping that emanated from the back wall. He stopped as he came across an empty beer can sitting on a brick buttress there; it was a Tennent's Super lager can and it looked new. The fact that it was sitting upright on the low wall precluded the possibility that it had been thrown over the fence from the road. He guessed at teenagers. Such a place would be attractive to teenage boys but there was just the one can, no other signs of Saturday-night revels.

Dewar followed the line of what he took to be the main pipe outlet from the boiler house. It ran above ground for twenty metres or so before disappearing vertically into the earth in some more scrubland to the east of the buildings. This could only mean that the pipe network must run underground. He started looking around for some likely means of access and came across an iron man-hole cover almost totally obscured by spreading cotoneaster branches. Dewar grabbed the handle and pulled at the heavy cover. It came away surprisingly easily to his way of thinking. He'd been expecting it to be stuck fast.

Dewar looked down into a shaft that dropped vertically for about two metres, then turned horizontally to the right through an arch leading into an underground tunnel. A series of iron rungs in the vertical section of the shaft tempted him down but he left the hatch cover open. It was his intention just to have a look into the mouth of the tunnel before returning to his car to fetch a torch, but he found to his surprise that he could see inside the tunnel. There were no lights, but a series of small armoured-glass windows in the roof provided just enough daylight to navigate by.

He could see he'd been right about the pipe network. The roof and sides of the tunnel carried long sections of steel piping with occasional pressure gauges set in them. The pipes were now cold and damp with condensation; the gauges read zero. He took in breath sharply as a rat suddenly scurried out from the gloom and ran over his feet to find a way past. He would not be alone down here.

He continued along the tunnel, mentally calculating where he was in relation to the estate. He reckoned he was just about at its eastern boundary when he reached the end of the passage. The brick wall he faced looked to be made from newer bricks than the ones outside. He supposed the builders of the Pines had filled in the old tunnel when they were working on foundations for the houses and blocked it off. It was not, however, the end of the tunnel complex because a smaller tunnel led off to the left.

Again there was just enough light to see his way ahead. Twenty metres more and he stopped in his tracks. He could smell something. He sniffed the air again to be sure. There it was again: it was cigarette smoke. Someone else was down here.

Dewar continued with caution, his pulse rate higher than it had been. The smell got stronger; his steps got slower. The tunnel broadened out into a square recess where he guessed an auxiliary pumping station had been sited, judging by the shadowy outline of machinery he could see there. He was looking at it more closely when two hands closed round his throat from behind.

'Got you, ya bastard!' rasped a voice in his ear. 'You'll no' be killin' me like you did Tam.'

Dewar hammered both his elbows back into his attacker's stomach and the man let go his throat with a gasp. He spun round but only to be met with a head butt to the face which sent him reeling backwards in pain. His attacker was on him again, a shadowy mess of tangled hair and bad breath, but apparently inspired by hatred.

Dewar slammed both his fists into the sides of the man's head and gained the upper hand again. Just to make sure, he unleashed a fierce punch into his stomach and the man fell to the floor like a sack of potatoes.

'Now, just what the hell are you talking about?' demanded Dewar.

There was just enough light for him to see that his attacker was wearing a raincoat buttoned unevenly over several layers of clothing judging by his bulk. He had a wild mane of dirty grey hair and a beard that seemed to sprout at all angles from his face. Everything pointed to his being a down-and-out, living rough in the tunnel. The lager can outside now made sense.

'You killed Tam, ya bastard and now . . . you're gonna kill me,' gasped the man. He was half weeping, half struggling for breath and clutching his stomach. Dewar regretted having hit him so hard.

'I don't know you from Adam,' said Dewar. 'And who's Tam?'

'Don't give me that shit. What fuckin' harm were we doin'? Eh? Answer me that?'

'What is this place?' asked Dewar.

'Don't give me that . . .'

The man stopped in mid-sentence as Dewar, growing tired of the impasse, grabbed hold of his lapels and brought his face up close. He rasped, 'Just answer the question.'

'The tunnels.'

'What tunnels?'

'The City Hospital tunnels, ya numpty.'

Alarm bells started to ring in Dewar's head. 'The City Hospital?' he repeated. You mean these houses out there are built on ground where the City Hospital used to be?'

'Every bugger knows that.'

Dewar's mind reeled with the implications of this news. He hadn't found a secret government establishment but he had found the site of an old hospital and that hospital had been the city's infectious-diseases hospital. He knew that because George Ferguson in Steven Malloy's lab had told him so! Dewar felt slightly light-headed as so much began to make sense. Ferguson had worked there for thirty years and this was the area where the smallpox vials had been unearthed. It all fitted. Ferguson was the missing link with the institute! Good old George Ferguson.

The virus hadn't come from any hi-tech reconstruction in the institute or indeed from any secret wartime research centre: it had come from an old infectious-diseases hospital, a place that had seen most of the diseases that afflicted humanity in its time.

'Tell me about Tam,' he said to the man on the floor.

'We lived here for more than three years. It was warm and even when the heating stopped it was still better than kissin' arse down the church places for a bowl o' soup.'

'What happened?'

The man raised an arm slowly and pointed. 'Through there,' he said. 'You'll need these.' He threw Dewar a box of matches.

Dewar frowned but followed the man's directions, moving cautiously in case of any kind of trap. There was a dark alcove to his left and he had the sudden sensation that he was no longer alone. The hairs stood up on the back of his neck as he took out a match and struck it. There, sitting propped up against the wall, like a rag doll at rest, was the blackened, charred corpse of a man, the flesh from his skull all but gone. The fingers of his right hand moved as a rat let go and dissolved into the darkness.

'Jesus Christ,' muttered Dewar, putting his hand to his mouth. He felt himself shiver all over.

'Why are you keeping him here?' he demanded as he returned to the man on the floor.

'I couldn't decide on a coffin,' came the sour answer. 'I report it and I don't have a home any more.'

'What happened?'

'One night the digger came and started working. We thought the builders were gonna fill in this bit of the tunnel, too, so Tam and me moved back but they stopped and went away so we came back. Then next night some bastard poured petrol down the hole while we were sleepin' here and torched the place. They burned Tam alive, poor bastard.'

'Where exactly did they pour the petrol down?'

'Along there.'

Once again, Dewar followed the line of the man's pointing finger. He passed the alcove with its grisly inhabitant and came to an earth wall blocking any further progress. He could tell the earth had not been there very long. It was still damp. It smelled fresh like a garden after rain, but there was also a smell of burning associated with it. He started to kick away at it but became dissatisfied at the progress he was making. He found a piece of metal that had once been part of a support bracket for the piping and pressed it into service as a digging tool. His first sign of success came when he felt a thin column of cool, fresh air on his cheek.

This inspired him to greater efforts and he succeeded in clearing a way up to the outside. He pulled himself up on to the grass and sat there for a moment looking down into the hole that Michael Kelly had made with his digger. He stood up and looked around to get his bearings. He could see that he was at the northeast corner of the Pines estate, about twenty-five metres to the north of the nearest house. That should be enough to work out, on a plan of the old hospital, what had once stood where he was standing now, but he thought he already knew the answer to that. He'd put money on this being the sight of the old microbiology lab where George Ferguson had worked for so long. The lab itself had been levelled to the ground but the underground access tunnels for heating and steam pipes had been left untouched because the builders weren't actually erecting anything on this plot. Ferguson must have known of some old storage facility for virus cultures and decided to make himself some money.

Dewar decided he'd better go back the way he'd come. He had to do something about the down-and-out. He wanted to assure him that no one had meant to kill his friend, that it had been an accident; but it was also true that he couldn't go on living there. There would have to be a full examination of the tunnel system just in case Ferguson's fire had not wiped out everything he'd left behind, and then the whole lot would probably be filled in for good. Dewar dropped back down into the tunnel and piled up loose earth behind him so that no one out walking his dog would see anything more than a dip in the ground. When he got back to where he'd left the down-and-out there was no one there. He considered giving chase but decided not to. The guy lived outside society; that was the way he wanted it; he could stay that way. He personally had more pressing problems to take care of. He made his way back to the derelict boiler house and climbed out of the hatch. He took out his mobile phone and called Steven Malloy.

As expected, Malloy sounded dry but there was no time to apologise for the previous evening. Dewar said. 'Are you alone?'

'Yes,' answered a puzzled Malloy. 'Why?'

'Because George Ferguson is the man we're after. Is he there at the institute?'

'What?' exclaimed Malloy. 'How on earth—'

'Is he in today?'

'He's on sick leave.'

'What?' exclaimed Dewar.

'He's not been himself recently. I told him to take some time off, sort out whatever was troubling him.'

'Jesus,' said Dewar. 'I know what was troubling him all right. Do you have his home address?'

'Of course.'

'I'll pick you up at the institute and we'll go over from there to confront him. I'll fill you in on the details on the way.'

'I just can't believe that George had anything to do with—'

'Trust me,' said Dewar. 'He's as guilty as sin.'

Dewar was about to begin wriggling under the wire again when he considered that there must be an easier way out, the one the down-and-out and his pal had been using for some time. He walked round the inside of the fence, examining all the posts until he noticed one that seemed loose at the base. It also coincided with its being the end of one stretch of wire and the beginning of the next. Dewar pulled at the post and it came away. He could now swing the section back like a gate.

'Cheers guys,' he muttered, replacing the post and hurrying back to the car.

# ⟋ Twenty-Five ⟍

**M**alloy was waiting on the steps of the institute when Dewar screeched to a halt.

'You look like you've been in the wars,' he said as he got in and slammed the door.

'It's been that kind of a day,' said Dewar. 'Where are we going?'

'Baberton Hill Rise, number seventeen.'

'Means nothing.'

'Start heading west. It's a housing estate on the far side of Colinton. Are you really sure about this? George has enough to worry about right now without any more shit blowing in the wind.'

Dewar told him what he'd learned at the Pines.

'Christ, whatever possessed him?' sighed Malloy.

'Try money,' said Dewar flatly.

'But why would the Iraqis approach George in the first place? They wouldn't know anything about forgotten virus stores or an old hospital.'

'They wouldn't. Ferguson must have approached them. It's my guess that Ali Hammadi confided in him when he was approached about making the virus the hi-tech way. These two were friends, weren't they?'

Malloy nodded. 'They had the occasional beer together.'

'When Ali took his own life Ferguson must have seen his chance and offered to provide the Iraqis with what they wanted – albeit from another source.'

'And all that stuff was just lying around in the ground. Jesus! Makes you think.'

'Thirty years ago there wasn't any legislation about what medical labs should and shouldn't keep. Every hospital laboratory had its own rules and made its own arrangements. Safety aspects were the concern of individual consultants, not a matter for committees and government legislation. I suppose as time went by, and the old staff retired or died off, old culture stores might be forgotten about or ignored if they were in out-of-the-way places like cellars or attics. Many old hospitals were built like medieval castles. Ferguson must have remembered about the old cellar store at the City's lab.'

'Turn left here,' said Malloy as they reached a crossroads.

Dewar slowed the car and turned into a suburban street lined on both sides with small semi-detached villas.

'It's about halfway along on the right,' said Malloy. 'Green door.'

'You've been here before?'

'I've driven George home a couple of times after lab parties. He never does anything by halves does George.'

Dewar stopped a little way before the house and asked, 'Are you OK about this or would you rather I called for police backup?'

'George and I have always got on,' said Malloy quietly. 'I'd like to hear his side of things before you do anything else.

As they walked up the garden path of number 17, Dewar could not help but reflect on the bizarre nature of the circumstances. They were walking up to the door of a suburban semi-detached house to accuse a man of bringing the scourge of smallpox back to the world and of being part of a conspiracy to plunge the Middle East into war.

The door was opened by a small, grey-haired woman who recognised Malloy and smiled. 'Steven! What brings you here? You've just missed George. Was it something important?'

'Missed him?'

The smile faded on the woman's face as she caught Malloy's air of tension. 'Maybe you'd better come in,' she said.

The two men were led into a small sitting room that seemed overcrowded with furniture. It was an impression mainly given by the presence of a large, old-style Chesterfield suite and the fact that a youth with spiky hair sticking up was lounging in one of the armchairs with his tongue lolling out of his mouth. He was well over six feet and broad with it, but clearly mentally subnormal.

'Don't mind Malcolm,' said Joyce Ferguson with a wan smile. 'He's happy watching television.'

'This is Dr Dewar,' said Malloy. 'He's here from London, investigating the smallpox outbreak.'

'How d'you do?' said Joyce pleasantly.

'Where has George gone, Joyce?' asked Malloy.

'I'm not sure myself, but he seemed very pleased about something. He said . . .' Joyce's voice faded. 'He's in some kind of trouble, isn't he? Oh my God, what's wrong? What's he done?'

'What did he say, Mrs Ferguson?' asked Dewar, willing her to complete her earlier sentence.

A distant look had come into Joyce Ferguson's eyes. 'He said . . . It was done. All our troubles would now be over. No more worrying about anything . . .'

Dewar and Malloy exchanged glances. 'You've no idea where he was going? None at all?'

Joyce shook her head. Malcolm made a loud guffawing sound as something caught his fancy on television. Joyce didn't take her eyes off the two men.

'Did he take anything with him when he left?' asked Dewar.

Joyce's eyes seemed to ask how Dewar could have known that. 'He was carrying something, a box he took from the garage, but I've no idea what was in it.'

Malloy looked at her. She responded, 'Something he'd been working on.'

'But you've no idea what?'

Another shake of the head.

'Where did he work on this whatever it was?' asked Dewar.

'In the garage.'

'Can we take a look?'

'It's locked. Quite a few houses round here have been broken in to and . . .' The words died on her lips.

'Do you have the key?'

'George keeps it. Oh my God, what's he done?'

Malloy put his arm round Joyce Ferguson. 'Joyce, do you have any tools in the house?'

'In the hall cupboard.'

Dewar went to look and came back with a Mole wrench and a long-handled tyre lever. He indicated to Malloy with a nod of the head that he should stay with Joyce while he went outside to deal with the lock. One good bend of the lever and one of the lugs holding the padlock snapped off the side door. He swung it open and stepped inside to feel for the light switch. He was now standing in a small, well-equipped laboratory.

Malloy came out to join him and stopped in his tracks, dumbstruck. 'No wonder our grant funds were a bit overspent,' he murmured.

'Tell me it isn't true,' said Dewar. 'Tell me he couldn't have grown up smallpox virus here.' Both men moved further in to examine the main workbench set up against the back wall.

Malloy looked at the equipment and grimaced. 'That's exactly what he's been doing, I'm afraid. These are all the things you'd need for virus subculture. He must have used the old vials to seed new cultures. It would have been relatively simple to grow up large amounts of virus if you knew how, and George knew how. Once you have the virus, you don't need much. Smallpox isn't a demanding thing to grow.'

'But the danger?'

'George is a first-class technician. He's handled viruses for years. Simple subculture wouldn't be nearly as hazardous as trying to create the virus from DNA fragments.'

Dewar looked at the assorted pieces of lab glassware and tubing. There were several bottles of clear fluid along the back of the workbench and a few smaller ones containing straw-coloured liquid. It scarcely looked as if it would satisfy the inventory of a kid's chemistry set. 'Where's the virus?'

'Not here,' replied Malloy. 'These bottles contain sterile buffer and culture medium. None of them have been infected with virus. But look here.'

Dewar bent down to peer into a beaker full of red fluid. He could see several broken glass vials in it.'

'It's disinfectant,' said Malloy. 'He put the old vials in here when he was finished with them but where are the new cultures?'

'Oh Christ, that's what was in the box,' exclaimed Dewar. 'That's what he must have meant when he told his wife their troubles were over. He's taken the virus with him. He's gone to hand it over to the Iraqis!'

'But where?'

Dewar pulled out his phone and called Barron. 'This is important! Is anything happening at your end right now?'

'No one's come out today as yet, if that's what you mean, but it's a bit early for them. They don't usually go round to the coffee shop until the back of three.'

'You're absolutely certain none of the Iraqis has left the building?'

'Absolutely. Why? What do you know that I don't?'

'The virus is on its way. The handover's happening today.'

'Where?'

'I don't know. It's going to be up to you and your men to follow any Iraqi who leaves – and for God's sake, don't lose them!'

'Roger that. I'll call you if something happens.'

'What now?' asked Malloy.

'Did Ferguson have a car?'

'A Ford Escort.'

'Then he must have taken it. It's not outside the house. Get the number from his wife. I'll get the police to put out an alert for it.'

Malloy went off to do this while Dewar took a last look round the garage before trying to restore the padlock mounting on the door as well as he could. He had plenty of time: Malloy seemed to take forever. When he finally did appear he said, 'Sorry. She couldn't remember the number. She's in a bit of a state. She had to look for the logbook.'

Dewar called the police with details of the car, giving instructions that its location should be reported as soon as possible. On no account were they to attempt to stop the vehicle or chase the driver. Dewar repeated the instruction so there was no misunderstanding. He didn't want Ferguson spooked into doing something stupid with the cargo he was carrying.

Dewar and Malloy drove back towards town, unsure what to do until they got word about Ferguson's whereabouts or of an Iraqi initiative. Dewar became more impatient with each passing minute. He checked his watch. 'What are the police doing?' he complained. 'Surely they must have found the car by now.' He called in to police headquarters to check for himself. Still no sighting of the car.

'Might be off the road,' suggested Malloy.

'In a car park, you mean?' said Dewar. He called the police again and asked that car parks in the city be checked. 'This has A-one priority!'

Half an hour went by with Dewar and Malloy just cruising around the city centre, waiting for news. At 3.40, Barron called.

'Siddiqui and Abbas have just left the building.'

'Don't lose them!'

'Not likely,' replied Barron. 'They're on foot.'

'What?'

'It looks to me as if they're just going round the corner as usual to the coffee shop.'

'Shit!' said Dewar. He couldn't bring himself to even contemplate a scenario not involving the Iraqis. He rested his elbow on the window ledge of the car door and brought the heel of his hand up to his forehead while he thought. 'That's it!' he exclaimed.

'What's it?' asked Malloy.

'The café! The Bookstop Café! That's where the handover's going to be. It's the one place they never arouse any suspicion by going to. They set it up that way by going there every day! They're regulars! Ferguson must be going to meet them there! Move it!'

Malloy drove. Dewar called Barron.

'The handover is going to take place in the Bookstop Café,' he said. 'The Iraqis' contact is one George Ferguson, male Caucasian, six two, red hair, early fifties. Is he there yet?'

There was a long pause. Malloy swung the car into Hanover Street and stopped at the traffic lights.

'Roger that. A male fitting that description is currently inside the café.'

'Is his car outside?' asked Dewar. He couldn't be sure whether Ferguson would have the virus with him or leave it in the car. 'It's a white Ford Escort.' He gave the number.

'Negative,' said Barron. 'What do you want us to do?'

'Ferguson and the Iraqis must not be allowed to leave. As long as they stay put take no action until we find his car. With any luck the virus'll be in the boot. Once we have that they're all yours.'

Dewar called the police again and asked them to concentrate their hunt for Ferguson's car in the area around the Bookstop Café, but on no account were officers to pass in front of the café. Ten minutes passed with still no sighting. Dewar could feel the sweat breaking out on his forehead. 'Come on, come on,' he urged impatiently. They were now sitting in Forest Road, just round the corner from the café. Dewar's impatience made him get out the car. He walked to the end of the road and caught sight of Barron, watching the café. He called him on the phone. 'Still inside?'

'Laughing and talking just like any other day.'

'And Ferguson?'

'He's joined them. There are a couple of books on the table in front of him that he's just bought. For all the world it looks like he's just having a cup of coffee before leaving and is chatting to people at a neighbouring table.'

'Just books? No boxes or parcels in front of him.'

'Not as far as I can see.'

Dewar looked towards Barron again and saw that he was using the medical school building on the other side of the street as cover for his watch on the café. 'The medical school!' he thought. The police wouldn't have checked the car park in the quadrangle. It was just conceivable that Ferguson might have left his car there. He said so to Barron.

'Want me to check?'

'No, you keep your eyes on the café. They might try to leave. I'll walk to the corner and cross the road. I'll only be exposed for a few seconds. If they're all inside the café, talking I should get away with it.'

Dewar pulled up his collar, stuck his hands in his pockets and walked to the corner junction with Teviot Place. He ran across the road and picked a moment when a bus was coming along to hurry up to the entrance of the medical school. The bus shielded him from view from the café. He looked around the quadrangle at the cars parked there. A man in uniform was walking among them, looking at windscreens for permits. Dewar looked along the line. At the far corner, nearest the building, was a white Ford Escort. He couldn't see the number but he felt sure it would be the one. He hurried over and saw that the number checked out.

Dewar informed Barron and the police. He needed help as quickly as possible to get inside the car but he didn't want patrol cars screaming into the quadrangle and uniforms running everywhere.

Barron said that he would send one of his men round. He was in plain clothes, so wouldn't arouse suspicion; he was more than a match for a Ford Escort.

'How long?' asked Dewar.

'About thirty seconds,' replied Barron. 'He's watching the café with me.'

It took the agent a further thirty seconds to break into Ferguson's car. Dewar searched the interior but found nothing. He pulled the boot release catch and hurried round to lift it up. There was nothing there apart from a travel rug, a few tools and a folding chair.

'Damn, damn, damn,' exclaimed Dewar. 'He left the house with it. He must have it with him.'

'In the café, you mean?' asked the agent.

Dewar nodded. He called Barron.

'All we needed.'

'But you said he doesn't seem to be carrying anything.'

'I can only see the top of the table. He could have a bag or a box at his feet for all I know.'

'Oh fuck!' exclaimed the agent at Dewar's side.

Dewar looked at him and then at what he was looking at. The old man who had been checking the parking permits was watching them and had a phone to his ear.

'He's calling the police!' said the agent. 'He thought we were trying to steal the Escort!'

Dewar called the police and tried to have the response cancelled but the sound of police sirens was already in the air and getting louder. 'Call them off!' he yelled into the phone but it was too late.

Two patrol cars came hurtling into Teviot Place and the people inside the café jumped to the wrong conclusion. Siddiqui and Abbas got up to leave.

Barron ordered his men in to stop them leaving the café. Dewar ran round to the front of the medical school leaving the agent to deal with the arriving police. 'Get the virus!' he yelled at Barron. 'Forget everything else. Just get the virus!'

Dewar was the last to enter the café. Ferguson had gone as white as a sheet and was sitting in a corner as if paralysed. One of Barron's men had charge of a box he'd taken from under the table and was guarding it with his body. Barron's men had pulled their weapons. Siddiqui was back sitting sedately in his seat as if nothing had happened. Abbas was looking distinctly more uneasy but he too had resumed his seat.

'Is that what you're after?' Barron asked Dewar. The agent stood back to let Dewar examine the box.

Dewar opened it and saw that it contained six individual flasks. 'I think so,' he replied. He looked at Ferguson and snapped, 'Well, is it? Do they contain smallpox virus?'

Ferguson nodded his head in hangdog fashion and then looked down at the floor.

Dewar squatted down in front of Siddiqui and looked him in the eye. 'Well, Professor? What do you have to say for yourself?'

Siddiqui looked at him disdainfully and said. 'I am an Iraqi national, here to liaise with students from my country. I have nothing to say.'

'And your relationship with Mr Ferguson here?' asked Dewar.

Siddiqui looked at Ferguson and said, 'I have never seen this man before in my life. He came in while my friend and I were having coffee as we always do at this time in the afternoon. I would like to go now please.'

'Lying bastard,' said Ferguson.

Dewar picked up the case that sat at the side of Siddiqui's chair and snapped it open on the table.

'I protest,' began Siddiqui but his protests fell on deaf ears.

Dewar lifted up the lid to reveal it was full of English banknotes. 'Well,' he said, 'I remember the coffee here being quite reasonably priced. You've got some explaining to do.'

Siddiqui's nerve held but Abbas snapped. He leapt to his feet and vaulted over the counter to snatch up a knife and hold it to the throat of the young woman who owned the café and who had been watching events with an air of bemusement.

Siddiqui rasped something in Arabic at him and it didn't sound complimentary, but Abbas seemed determined to make his own bid for freedom. 'Let Susan go,' said Siddiqui, this time in English. 'She has always treated us with courtesy. Perhaps she might even forgive you this misunderstanding . . . if you let her go!'

'Drop your guns,' demanded Abbas, ignoring Siddiqui and now looking wild-eyed, like a trapped animal.

'I'm sorry,' said Barron calmly. 'But no.'

'I'll kill her!' threatened Abbas.

'I hope not, but we will not be putting down our guns.'

'They don't say that on television!' complained Susan as she struggled to breathe with Abbas's arm round her throat.

'I mean it!' threatened Abbas.

'I mean it too,' continued Barron. 'We have charge of the virus. Laying down our weapons would mean relinquishing that charge. My orders do not permit that. Killing the young lady will accomplish nothing. I'll just kill you afterwards.'

'I don't want the virus! It was Siddiqui's plan. Everything is Siddiqui's plan!'

'Shut up!' said Siddiqui, losing his cool for the first time.

Dewar kept trying to catch the café owner's eye while Barron and Abbas continued their stand-off. He finally succeeded and started trying to direct her attention to the coffee pots standing on the counter in front of her. Steam was curling from their spouts. She had been about to serve them when all hell had broken loose. Dewar saw that she had understood what he was getting at.

'Put down your guns!' said Abbas, now sounding desperate.

'No deal,' said Barron.

Dewar nodded and the young woman grabbed one of the coffee pots, flinging the contents back into Abbas's face. He screamed out in pain as the scalding fluid met his eyes, and he dropped the knife. Dewar vaulted over the counter and brought him to the floor, where two of Barron's men took over.

'Are you all right?' he asked the owner, who was standing with both hands to her face. She nodded mutely.

'Time to get these two out of here?' said Barron, looking to Dewar.

Dewar nodded. 'But leave Ferguson.'

Barron and his men escorted the Iraqis out to waiting cars. Dewar lifted the box up off the table and put it on the service counter while he took out the flasks one by one.

'You'll bring him?' asked Barron as he was about to close the door.

Dewar nodded. Malloy squeezed in before the door was closed. 'Looks like I missed it all.'

'It's over,' agreed Dewar wearily.

'Why?' Malloy asked Ferguson, who was sitting with his head in his hands.

Ferguson looked as if he had aged twenty years in the last half-hour. His shoulders sagged and he had the air of a man about to face the gallows. 'I needed the money,' he replied.

'But Christ! Smallpox!' exclaimed Malloy.

Ferguson shook his head. 'That wasn't the plan.' he said. 'It all went wrong.'

'What d'you mean?'

'I never intended to give them variola major,' said Ferguson. 'That's alastrim in the flasks.'

'Oh God,' said Malloy.

Dewar looked at him for an explanation.

'Alastrim is a mild form of smallpox. It's practically indistinguishable from the real thing in lab tests but when they came to use it it wouldn't be anything like as effective as the real thing. The whole Iraqi plan would misfire.'

'I took the alastrim vials and left the variola major cultures in the cellar along with the other stocks until I had time to destroy them. I never dreamed anyone would want to steal them.'

'The guy on the digger thought the vials contained drugs so he helped himself to a few.'

'Shit.'

'So it was just bad luck he picked the smallpox ones,' said Malloy.

'I suppose,' agreed Dewar. 'It could have been typhoid, tuberculosis, cholera, God knows what else. But you're still responsible for the outbreak,' Dewar accused Ferguson. 'All the people who've died, the ones who'll never see again and the fact we've now got smallpox back in the world. And all because . . . you needed the money.'

'I did!' retorted Ferguson with some semblance of spirit. 'The bastards are putting me out to grass after thirty years with a pension that won't pay the fucking gas bill. Joyce has cancer and who's going to look after Malcolm when we're gone? He needs long-term care. That takes money. Money I don't have!'

Neither Dewar nor Malloy could think of anything to say. After a long pause, Dewar said simply, 'Let's go.'

Dewar drove. Malloy sat in the back with Ferguson. They were about to start heading down the Mound on their way over to police headquarters when Ferguson suddenly pleaded, 'Let me see Joyce and Malcolm one last time. Just a few minutes together then I'll come with you and cooperate fully.'

Dewar thought for a moment, then said, 'Five minutes, no more.'

'Thanks. You're a decent bloke.'

They drove over to Baberton in silence and Dewar parked outside Ferguson's house. He could see that Joyce had come to the window. She looked small and fragile.

Malloy said, 'We have your word?'

'I promise,' said Ferguson. 'I will not try to run away.'

'Five minutes,' Dewar reminded him.

Dewar and Malloy sat outside in the car while Ferguson, gathering Joyce in his arms, disappeared inside. Five minutes passed with no sign of his return. 'Another couple,' said Dewar.

'Right,' said Dewar after ten minutes had gone by. 'Let's fetch him.'

Dewar rang the bell. There was no response. He tried again. Nothing.

Both men ran round the back of the house, half expecting to find the back door flapping open and Ferguson gone, but the back door was locked. Dewar shrugged and put his shoulder to it. It gave after the second challenge.

Ferguson, Joyce and Malcolm were all lying together on the living-room floor. The television was on but they were all quite dead. There was a vague chemical smell in the air.

'Cyanide,' whispered Dewar, freeing a small brown bottle that was still in Ferguson's hand. 'Poor bastard. I guess this was plan B all along. The Iraqis just provided an alternative scenario for a few weeks.'

'Oh George,' whispered Malloy.

TEN DAYS LATER

'Tell me it's really all over,' said Karen as she and Dewar

travelled south together on their way back to London. Ian Grant was well on the road to recovery, the outbreak in Edinburgh was under control and people were being vaccinated in circles of ever-increasing radius from the city to ensure that the virus would find it difficult if not impossible to spread. With a bit of luck it would be contained and the Earth would be free of it again.

'It's over,' smiled Dewar.

'What will happen to the Iraqis?'

'George Ferguson's death will provide the authorities with the excuse they need to avoid any kind of public trial. No testimony from George means no trial for Siddiqui means no embarrassment for the establishment. Nobody comes out of this affair with any credit.'

'So it will all just be swept under the carpet?'

'That's my guess.'

'But surely there will be demands for an inquiry?' insisted Karen.

'For some politicians, calling for a full public inquiry is a way of life. They do it so often that nobody takes a blind bit of notice any more. Their requests will be denied and armies of spin doctors brought in to make sure everyone concentrates on the fact that the epidemic is over and the disease has been contained. Celebration and services of thanksgiving will be the order of the day.'

'Doesn't that make you angry?'

'Just numb.'

'Will you get leave?'

'I'm presenting my report at the Home Office tomorrow morning, then I'm all yours. How about you?'

'My leave started this morning.'

'Shall we go away for a few days?'

'Where?'

'Scottish Highlands? Very few people and lots of fresh air.'

'Deal,' smiled Karen.

When Dewar finished delivering his report on the happenings in Edinburgh he was met with a wall of stunned silence. There were about thirty people in the room, the Home Secretary and Secretary for Defence were sitting in the front row beside Macmillan.

'Dr Dewar, I think we owe you a debt of gratitude,' said the Defence Secretary. 'Thanks to your efforts, a potentially disastrous scenario in the Middle East has been averted. There are already signs that Saddam will now back down and allow the UNSCOM inspectors to resume their work.'

'Until the next time,' said Dewar.

'Almost certainly true, I'm afraid. But I'm sure we can all learn from this experience.'

'I must say I'm pretty alarmed at how close he came to getting what he wanted. I thought we had all sorts of safeguards with respect to microorganisms,' said one of the politicians in the second row. 'It seemed almost . . . easy in the end.'

'It was,' agreed Dewar.

'Dr Dewar, are you suggesting that all the legislation we've brought in, all the regulations we've imposed about the storage and handling of dangerous viruses and bacteria, count for nothing?' asked an official from the Health and Safety Executive.

'In this instance, sir, they were irrelevant,' said Dewar. 'In the final analysis, all it took was one lab technician and a few glass bottles in his garage and we had a biological nightmare on our hands.'

'Just how many of these old infectious-diseases hospitals do we have out there?' asked the Home Secretary.

'Several hundreds, sir,' came the reply from the back.

'And how many are being pulled down?'

'Almost all of them, sir; they're no longer required. We don't have the epidemics we used to . . .'

There was a very pregnant pause before the Home Secretary turned to Dewar and said, 'And it's conceivable that many of them have forgotten stores of bacteria and viruses?'

'It's a distinct possibility,' Dewar agreed.

'Then all our efforts at containing dangerous microorganisms in strictly controlled environments . . .?'

'Are excellent in their place, sir.'

'What does that mean?'

'It means, sir, the animals in the zoo are perfectly safe. It's the ones in the forest we have to worry about.'